D1417423

Stay in touch with Rawlin to get free books and offers.

SIGN UP NOW

JACK HUNTER

HEADSHOT

RAWLIN CASH

ONE

In Manhattan's Civic Center, between a federal court-house, an FBI field office, City Hall, and One Police Plaza, stands a twelve-story high, rust-colored, brick fortress. The windows are opaque slats. Federal marshals man the gates. The receiving area is an underground, bomb-proof bunker, its concrete three times thicker than that of the Führerbunker built by Hitler to withstand the destruction of Berlin.

It is among the most secure facilities ever built on US soil. The *LA Times* called it the Guantanamo of New York. Journalists and civil rights activists have sought information from the inside for years.

On a normal operating day, no one goes in and no one comes out. The building's services are so automated that almost all staff and guard duties are performed remotely. Food delivery, cell rotation, and prisoner processing is completely automated. There is a control center in the basement where guards monitor every process and function on screens. In the event of an emergency, authorization from the attorney general is required to enter.

The building is as close to a legal blackbox as the US constitution will allow.

In 2011, the *New York Times* learned of the entry procedure from a former inmate, a Saint Petersburg computer science graduate who'd built a server-farm in Rockville, Maryland. He was eventually found not guilty of espionage and released. The story published a month later read like something from a science fiction novel.

The only way in is through the basement. A bus pulls up to a receiving bay, a single prisoner gets out, and federal marshals tell him to strip. The prisoner can still remember the daylight he was in just a few minutes before. Unless he is released, transferred, or required to make a court appearance, he will not see the sky again until the date of his release. In a tiled room he is strapped to a chair and his head is shaved. He is showered. The water smells like the over-chlorinated swimming pools of his childhood. He squats. He coughs. Someone puts a finger in his ass and someone else checks his mouth. He puts on an orange jumpsuit which has a number and the words Federal Correctional Center stenciled on the back.

He is shackled at the ankles and wrists. The shackles are connected to a chain around his waist and are locked and unlocked remotely. He is brought barefoot to a large electronic door like the sealed door of a submarine. Through the door is a long tunnel, forty feet below street-level, and he is instructed to walk to the door at the other end. He walks alone. The first door locks behind him. The second remains locked until he reaches it. The doors are controlled remotely by guards watching on monitors. There is no local override. Any interruption in the feed to the control center and the doors cannot be opened.

Beyond the second door is an open elevator. The prisoner looks at the elevator. There are no buttons. There are no guards. It is obvious what he must do but even so, he is confused. A voice on an intercom tells him to enter the elevator but it cannot rush him. The elevator contains a cage large enough for him to stand in. He can look into it for a minute or an hour, but eventually he must step inside. It locks behind him and he is taken to his floor.

Each floor is self-contained. Only a handful of technicians have ever set foot on more than one floor. The highest priority prisoners exit on the tenth. The confinement conditions are so severe the United Nations has lodged formal anti-torture complaints with Washington.

This is 10 South.

The prisoner will not speak to another living soul for the duration of his sentence. He will never meet another inmate. He will never face a guard or member of prison staff. For twenty-three hours a day he will be in a sealed, windowless cell. He is constantly monitored by four high-resolution cameras. Food is delivered by machine. The fluorescent lighting will never be turned off, never dimmed. It is so intense that within six months he will suffer measurable sight degradation. Within six years, a significant proportion of prisoners are blind or close to it. For one hour each day he will visit a small exercise room. He will not be escorted. His cell will unlock and an LED light strip will lead him to the room. The room has an opaque window that lets in natural light but cannot be seen through. The room contains a treadmill, a bike, and a rowing machine. After an hour he returns to his cell or is subjected to an auditory alarm that increases gradually from one-hundred-twenty decibels, about as loud as a chainsaw, to one-hundred-fifty decibels, at which point there is a risk of eardrum rupture.

This is the pinnacle of penal security. This is the place

where the highest-risk prisoners in the world end up. The Al-Qaeda leaders who stood trial ended up here. The terrorists who bombed the embassies in Nairobi and Dar es Salaam ended up here. The perpetrators of classified attempts to assassinate senior government officials, including President Bush in 2002 and President Obama in 2010 and 2014, ended up here.

This is not a place for serial-killers or psychopaths, rapists or child molesters. This place, this level of confinement, this degree of isolation, is reserved solely for enemies of the state, people so dangerous they don't just threaten the law, they threaten the nation that wrote the law.

The United States has the most powerful military of any nation or empire of any era in history in any part of the world. Active and reserve personnel exceeds two million. Annual expenditure exceeds six-hundred billion. It has over thirteen thousand fixed and rotary-wing aircraft, six thousand tanks, thirty-eight thousand armored fighting vehicles, two thousand self-propelled or towed artillery vehicles, and over a thousand rocket projectors. Total naval strength is four-hundred-fifteen vessels, including twenty aircraft carriers. It has a current usable nuclear stockpile of four thousand warheads, two thousand deployed. Nuclear strike range is ten thousand miles from land, seven thousand from sea. Nowhere is out of range.

Absolute supremacy can be projected to any theater.

Absolute power can be brought down on any actor.

Absolute destruction can be delivered to any spot on the globe.

This prison, this anonymous high-rise that could be mistaken for a medium-grade municipal office building, contains the people, the men, who threaten that power.

It has six cells.
It is hell on earth.

TWO

Segundo José Heredia, also known as El Sucio, or the Dirty, is not your average drug lord. When he was arrested crossing the Mexico-Guatemala border in 1993 and sentenced to thirty years, he didn't just escape Federal Social Readaptation Center Number 1 in Almoloya de Juárez.

Escaping is what your average drug lord would do.

El Sucio went on a kidnapping spree. His men snatched the governor of the prison, four-hundred-twenty of the four-hundred-twenty-six prison guards, as well as over a thousand wives, girlfriends, parents, children, grandparents, and grandchildren of those guards. Governor, guards, men, women and children, he rounded up over sixteen-hundred people.

And he didn't just kill them.

That wouldn't have sent the message he wanted to send.

Instead, he took over the Toluca City Sewage Treatment Plant, blew open the thirty-foot deep raw sludge tank, and forced his sixteen hundred captives into it. They floated for as long as they could, and then they sank.

No one survived.

As a side effect, half a million people in Toluca, Metepec, and San Mateo Atenco had no sewage treatment for six weeks. The stench reached the Mexican parliament, forty miles away, at the National Palace.

And more was to come.

Within a year, the Guatemalan president was dead, assassinated by sniper from a helicopter while on vacation in Cancún. So many attempts were made on the Mexican president that he was forced to resign his office, go into hiding, and has not been seen in public since.

El Sucio walked free and grew his cartel with impunity. It would be decades before another Mexican president attempted to stop him.

And then, in 2013, El Sucio was captured for a second time when the Mexican army launched an all out assault on his convoy in Chihuahua. It was the biggest military operation on Mexican soil since the days of Pancho Villa. Four thousand troops were involved. Six hundred were killed. In less than a month, while still awaiting trial, El Sucio escaped Federal Social Readaptation Center Number 2 in the state of Jalisco through a tunnel from his cell to a barn four miles away. The night of his escape, fifty-eight Guadalajara city buses blew up during rush hour. The death toll exceeded eleven hundred.

The struggle against the cartel continued, but eventually the Mexican government was forced to admit de facto defeat when it pulled the entirety of its military, as well as all federal and state law enforcement personnel and all judges out of the province of Sinaloa. In the preceding twelve months, total federal and state casualties in Sinaloa exceeded thirty thousand. Civilian casualties exceeded one hundred thousand.

Wars had been less deadly.

The city of Culiacán, El Sucio's birthplace, had long been a no-go area for government forces. When that area suddenly expanded to include all of Sinaloa, a full fortieth of Mexico's territory containing three million people, the international community took notice. It was the biggest threat to global order since the Islamic State declared the Caliphate in 2014.

The Mexican army set up checkpoints on all roads in and out of the state. The airports were closed and the airspace patrolled jointly by the Mexican and US Air Forces. Residents were notified officially by the Servicio de Administractión that they were no longer required to pay taxes.

No one paid closer attention than the US military.

This threat wasn't halfway around the globe in Afghanistan or Iraq, it wasn't on the Korean Peninsula, it wasn't in Palestine, it was on their doorstep. If some drug dealer wanted to launch rockets over the fence into US territory, it wasn't going to happen on their watch.

The politicians urged caution, they didn't want to create panic, but the joint chiefs closed ranks. In a heated argument with the president, the attorney general, and FBI Director Willis Chancey, who all wanted to tread softly, the chairman of the joint chiefs, Harry Goldwater, threatened to resign if extraordinary measures were not put in place. The national security advisor backed him up.

The president responded by providing comprehensive military support to Mexico, enhancing security along the southern border, calling up thousands of additional troops for deployment in California and Texas, and fully funding the border wall. The prototype for the wall approved by congress was to stretch the full two-thousand miles from the

Las Palomas Wildlife Management Area in Brownsville, Texas, to San Ysidro south of San Diego, California. It was a forty-foot high concrete barrier with high-tech, full-spectrum surveillance, experimental anti-climbing measures, and sensors capable of detecting underground vibrations to a depth of two hundred feet. The price estimate was not publicly disclosed, but the project was hailed by both the president and lawmakers as the largest and most ambitious manmade structure built since the completion of the Great Wall of China by the Ming Dynasty in the sixteenth century.

Within months, the joint chiefs were proved right.

Satellite imagery of Sinaloa showed new air fields, anti-aircraft installations, and the initial phases of construction of what appeared to be missile launch pads. In January, US and Mexican patrol aircraft were shot down by cartel pilots flying Sukhoi Su-27 fighter jets. The Department of Defense's best guess was that the jets, and possibly the pilots, had been purchased from Belarus, which had inherited thirty of them from the Sixty-First Fighter Aviation Regiment after the fall of the Soviet Union. Since 2010, NATO had not been able to account for the location of the fighters, and when one of them was shot down in Angola by a terrorist with a shoulder-mounted SA-14 Gremlin rocket launcher, it was confirmed that the Belorussians had sold them to the highest bidder. Evidently, the cartel had been one of the buyers. The number of jets in their possession was unknown.

The official position, supported by a joint report by the DEA, the FBI, the DoD, and the CIA, became that the cartel of Segundo José Heredia, also known as the Sinaloa Cartel, had graduated from a law enforcement issue to a full blown military threat. A bipartisan congressional report concluded, 'Heredia's cartel has verifiable and confirmed military hardware capable of launching a credible military threat to US territorial integrity.'

El Sucio could wage war on the United States.

The most up to date DoD analyses estimated he was capable of posing a more significant challenge to the military than all but twenty-one of the world's sovereign nations. The DC-based Fire-Power Analysis Center put the cartel's military capability on a par with Israel. And it noted, 'unlike sovereign militaries, El Sucio, as his name suggests, can be expected to fight dirty.'

THREE

When the cartel took over Sinaloa, El Sucio was already the most wanted man in the history of US law enforcement. He had been federally indicted in fourteen federal court districts for drug trafficking, bribery, murder, torture, rape, and in one count, cannibalism. According to an indictment filed in the northern district of Illinois, he had ordered that three members of a rival Chicago drug gang be boiled alive in a nine-hundred gallon oil-fired water tank. After thirty minutes, El Sucio cut flesh from the bodies and served it on skewers to his men.

Across all US state and federal courts, he was listed as a defendant or codefendant on over two thousand indictments, accounting for over forty thousand murders.

The president, in discussion with the military and the government of Mexico, was weighing a number of options. The military and the CIA wanted to move aggressively to contain the threat. The FBI and attorney general argued for a more law enforcement based approach.

The team that apprehended Osama Bin Laden was consulted.

After rejecting the possibility of US Army units crossing the border into Sonora and Chihuahua in force, plans were drawn for an operation resembling the intervention in Iraq against ISIS. Limited US ground troops would assist the Mexican army on the ground, while four US carrier strike groups would provide massive air support from the Gulf of California.

The operation was given the codename Everglade.

Based on the ISIS experience, Everglade would take years to degrade the cartel's fighting power, and there was an extremely high risk of major counter attacks on US soil during the process.

Parts of southern Texas and California would almost certainly experience air and missile strikes.

It would be a grim operation.

The cartel was expected to fight to the death.

No one relished the prospect.

But it was the best option on the table.

And then, while plans for Everglade were being finalized, El Sucio was arrested.

It came from nowhere.

A complete surprise.

A single, uniformed police officer in the Mexican resort town of Cabo San Lucas thought he recognized Heredia on a beach with his family. He called in the sighting. The Mexican federal forces ignored the report, not regarding it as credible. The state governor was skeptical but authorized a local tactical unit to make an arrest. Without notifying the military, and without the assistance of US or Mexican special forces, a squad of fifteen men and three helicopters moved in on a luxury beach villa outside Cabo.

An hour later, with six casualties, none fatal, El Sucio

was in the custody of the Cabo San Lucas municipal police force.

No one could believe it.

In Mexico city, the president ordered that fireworks be set off.

The day after the arrest, he flew to Washington to sign a waiver of specialty in front of the television cameras. The US secretary of state and six-hundred marines travelled to Cabo the same day. The next day, the Nimitz-class aircraft carrier, USS Theodore Roosevelt, arrived at Cabo's small port.

It was the fastest extradition in US history. El Sucio had escaped Mexico's highest security prisons, not once but twice, and no one, least of all the Mexicans, wanted to risk that happening a third time.

Within forty-eight hours of his sighting by the Cabo police officer, El Sucio, the most dangerous man on earth, was in the custody of the US Navy, locked up in the brig of the USS Roosevelt. The next day, four transport helicopters, one principal and three decoys, took off from the deck of the Roosevelt. The principal landed at Naval Air Facility El Centro in Imperial County, California, where El Sucio was transferred to the hold of a C-130J Super Hercules. Seven hours later, that plane landed at Stewart Airport in Orange County, New York, where a military convoy was waiting. An hour later, El Sucio was on lock-down in 10 South.

The president held a press conference thanking all agencies involved in the handover and transport of the prisoner, and announcing that his administration would be seeking the death penalty. He said El Sucio was responsible for more than ninety-percent of the illegal narcotics flow into the US, and that his capture proved the president's commitment to law and order. He promised that justice would be swift, and that every legal step would be taken to expedite the trial.

He wasn't lying.

Government lawyers took unprecedented steps to expedite El Sucio's trial. In consultation with the attorney general, the state department, federal prison administrators, and the New York City Police Department, it became increasingly clear no one wanted to hold the bag on El Sucio for longer than necessary. Every hour he was in custody was a risk. If he were to escape, careers would be ruined.

Elections would be lost.

Blood would be spilled.

The first taste of that blood came on day three of El Sucio's custody, when armed gunmen overran a US border post at Tijuana, killing four border agents and going on a shooting spree in downtown San Diego until they were killed by police. The total death toll was seventy. The next day, two men on two separate flights from Mexico City were found in possession of bomb making materials and arrested. A day later, a bomb at a shopping mall in El Paso killed twenty-three people.

Pretty soon, the FBI had threat assessments on the president's desk showing just how vulnerable the prison really was. It wasn't a military facility and hadn't been designed to withstand a military-grade attack. If the cartel made a move in force, they would overrun it. The CIA's scenarios, using confirmed military hardware known to be in the cartel's possession, were even worse.

The president was worried.

After two more attacks in El Paso that killed eight civilians and a police officer, he was pissed off.

"You guys handed me a ticking bomb," he said to the lawyers who'd negotiated the extradition.

"If this guy gets out, it'll be the biggest cluster fuck since 9/11."

He wanted Heredia standing trial immediately. The danger of holding him grew worse by the day. He told the attorney general and the prosecution team that the risk of an attack on the prison was grater than the risk of political or legal fallout if the trial was rushed. He wanted every rule bent. Every door opened.

"Get me a death sentence on this guy by the end of the month or I'll get a new lawyer," he told the attorney general. "I want this guy judged, juried, and hung before the cartel blows up half of New York trying to get him out."

An intern in the room said a prisoner hadn't been executed that fast in the US since the 1890 case of James J Medley.

The President looked witheringly at the intern before leaving the room.

A day later, explosive material was detected in a decommissioned service tunnel beneath the federal court building for the Southern District of New York. That court, located just across the street from 10 South and linked to it by secure tunnel, was the obvious venue for El Sucio's trial.

The president went ballistic.

The same day, without consulting the attorney general or federal prosecutors, he announced the trial date at a White House press conference. The trial would begin the following Monday, and the entire slate of the federal court for the Eastern District of New York would be cleared to make room for it.

The Mexicans had initially granted extradition only to the Southern District of California and the Western

District of Texas. That detail was remedied with a single phone call which the attorney general was forced to make in front of the president.

"Was that so difficult?" the president said after the call.

"No, sir."

"Now get me the death warrant," the president said, before storming out of the room.

The courthouse for New York's Eastern District was located directly across the Brooklyn Bridge from 10 South. From the prison's underground receiving area, the convoy would have to travel just six hundred feet to the bridge. The bridge would be completely closed to traffic and helicopters above would have a clear line of sight for the entire journey. The courthouse on the Brooklyn side backed onto the ramp of the bridge. From the end of the ramp, the convoy would drive on public streets for just two hundred yards before entering the courthouse's secure loading bay.

The convoy would travel at an average speed of thirty miles per hour and the journey would take one-hundred-twenty seconds.

During the press conference, the president stated, "EDNY is the most secure federal court building in the country. It definitely will be on Monday morning when this trial begins. We'll have over a hundred sharp shooters with sights on every angle and every approach. And let me tell you, I can vouch for these sharp shooters. When they shoot, they don't miss."

There was mild applause in the press room.

The president had been assured that unlike SDNY, EDNY had zero risk of an underground attack. There were no subway lines beneath the building. The sewers would be sealed. The courtroom's entrance and the holding area where El Sucio would sit during the trial would be reinforced with bomb-proof concrete. There were more available K-9 units with bomb detection training in New York than anywhere else in the country. Screening in and out of the building would be handled by TSA with new radiation and x-ray equipment that was the most advanced in the world.

The president made a point of speaking with the TSA team that would handle the screening.

"Sir," the leader of the team assured him, "when that courthouse opens, we'll know if someone approaching the building has thyroid cancer before they even get to the door. We'll pick up the Iodine 131 from thirty feet away. If they had a heart scan, we'll pick up the Thallium 201 from two hundred feet away. This is not the type of screening you've seen at the airport. Nuclear material, biohazard, and over eight hundred chemical compounds used in explosives will show up on these screens before they even reach the lobby. I could tell you which of the lawyers used cocaine to get his juices going for the opening arguments, or which of the witnesses smoked menthol."

"Jesus."

"Yes, sir."

"Why don't we use this stuff at the airport?"

"Oh, we will, sir."

The challenges didn't stop with securing the building. Witnesses, investigators, lawyers, even the judge, would be at such a high risk of assassination that they would require protective measures possibly for the rest of their lives.

"We can have the jury watch the proceedings remotely, sir," the attorney general told the president. "They'll be located in Albany, watching from a location secured by the military. During deliberations they will communicate with each other electronically. They won't see each other's faces.

Only the judge and a handful of people in the justice department will ever know who they are."

"And what about death row?" the president said. "I can't put this guy back in jail after the trial. The whole point of this is to get him off our hands."

"Federal death row and the federal death chamber are at the special confinement unit in Terre Haute."

"I can't send this guy to Indiana."

"No, sir."

"We'll need an exception."

"Of course, sir."

"We need to carry out the execution in 10 South. I don't care how they do it. And it will be immediately after the trial."

"What about appeals, sir?"

"No appeals."

"That's a big exception."

"Get the paperwork written up. This guy is a threat to the country as long as he breathes. I should have had him killed as soon as he got onboard the Roosevelt."

The attorney general didn't respond.

The president looked at him. "Oh, and tell your intern I read the case of James J Medley. He lost."

FOUR

"This is a fucking shit show," Fawn Aspen said as her cab pulled up to the Saint Royal.

"You sure you want to get out?" the driver said, taking in the scene.

There were police cars everywhere. Ambulances. A firetruck. Blue and red light reflected off the wet street. A traffic cop was waving them through the intersection.

She handed the driver a twenty and got out of the car, pulling her black trench close against the night air. Her breath billowed. It was cold for November. It felt like it might snow.

She stood on the sidewalk across from the police cordon and took in the scene.

Maybe forty city cops. The target was dead so the paramedics had been held back. The hotel staff were inside, she could see them giving statements to police through the rotating lobby door.

It didn't look like the FBI was there yet, but they would be. No way they'd let DC Metro handle this. From where she stood, she could see the gates of the White House on Lafayette Square.

The oval office wasn't a thousand feet away.

Armed members of the Secret Service were visible on the lawn and roof.

"Jesus H. Christ," she said under her breath.

It wasn't every day that someone shot a congressman this close to the president's office.

She crossed the street and approached the police officer in command.

She flashed him a false Capitol Police badge. "One of ours?"

"Looks like it ma'am."

She pulled a pair of black leather gloves from her pocket and put them on.

"I heard Gabriel Dayton," she said.

The officer was distracted, keeping an eye on twenty different things at once. He had to prevent potential witnesses and hotel staff from leaving, preserve the crime scene, and keep the street clear and pedestrians moving.

Fawn let her coat fall open, flashing just a hint of cleavage.

"Can you tell me what happened before the Feds show?" she said.

He gave her a second look over.

"Sniper," he said. "One bullet. One casualty. That window over there."

She looked at the broken window, cordoned off by police tape. Inside, in the warm glow of the hotel, she could make out the slightly bemused look of a George Washington portrait.

"Head shot?"

"Yes, ma'am."

She looked around at the surrounding buildings. There were a number of spots where a shooter could have been positioned.

"When exactly?" she said.

The cop shrugged. "Thirty minutes?"

A Fox 5 van pulled up and a crew started setting up a camera. She pulled up her collar.

"Thank you," she said to the cop, crossing the street back to the open sidewalk.

She looked up and down the street for a cab while lighting a cigarette. She'd taken two puffs when she spotted one. She stamped it out on the ground and stepped into the cab.

"Dupont Circle," she said. "Select Bistro."

A few minutes later she was in a booth in the restaurant. Her boss, Director of Paramilitary Black Ops, Jeff Hale, was sitting opposite her. He was eating a French blood sausage with mashed potatoes, golden with butter.

"Dayton, right?" he said, taking a bite.

She nodded.

He raised his hand to the waitress and asked for a second wine glass.

Fawn didn't bother to turn him down. He never took no for an answer anyway.

The waitress poured her a glass and she took a sip.

Hale waited for the waitress to leave before continuing.

"That's three today," he said. "Judge Hoffman, Jake Dillons at Treasury, and now the congressman."

"Do you think there will be more?"

Hale shrugged. "For all we know, they could be after the entire government."

"How did this get by us?" Fawn said.

Hale let out a laugh and put another piece of the sausage in his mouth.

"We'll get to the bottom of it."

"Or we'll be blamed for it," Fawn said. "Three assassinations. No warning from us? They'll call it a conspiracy."

"Lets just hope none of these three had something against us."

"Motive. That's all we need."

Hale nodded. He forked some potato and put it in his mouth.

"Is that apple sauce?" Fawn said.

"You want to try?"

She shook her head. His fork in her mouth was just the kind of thing that would get his blood flowing.

"You should order something."

"If I don't get home to Mitch soon, he'll get pissy."

"Bitchy Mitchy," Hale said, cutting another piece of sausage.

Fawn shrugged. "C'est la vie," she said, finishing her wine.

"So you're not going back to the office?" he said to her as she put on her coat.

"I was there all day."

"Three assassinations, Fawn."

"Are you going back?" she said.

Hale sat back in his seat, defeated. "Be there at seven then. This thing has put us in the shit."

"Thanks for the wine," she said.

Outside she lit a cigarette. Her apartment was just a few blocks from the restaurant so she walked. When she got home Mitch was waiting for her.

"So you decided to come home," he said.

"What's that supposed to mean?"

"You know."

She sighed. She was getting tired of this. They'd been dating a year, it had started so well, but lately he'd been getting jealous.

She was still smoking a cigarette when she entered the living room. She knew it pissed him off but it was her apartment.

"Where were you?"

"What do you mean, where was I? At work."

"It's after nine."

"Do you watch the news, Mitch? It was a crazy day."

"You got home late last night too."

"So sue me. I had a drink with a colleague last night."

"That must be nice."

She walked up to him, she could usually mollify him with some affection, but he pushed her hands away.

"Baby," she said softly. Her voice had always given her power over men. She'd have made an excellent phone-sex operator.

"Why do you have to be such a bitch, Fawn."

"Baby," she said again, but her heart really wasn't in it.

He was right. She was a bitch. She couldn't help it. He was a nice guy, sweet, a nurse at George Washington. Was it her fault he needed her more than she needed him?

"Tell me something," he said. "Last night, was it Celeste you had the drink with?"

Celeste was a twenty-eight-year-old brunette analyst who Mitch had met when she came to Fawn's birthday party earlier in the year. She'd been wearing a Charlie Chaplin suit, complete with mustache. Her shirt was thin cotton and her braless nipples were visible through it. Mitch said she looked like a slutty Hitler. Fawn never told him

she'd had an affair with Celeste before they met, but somehow, the chemistry, he knew.

"So what if I was?"

"Was anyone else there?"

"What is this about, Mitch? Why do you want to start
a fight?"

"Because I'm living with a fucking dyke, that's why."

FIVE

Fawn slept in. After the fight with Mitch she'd gone to a bar. When she got home around midnight he was gone. His stuff was gone. He'd packed a year of his life in one hour. She didn't know where he went but he had family in the area, he'd grown up there and gone to school there, he had a million options.

She briefly thought of texting him and trying to make up but she knew she didn't want to.

The apartment was fine without him. It was nice to have the space to herself.

She texted Hale.

What time did we say?

She put on the kettle and took a shower while it boiled. It was whistling when she got out. There was a text from Hale.

You slept in.

She tapped out a reply.

I'll be there by 7.30.

She made coffee and got dressed, rushing the makeup. She had the TV on in the background and the assassinations were all over CNN. Still just three of them. With any luck, that would be all of it. She put coffee in her travel mug and was in her car before seven. The worst thing about working at Langley was getting there. Everything else in DC was so compact and accessible. The CIA, on the other hand, occupied a sprawling campus ten miles out of town. Her first day working there, six years earlier, she'd tried to take transit. She was an hour and a half late.

She put on the radio and learned that all three of the assassination targets had been in Seattle recently. A state senator had been thrown off the roof of a parking garage there a month ago.

She was at Langley twenty minutes later and for once, parking wasn't a battle.

She hurried through security, picked up another coffee in the lobby, and was in the conference room by Hale's office at seven thirty on the dot.

Hale wasn't there but that was all right. The office was peaceful. She sipped her coffee and thought about Mitch. Now that he was gone he didn't seem so bad. He was good-looking. He had an amazing body. The sex was amazing. She'd thought so.

She hoped he did.

She ran her hands quickly over her hips, her breasts. She was sure she was still attractive. She was thirty-two and in the best shape of her life. She was required to do all the physical training of a field operative. She could climb walls, dodge bullets, jump out of moving vehicles, all that CIA crap.

She knew Mitch hadn't left because of her looks.

She didn't appreciate being called a dyke though. She appreciated cock as much as the next girl. More even. It just wasn't the only thing she appreciated.

"Sleeping beauty," Hale said as he strode into the room.

He was holding a folder in one hand and a porcelain coffee cup on a saucer in the other.

"Don't flirt with me," she said. "You're not my type."

"Oh, I wouldn't say that. I never met a girl in this building that didn't have daddy issues."

"Jesus, Hale. Do me a favor and don't say that to anyone else. Unless you want to end up defending a lawsuit."

"God, can't a guy make a joke?"

"Sure he can. If he doesn't mind losing his job."

He took the seat opposite her and put the folder on the table. He didn't say anything.

"You going to tell me what you've got, or am I going to guess?"

He rose an eyebrow at her as he opened the document. "Bet you didn't think I'd have the assassinations solved already."

She smiled. "Let me guess. Someone on a list booked a flight from Seattle."

Hale laughed.

"Not quite, but sometimes this shit is too easy."

"So you wanted me in early to witness your accomplishment?"

"Fawn," Hale said magnanimously.

She hated when he was like this. With the Seattle connection, a team of monkeys could have solved this thing.

It wasn't rocket science. And it wasn't their responsibility either. This was FBI jurisdiction.

"Has he been arrested yet?"

"No."

She looked at him as he stirred his black, sugarless coffee with a spoon.

"What are you plotting?"

"Read the file first."

"The suspense is killing me," she said, taking the file and rising to her feet.

"You eaten yet?" he said as they left the conference room.

"Thanks but no thanks, Mr. Weinstein."

SIX

Hale waited in the lobby bar of the Ritz-Carlton in George-town. He sipped his old-fashioned and watched the clock. She was twenty minutes late. He didn't mind. The wait would be worth it. It was early evening, about six, the busiest time of day for the upscale after-work bars in the area. Hale had a table reserved and they'd hold it all night if he told them to.

The screen above the bar was showing CNN. He watched the cavalcade of armored vehicles crossing the Brooklyn Bridge.

"Disaster, waiting to happen," he said to the bartender.

The bartender stopped what he was doing and turned to watch. There must have been fifty vehicles in the procession. Armored trucks, humvees, police cruisers, even police on horseback. What good would horses do in an emergency, Hale thought.

Two police helicopters with sharp-shooters flew over the procession and he'd heard there were shooters on the towers of the bridge, the roof of the prison, and the roof of the courthouse too.

"I don't know why they didn't just kill him when he was on the ship," the bartender said.

The security measures and risks surrounding El Sucio's imprisonment had been all over the news for weeks. Hale had fought them on every single detail, but once El Sucio was on US soil, no one cared what the CIA thought.

"We're a nation of laws, Billy," Hale said.

The bartender had a line of orders and got back to work. Hale ordered another old-fashioned.

"Mr. Hale, I'm so sorry."

A hand touched his shoulder.

He turned to see the sexiest piece of ass since his morning conference with Fawn.

"Jasper. I was beginning to worry."

"I got called back by the editor just as I was leaving."

He looked her up and down.

"If you were mine, I wouldn't let you leave either," he said.

She looked at him and then looked away. She was coy but they both knew the real reason this meeting was taking place. It wasn't to discuss the finer details of the *Washington Post's* editorial policy. Jasper Marten had been working at *the Post* for all of six months. She was twenty-five, just out of journalism school, and to say she was still making a name for herself would be to overstate the impact she'd had on the world of journalism. When Hale met her at a routine press announcement at Langley five days earlier, she'd been holding the CIA correspondent, George Hancock's, coat.

"What are you having to drink?" he said, beckoning Billy over.

"Oh, how about red?"

"I won't hear of it," Hale said. "We'll have wine with dinner. Before, it'll be strictly cocktails."

"Dinner?" she said.

"I wouldn't get you to come all the way down here for nothing," he said.

"Oh, this story is hardly nothing, Mr. Hale. Honestly, it's the first time the editor even spoke to me. I don't think he knew I existed until you called."

"Well, he knows now," Hale said.

Hale was beginning to wonder if she really was innocent enough to think he just wanted to do her a favor. It almost made him feel guilty. This girl could have been his daughter.

She crossed her legs and settled in next to him. She was stunning. However guilty he felt, he knew he lacked the self-control not to go through with this.

"Billy, she'll have a French Seventy-Five."

She smiled at him awkwardly and he allowed his gaze to wander over her breasts, which were covered by a professional, navy-blue office dress and white shirt, the collar neat and crisp over the neck. The dress was cut at the knee, and below, her slender ankles dangled in their high, black stilettos. She wore a young, fresh perfume. Her hair was rich, wavy, straight out of a shampoo commercial.

When the bartender brought her drink Hale raised his glass.

"To your career," he said.

She smiled.

She was about to learn, if she hadn't figured it out yet, what business she was really in.

They made small talk over the drinks and he had the bartender bring another round as they were shown to their table. He asked her where she was from, Bethesda, where she went to school, Columbia, where she was living, U

Street. She was too meek to steer the conversation to the subject he'd promised her.

For dinner he had the choucroute garnie. She had scallops. He ordered white wine from Quebec, it was biodynamic, whatever that meant, and he poured her big bowls of it. It was doing its job. By the time the waiter brought the dessert menu, her cheeks were flushed and she was swearing about her editor, who was a complete and utter asshole who treated her like a child. He hadn't wanted her to come to this meeting. He'd called Hale a dirty old man.

"He's older than me," Hale said, taking it in stride. He'd been called a lot worse.

"He said there's only one reason you'd meet a young, pretty journalist."

"So he thinks you're pretty," Hale said.

She laughed.

"One thing I can promise you," Hale said. "I may be a dirty old man, but at least I'm honest."

She looked into his eyes. "Are you, Jeff Hale?"

Hale looked at her, looked into her fresh, bright, twenty-five-year-old eyes. They were the color of the emerald on the ring on his wife's finger. It had belonged to his grandmother. She'd brought it across from Ireland a hundred years ago. He gave it to his wife for their thirtieth anniversary.

"I'll be honest with you," he said.

"Please do," she said.

"I'm a good friend. You play nice, I'll play nice. I won't stab you in the back."

"I think I could live with a friend like that," she said.

Her foot had released itself from its Neiman Marcus shoe and was sliding up the inside of his thigh. He looked down at his lap. There it was, her delicate foot, red paint on the toes, covered in nude pantyhose.

He wished he was stronger. He wished he could turn this down.

He asked for the bill and charged the meal to his room. He was using his expense account for this little tryst. Fuck accounting. They could live with it or they could have him censured. He had to do what he had to do.

"You got a room?" she said.

He took her by the hand and led her to the elevator. She didn't offer a moment's hesitation. They stood next to each other in the elevator in silence. When it stopped he led her down the corridor. She waited behind him while he opened the door. He had to swipe the key a few times for it to work.

It was quiet in the room. Too quiet. Neither of them spoke. He closed the door and turned to her, taking her face in his hands. She let him kiss her on the mouth. She tasted earthy. He pulled down the zip on the back of her dress and when it came off, he saw that she hadn't been wearing a shirt after all. The collar and cuffs were a trick, sewn into the neck and sleeves of the dress.

Her underwear was a matching set, a black and pink Victoria Secret bra and thong. He removed them, tearing the pantyhose, and she got on her knees.

As she opened the zip of his pants, he said, "the shooter of the three targets yesterday is the same man who killed the state senator in Seattle a month ago."

Jasper looked up at him.

"Everyone already guessed that much," she said.

He put his fingers through her hair.

"The FBI will discover that all four men were receiving money from the same source."

"Go on," she said.

"That source," he said, gasping, his fingers gripping her head tighter, "is the government of Saudi Arabia."

While Jasper cleaned up in the bathroom, Hale went to the minibar and took out two bottles of Peroni. Thirteen bucks each. He opened them and took a long swig from his. On the desk was a file containing a typed transcript of a meeting that took place at the Saint Royal hotel five years earlier between Congressman Gabriel Dayton and a representative of the King of Saudi Arabia, a man named Jamal Al-Wahad. The transcript was accompanied by black and white photos of the meeting.

Hale put the second beer on top of the file and then sat on the bed and turned on CNN. No new developments in the assassination story.

Jasper emerged from the bathroom fully dressed. She looked as put together as when they'd entered the room.

"You're not staying the night?" he said.

"Oh," she said, awkward now. Embarrassed by what they'd done. "I don't think I can."

He nodded and kissed her as he walked past.

"I'm just going to take a quick shower," he said. "There's a beer by the desk if you want."

When he came back from the bathroom a few minutes later she was gone, along with the file. Her beer was still on the table and he didn't see the point in wasting it. He picked up his phone and dialed Fawn's number.

"Boss?" she said. He could hear the sounds of a busy bar in the background.

"Fawn, are you at the office?"

"No. Are you?"

He smiled. "I need you to go back down there. There are four files in our surveillance archive relating to the assassination targets. I'm sending you the reference numbers now. I need you to print them out and put them in *the Post's* drop box."

"We're leaking them?"

"Yeah."

"I take it your little date was a success."

"Very satisfactory," he said.

SEVEN

Hunter looked at the departure screen. He was at JFK. He'd been able to get a late flight to Toronto, where he'd transfer to an Air Canada flight back to Fairbanks. He had some time to kill. The terminal was quiet.

A Starbucks was open and he asked the girl working there if there was a bar. She directed him down the corridor and a few minutes later he was sitting on a stool with a bottled Budweiser in front of him. The TV was showing sports. He was the only customer.

"Late flight?" the girl working the bar said.

He nodded and glanced at the TV. "You got CNN on that?"

She found the remote and switched the channel.

The only news other than the assassinations was the El Sucio trial. He watched the screen as a convoy of fifty vehicles made its way across the Brooklyn bridge. Broad daylight. Snipers, dogs, helicopters, humvees. They even had mounted police.

"Disaster waiting to happen," he said.

The girl looked at the screen and nodded.

"You still serving food?"

"Just what you see there," she said, pointing to a display case containing cold snacks, sandwiches, the kind of things he could have bought at the Starbucks.

"What do you recommend?"

She shrugged. "The corned beef."

"I'll take it."

She grabbed it for him, opened the wrapper, and put it in a microwave.

He turned back to the TV. It was as if the president was daring the cartel to attack. Hunter played through possible scenarios in his mind. How he'd do it if he was the cartel. There were so many options it wasn't even funny. People were going to die in New York over this. It was just a question of how many.

The girl served his sandwich.

"You're in for a treat," she said.

He took a bite and asked for ketchup. When he got back to Fairbanks he'd go to Lacey's and order the biggest steak on the menu. He knew he might not have that freedom much longer.

It wouldn't take long for the feds to join the dots. Since leaving Seattle, he'd covered his tracks perfectly, but if anyone found out the targets all had a hand to play in the death of his wife, they'd come looking for him.

He knew how to stay off the radar, he'd spent years dodging the CIA, but the second he got the call telling him Chianne and the kid were missing, he quit worrying about that. He bought a plane ticket to Seattle knowing it would raise a flag on a computer somewhere in Langley. It was just a matter of time now.

Hell, he'd order two steaks.

And he'd savor every bite.

No regrets.

The men who'd killed his family had to die, and whatever followed was small potatoes next to that.

When he met Chianne two years earlier she was a nineteen-year-old diner waitress with a three-year-old daughter, an alcohol problem, and more bills than she could handle. He was an AWOL CIA assassin who couldn't sleep at night from the things he'd done. At thirty-three, he was almost twice her age.

But whatever it was between them, it worked. They were a balm to each other's wounds. Looking after Chianne and the kid kept him focused. It kept his demons at bay. It stopped him focusing on what he'd done for the government. And what the government had done to him. He wouldn't have said it for fear of jinxing it, but with Chianne he'd been happy. Happier than he'd thought possible.

And Chianne had done well with him too. She'd cleaned up her act. The kid was doing well. They'd made a life together.

And then it was gone.

He looked up at the TV.

The newscaster was talking about El Sucio's past. He'd escaped every prison he'd ever been put in. And he'd gone after the prison workers afterwards, mercilessly hunting down everyone, from the governor right down to the women who delivered the tortillas on bicycles. Apparently, the guards at 10 South were having their families put into protective custody.

"What a shit show," Hunter said.

The girl looked at him but she hadn't been watching the TV.

"You want another beer?" she said.

He nodded. He hadn't slept in days. His eyes were heavy. He looked at the departure screen. Not much longer to wait.

"How much do I owe you?" he said.

EIGHT

Fawn sat at her desk and read the file, cover to cover, for the third time. It was getting late. If Mitch had been at home waiting, this was about the time she'd have begun worrying about him.

Hale knocked on the door.

"You burning the midnight oil?" he said.

She hadn't spoken to him since the night before and she had questions. She'd double checked every salient detail in Hunter's file, she'd confirmed everything she possibly could, but there were gaps. Some details were classified, they'd come back so redacted they'd be useless. Others, even the government wouldn't have knowledge of. Hunter had been masterful at covering his tracks.

"I'm calling it a night soon," she said.

"Mitch will be getting pissy," Hale said.

Fawn shook her head. "No he won't."

Hale cleared his throat. "I was about to make some coffee."

"Shouldn't you be getting home," Fawn said, looking at her watch. "It's after nine."

Hale sighed.

Fawn looked up at him. She arched her back and stretched out her arms.

"Come on," Hale said. "Time for coffee."

She followed him to a small break room and he put a capsule in the machine. The room was comfortable, a major upgrade from the plastic chairs and fluorescent lights she'd gotten used to at SIGINT. This room was more like a business class airport lounge with upholstered furniture, comfortable lighting, and a well-stocked snack fridge. She grabbed an apple from a metal bowl by the coffee machine and took a bite.

"You skipped dinner," Hale said, handing her a cup of coffee.

"I'm watching my figure," she said.

Hale grabbed his own coffee from the machine and they sat at some sofas by the window. They had a five-star view of a two-hundred-thousand-square-foot parking lot. It was almost empty now and the lamps on the asphalt made it look like some sort of futuristic agricultural facility. All the scene needed was some workers, stooping over the concrete, to complete the picture.

Fawn had the file with her and she put it on the table.

"So this Jack Hunter, he's one of ours?"

"He was," Hale said. "Praying Mantis. The Enhanced Operative program."

"Enhanced Operative?"

Hale shrugged. "They've got to have a name for everything."

"Is the program ongoing?"

Hale shook his head.

"Who was cleared?"

"The president, director of national intelligence, director of the CIA, the joint chiefs."

"Who handled the program?"

"Yours truly," Hale said.

"And you never told me?"

"It's been on ice since Hunter went AWOL."

"He was the only operative?"

"There were eight. He's the only one still alive. He went underground after a particularly bloody fuck up in Afghanistan. His team got wiped out. It wasn't his fault."

"Four years ago?" Fawn said.

Hale nodded at the report. "You've done your homework. What do you want to know?"

"Will you tell me the truth?"

"Depends."

"We've got some damage control to do, boss."

"I'll tell you as much as I can."

Fawn flipped open the document. She'd made notes on the inside cover and went through her questions, one by one.

"Apart from the eight operatives, how many were on the Praying Mantis team?"

"Here in Langley there were twelve."

"When did you disband the team?"

"After Hunter went AWOL. He was the last of the assets. Without him there wasn't any need for the team."

"Where are they now?"

"Still here. All twelve. Other programs."

"You can vouch for them?"

"They're good, Fawn."

She put a line through the first item on her list and moved on.

"Hunter went AWOL four years ago?"

Hale nodded.

"How long was he dark?"

"First two years. Then he showed up in Fairbanks, Alaska. Got married."

"Who knew about that?"

"Only me. And now you?"

"What about the director? The president?"

"Just me."

"Is Jack Hunter his real name?"

"Not by birth, but it's a legal name. And no, none of the twelve from the original team knew him by that name. He acquired it afterward."

Fawn put down her pen and looked up at Hale.

"Why didn't you report up the chain when you found him?"

Hale shrugged. "A hunch."

She knew Hunter would have been neutralized at that point. Hale had gone out on a limb. That was the thing about Hale. For all his faults, he was a loyal son of a bitch. If Hale threw someone under the bus, it was only because it was operationally justified. He never did it purely for expedience.

She picked up her pen.

"Okay," she said. "Very noble. Now he's gone haywire and killed a state senator, a federal judge, a treasury executive, and Congressman Dayton."

"Yes," Hale said.

"You don't look worried."

"I'm worried."

Fawn shook her head. "Jesus, Jeff. You've got your ass hanging out here. Did you see that Dayton launched a presidential bid the day he was shot."

"I was aware of that."

Fawn's voice rose. "How long did it take you to figure out this was Hunter? For Christ's sake. How long do you think it will take for someone else to figure it out?"

"They won't."

"You're kidding me. He's flying around on a fricking MasterCard, Jeff. You're in the shit."

Hale leaned forward and put his hand on Fawn's knee.

"I'm flattered you're so concerned for my wellbeing," he said.

"I'm your underling," Fawn said. "You go down. I go down."

"We're not going down, Fawn."

Fawn let out a long sigh. She leaned back in her chair and pushed Hale's hand off her knee. She brought her coffee to her lips. It was good coffee. Strong. That George Clooney knew his shit.

She forced herself to calm down, then she said, "What am I not seeing?"

Hale flipped a few pages forward in the file. He opened the section on what had happened last month in Washington State.

"His wife was murdered," Hale said.

"And her child. It's all over the news. Picked up nationally, I might add. Police officers dead. Prostitutes dead. It's like a Netflix original."

"I'd watch it."

"That's the problem," Fawn said.

"But no one's linked the wife's death to the state senator's death."

"Not yet, but that got major airtime too. He was thrown from the roof of a parking lot. You couldn't wish for a better story if you were a reporter."

"Couldn't you?"

She looked up at him. He had that look in his eye.

"What are you planning, you sly fuck?"

"You should go home and get some sleep. Pick up a copy of *the Post* in the morning."

"That's why you wanted those files flagged," Fawn said.

Hale smiled. "Get going. You've got another early start tomorrow."

"I'll be here."

"Not here. You're flying to Fairbanks."

"What? I'm not going anywhere near your enhanced operative," she said, emphasizing the last two words.

"Oh, you're going. And you're recruiting him."

"The fuck I am."

Hale was enjoying this. "Pack warm. Your plane leaves at seven."

NINE

The alarm on Fawn's phone was set for four AM. She groaned as she shut it off and got out of bed. A quick shower, brushed her teeth, that was it. She could do her makeup in the cab. She hadn't packed the night before so she threw a few random toiletries, some underwear and a few shirts in the Louis Vuitton shoulder bag Mitch had given her for Christmas. He had taste, that was one thing you could say for him.

She didn't bring any paperwork, or the two-pound government-issue brick the CIA passed off as a laptop.

The cab honked while she was still waiting for the kettle to boil.

"Fuck," she said as she shut it off and grabbed her bag.

"Dulles," she said to the driver.

He was Mexican and had the radio tuned in to a Spanish language talkshow discussing the El Sucio trial.

"What do you make of all that?" she asked him.

"Ma'am?"

"El Sucio? El cartel?"

"Oh, no sé."

"I hear he's a hero in Mexico."

"A hero? Más o menos," the driver said, moving his hand back and forth. "You know, in my town, there was a singer who wrote songs about him."

"Like Robin Hood," Fawn said.

"He escaped the government. He made them look foolish. In Mexico, if you make the government look foolish, you are a hero."

"But he also killed people."

"Sí. So many people. Thousands and thousands."

"Are Mexicans glad he'll see justice?"

"If he sees justice they will be happy. But he's been caught before. Men like El Sucio, they don't go down without a fight."

"You think there'll be an attack?"

"If I owned bombing planes and I was in prison I would tell them to use the planes, wouldn't you?"

Fawn nodded. They were close to the highway and were passing an open gas station. "Would you mind if we made a quick stop."

"No problem."

As she got out, she asked how he took his coffee.

She was back a minute later with two coffees and an early edition of *the Post*. The story was on the front page.

Assassination victims all linked to Saudi Arabia.

She read the article. It appeared the Saudis had been supporting certain US politicians for years, aiding their careers, contributing to their campaigns, and receiving preferential treatment in return. It wasn't exactly news. The Saudi government spent billions in Washington every year and pretty much everyone had had a taste. But the fact these four had been specifically aided, and were now all dead, all assassinated, that was going to ruffle feathers.

"Hale, you son of a bitch," she said to herself.

She didn't doubt for a second it was true. Hale wasn't the type to make up a story. No. His style was to use true facts to tell his lies. They worked so much better.

No one would be looking at the murder of a native woman in upstate Washington any more. This would be an international story. The Saudis could be reliably depended on to make things worse for themselves. They would over-react and their arrogance would fuel the media. This story would be about Saudi Arabia from here on out.

It suited Hale to take the heat off his former asset, but Fawn wasn't so sure how she felt about it. Hunter wasn't just a political liability, from what she could make out he was a murderous lunatic. He'd been trained by the CIA's most sophisticated operative program to be as lethal as it was physically possible to make a man. When rappers said there were six million ways to die, this guy's methods were what they were talking about. And he'd gone haywire.

Recruiting him was the stupidest thing she could think of. If he said yes, she and Hale would both live to regret it. She knew that, and made up her mind not to be too persuasive when she delivered Hale's message.

She looked up at the driver. "You got any of that music? The El Sucio songs?"

"Narcocorridos? Sure. I can find something."

He flicked through his phone while passing a huge truck. A moment later, they were listening to a ballad of El Sucio's bravery and heroism in the face of government oppression.

The airport was empty and check in went smoothly. She was flying business class with a short layover in Seattle.

She bought coffee and a croissant while waiting to board and as soon as the plane was in the air she asked the hostess for more coffee.

The plane was only half-full and the hostess had plenty of time for her. She brought two cups of coffee and Fawn noticed her breast touch her shoulder as she leaned over. She smelled of cinnamon.

"Thank you," Fawn said.

The hostess was petite with short black hair cropped at the neck. Her oval eyes reminded her of Celeste's. Maybe she'd look Celeste up when she got back. They worked in the same building after all.

When they landed in Seattle, Fawn was sorry to say goodbye to the hostess. She gave her a smile but doubted she'd remember her in five minutes.

She had an hour to kill between flights and bought more coffee and called Hale.

She called his cell but was redirected to his secretary. He's flying today, the secretary told her.

Fawn wondered where he was going.

There was a TV showing the news in the lounge and she half-watched it. It was another big day in the El Sucio trial. Security had been heightened all over New York after a number of bomb scares were called in. The Brooklyn Bridge was completely closed to traffic all day.

She slept on the next flight, which was five hours, and was in Fairbanks by one PM local time. It was time for dinner back in DC and she was hungry. She'd mercifully slept through the on-flight meal.

At the terminal in Fairbanks she picked up a car from the Hertz desk and drove to her hotel. It was freezing and she hadn't brought anything warmer than the Burberry trench coat she wore back in DC. It wasn't nearly enough.

She tried calling Hale again but his phone was still off. She let the valet take her car at the hotel and checked in. In her room she ordered a burger and fries and ate it on the bed with the TV on.

She freshened up before leaving the room, cursing her impractical short skirt, heels, and light coat. She prayed she wouldn't be in Fairbanks long.

TEN

Hunter went straight to Lacey's from the airport. He had the steak and eggs with A1 sauce and brown toast. He relished it as if it was the last meal he'd ever eat. It was still early when he got back to his apartment and that's when it hit him. The place had Chianne and the kid written all over it. He saw them in the dishes in the kitchen, the food in the pantry, the kid's DVDs scattered under the TV, the bedrooms. He couldn't breathe.

He took a shower and lay on the bed but couldn't sleep.

He went out and bought some groceries, the very basics, coffee, milk, cereal, jerky. He tried the TV, watched a guy and his wife renovate a house in Atlanta and flip it for a forty-grand profit. Around five in the evening he had another shower and punched a hole in the wall through tile.

His fist was bleeding and the water at the bottom of the shower ran red.

Afterward, as he was drying off in the bedroom, he heard a dog bark. A car had pulled into the lot. There was a change in the lighting from the lamp outside the bedroom.

His instincts kicked in. He knew they'd be coming for him and, at this point, he wanted them to come.

Staying here, in this apartment, the memories of Chianne and the kid on everything, was torture.

He threw the towel on the bed and walked slowly through the hall to the front of the apartment. He stole a glance through the lace curtain. There was a woman approaching. He'd have noticed her a hundred miles away in her two-thousand-dollar coat and high-heels. You didn't dress like that in Fairbanks in November.

She wasn't the tactical team he'd been expecting. He looked out over the parking lot, the approaches to the door, then went back to the bedroom and checked out back. It looked like she was alone.

She knocked on his door.

He grabbed the towel and went to answer, wrapping it around his waist. He didn't look at her when he opened the door, but checked both sides of the building before ushering her in. It was freezing outside and neither of them was dressed for it.

"You CIA?" he said.

She nodded.

"Hale send you?"

She nodded again.

"I'm not going back."

She looked him over and he suddenly felt naked.

"I'll be right back," he said, and left her standing there while he went to the bedroom. He came back in jeans, a white t-shirt and a red and black flannel shirt. Fawn was sitting in the living room. He took the sofa opposite her and started pulling on thick, wool socks.

"They didn't tell you about the weather before they sent you?" he said.

She shook her head. "I didn't have much time to pack."

"Temperature will be below zero tonight."

Fawn looked upset at the prospect. "Fuck," she said.

Hunter got up and put on water to make coffee. While it boiled, he went into the bedroom and grabbed Chianne's winter coat and some boots. He brought them to the living room and left them on the table.

"You can borrow these."

"I couldn't."

"Sure you could," he said.

She was visibly shivering.

He went back to the kitchen and returned with two mugs of black coffee.

"I've got milk," he said. "No cream."

"Black's fine."

He sat down across from her and took her in. She looked like a tall glass of water. He didn't usually go for short hair but her's looked good, stylish, like something from Paris. Her features were delicate, her skin pale almost to the point of translucence. A stiff breeze would blow her away. He wanted to get a blanket from the bedroom and put it over her.

"My name is Fawn Aspen. I work in," she hesitated. CIA officers aren't used to ever saying their jobs aloud. "I work with Jeff Hale."

"Black Ops," Hunter said. "No need to be coy with me."

"You worked for Hale until four years ago?"

"I served my country. Hale happened to be there."

Fawn smiled.

"I'll cut to the chase."

"I'll save you the hassle. I'm not coming back."

She didn't look surprised.

"Maybe I'm here to arrest you," she said, smiling.

Hunter smiled back and took a sip of his coffee.

"One little girl?"

That hit the mark.

"There's no need to be rude," she said.

"I just want to be clear. I wouldn't go back to Langley if my life depended on it."

"Your life does depend on it."

He sipped his coffee and sat back on the sofa.

"We're on the same page then."

She sighed and got up to leave.

"Please do me a favor and put on the coat and boots before you go."

She looked at him and glanced toward the window. Snow flurried across the parking lot. Reluctantly, she put on the snow boots and the huge parka over her coat. They didn't match her pencil skirt and silk blouse but she looked a lot less foolish in them.

She left with her shoes in her hand.

ELEVEN

Hunter watched Fawn walk down the steps to her car. It was a Chevy Impala with the rental company's logo on a sticker in the windshield. He noted the plate number. She turned left out of the parking lot and set off in the direction of the airport. He kept watch of the lot for about a minute, then threw on some boots and a coat and ran down to his truck. He set off in the same direction and caught up to her a few blocks later. Her red car was easy to tail and he kept five or six cars back to make sure she didn't notice him.

Something about her visit was just a little too easy. The CIA wasn't in the habit of giving you options. He was going to follow her and see if he could get a clearer picture of what was going on. He believed that she worked with Hale, and he knew Hale wanted him back. Praying Mantis had been a major investment, a major asset. Hale had spent the better part of his career getting it up and running. It was his baby. Now that he had some leverage over Hunter, he'd want to make maximum use of it.

It was clear Fawn was headed toward the airport so Hunter gave her a lot of room and took a few precautions to detect any tails that might be following him. He bungled an intersection, getting caught trying to make a left turn after the light had turned. Some people honked but no one turning left after him. When they got close to the airport, Fawn turned off toward the hotels. It was the usual cluster of brandnames, Best Western, La Quinta, Candlewood. She pulled into the Hampton Inn and parked. She entered without luggage, still wearing the boots and parka he'd given her, still carrying her fancy shoes.

Hunter drove past the hotel and made a round of the block. He pulled into the lot of a fast food place across the street from the hotel. He could see the hotel entrance and Fawn's car from where he was.

He kept the engine running so the heat would stay on and turned on the radio. There was a lot of talk about the El Sucio trial. There'd been a bomb scare at the court building and the place was still on lockdown. No one at the trial had been able to leave the building. There'd also been a big story in the *Washington Post* about the assassinations. The targets had all been mixed up in some scandal involving Saudi Arabia. If it was true, it was the first Hunter was hearing of it. He'd gone after them because of what happened to his wife. Nothing more.

He wondered if the Saudi connection had something to do with the group the state senator had told him about, the Society of True Blood. He'd assumed it was something racist, like the Klan but against natives. Maybe there was more to it.

He didn't care.

It was convenient they hadn't connected the assassinations to his wife's murder, but Jeff Hale had, and this Saudi connection could easily be some misdirection from his

department. Hale had always been an expert at manipulating the press.

Hunter stamped his feet to get some blood flowing.
He'd been sitting there an hour and it was cold despite the
running engine. He looked across the lot at the fast food
restaurant and wondered if they served coffee. If they didn't
there was a gas station at the corner of the street that would.

He was about to go find out when someone rapped on
the passenger-side window.

It was Fawn.

Some stakeout this was.

He leaned over and opened the door. She got in and
turned the heat on full.

"You staying out here all night?"

He shrugged. "I was making sure you got home safely."

"I know what you were doing."

"You here alone?"

"Hale is en route. He's landing soon."

"Oh, great. I knew our meeting had been too easy."

"You might as well come inside," Fawn said. "Save me
and Hale a drive back across town."

Hunter looked at his watch as if he had somewhere else
to be.

Fawn had her hands over the heat. "Drive us closer to
the door," she said. "There's a bar inside."

Hunter sighed "Is there a restaurant?"

TWELVE

Fawn led the way to the hotel bar. She'd already had a scotch while waiting to see if Hunter would come inside on his own. He'd been stubborn. She had to go back out in the cold to get him. She did it more for the company than any operational reason.

They sat in the lounge next to a fireplace. The lobby was a mix of rustic cabin and the generic corporate décor of a chain hotel. There were a few other business types in the bar, a guy alone by the window, a man and woman eating dinner, a man on a laptop peering at his screen.

Fawn was grateful for the fire. She was still wearing the snow boots Hunter had given her and she didn't want to take them off, despite how they looked. In this weather, her Manolo Blahniks were the less appropriate option.

The waitress came over and Fawn ordered a glass of white wine. She watched Hunter as he looked over the options.

"What beers do you have by the bottle?" he said.

The waitress ran through them and Hunter picked something domestic. He also asked for the food menu. Fawn had been planning on waiting for Hale but decided she'd eat with Hunter if he ordered something. Not that she was hungry. It just felt like the polite thing to do.

"What are you having?" he said as he scanned the menu.

Fawn shrugged.

He handed her the menu and beckoned the waitress.

"I'm going to have the steak, medium rare, with french fries," he said. "And my friend will have the calamari."

He looked at her with a challenge in his eye that made her smile. The waitress was already writing the order.

"No, I hate calamari," Fawn said.

Hunter sighed. "The seafood pasta then."

"No," Fawn said.

She began reading the menu and Hunter grinned at the waitress, shaking his head.

"She's going to order for herself. Let her get anything she wants."

Fawn didn't know if he was teasing her or being serious. She felt like kicking him on the shin. She could tell this was going to be one of those CIA sparring matches where they both tried to get as much information from each other as they could while giving away as little as possible.

"I'm going to have the house salad, with salmon," she said, "and we'll take the breaded mushrooms too."

The waitress nodded and left and Fawn looked at Hunter.

"So you're a funny guy," she said. "Hale never mentioned that."

"I'm surprised," Hunter said. "I had him cracking up every time I came back from a mission with my report."

"I bet."

"You know Hale. Nothing tickles his fancy more than a good kill."

She was surprised he said that. It was straight to the point. No playing around.

"That much is true," she said.

"How long have you worked with him?" Hunter said.

Fawn wondered how much she should say. "A few years."

He nodded. "How are you liking it?"

"It's fine."

"Did you always want to work in intelligence?"

She shook her head. "I was a math PhD at Berkeley. I interviewed for a few defense contractors. They had me take some tests and next thing, the CIA contacted me."

"So math's your thing?"

"It was."

"I'm surprised they've got you under Hale. His operations aren't usually very," he paused, searching for the word, "analytic."

"No," she said, "but we worked together frequently in my first posting. He had more intercepts to decode than the rest of the departments combined. Eventually, he just popped the question."

Hunter laughed.

She'd chosen her words deliberately. She meant to imply something sexual might be going on. She wanted to get Hunter to pry into her personal life, her relationship with Hale. It was a manipulation tactic she'd been taught at Langley. If a man overstepped in some way with a woman, he was very likely to pay her back in another. A little quid pro quo. Her goal was to get him to say something that could be interpreted as hurting her feelings in some way.

"You impressed him," Hunter said, probing.

"His new project required someone with my," she looked up at him before finishing the sentence, "skills."

Hunter looked at her for a few seconds. She knew what he was thinking. She was young. She wasn't unattractive. Everyone knew Hale's reputation.

He was wondering if she slept with the boss. He wanted to know what box to put her in. Was she a real operative, someone to be wary of, or was she one of Hale's playthings?

The smart thing would be to let him believe the later.

But something about him, the way he looked at her, the way his eyes probed her, made her hesitant to give him that impression of her.

Who was manipulating who, she wondered. After all, he was CIA-trained too.

He didn't take the bait. He kept it professional.

"He's got some new scheme cooked up to take the place of Mantis, doesn't he?"

The waitress arrived with the mushrooms. Fawn waited.

"Yes, but I don't think his heart is in it the same way. He still talks about the old days. The eight of you. The capabilities you were developing."

"He saw us sneaking into the Kremlin and stealing Putin's porn collection."

She blinked. Maybe he was taking the bait.

"Oh, porn is exactly what he'd steal."

Hunter laughed. Fawn was surprised how pleased that made her.

Hunter said, "Do you like working with him?"

She looked at him. He was definitely probing.

For some reason she felt embarrassed. She cared more than she should what he thought.

"What do you think?" she said.

He looked her over then looked away.

Fawn felt her cheeks flush and was glad he wasn't looking at her.

He didn't know what to make of her, and she wasn't sure what she made of him either. He certainly wasn't what she'd been expecting. He'd been funny with the waitress. The look in his eye when he spoke to her was open, unguarded. He was straightforward. He didn't play games. He told it like it was. He hadn't taken the bait when she'd tried to manipulate him, and as far as she could tell, he hadn't set any traps of his own for her either.

That, or he was just better at this game than he seemed.

She doubted that.

He ate a few mushrooms, picking them up from the bowl with his fingers. Was that a false intimacy, something to get her guard down? It would have been if she'd done it.

She wanted to trust him.

She had the impression she could ask him about his time at the agency and he'd tell her the truth. She could ask him who she needed to be wary of and he'd tell her. She could ask him if she could really trust Hale, if she could really trust the director. She felt she could talk to this man, and that wasn't a common feeling in their line of work.

She decided to test the ice, see how he responded.

"Do you miss Langley?"

"It's hard to miss something when you still dream about it every night," he said.

"Nightmares, you mean?"

He nodded.

Fawn had read about some of the side effects of the enhancement process that had been used in Mantis. Insomnia, depression, paranoia. Three of the eight subjects had killed themselves stateside. Another three committed suicide by enemy fire. They'd exposed themselves need-lessly, inexplicably. The seventh died in a helicopter crash. He was the only person on board and had not been under fire.

None of the dead Mantis operatives, as far as she could tell, had needed to die. Their training promised to make them invincible, and some people still believed it had. Invincible to everything but themselves.

Hunter was the only one left.

She was surprised how willing he was to talk.

"Can I ask you something?" she said.

He shrugged. "Go ahead. I can't promise I'll answer."

She took a sip from her glass.

"What do you think happened to your colleagues?"

"The other seven?"

She nodded.

He was about to answer when the waitress arrived with their food.

"Thank you," Fawn said.

"You two need anything else?"

Hunter shook his head.

He waited for her to leave, then leaned back and took a breath. He wasn't upset she'd asked, but it was clear it wasn't easy for him to talk about it.

Fawn took a bite of her salad, it was very bland, and waited for him to speak.

He was looking at her and hadn't touched the steak. It looked a lot better than her salad.

"I'm no psychologist," he said. "I'm a simple guy. If there's a simple answer, that's the one I'll take."

He cut a piece of steak and put it in his mouth.

"And what's your simple answer?" she said.

"Combat stress. No big mystery. Veterans have been

coming home with trauma for decades. Those situations. Those things we see. They fuck us up."

"Simple as that?" she said, poking at the salmon with her fork.

"Simple as that. Praying Mantis was intense. It was traumatic. So, you know, it fucked everyone up."

"So you just put it down to PTSD?"

Hunter held his hands open to her like he was showing her something. "Did you see the mission files?"

"I've seen the blue ones."

"Not the others?"

"To be honest, I don't even know if they still exist."

Hunter nodded. It wouldn't be surprising if Hale had destroyed the most damning records of a cancelled program.

"We did some fucked up shit," he said.

"Yes we did."

"Worse than your normal war stuff."

"Yes," Fawn said.

"And the red files, they'd be worse than what you've seen."

"Yes they would," she said.

"Now imagine you're the guy doing that shit. The fallout. The collateral damage. All that's on you. Something so dirty even the CIA doesn't like to touch it. They delete every record proving it ever happened."

Fawn nodded. She wanted to believe him. She wanted to believe the suicides were nothing more sinister than PTSD. It was certainly possible. Plausible even. Those were some heavy missions. And the men had been sent in alone. No cover. No rescue. Complete disavowal if anything went wrong. That sort of stress fucked with a man. It didn't stop just because the mission stopped.

PTSD. It was possible.

But something in her gut told her there was more to it. And she felt Hunter knew more than he was letting on.

There were too many deleted files for someone not to be hiding something.

Mantis had delivered results that were unheard of prior to its initiation. Those operatives were wrecking balls when they got into it. They singlehandedly gutted organizations and cells that had threatened national security for decades.

There was no way the government would pull the plug on a program like that unless something had gone seriously wrong. Seven dead operatives, a little PTSD, that was nothing compared to those results. It gave her pause. She'd seen the dark side. It was very difficult to unsee that stuff, and to see your own government in the same light afterward.

Someone had hit a kill switch. She was sure of it.

She'd seen so-called self-destruct mechanisms, physical and psychological, built into black-ops programs before. Methods that could be used to ensure that an operative wouldn't go off the rails after a mission. Suicide was a very practical strategy in certain cases. None had been approved during her time with Hale, but they'd definitely been used before her arrival, when a different team had been working for him.

Suicide, or self-destruct as the documents referred to it, would definitely have been part of the Mantis parameters. From what she'd seen of the enhancement program, there was no way the government could risk those operatives going rogue. It would be like unleashing smallpox and hoping it only killed the enemy.

The administration would have demanded a surefire way of pulling the plug. And deep down, she knew Hale would have given it to them.

Hunter had finished his food and his second beer.

If he'd been subjected to some self-destruct measure, it certainly didn't show. He was damaged goods, that much was clear, but like he said, a lot of soldiers were damaged goods.

It certainly didn't look like his brain had been fried. He was functioning. If it wasn't for the fact he'd just assassinated four members of the government, Fawn would have thought he was less fucked up than most of the guys she'd dated in the last five years.

She could see why Hale had let him live.

It would be a crime to kill a man like this after the things he'd been through. The things he'd done.

"Hale will be here soon," she said.

Hunter nodded. He didn't seem anxious at the idea of seeing his old boss.

"Anyway," he said, "those days are behind me. You're the one we should be worried about."

"What do you mean?"

"You know what I mean."

"No I don't."

Hunter ordered them another round.

"Sure you do," he said, and left it at that.

Fawn was confused. Had he just taken her bait? If he had, he'd done it in a way that didn't make him owe her a thing. She'd exposed herself for nothing. Hunter had decided he didn't need to know for certain. The suggestion she was sleeping with Hale was enough to justify his comment.

He seemed to know exactly who she was, what kind of person, and how she felt about the life she was living.

"I'm not sleeping with him," she blurted.

Hunter smiled.

Fawn was upset with herself. "If that's what you were suggesting," she added.

Hunter let out a sigh and leaned back in his chair, very satisfied with himself.

"Check mate," he said.

She'd fallen for it. She'd told him what he wanted to know without him having to ask. He'd taken the bait from the trap without touching the trigger.

There was a TV behind the bar and some breaking news flashed across the bottom of the screen.

Major Terrorist Attack in New York. Multiple Casualties. This is a Developing Story.

"Turn that up, would you?" Hunter said to the waitress.

THIRTEEN

Hale was in a shitty mood as he hurried through the Fairbanks terminal. There were fourteen missed calls on his cell. All required encryption that couldn't be provided over the airline's onboard wifi.

"Fuck off," he said to his phone as he hurried down the escalator.

The world wasn't going to end just because he'd had his phone off for a few hours.

What was it about escalators that made everyone fucking stand around like a complete zombie? Just because the stairs moved didn't mean you lost the power to walk. He squeezed past an overweight businessman and when he felt the first blast of the Alaskan winter through the terminal doors he wanted to punch someone.

This was the last place on earth he wanted to be. He'd been glad to send Fawn to take care of it, but even as he read his perfectly placed story on the front page of *the Post*, Jasper Marten's first byline, he realized this was something he needed to take care of personally.

There was no way Hunter was going to say yes to

Fawn's request. He'd sent her unprepared. He hadn't explained to her the importance of recruiting him. He'd say no and she'd accept his answer and come home. The more he thought about it, the more he knew he couldn't let that happen.

Hunter simply could not stay off the leash. He'd murdered a presidential candidate, for fuck's sake. Sure, he had a good reason, but still.

Fawn had been right. His ass was way out in the wind on this.

He'd fucking recruited Hunter personally.

Either Hunter came back to heel, or his hand would be forced.

Hunter was a good soldier. He'd done everything asked of him and more. He deserved one last chance to come in from the cold. And Hale had to give him that chance personally.

He found the stop for the hotel shuttle and pulled his coat around him. It was nowhere near adequate for the weather. And of course the shuttle took forever.

He waited impatiently. He'd have called his secretary but it was so windy he'd have had a hard time hearing her on the phone. He decided to call from the shuttle.

It was another five minutes and he felt every single second.

"Where have you been?" he said irritably to the driver.

The driver made a face. "They don't have coats where you're from?" he said.

Hale muttered under his breath and took a seat at the back. He was the only passenger. He called his office to find out what was so urgent it couldn't wait.

"Sue, it's me."

He watched the driver as he spoke.

"Yeah, I just landed."

The driver took corners like he was in a race.

"Picture the north pole with the heat turned down."

She asked him if he'd seen the news and he said no. There'd been no screens in the terminal.

The next words out of his mouth were, "Holy mother of fuck."

She said they were calling it the worst attack on US soil since 9/11. They were nowhere near a final count but the casualties were already in the thousands.

He'd been out of DC less than twelve hours and the country was falling to shit.

This was going to be big. This was going to be all hands on deck.

He remembered everything that happened after the World Trade Center. The complete reorienting of foreign policy. The mistakes that were made. The losses that were compounded. The careers that were won and lost.

Whoever played this right would end up director of the CIA. Someone was going to do it.

And one thing was for certain. The current director was history. No way he'd survive this.

As the shuttle pulled up to the door of the Fairbanks Hampton Inn, Jeff Hoffelder Hale, Director of Paramilitary Black-Ops, the minuscule, insignificant, dirty little secret of the directorate of operations, itself a dirty secret of the intelligence service, decided how he was going to respond to the greatest opportunity to present itself to him in his entire career.

This attack, this atrocity, was going to make him a mother-fucking king.

He grabbed his bag and stepped off the shuttle without speaking to the driver.

Inside, he found Fawn and Hunter at the bar, sipping drinks and watching the news coming in from New York.

"Aspen, Hunter, don't get up," he said, walking over to them and beckoning the server.

"Have you seen this?" Fawn said.

"I was just notified by Sue. I haven't seen shit. How bad is it?"

"It's bad, boss."

"Thousands of casualties," Hunter said.

Hale looked at Hunter and then back at the screen. It was strange. The man had gone dark for two years, and remained in hiding for two more even as Hale tracked him. Hale could have had him killed at any moment. There were several times when he came close to making the order. Now, they were sitting in an airport hotel bar, watching the news like nothing had happened.

"Whatever he's having," Hale said to the waitress.

The three of them couldn't believe what they were seeing. There'd never been carnage on the streets like this before. Not ever. Hale realized this was going to turn out to be the deadliest attack in the nation's history.

And then it flashed across the screen.

Death toll exceeds Pearl Harbor, making this the second deadliest attack to take place on US soil.

The waitress brought the drinks and Hale wondered how the fuck he was going to get Hunter to help him again. After everything that had happened, he wondered if it was even possible.

When he'd stepped on the plane at Dulles twelve hours earlier, he'd come here hoping to save a good man's life. Or, more accurately, of persuading him to save his own life.

Now, the stakes had gone all the way to the top.

The message along the bottom of the screen was updated.

Death toll exceeds 9/11, making this the deadliest attack in US history.

FOURTEEN

The operation to free Segundo José Heredia from US custody was a plan with many moving parts. The details offered a sinister view into the minds of those running the cartel in his absence. The level of carnage, the purposeful targeting of civilians to create diversions, resembled the methods of a terrorist organization. But the resources of the cartel, and tactics used, were military in scale.

The cartel had discovered long ago what all ruthless military forces in history knew. Whoever is willing to get the most blood on his hands has the advantage.

There was no way the US would be prepared for the ferocity of what they were planning.

El Sucio's transportation between the prison and courthouse was the obvious point for an attack. The cartel knew it, but the authorities also knew it. At the scheduled transportation times to and from the courthouse the security was so tight, and was arranged in such a way, that any kind of escape attempt would result in El Sucio's death.

Given the political implications of an escape, the President, the FBI Director, and the heads of all supporting agencies had devised a system that would make live escape almost impossible.

Officially, security was the responsibility of three agencies, the city of New York, federal prison marshals, and the FBI. The marshals secured El Sucio's person. They were responsible for the prison, the armored vehicle that moved him between locations, and his person while in the courthouse.

The city secured the courthouse itself, provided an escort for the transportation convoy, and ensured conditions surrounding the prison and courthouse were secure. They closed the area to traffic, had sharp shooters and helicopters on overwatch, and monitored movement on the ground. The FBI played a coordinating role. They had hundreds of agents on the ground, but the bulk of their work was providing intel. They were monitoring cartel movements and activity across the US and Mexico, liaising with the military and the intelligence services, and ensuring that nothing unforeseen entered New York from outside the city.

Unofficially, the president also ordered the military and CIA to be on standby. Neither could be legally used to play a law enforcement role on US soil, but the slightest hint of an external threat and they would be called in. Given the upgrading of the cartel to the level of a sovereign enemy, use of the military would be justified in a range of scenarios.

From the outset, the security operations were well-managed and resourced.

Communication and coordination between the three branches on the ground was impeccable. The FBI director, Willis Chancey, took personal control of the operation and set up a command center at the New York FBI field office, conveniently located just across Foley Square from the prison. He took over an entire floor of the building and had three-hundred agents working on the constant stream of data coming in from FBI offices across the country, as well as from the CIA, the DoD, the DEA, and New York's law enforcement agencies.

Taking over personally was a political risk. If anything went wrong, Chancey's career would be on the block. Chancey knew this but had decided the opportunity was worth the risk. The case had the president's personal attention as well as round the clock press coverage. Chancey personally held a press conference in the lobby of the FBI building every morning before El Sucio's transportation. It became clear to everyone who knew him he was considering launching a bid for higher office as soon as the trial concluded.

Each morning of the trial, El Sucio went through the same security procedure he'd gone through when he first entered 10 South, only in reverse. His automated cell released him and if he didn't follow voice directions given through an intercom he would be subjected to the one-hundred-fifty decibel, eardrum rupturing, auditory stimulant. If that didn't work, federal marshals were authorized to enter the prison and physically move him through the process. That didn't prove necessary and El Sucio showed every sign of compliance as he followed the LED light strip to the elevator, entered a holding cell, stripped naked, went through a chlorine shower. He then allowed himself to be shackled and entered an eighteen-inch-thick steel sarcophagus.

The sarcophagus resembled a huge, steel coffin. It had been custom built at the Derecktor shipyard in Mamaroneck, New York, out of steel plate graded for nuclear submarines. It had its own oxygen supply, temperature control, and closed ventilation system. It manufacturer joked that if there was a nuclear attack on the city, the man in that sarcophagus was the only person guaranteed to survive. Chancey had a keen interest in ancient Egypt, and inspired by the stone engravings on the coffins of the pharaohs, had included an embossed seal of the United States on the sarcophagus.

The sarcophagus weighed over a ton and a special crane traveled with the security convoy to load and unload it.

Also like the tombs of the pharaohs, it contained booby traps. Three glass vials had been built into the locking mechanism and any attempt to tamper with the lock or excessively shock or vibrate the case would cause them to break. It was feared that a large pothole or an accident loading or unloading the sarcophagus would cause them to break. Their insertion had not been authorized by the president who was purposely kept in the dark to allow for plausible deniability.

The trap was Chancey's idea and only the small team responsible for handling the sarcophagus knew of its existence. An engineer in the FBI's bomb squad had constructed the device. The vials were placed within the gears of the locking mechanism. The largest contained distilled water, while two smaller vials contained sulfuric acid and sodium cyanide crystals. If the trap was tripped, the three substances would mix, creating hydrocyanic gas. The use of this gas for executions had been ruled cruel and unusual punishment by a federal appeals court in 1996, but the Supreme Court overturned the decision.

It's use as a security measure to prevent El Sucio's escape was undoubtedly a violation of the constitution.

Unlocking the sarcophagus could only be performed by

an agent aware of the device and familiar with how to open the lock without setting off the trap.

At any time, Chancey could remotely unlock the sarcophagus. This was ostensibly for the prisoner's safety and had been authorized by the president. Only Chancey knew that using the remote would also set off the trap, giving him an effective kill switch over the prisoner.

That is what made him confident enough to stake his career on the outcome.

The convoy consisted of the primary armored vehicle as well as an alternating number of decoys. The lead agent on site decided randomly each day which vehicle would contain the prisoner, and the drivers, who were randomly selected from a pool and were never given the job twice, decided the order of travel of the vehicles among themselves. The decoys were loaded so the drivers, or anyone else trying to judge the bearing of the vehicles, would not be able to tell which carried the weight of the prisoner. The drivers were shown to the vehicles after loading, and they never knew which of them carried the prisoner. By the time the convoy left the prison basement, no one at all knew which truck the prisoner was in, and all were given equal priority.

Fifteen minutes prior to the convoy's departure in either direction the airspace over Manhattan was cleared of all aircraft deemed capable of tactical maneuver. This meant all helicopters and small planes were grounded or rerouted. Pilots were informed in advance of when this would likely occur. Any failure to clear the airspace would be enforced by NYPD helicopters who were authorized to use force.

Commercial jet traffic was unaffected but security was heightened at the airports, and fighter jets were on standby at Otis and Langley Air Force Bases, with two squadrons airborne over the Atlantic during convoys.

The Brooklyn Bridge, and the entire surface route from the prison to the courthouse, was under twenty-four hour surveillance. Tampering with the route was impossible. Parked vehicles, street vendors, and all non-government traffic was prohibited along the route. Residents and business owners were interviewed, vetted, and informed of restrictions that would be in place for the duration of the trial. They would be unable to leave or access their buildings while the convoy was in motion, and would require police escort at other times. Pipes and tunnels beneath the route were checked and monitored daily by a special team of MTA workers.

The day of the attack began like all the others. El Sucio was escorted to the courthouse as normal, and the court proceedings went on all day without interruption. It was only as the proceedings came to a close in the evening, and preparations were being made for the convoy to return to the prison, that something began to happen.

The first part of the cartel's strategy was to prevent the return convoy. If the convoy moved, the Air Force would have fighters in the air and NYPD would clear the skies.

There was a near infinite number of ways to cause a disruption that would achieve their objective, and the method settled on by the cartel was car bombs. New York was a car bomber's paradise. The streetscape was compact and crowded. An explosion in that environment during the evening rush hour would cause massive casualties. The cartel also had ample experience building and deploying car bombs, having used them all over Mexico for decades. The chemicals, fertilizers, and electronic components necessary were readily available in large quantities.

Thirty minutes before the attack, a team of ten gunmen took over a UPS depot in New Port, New Jersey. They loaded thirty-one delivery vans with hundreds of pounds of explosives, equipped them with cellphone activated detonators, and had a team of drivers scatter them all over the city. Because the bombs could be activated at will, the vehicles could be double parked in high security locations and detonated before the police had a chance to move them.

The first explosion took place when a cartel driver double parked a van in the middle of Times Square. He simply turned on the hazard lights and walked away. At the same time, another driver pulled over while crossing the Manhattan Bridge and blocked an eastbound lane. A third driver was outside the Fulton Street subway station close to Wall Street. A fourth was at One World Trade Center. Three vans were parked along the busiest shopping area of Fifth Avenue, close to Trump Tower, with another around the corner on Park Lane. Three more were in Brooklyn Heights, in the vicinity of the courthouse, and certain to cause the Feds to cancel the return convoy. The rest of the vans were scattered all over Manhattan and Brooklyn, at the discretion of the driver, who received a phone call one-hundred-sixty seconds prior to detonation. At that point, the driver simply stopped the vehicle where ever he happened to be, got out carrying a fake UPS package, and did not look back.

All but one exploded successfully. The Trump Tower van was approached immediately by police and the driver panicked. The van was apprehended and the detonator disabled before the cartel knew what was happening.

The other thirty went off without a hitch, killing a combined total of over fourteen-hundred-sixty civilians in what would have been the second largest terrorist attack on

US soil in history, had that been the end of the story. The Times Square explosion alone killed over a hundred people, while the two successful Fifth Avenue explosions together killed over one-hundred-fifty.

Thirty simultaneous bombings across the city caused catastrophic carnage. The security response was massive and immediate. The cartel had excellent intel on the city's anti-terrorist response measures. Because of 9/11, New York had what was widely believed to be the most sophisticated, well-rehearsed, and comprehensive anti-terrorist measures of any major city on earth.

But if a terrorist organization knew what those procedures were they could be used against the city. The cartel had put sharpshooters in position all over the city. Many were overlooking bomb sites. Inspired by the practice in Iraq and Afghanistan of firing a second missile at a target a few minutes after the first, these snipers took out first responders and rescue workers as they arrived at the scene.

This not only delayed rescue work and increased the lethality of the bombings, it also caused the city to divert more resources than normal to the bomb sites. The forces ordinarily kept in reserve to respond to follow-on attacks or pursue perpetrators were forced onto the streets to track down the snipers. The snipers were well trained, knew how to stay concealed, and took effective evasive measures for the urban environment they were in. Many went uncaptured for hours, killing dozens more in the streets below.

Even though the FBI and the city new immediately that the attacks were related to El Sucio, the scale of them and the mounting death toll forced them to call in units from the vicinity of the courthouse.

The cartel knew courthouse security protocols would require El Sucio be taken to a hard room below street-level.

This was done, and essentially kept him pinned down while the escape plan proceeded. Had he been taken to the sarcophagus, the cartel wouldn't have been able to free him without risking tripping the trap.

A separate attack was aimed at taking out the city's air response capability. The New York Police Department operated eight twin-engine Bell 429 patrol helicopters out of Floyd Bennett field in southeast Brooklyn. The cartel attacked this facility by speedboat across Jamaica Bay. Fourteen men armed with Heckler and Koch MP5 submachine guns and M320 grenade launchers stormed the facility. The M320's were armed with 40x46 millimeter low-velocity rounds, which were deathly effective in the close-quarter combat that followed. The facility was completely unequipped to respond.

The gunmen overran the facility and destroyed the three helicopters on the ground. The other five were already responding to the mayhem in the city. Because of the chaos they were not notified of the attack at the airfield and all five returned for refueling, where they made easy targets for the grenade launchers.

There are three high-capacity commercial helipads on the southern half of Manhattan, one in Chelsea near the terminus of the Lincoln tunnel, one on the FDR between the UN building and Bellevue Hospital, and one serving Wall Street from Pier Eleven, a few blocks from the Brooklyn Bridge.

Because of the timing of the attack, the air force was on standby but not airborne. The bombings were picked up instantly by NORAD. Jets were mustered, but the specific units allocated to El Sucio were still on standby, hundreds of miles away in Virginia and Massachusetts.

The cartel launched nine Agusta Westland 101 helicopters, three from each helipad, carrying ten men apiece and heavy assault weaponry. This included the grenade launcher used in the Jamaica Bay attack, as well as the smaller M203 variant attached to machine guns. The choppers were also armed with FIM-92 Stinger rocket launchers. These had been purchased in Yugoslavia, left over from the NATO mission there, and were armed with annular blast pattern high-explosive warheads and infrared, surface-to-air homing capability. They were overkill for ground targets but that didn't matter to the cartel.

As the helicopters crossed the city, the men fired hundreds of grenades at random onto the streets below. This devastation increased the general chaos but also drew heavy fire from ground-based police.

The helicopters from Pier Eleven were the first to arrive at the courthouse. They concentrated fire at the police and marshals at the court while trying to stay out of range of return fire. Police sharpshooters on the two-hundred-seventy-foot-high towers of the Brooklyn Bridge proved effective and took down two choppers before the rest arrived.

With the seven remaining choppers in formation, fire focused entirely on the heavily guarded front of the court-house. The objective was to demolish the entrance and neutralize the court's defenses so that a ground team could enter the building. They had complete schematics for the building and surrounding tunnel system and knew exactly where to go.

The attack successfully destroyed the front of the court-house, killing hundreds of police officers, federal marshals, and civilians. Their objective was complete by the time the jets arrived.

The jets scrambled by NORAD approached along the

corridor of the Hudson. Four F-22 Raptors traveling at a supercruise of mach 1.82, over twelve-hundred miles-per-hour, and an altitude of just eight-hundred feet. They were lower than many of the adjacent skyscrapers and the deafening thunder shattered fifty-million dollars worth of glass along the East River. They were so fast people on the ground only heard them. In a single pass, the four jets fired eight AIM-9 Sidewinder missiles. The cartel's choppers exploded in a single instant, crashing onto Whitman Park, the Korean War Veterans Plaza, and the roof of the New York City Emergency Management Department.

By then, over fifty heavily armed cartel men were swarming across the Brooklyn Bridge Plaza toward the courthouse in tactical formation. They managed to fire heat-seeking Stinger rockets at the fighters but missed.

The men entered the courthouse shooting everyone in their path. Over two hundred people including court staff, police officers, federal agents, witnesses, and a number of federal judges were killed. Hundreds more lay wounded in the building, prevented from leaving by the firefight still taking place between cartel mercenaries and the police outside. Once inside, cartel men went straight to the hard room where El Sucio was being held, blew open the supposedly blast-proof doors, and killed all the guards.

CCTV footage of the moment showed a cowering El Sucio, his hands over his ears, being taken from the room by the gunmen and brought to a lower level of the basement. The service tunnels leading into the courthouse had been sealed with concrete prior to the trial as an added security measure. The cartel blew them open with plastic explosives.

Within half a mile of the courthouse, there were hundreds of potential points of egress into neighboring buildings, city service tunnels, and subway tunnels. There was no way of predicting where the men would come up, and even if there was, a response strong enough to counter the machine guns, rockets, and grenade launchers would have taken longer to muster than the time available. In the event, dozens of police followed the cartel into the tunnels where they were killed by booby traps left for them.

Minutes later, the entire court building collapsed after massive explosions detonated at the Borough Hall, Court Street, and Brooklyn Bridge subway stations, completely collapsing the stations and plaza above, and sucking the Saint Ann of the Holy Trinity Church into a crater five-hundred feet across.

For hours after the escape, car bombs, snipers, and grenades continued the wreak terror across the city. By dawn the next morning, with the city still in a state of shock, many cartel men had not been apprehended and were able to simply put away their weapons, leave their positions, and disappear into the city. It was later estimated that over two-thousand combatants had been involved in the operation, making it the largest military incursion on US territory since Pearl Harbor, and the most deadly since the Civil War.

During the night, a small explosion was detected at the Owls Head Wastewater Treatment Plant near the Brooklyn Army Terminal. Surveillance later showed eight men, including El Sucio, running on a sidewalk from the water plant, along Shore Parkway, to the Bay Ridge Pier. A speed-boat waiting for them took them across the river to Bayonne, New Jersey where they entered a large warehouse. Nine vans came out of the warehouse a few minutes later. The vans traveled by different routes to the Holland Tunnel, where their movement could no longer be tracked by satellite. CCTV in the tunnel had been destroyed in advance.

The vans were abandoned in the tunnel and it was still unknown if the cartel left the tunnel on foot, in other vehicles, or through service tunnels accessed from within.

The total number of casualties during the 9/11 attacks was two-thousand-nine-hundred-ninety-six. That included those on board the planes, at the Pentagon, and at the World Trade Center, as well as the hijackers themselves. At Pearl Harbor, two-thousand-three-hundred-thirty-five service personnel and sixty-eight civilians were killed.

The final count from El Sucio's escape was nine-thousand-six-hundred-eleven.

That included casualties from the truck bombings, the indiscriminate grenade attacks from the helicopters, the attack on the courthouse, the explosion of the courthouse, and the bombings at the three subway stations, as well as the open fighting that took place on the streets for hours after the escape.

The President went on the air to declare a state of national emergency.

The city of New York was put under martial law.

The biggest manhunt in history was initiated.

And El Sucio was gone.

FIFTEEN

Hunter, Fawn and Hale watched the TV screen in horror as the details came in. It would be days before the full extent of the attack was known and a full casualty count released, but it was clear the scale was catastrophic. When fighter jets hurtled down the East River, shooting helicopters from the sky with sidewinder missiles, Hale stood up and excused himself.

"I better get us a flight back to DC," he said to Fawn.

"Yes, sir," she said without taking her eyes from the TV.

Hunter watched him take a seat at the far end of the bar, out of earshot. He was talking on the phone and it was clear this attack would involve him directly.

Hunter doubted there was any branch of the security services this wouldn't involve directly.

"What are you going to do?" Fawn said, looking at him.

Hunter shook his head. "Don't make like this is the reason we're sitting here. I told you I'm never going back to Washington."

"Your country is at war."

Hunter sighed. He'd done his service. He didn't see why a new war, however brutal, had to involve him.

"We're always at war," he said. "And always will be."

Fawn couldn't argue with that.

Hale hung up his phone and came back over to them.

"Watch this," Hunter said to Fawn. "He's going to say this changes everything."

"It does change everything," Fawn said.

Hunter looked at her. Her hand was trembling. She was watching the news in rage. Every gun shot, every explosion, was personal to her.

He could see why she'd signed up with the agency. It wasn't a career move. She was a patriot.

Like he'd once been.

Hale took his seat but said nothing.

Hunter looked at him.

"What are they saying?" Fawn said.

Hale didn't respond.

Fawn put a hand on his arm. That brought him back to the present.

"They're getting a plane ready," Hale said. "Commercial traffic is grounded. We have to fly out of Eielson."

"You look pale," Fawn said.

Hale shook his head. "It's Chancey. He was in the building."

"The courthouse?"

Hale nodded.

"Jesus, Jeff," Fawn said.

Hunter had never met Willis Chancey, the FBI director, but he'd heard of him. He'd been director four years ago when Hunter was still at Langley. He and Hale fought over everything. The El Sucio case, which was a jurisdictional free-for-all, would have had them at each other's throats.

"That could have been me," Hale said. "I fought them all the way. Look at that shit," he said, nodding toward the TV. "Does that look like a law enforcement issue to you?"

"It looks like a war," Fawn said.

Hale nodded.

"It does. They wouldn't let me anywhere near it."

"That wasn't your decision," Fawn said.

Hunter looked at her. He knew from the way they were talking she'd been telling the truth when she said she hadn't slept with Hale. That meant she was there on merit.

Hale let out a deep breath. "Fuck me," he said. "I had coffee with him two days ago. He wouldn't budge. Said he had the whole thing tight as a knot."

"No one could have seen this coming," Hunter said, looking at footage of the explosion at Times Square.

Hale looked at him. "And what do you have to say for yourself, soldier?"

Hunter didn't answer. There was no point arguing at a time like this. It was a national tragedy. Nothing he could say would sound right.

"What if I told you I could put you on this?" Hale said. "What if you could be the man who put a bullet in El Sucio's head."

"I'm done putting bullets in people's heads," Hunter said.

Hale let out a quiet laugh.

Hunter watched him.

"We all know that's a lie," Hale said.

"Fuck you," Hunter said.

"I can put you in Seattle and DC for the four assassinations."

"That was personal," Hunter said.

"I know that," Hale said. "I know what they did to your wife and her girl."

"Our girl," Hunter said.

"I also know you work for Alaska State Predator Control."

"So what?"

"Once a hunter, always a hunter. Isn't that what they say?"

"I never heard anyone say that," Hunter said.

Hale looked right at him. "Come back to me, Hunter. I can give you what you want. I can give you the only thing you want."

"And what's that?"

Hale made a gun with his hand and pointed it at Hunter. He cocked his hand as if the gun was firing.

Hunter stood up to leave. He wanted to tell Hale to go fuck himself but the tragedy unfolding on the TV made the mood too solemn.

"Sorry you both flew up here for nothing," he said.

"Don't give me that," Hale said. "You know where you belong."

"No I don't," Hunter said.

"You know you want to come back into the fold."

"I'd rather die, Hale."

"And maybe you will die."

"You going to call me in?"

"You know I can't let you off the leash. You're a liability. If I ever had a doubt, the assassinations proved it."

Hunter looked at them both for a minute and said nothing. Fawn's eyes were even more intense than Hale's.

"You do what you have to do," he said to them.

SIXTEEN

Fawn and Hale flew back to DC on a military plane out of Eielson Air Force base. Hunter drove them to the base. He'd been ready to leave them at the hotel bar but Fawn went out to the parking lot after him. The wind was howling out of the mountains and when he saw how cold she was, his tone softened.

"Come back inside," she said. "You know how he is."

"And that's why I don't want to work for him."

She could understand that. She'd seen first hand the effects their work could have on men in the field. She could only imagine what had caused Hunter to go AWOL when everything in him had been trained to report back to command.

"I've got to leave my rental here," she said.

He followed her back inside and waited in the lobby with Hale while she went upstairs and got her things. He and Hale didn't speak to each other.

A few minutes later, the three of them were squashed together on the bench of Hunter's truck, Fawn in the middle. They drove in silence.

As they approached the base, Hale finally spoke.

"We're at war," he said. "Every man has a part to play."

Hunter said nothing and Fawn was glad. She didn't want another argument.

Hunter brought them as far as the security checkpoint at the entrance to the base and let them out. He squeezed Fawn's hand as she left.

"So long, Hunter," she said.

"So long, Agent Aspen."

She smiled and watched as he turned the truck and drove off into the darkness. The world was a harsh place for a man like him. She'd seen it in his eyes. She'd seen it in the empty apartment he'd shared with a family who was now dead. She wondered what would become of him.

A guard from the checkpoint drove them to the base terminal. The atmosphere inside was somber, the personnel all huddled in front of a TV in the lobby. Everyone watched with growing horror as the gunfighting and bombings continued in New York. It had been going on for hours and every minute, the bodycount rose higher.

Fawn looked around the terminal and couldn't help admit she felt the same way as Hale on the question of duty. She knew Hunter was fucked up. She knew he'd done more than anyone for his country. But he was also one of the few people with the training and expertise to make a difference at a time like this. Every man had a part to play. She believed that.

On the TV, video from someone's cellphone showed a young girl crying as she stood alone in the middle of a Harlem street. She was holding a teddy bear. Anyone who approached her was shot by a sniper. There must have been ten bodies in the street. The little girl stared helplessly at the camera. The sniper was using her as bait.

"How could this happen?" a woman said.

No one answered.

Fawn knew many of those present had served in Iraq. She had served there too. None of them could ever have imagined they'd see street fighting like this in their own country.

Car bombs. Snipers. Helicopters. Screaming children. The billowing black smoke that can only come from war.

The footage they were watching was surreal.

Unedited social media feeds were streaming the carnage live. Hundreds of people's last moments were being broadcast. A news reporter for one of the local New York stations was shot by a sniper while reporting live to the camera. Fighter jets thundered overhead. The death toll was going to be beyond anything the nation had ever seen.

And so would the political fallout.

"Are you Hale and Aspen?" an Air Force pilot asked as they stood with the other personnel in front of the TV.

Hale nodded.

"I'm your pilot. We're ready for takeoff as soon as you are, sir."

They followed the pilot onto the tarmac and Fawn realized she was still wearing the coat and boots Hunter had given her.

What was Hale going to do about him, she wondered, as she climbed into the plane.

On board, she was relieved to see the plane was mostly empty. A few military personnel were in the back. They nodded and she and Hale nodded back but no one introduced themselves. They sat in the front row because it had the most legroom.

Hale had three seats to himself on one side of the aisle,

and Fawn had three on her side. She sat next to the window and closed her eyes.

They waited about fifteen minutes before taking off.

When they leveled off, she said to Hale, "What are you going to do about him?"

He thought for a second then said, "This morning when I woke up, Jack Hunter was the most important thing in the world to me. I wanted him back and I would have done anything to avoid having to order his death."

"And now?"

He looked at her. "Honestly, now I couldn't care less what he decides. If he comes back, I could use him. Washington's going to be an absolute shit show and having someone like him up our sleeve would be useful."

"And if he doesn't come back?"

Hale said nothing.

Fawn got up and went to the coffee station. She filled two styrofoam cups with the thick, black liquid and went back to her seat. She handed Hale a cup.

"I've never known you to turn on one of your own, boss," she said.

Hale smiled thinly. "I've done it, Fawn. I've done it plenty of times. You're just lucky not to have had to witness it."

"When?"

"You don't want to know."

"Sure I do."

"It would change your view of me."

Fawn smiled. "Right. Because everyone knows how I idolize you."

"I know the impression you have of me," he said.

She looked at him and he looked back, locking her gaze. She looked away.

"You don't know what I think," she said.

He let out a mirthless laugh.

They both sat quietly for a few minutes. It was Hale who broke the silence.

"It's been one hell of a day," he said.

"Did you speak to Langley?"

"I called from the base," he said, "but the central system's down. I couldn't get through to anyone who'd have a clue what's going on."

"How exposed are we?" Fawn said.

"Not as exposed as Chancey."

As soon as he said it he remembered Chancey was probably dead.

"It's okay," Fawn said.

"I forgot."

"It's okay."

Hale got up and fixed himself a drink. He offered one to Fawn but she asked for more coffee.

"Are you really going to turn in Hunter?" she said.

He shrugged. "I don't know that I can leave a man like that walking around. He's too dangerous."

Fawn sipped her coffee and peered out the window at the flashing light on the wing.

She agreed.

SEVENTEEN

When the plane landed late the following morning Hale was exhausted. He hadn't slept on the flight and poured himself a few drinks too many in compensation. He woke Fawn who was asleep in the row next to him and they went into the terminal together.

For security reasons they'd been diverted to Langley Air Force Base, two hours by car from DC.

The atmosphere inside the base was very different from back in Fairbanks. Eielson was thousands of miles away from the attacks, a full five timezones from the capital. The personnel at the base had been angry, they'd been horrified, but they were removed from it.

Here, close to the heart of the nation, a place where cabinet members and generals were often seen in person, things were personal. Things were visceral. Victims had been flown in from New York to local hospitals. Fighter jets had used the base for refueling. In the arrival hall, the men and women in uniform watching the TV screens were in shock. And as Fawn and Hale stood on the sidewalk outside the building, waiting for Hale's town car, Hale began to feel the depth of the wound that had been inflicted on the nation.

There were no two ways about it. This was a stab to the heart. Ten thousand casualties.

This would change everything.

He'd spent the night on the phone, speaking to all the heads of service he could reach. His boss, Director Gee Jonson, and the national security adviser, Andrew Antosh, were on the same page. They knew the battles he'd fought with the FBI over El Sucio's security. They agreed that none of this would have happened if the CIA had played a more prominent role. It had been the president's call to give control to the FBI, under advice from the secretary of state and the attorney general. Undoubtedly, that had been the correct legal decision, the correct decision constitutionally, but tactically, militarily, it had been an unmitigated disaster.

It had opened the door for the attack.

It had allowed a military foe to go up against domestic law enforcement agencies.

It pitted NYPD officers against grenade launchers and rockets.

Heads would roll.

Hale wasn't sure the president himself would survive the backlash.

While Fawn slept on the plane, Hale had gone through his rolodex and touched base with the head of the NSA, the head of the Defense Intelligence Agency, Homeland's head of intelligence analysis, his contacts at the DEA, and even an old CIA colleague who now worked at the Department of Energy's intel office. Without saying it in so many words, he dropped hints to all of them that Mantis was on the table.

These were desperate times.

The military wanted to redeem itself.

The politicians wanted to save their skins.

Mantis, the most effective assassination program in the history of the agency, would be too tempting to turn down.

Hale knew the intelligence community would back him up. Even his enemies would support reinstating Mantis. This was a time for the CIA to stand as one and everyone knew it.

Chancey's body had been found in the courthouse, riddled with nine millimeter bullets, but his successor, Daniel Moynihan, was already trying to shift responsibility. That wasn't going to go down well at Langley or the Pentagon.

Hale had spent half his career fighting with the DoD. Now they would stand together.

He'd tried to call the joint chiefs from the plane, and had placed separate calls with the DoD, the army intel branch, and the air force intel branch. No one from the military had returned his call, so when his cell rang, and it was the Pentagon, he was surprised.

He was in the back of his car with Fawn, a privacy screen between them and the driver.

"This is Jeff Hale," he said into the phone.

An automated voice said, "Please verify for Bluebird."

Bluebird was code that the president would be on the call.

"Bluebird," he said to Fawn, who was sitting next to him, touching up her makeup with a compact.

She knocked on the security screen and told the driver to pull over so they could give Hale privacy. The driver stopped at a gas station and she went to go freshen up in the washroom.

Hale went through the verification process, which

involved typing a code into the phone's keypad, saying a voice analyzed passphrase, and attaching a physical verification device to the phone.

After verification he was put on hold, standard practice for a call of this nature. He could picture the scene at the Pentagon. The president, the vice-president, and the joint chiefs would be in a secure briefing room. Gee and Moynihan would have received similar calls to his and would also be on hold.

Hale waited on the line and prayed they'd want to speak to him.

He knew exactly what he was going to say.

A moment later, he heard the ambient noise signifying he'd been put on speaker, and the voice of the chairman of the joint chiefs, Harry Goldwater, addressed him.

"Hale, you're on with the president and the joint chiefs. We want to know what Black Ops can offer."

Hale didn't miss a beat. He'd been expecting to have to fight for a seat at the table. Now that they were offering it to him, he wasn't going to blow it.

"We can take out El Sucio, general."

"Have you got an operation with the capability?"

"Praying Mantis, sir."

There was a pause on the other end. The phone went mute.

The next voice he heard was the president's.

"I thought Mantis was down, Jeff."

Hale took a deep breath. It was now or never.

"Negative, sir. I've got an active agent and we're ready to go. Just give me the word."

He was back on mute.

He took another deep breath. He was putting his neck out.

He hadn't told anyone about Hunter. Until last night, the entire chain of command believed Mantis was completely out of action and all operatives dead or missing. Given the dangers Mantis had created during its operation, there was no way Hale could have resurrected it. It was done. If anyone had found out he'd been hiding Hunter, it would have meant the end of his career.

But this was a different world. A more dangerous world. And whoever had the most dangerous weapon had the most to offer. And the most to gain.

The phone came back on and he recognized his boss, Gee Jonson's voice. He hadn't counted on Gee being in the briefing room in person.

"Hale, which agent have you got in action?"

If this conversation had taken place a day earlier, Hale would have been facing a lengthy prison sentence for the information he'd withheld. Now, it might make him head of the CIA. Gee knew it. Hale knew it.

"I've got Tooth Fairy, sir."

He could hear the strain in Gee's voice. He was in an uncomfortable position. He was admitting to the president and the entire military that Hale was the most useful man they had in the CIA, and that Hale's operative was the man most likely to give them the result they needed.

Gee had beaten out Hale in the contest for CIA director by a hair. It had been the biggest victory of Gee's career. The biggest blow to Hale's. Now the table was turning.

"It was my understanding Tooth Fairy went dark four years ago."

"I had a trace on him, sir."

Keeping that secret had been the biggest gamble of

Hale's career. It could have destroyed him. Now it was going to make him.

"You had a trace, Jeff?"

Hale had to keep the conversation moving. What was important now wasn't how they'd acquired a weapon, but what that weapons was capable of.

"Sir, Agent Aspen and I have already made contact. Tooth Fairy is ready to go."

The phone went silent again. He knew this was creating a stir in the room. Mantis had been the most effective operation the CIA ever created. Tooth Fairy had been its most effective asset. It's most lethal.

And it's most dangerous.

When the shit hit the fan, Mantis had proven everyone's worst fears. They'd unleashed a weapon they couldn't control. A weapon that threatened them all.

Not that Hunter could remember that. Hale was confident of that much. He'd been watching Hunter closely for two years, and everything he'd seen supported the conclusion those memories had been effectively erased.

Hale didn't like to think back to those times. Those operations were the biggest mistake of his life. And the biggest regret.

The memory of Hunter's last operation, Blackstone, kept him up at night.

He couldn't understand how something so good, and someone so good, could become such absolute evil.

'Haywire' was the word the pysch team had used. With all their expertise and all their fancy degrees they couldn't come up with anything more scientific than that.

What they'd done to Hunter would haunt Hale for the rest of his life.

Unless, somehow, he could turn things around and redeem him.

Hunter had been twenty-four when Hale recruited him. Hale chose him personally. He was a graduate of the CIA's most elite recruitment program, a secret program operated by Hale's Black Ops division to train the operatives necessary for the most treacherous missions the US conducted overseas.

The longterm survival rate of recruits was less than fifty percent. Hunter knew that, and still he volunteered. He never flinched. Not when they taught him the thousands of ways he could kill an opponent in hand-to-hand combat. Not when they taught him the genetic predispositions of each racial group, and the ways those traits could be used to weaken an enemy physically or psychologically. Not when he was taught the limits of human endurance to pain, fatigue, extreme temperature, extreme depravation, and experimental ways to overcome those limits.

Hunter had signed waivers for gene therapy, for chemical enhancement, for radiation treatment, for psychological manipulation and altering, for memory interference, for the insertion of electronic devices in his body, for the erasure of his civil records and constitutional rights. He even signed a waiver allowing the government to kill him if his existence became a threat to an operation.

Hale had gone through every document, in person, with the recruit.

That man knew what he was signing up for.

And he didn't flinch.

There was only one thing Hunter ever complained of during the entire recruitment process. He didn't like his codename.

Hale could picture the scene in the briefing room.

They'd want Tooth Fairy. The president would definitely want him. But they'd also remember what had gone wrong last time.

The phone clicked back on.

"Hale, this is Gee. Is there any deterioration in Tooth Fairy's readiness?"

Hale was lying through his teeth, but he had to give them what they wanted to hear.

"Readiness has been maintained, sir. Psych, physical, tactical, good to go."

There was another brief pause and then the president came back on.

"Hale, I want to know your assessment on this guy. No bullshit. Last time I heard the words Tooth Fairy, it was in relation to a bloodbath that made the rest of Mantis look like a walk in the park. What is the likelihood we're going to see that sort of outcome again?"

"I understand the concern, sir. I regret that operation every day."

"And are we going to get a repeat, Hale?"

"Everything suggests the operative has no memory of that incident, sir. In four years, nothing has gone wrong."

"The self-destruct failed," the president said. To Hale's knowledge, this was the first time a sitting president had acknowledged the existence of such measures.

"Yes it did, sir."

"But the memory wipe worked?"

"I believe so."

"I told you not to bullshit me, Hale."

"Of course not, sir. It looks like the wipe worked. There's no way for me to know what the man remembers for sure. If we brought him in for assessment we'd get a better idea."

"No contraindications at all in four years?" the president said.

Hale thought of the assassinations that had rocked the capital just a few days earlier. The president himself went on a rampage looking for the culprit. Hale closed his eyes.

"No contraindications, sir."

"What's he been doing for a living?"

"Predator control, sir."

"Predator control?"

"He hunts wolves for the Alaska wildlife department."

There was a pause on the other end but the line did not go mute.

"I don't think we're going to want an operative like this walking around unleashed once the operation's over," the president said.

"I understand, sir."

"Are you sure, because it looks to me like you were keeping this guy to yourself the last couple of years?"

"Yes, sir," Hale said.

He knew he shouldn't say more than that. No explanation. No apology. Everyone wanted this operative and Hale was the only one who could deliver him.

The fact the president was saying they would likely order Hunter's death once the mission was over only concerned him a little. He knew a successful mission would change that. And an unsuccessful mission, well, maybe it really was for the best not to have a man like Hunter walking around free.

"Is that all you have to say?" Gee said.

Hale spoke, but addressed the president, not his boss.

"Mr. President, if you give us the mission, I swear it will get done. The operative will go in, there'll be a mess, but one way or another the target will end up dead. It's a virtual certainty, sir."

"A virtual certainty," the president repeated, before putting him back on mute.

Hale was still on hold when he motioned for Fawn and the driver to come back to the car. He needed to be in Washington ASAP. Fawn got back in next to him and gave him a coffee.

They were back on the road when Goldwater came on the line.

"It's just me, Hale. You've got the mission. There's going to be some shit over keeping Tooth Fairy under wraps but I'm sure you knew that much already. And you're point on this. You're answering directly to the president, not the director."

"I understand, sir."

"We'll get all our best intel sent over to you. It's for Black Ops only. Not to be shared with Gee."

"I understand, sir."

"If Gee gives you any trouble, contact me. The president will make you director if he thinks it will get El Sucio's head on a spike."

"It will, sir."

Goldwater laughed. It was always the same. Every disaster, every battle, every war, it was always about the careers in the end.

"We'll see," he said. "I think you're aware we're going to war with Sinaloa."

"I was not aware of that, sir."

"Well, we are. The president is seeking a declaration from congress today. You will be outside that process. Strictly paramilitary."

Hale's directorate was paramilitary by definition. His

title was Director of Paramilitary Black-Ops. This mission couldn't have been designed more perfectly for him.

"We'll stay out of your way, general."

The general hung up and Hale let out a long sigh. He smiled at Fawn.

"We got the job?" she said.

Hale nodded. "And we need Hunter. I promised them Hunter. I said he was already operational."

Fawn shook her head. "And why would you go and do a thing like that?"

Hale shrugged. "You know me. I aim to please."

"You have a dozen other operatives you could have given them."

"They didn't want another operative. If I didn't give them Hunter, they'd have given this to Gee."

"But you don't have Hunter. You heard what he said. He'd rather spend the rest of his life in a federal prison than another day working with you."

"He's just forgotten all the things he loved about working with me."

Fawn took a sip from her coffee.

"That's something I can relate to," she said.

Hale smiled. He was pleased. This was the mission of the century and it was all his. He wasn't answerable to Gee. He went straight to the top.

It was an assassin's wet dream. He'd have everything he wanted, everything he needed, and no one interfering. There'd be no holding back. For once, the gloves could really come off.

And it might even make him director.

There was just one problem.

This was a hunt, the biggest hunt since Osama Bin Laden, and he didn't have his hunter.

EIGHTEEN

Hunter woke at dawn and had a cold shower. Something was wrong with the water heater but he didn't look into it. It was only him in the apartment and cold water wasn't going to kill him.

He went to Lacey's and avoided looking at the newspapers or TV screen. He took a booth facing the counter and looked over the menu.

"What can I get you today?" the waitress said.

He remembered being there with Chianne and the kid and the same waitress serving them. They'd had pancakes with berries and whipped cream.

He ordered over easy eggs with sausage and toast. He ate it with coffee and thought about what had happened the day before. After Fawn and Hale left, he'd watched the news for as long as he could bear it, then lay awake on his bed staring at the ceiling.

He ate the eggs and sausage and afterward went to the police station to see if they had any jobs for him. He'd left the house with his rifle and equipment and prayed there was something for him to do, anything, so that he wouldn't have to go back to the apartment and feel the walls close in on him.

"We got a call," the woman at the desk said when she saw him coming in.

"A wolf?"

"A big one. Down in McKinley Park."

McKinley Park was over an hour south of the city. A tourist place for hikers and kayakers exploring Denali.

"What's the pay?"

"Five hundred."

"That much?"

"Apparently this is something nasty."

"Will you call ahead and tell them I'm coming?"

"Will do," she said.

Hunter wrote down the name "Grizzly Bear Center," and went back to his truck.

He had with him a new Remington 700, adjusted for the .300 Winchester cartridge. The modification was an army request to give snipers in Afghanistan extra range and accuracy. The gun was heavy for a rifle and the recoil packed a bit more punch than he liked, but for taking down a wolf it was unparalleled.

He picked up more coffee from Lacey's on his way out of town and couldn't help turning on the radio once he was on the open road.

The attack on New York had been devastating. The more reports came in, the worse the story got. At one point, the news report said, cartel men had been lobbing grenades straight from helicopters onto the streets. Dozens of car bombs had gone off.

Hunter had seen up close the kind of carnage an attack like that could cause. There were times in his life he'd become numb to it. There were times he thought the violence would swallow him up like a wave.

His last mission.

Something went wrong.

Something inside him cracked.

After that, he knew he had to end things. His options were to kill himself or go completely dark and never come back.

The mission had been political, ordered directly by the president two days before the midterms. It was the president's first term and things were going badly. He needed a win.

And that win was to be a high-value Al-Qaeda target known as the Butcher of Kabul. The media had built him up back home. He'd captured some US marines and uploaded their torture videos to YouTube. Everyone wanted him dead.

One of Hale's SIGINT teams got a lead on him. They'd honed in on a two-block area in the south of the city that contained a large open-air market. The place was a maze of vendors, tents, and vehicles, packed every day with thousands of Kabul residents. It was one of the busiest and most densely packed places in the city. Even in the best of circumstances, it would have been a nightmare of collateral damage.

And these weren't the best of circumstances.

There was no time to draw up a plan of attack. With the time zone difference, it was just twenty-eight hours before polls opened on the east coast when the president told Hale to send in Tooth Fairy.

It wasn't Hale's fault. He'd told the president the mission would be a disaster, that they hadn't yet pinned down the Butcher, that they needed time to make a plan.

The president said if Tooth Fairy couldn't go in and kill one overweight, middle-aged Afghan, then how had the CIA spent two years and twelve million dollars training him?

He said the Butcher would be useless to him after the election. He wanted him now.

And that's how it had to be.

Hale did what he could. He assembled a team of eight marines to go in with Hunter. They set up the bare bones of a plan, which required the marines to start a noisy search of the market. Hunter would be on overwatch. The plan, such as it was, was for the marines to flush out the Butcher. When he ran, Hunter would be waiting. There would be satellite surveillance to help track him.

Hunter didn't like the plan.

Not one bit.

In the briefing he said they'd never find the target with such a small team in a market that size. He said satellites wouldn't see shit in that environment. He said sending eight men into that market was suicide.

The general in command listened to Hunter's concerns and then told him to sit down. He had the president on video conference and he was patched through. The president wished the men good luck, told them he was personally waiting for news of their success, and said it was his personal wish that the shooter use a Barrett M82 rifle.

Hunter couldn't believe it.

Hale told him after the briefing that the president was holding a rally in Christiana, Tennessee, later that day and the Barrett factory was located there. He wanted to announce the kill at the rally. It would get good play the day before the midterms if he could say a Barrett gun made the kill.

"What the fuck are we doing?" Hunter said.

"Just do what they say," Hale said. "It's the official state rifle of Tennessee."

"The official state rifle? It's overpowered."

"All the better to kill the butcher," Hale said.

Hunter shook his head. That wasn't how it worked.

Thirty minutes later, he and eight marines were dropped off at the north end of the market by two humvees. Hunter went through a café that hadn't been pre-screened, kicked down a door, and went up to the roof. It was a three-story building overlooking the market. He hauled the thirty-pound Barrett M82 semi-automatic sniper system with him. It was bulky and meant he lacked any maneuverability if the situation changed.

The gun had been designed to take out Soviet tanks at long range.

The Coast Guard used it to take out ship engines.

There wasn't a light armored vehicle in production it couldn't disable.

It was a good gun. A very good gun. But it was the wrong weapon for this mission.

Its steel magazine held ten .50 BMG heavy machine-gun cartridges.

It packed a punch. At 1.4 miles, it delivered three times the force of a 9mm bullet at point blank range. But it wasn't accurate to that distance and it kicked like a mule. It was semi-auto but you couldn't hold it for repeated fire. It was a jackhammer.

The plan made no sense.

Hunter set up the gun quickly and watched the marines, who were moving through the market, showing everyone pictures of the Butcher and asking in english if they knew where he was. In minutes, a mob began to form.

It was a disaster in slow motion and Hunter had to watch it all unfold from his position.

"Crowd gathering to your right," Hunter said in his radio.

The marines veered left but the crowd followed them. They continued their job of trying to flush out the Butcher but the crowd grew bigger and bigger. There was no way it could end well. They didn't have nearly the resources to contain a mob like that once they got angry.

"They're behind you now," Hunter said. "This is going to get messy. Get through the market and I'll call for extraction."

"Roger that," the marine commander said.

The marines quickened their pace but the crowd grew thicker and slowed their progress. They made their way slowly to the far end of the market and Hunter kept eyes on them, making things didn't get too hairy.

"This is Tooth Fairy requesting extraction on the south end of the market."

He waited for the confirmation. "That's a negative, Tooth Fairy."

"Fuck," he said as he watched the crowd coming toward the marines from all sides.

He heard a shout behind him. Four men were on the roof. They'd followed him up from the café and were ready to give him trouble. One of them was carrying a Soviet-era AK-47 and pointed it at him. Hunter drew his sidearm and hit the man twice in the chest.

Before the man hit the ground, Hunter was running at the other three. He shot one in the forehead as he ran and leapt, kicking the other in the neck and disabling him instantly. He landed behind the fourth man who was now running for the door back into the building. Hunter sprang after him and grabbed him round the neck from behind. A few seconds struggle and he was unconscious.

He could hear shouting in the marketplace now. He ran back to his position and saw an angry mob had surrounded the marines. They were shouting and throwing things.

"Abort, abort," he said into his radio but it was too late for the marines to do anything. They were surrounded by hundreds of people who wanted their blood.

Hunter could see what was going to happen. In minutes, the crowd would be ripping the men apart, limb from limb.

"We need extraction now," Hunter said, knowing that command was watching everything in high definition from the satellite feed.

He took aim at an Afghan man that was instigating the crowd. When the man grabbed one of the marines by the uniform, Hunter pressed the trigger.

The .50 Browning cartridge is five and a half inches in length. At its base it is half an inch thick. It weighs an ounce and a half and leaves the barrel of the M82 at three thousand feet per second, three times the speed of sound.

The first round hit the instigator. The man's head exploded like a watermelon. The bullet passed through him and hit the man next to him. The deafening sound echoed over the market and people began to scream and run.

The recoil knocked Hunter out of position.

The crowd backed off slightly but only for a moment.

Hunter re-aimed and fired at another man in the crowd. Another bang. A man's chest exploded. Panic began to spread through the market.

The crowd rushed in at the marines and began punching and kicking them.

The marines fought for their lives, firing their weapons

repeatedly into the mob that was overwhelming them. Their weapons were quickly ripped from their arms. The crowd clawed at them, ripping their flesh, tearing at their limbs.

Hunter fired again and again. The huge bullets hit the crowd but by now there was so much chaos they made no difference. He could see the marines literally being ripped apart.

And then a grenade exploded right at the center of the mob.

One of the marines must have pulled the pin.

The carnage was like something from a zombie movie. Human flesh flew in every direction. And then a second grenade blew, and a third. The marines were ending it in the only way they could.

The explosions scared back the crowd but four marines had been blown to bits by the explosions.

Hunter kept firing, pushing the mob back with the devastating force of the bullets.

When the magazine was empty he abandoned the rifle and leapt down to street level, using the roof of the adjacent building and a wooden fence to get down the three stories.

There was still no word on backup.

Using his sidearm he cut a path to the marines. Three were alive. About thirty members of the mob had been killed by the gunfire and grenades.

"ETA?" he screamed into his radio, looking for a way to get the marines to an extraction point. "We're at the south end. Five men down. We need evac now."

There was no answer. The crowd was beginning to re-form.

Hunter told them to stay back in Arabic.

And then he heard it. The unmistakable sound of an air

strike. The whoosh through the air. The base thud in the ground. The massive explosion at the far end of the marketplace, a few hundred yards away. If he'd still been on the roof of the café he'd have been hit.

He went deaf. His vision blurred. The air was thick with dust. Daytime turned instantly to night. He swung wildly in different directions, seeking a bearing. As his senses came back to him, another strike hit. This one was closer, about midway through the market.

The shockwave hit them like a freight train.

The next strike would kill them.

The marketplace had been packed with people. Casualties would be in the hundreds.

Hunter tried to listen through the chaos, the ringing in his ears, the screaming of injured survivors. He knew the sound of the Rockwell B-1 Lancer. He knew the sound of its eight-hundred-mile-per-hour engines. He knew the sound of its satellite-guided payload.

If he heard it again, he was already dead.

But it didn't come.

Not yet.

He was still with his men. Only one was conscious now.

"Can you walk?" Hunter shouted to him.

The man couldn't hear him, or if he could, he didn't understand.

The man was in shock.

Hunter looked at his watch and started counting. In the back of his mind he knew, if he heard the sound of the next strike, they were already dead.

"We've got to move," he shouted at the marine.

And then it happened. He heard the strike.

Everything went black.

NINETEEN

When Hunter regained consciousness, two days had passed. He was under twelve feet of rubble. Somehow, beyond all logic, he was alive.

Barely.

When he got out of the rubble he was so dehydrated he could barely think.

Everything in his body, everything in his mind, told him to report back to Hale. To make contact. But something deeper stopped him.

He accepted help from some locals. He spoke the language. He rested up in a bombed out building a block from the marketplace. He read about the attack in the Afghan newspaper brought to him by the man who'd helped him. Back home, the president had hailed the mission as a huge success. At his rally in Tennessee he'd said the Barrett gun fired the kill shot. The president's party did better than expected in the midterms.

And something was stopping Hunter from reporting in.

It went against everything he'd been taught.

The training he'd received at Langley went to

extraordinary lengths to ensure he remained obedient to the chain of command. The government did everything in its power to make it impossible for a Mantis agent to go rogue.

He went through psychotherapy. He went through hypnotherapy. He had electronic trackers implanted in his body. The agency was willing to go to any lengths to maintain control.

At a veterinary surgery a few blocks from the market, Hunter had the tracking device in his calf muscle removed. After the procedure, the vet showed him that the device was also capable of releasing a number of substances into his bloodstream. He couldn't tell if it had been used. Hunter later brought the device to a medical lab and learned the substances could be used to promote certain behaviors such as increasing compliance, causing severe depression, or causing cardiac arrest.

The rumored kill-switch, or self-destruct switch, had been put inside him.

And all he could think was that he'd known the other Praying Mantis agents weren't suicidal. He knew those men. He'd been able to get a read on them. The reason they'd killed themselves was the drugs in that device.

He was sure of it.

And that's when he went dark.

Four years passed.

Now, he was driving on a lonely stretch of Alaskan highway, listening to the reports still coming in from New York.

Hale said everyone had a part to play.

As he listened to more details of the attack, he felt more and more strongly that Hale was right.

Segundo José Heredia was a man gone bad. Someone

had to take him out. It was no different than the work he did for predator control. When an animal turns, you killed it.

Simple as that.

Hunter had read all about El Sucio. He knew what he was capable of. He knew of the upgrade of the cartel to military-level threat.

If he went back to Langley they'd send him after El Sucio.

He was a hunter, and they had a wolf that needed putting down.

It was the only thing he knew how to do.

It was the only thing he was good at.

And there might not be another man alive capable of pulling it off.

, McKinley was a tiny town, a single main street and a few dirt side streets, and Hunter had no difficulty finding the Grizzly Bear Center. He went inside and told the receptionist who he was.

She was more upset than he'd expected.

"Thank God you're here," she said, texting her boss on the phone. "It's been horrible."

"What happened?"

"School tour. We do tours with kids. Show them nature. Take them to see the glacier, that sort of thing."

It was clear from the building that was what they did. There were science displays, kid-sized tables for sitting and coloring, or listening to a park guide explain the flora and fauna.

"I see," Hunter said.

"Early this morning, we had a group of fifth-graders go out with Sandra."

"Is Sandra here?"

"She's on her way. That was her I just sent the message to."

"Who got hurt?"

"All of them, I think."

"All of them?"

"Sandra and eight kids. The wolf attacked and they were terrified."

"And someone got killed."

The woman began to cry and Hunter gave her some time.

"Two. That's what I hear. Two kids."

"Where is Sandra now?"

"I don't know. They took her to the hospital in the city. Then the police station. Then she said she was coming back here."

Hunter asked for a phone and called Sandra. It took a few rings for her to pick up.

"Hello?" she said.

"Ma'am, my name is Jack Hunter. I'm with predator control. I'm going to go out and kill this wolf for you."

Sandra was crying. Hunter could tell she was in a car.

"I'm almost there. About a half hour out."

"You're driving alone?"

"No. I'm with a police officer."

"Can you tell me where the attack happened?"

"It was at the State Park. Just head south through Cantwell. Keep going about twenty minutes. You'll see the sign. There's a place to park by the highway and view the glacier."

"It's signposted?"

"Yes. There's a sign and a picnic area. Park there and go up toward the glacier. It's not far. You'll see the kids' back-packs and things. Probably some blood."

She burst out crying again and Hunter handed the phone to the woman. He thanked her and went back to his truck. He drove to the place Sandra had described. He parked and could see from the highway the backpacks and belongings of the children. There were two police cruisers there, each with a cop in it.

Hunter went up to them. They were both young, mid-twenties. One was a man. One was a woman. The man lit a cigarette and offered one to Hunter and his colleague. The woman declined. Hunter took one and the cop lit it.

"Any sign of the animal?" Hunter said.

"Nothing. We've been here two hours. I'd say he's long gone."

"Guess I got a walk ahead of me," Hunter said.

"You're going after it?" the woman said.

Hunter nodded.

He went back to the truck and got his rifle and bag and told the cops he might be gone overnight.

"You don't have any camping gear," the woman said.

Hunter nodded. "I don't plan on stopping until this is done."

He left the police and made his way up the slope toward the glacier. There was blood on the clothing and backpacks that lay strewn on the ground. He picked up the wolf's trail and started out west toward the mountains.

He brought the bare minimum with him, his rifle, thirty-rounds of ammunition, some jerky, some unsalted peanuts, some basic survival equipment. He had everything he needed to navigate, build a fire, cut wood. He knew the territory well, although he'd only been in Alaska a few years. It was about as far as he could get from the west Texas ranches of his youth, but at the same time, about as similar a place as you could find. The same lonely highways, the same stoic people, the same weight of nature, like a force exerting its will on the country.

He felt at home in Alaska. And he felt at home hunting wolves.

Wolf hunting was a lost art in Texas. He could remember the stories from his grandfather. He could remember looking at his grandfather's things in the barn. He could remember wanting to be like his grandfather.

In his grandfather's time the Sierra de la Madera was full of wolves. They roamed freely across the US Mexico border, harassing cattle and sheep and attacking the occasional homesteader. His grandfather showed him all the old equipment, the tools of the trade, and Hunter held them in his hands like artifacts from another world. The long-spring coyote traps. The larger cougar and bear and wolf traps. The iron-toothed traps. The springs and stakes and chains. The old, cloudy jars full of lard and grease, liver and gall, kidney and entrails. The scents that were used to lure the cunning, intelligent wolves, even as they became so rare, so suspicious, that they wouldn't go anywhere a horse had been for days after.

His grandfather told him the wolves became so cautious he had to wear bearskin slippers every time he dismounted. And his horse had to wear them too. If he buried a trap, he couldn't use a steel shovel for the smell it left.

At the very end, when the wolves were so rare they wouldn't even follow the scent of their own kind, he resorted to using exotic elixirs made from the strangest parts of the strangest animal innards.

Hunter's grandfather remembered the last wolf he ever killed.

"Ain't heard another one howl since," he told Hunter.

His grandfather was proud. A job completed. The wolves gone.

Hunter found it sad.

He looked out over the mountains now, the largest range on the continent, and breathed in the icy air. It was warm in the sunlight but the temperature would drop rapidly after dark. He was gaining altitude. He hadn't lost the wolf's trail and could tell it was moving aimlessly. It circled back on itself. It turned around at a river. After three hours of walking, he wasn't that far from where he'd started.

He was following the general direction of the glacier through a valley between two peaks, known locally as Moose's Tooth and Rooster's Comb. When he reached the ridge of the glacier, he stopped for some water and jerky. He always ate the jerky first. The peanuts were for the journey home. He didn't like the taste of unsalted peanuts but they were cheap and light and gave him the fuel he needed.

He was sitting on a long ridge. Ahead of him on the east facing slope he got his first sight of the wolf. It was an enormous female and in her mouth was the arm of a human child.

His grandfather often told him of the wolves gone bad. It wasn't unusual back then. Children were often taken. An animal that intelligent was bound to lash out at the force that threatened its existence so utterly.

Hunter had always been thrilled by the stories.

He rooted for the wolves, even though he knew they lost in the end.

The same thing was happening now in Alaska. More and more wolves were turning. He never had to wait long for a job. It was like when he was at the CIA. There was always someone, somewhere, who had gone bad and needed to die.

He pulled out his rifle and began to set it up on the ridge. He didn't think he'd get a shot off, not yet, but the wolf stuck around. It waited.

It seemed to want what was coming.

It seemed to know it had gone against its nature.

Hunter had seen it before. The wolf that went bad knew it had to die. The men the CIA sent him after sometimes knew the same thing.

There was an order to the world. There was a law.

Not a law written on paper, but a law written into the blood of every creature. The lowliest creature knew that law. The scorpion, the rattlesnake. If a wolf forgot it, if a man forgot it, then someone had to go out with a rifle and set things right again.

He attached the scope to the gun. The wolf was at the outer limit of what the rifle was capable of.

Almost a mile away.

It looked in his direction. He peered through the scope and saw it had abandoned the child's arm. He aimed at its heart.

As he pulled the trigger, he knew he would accept Hale's mission.

TWENTY

The FBI Headquarters in Washington DC is housed in the J. Edgar Hoover building.

The building is not hidden away in the suburbs like the CIA campus. It's right there on Pennsylvania Avenue, halfway between the White House and the Capitol.

It's an eleven story, three-million-square-foot concrete behemoth with an additional three stories underground. It took ten years to build and was inaugurated by President Nixon in 1972.

The explosion that tore through its fourteen floors, just one day after the attack on New York, marked the biggest attack inside the capital since General Ross sacked the city for the British in 1814. Ross and his generals had a banquet in the White House, then burned it down along with half the city.

El Sucio had to satisfy himself with a delivery truck from the FBI's storage facility in Bethesda, Maryland. The truck pulled into a loading bay around dusk. It was packed with five thousand pounds of ammonium nitrate fertilizer, nitromethane, and diesel fuel.

No one paid any attention for thirty minutes, until one of the guards noticed that the driver's signature wasn't on his list.

He walked toward the truck armed with a clipboard, a pen, a radio, and a 9mm semi-auto Glock. As he approached the truck, the driver leapt from the cab and ran. The guard gave chase.

Thirty seconds later the truck exploded.

Security camera feeds, which were transmitted offsite by secure fiberoptic cable, went dead not just at the Hoover building but at every federal facility within twenty blocks of the explosion, including the Capitol, the Supreme Court, and the White House.

The detonation was heard fifty miles away and was measured by the seismic monitoring station at Dulles as four on the Richter scale.

The front half of the building along Pennsylvania Avenue was vaporized, along with eight hundred FBI employees. Shattered glass within a three mile radius killed thirty more people and injured hundreds of others. The glass at the White House shattered. Fire alarms and the sprinkler system in the Capitol were triggered.

Daniel Moynihan, who had taken over as head of the FBI less than twenty-four hours earlier was among the dead. His body was so badly burned it had to be identified by DNA.

The president, at that moment, was addressing both houses of congress seeking a formal declaration of war against the province of Sinaloa. He was evacuated by helicopter to Andrews Air Force Base and taken out of the city in Air Force One. It was the second day in a row he'd been subjected to evacuation.

Within thirty minutes, executive orders were being

transmitted from Air Force One in preparation for the imposition of martial law. Certain orders addressed directly Article 1 of the Constitution and the suspension of habeas corpus. A request was made to congress to repeal the Posse Comitatus Act of 1878, which would allow the president to use the army and air force for the purposes of domestic law enforcement. He also requested that congress exercise its Article 1 power to federalize the national guard and call up the militia to 'suppress insurrections and repel invasion.'

In the space of thirty minutes, the president had requested unprecedented powers that had not been exercised in centuries and that completely altered the constitutional standing.

Congress was called back into the capitol, which was still wet from the sprinkler system. The lawmakers filed into their respective chambers, their seats covered in shattered glass.

By midnight, they had declared war on Sinaloa and granted the president all of the powers requested.

Immediately, national guard and active military units were taking up defensive positions in every large city across the nation. All air and rail travel was suspended. Schools, post offices, and public buildings were closed. The army erected roadblocks on interstate highways.

But even as the forces mobilized, more bombs went off.

Federal buildings in Montgomery, Phoenix, Little Rock, Los Angeles, New York, Denver, Miami, Dallas, Houston, and Baton Rouge were attacked.

All the attacks were similar. Vans and trucks laden with explosives were parked in or near the buildings and detonated remotely.

The military began to close down urban centers,

preventing crowds from forming, moving parked vehicles, and closing streets.

In the space of a single night the country realized it was at war.

And it realized this war was going to be different from every other.

It was going to be fought on US territory.

As the night went on, and news of attack after attack kept coming in, executive and congressional orders were passed in a steady stream. Soldiers moved in to secure every state capital, every bridge over a major river, every railroad tunnel, every metropolitan transit system, every airport, and every sea port. The roadblocks on the interstates began turning traffic around. Likely bombing targets including sports arenas, shopping malls, and federal buildings were closed. The entire southern border was closed. Travel restrictions were imposed on eighty-four countries.

Media controls were imposed. Internet traffic ground to a halt. Cell phone grids shut down.

And at four AM, after eleven major bombings had been reported and the death toll was estimated to be in excess of five thousand people, the president addressed the nation.

His location was not disclosed but it was clear he was not still on board Air Force One. No press was present. He was standing at a podium draped with the American flag and the microphone visible in the frame was a field mic, used on the road and not in studios.

The broadcast, which was played on a loop on all television channels and emergency radio frequencies, and which flashed across mobile devices using a government emergency broadcasting protocol, made it clear the nation had entered a new era.

"My fellow Americans," the president said. "I stand before you no longer as a politician, but as a soldier. As Commander in Chief, my primary responsibility to this nation is to protect it. And make no mistake, protect it I will. Tonight, we have been subjected to an unprecedented attack. Bombs have gone off at federal buildings in eleven states. The headquarters of the FBI has been destroyed. Thousands of federal employees, men and women who gave their lives for their country, are being mourned. And more will follow. Our foe is well-equipped, and he is desperate. He will fight like a dog. But we will direct the full force of the world's most powerful military against him, and we will destroy him. Tonight, I have passed a number of emergency measures that will give our military the powers they need to wage this war, both inside and outside our borders. I trust that our nation will stand as one during this difficult time. God save America.

Immediately after the address, Hale's phone rang.

He was in a bar in downtown Washington watching the news with a group of CIA employees including Fawn.

The call was from the Pentagon.

"Fuck," he said to Fawn, showing her the screen.

She followed him out to the street and lit a cigarette while he went through the verification process for Bluebird.

When the car arrived, she opened the door for Hale and got in the front with the driver. They couldn't hear what was being said in the secure compartment.

Hale waited on hold.

When the president's voice came on he sounded frail. Hale had watched his address carefully, searching for any sign of weakness. They'd entered a new world and he had to know what kind of commander in chief he was going into battle with. He'd been working with this president for six years, he'd been involved in countless missions, but the stakes had never been like this. It had never been life or death.

Now, there were thousands of bodies in the streets, martial law had been declared, and any mistake from the president could lead to disaster.

There were the military risks, but those weren't the ones that worried Hale.

What worried Hale most was the risk of treachery.

Crucial aspects of the constitution had been set aside indefinitely. If a man had ever been tempted to grab power, to hold onto it, now would be the time.

And the threat wasn't just from the president. There were countless senior officials, including Hale himself, who could use this situation to seize power in some way.

"Mr. President," Hale said.

"Hale, I'm making you director of the CIA."

"Sir?"

"The only thing I care about is catching and killing El Sucio."

"Sir," Hale said again, "are you sure this is the time for personnel changes."

"Haven't you heard?"

"I'm sorry, sir. I'm not sure what you're referring to."

"I'm very sorry. I thought you knew."

"What happened, sir?"

"There's been an attack at Langley."

Hale felt light headed. He peered through the glass at where Fawn was sitting next to the driver. Her phone had just lit up and he saw the expression on her face as she got the news of the attack on Langley."

"A bomb?"

"I don't have details to give you," the president said. "I'm sorry, but Gee Jonson was among those killed."

"Jesus," Hale said, his head spinning.

"You're head and you get me El Sucio, you hear me? I want Tooth Fairy in play. I don't care what the risks are. I don't care what the collateral is. You get this guy before he brings our country to its knees."

The line went dead. Hale took a deep breath. He hadn't been expecting this. Head of the CIA. It was something he'd fantasized about many times but never under such circumstances.

He opened the partition between him and the driver.

"How bad is it, Fawn?" he said.

"They don't know yet, sir. It appears to have been another vehicle bomb."

"Jesus, you'd think they'd be stopping those fucking vans by now."

"It looks like it was a big attack, sir. All the others were big. This one wasn't any different."

Hale looked at her. They both knew this meant hundreds of casualties. On a normal night, the building contained a skeleton crew. About a quarter as many employees would be present as during the daytime. But tonight, half the agency would have been called in. Hale's own team had been called in. Hundreds of people would have been in the building.

"Is this ever going to stop?" Fawn said.

Hale wanted to reach out and comfort her but he knew she wouldn't like that. She already thought he took too many liberties. He told the driver to drop her at home.

"Try to get some sleep," Hale said.

"What about you? What are you going to do?"

"I'm going to make sure Hunter's on the next plane out of Fairbanks."

"Is that what the president wanted?"

"Yes. He also wanted to make me CIA head. Jonson was killed in the blast."

Fawn looked at him and he wasn't sure he could read what it was she was thinking. She hadn't been close to Gee. No one had. But that didn't mean his death wasn't a shock.

"I'll get Hunter," she said. "You've got other things to take care of."

"Nothing's as high priority as getting Hunter," he said.

"And that's why you can leave it with me," she said.

TWENTY-ONE

When Hunter got back from the wolf hunt, the attack on the FBI was all over the news. As he drove back to the city, reports started coming in from around the country of more attacks. He'd been on his way home but when he got to the city he went straight to Eielson.

Security at the base wouldn't let him past.

"If you don't have a pass, I can't give you one," the guard said.

"The CIA is going to be looking for me."

"If they are, someone will let me know."

Hunter sighed. It was eleven PM. It was four in the morning on the east coast. The president's address came in over the radio and Hunter and the security guard listened to it together.

"Do you have an FBI liaison officer or someone in there?"

"Most I could give you is the colonel, but I'm not calling him at this hour."

"You were on duty when I was here last night, weren't you?" Hunter said.

"I remember you," the guard said. "I remember the truck."

"And that isn't enough for you to call the colonel?"

The guard sighed. He knew Hunter was who he said he was, but procedure was procedure. If someone needed to speak to him, they could radio down to the gate and get the man a pass.

"You can come in here for a minute," the guard said, opening the door to his post.

Hunter stepped inside and stood next to the guard. The guard opened a binder and ran his finger over the duty list. He picked up the phone and called the colonel's office. No one answered. He called the head of security and said there was someone there for the CIA. Hunter waited while the guard spoke to his superior. The guard told Hunter to name the two people he'd dropped off the night before. Hunter named Jeff Hale and Fawn Aspen.

The guard nodded and said someone was on their way.

Hunter waited and a few minutes later a jeep showed up with the base's head of security in the passenger seat. The man was a little overweight, about fifty, with thin hair.

"You with the CIA?" he said.

"Sort of," Hunter said.

"I haven't received anything about you."

"You will," Hunter said.

"We just got word there's been an attack at Langley," the man said.

Hunter nodded. He wondered what that would mean for his chances of getting to DC anytime soon. Regular air traffic was already grounded. It would be days, maybe weeks, before the airports reopened.

"I guess you can come with me," the head of security said.

Hunter got in his own truck and followed the guard.

The staff at the base were all standing in front of the TV watching the news as it came in. The situation kept getting worse. The president's address had done little to calm things and Hunter could hear the edge of panic in the newscasters' voices.

"What did you make of the president's address?" he said to the head of security.

"Call me Murphy," the man said.

"Alright," Hunter said.

Murphy led him to the coffee machine and poured them each a cup.

"I don't know what I made of it," Murphy said. "That was a lot of laws to be changing all at once."

"Yes it was," Hunter said.

"And what did you make of it?" Murphy said.

"I thought it was a good address."

Murphy nodded. "Yeah, I guess I did too."

They sat at a table and sipped their coffee from plastic cups, watching the news on the big screen. About ten minutes later someone came over with a cell phone.

"Are you Jack Hunter?"

"Yes I am."

"This is for you," she said, handing him the phone.

"This is Jack Hunter," Hunter said.

"Hunter, this is Fawn Aspen. You're at the air force base?"

"Yes I am."

"I take it that means you're ready to get on a plane."

"Yes, ma'am."

There was a second's pause, then Fawn said, "Thank you."

TWENTY-TWO

Hunter thought they'd fly him straight to DC. The carnage at Langley was even worse than at the FBI headquarters. But the flight was to El Paso.

The plane was a lot more comfortable than he was used to. It was a small jet, like something the CEO of a corporation would fly on, and he was the only passenger. There was an air hostess and once they were in the air she asked if she could get him anything.

"How long is this flight?" he asked her.

"Ten hours. We'll be arriving 2PM local time tomorrow."

"You'll be well and truly sick of me by then," Hunter said.

She smiled but she didn't deny it.

Hunter had some coffee and he tried not to keep looking at the air hostess while he drank it. She was sitting at the back of the plane. He was at the front. The two pilots were civilian and they opened the cockpit door to speak to him. They told him about the route. Said they had the sky to themselves. There was only a handful of planes airborne over the entire continent.

Hunter thanked them for the information.

He asked if they were on a government craft.

They said they'd been chartered by the government but were a private jet service.

They shut the doors and Hunter asked the hostess if there was a shower on board.

"Yes, sir, at the back there. You'll find everything you need."

"You wouldn't have a change of clothes or anything like that, would you?"

He was still in his hunting clothes and they weren't clean. Sitting on the white leather upholstery made them seem even dirtier.

"You'll be able to find some sweats and white t-shirts. We don't have a suit or anything."

"Okay," Hunter said.

He went to the back of the plane and took a long, hot shower. He was impressed. The bathroom was like a fancy hotel bathroom, complete with mini soaps and mini shampoos. He washed up as best he could, shaved, and put on gray sweats and a fresh white Calvin Klein t-shirt. There were some disposable slippers and he put a pair of those on too.

"How do I look?" he said to the hostess.

She shrugged. "Better than before."

He smiled and told her his name was Jack. She said her name was Keira. She had red hair and he asked if she was Irish. Her grandparents had come over. She grew up in Houston.

"I'm the only passenger so I'm not going to make you

wait on me," he said. "If you want to get some shuteye, you go ahead."

"Thank you," she said.

"If I need anything I'll let you know."

She nodded.

"I need a phone," he said.

She smiled and showed him how to use the phone in the console next to his seat. He called the number Fawn had given him and waited for her to pick up.

It rang four times before she answered.

"I woke you, didn't I?" he said. "I shouldn't have called."

"No, it's fine. You're enroute to El Paso, correct?"

"You going to be there when I land?"

"Yes."

"What about Hale?"

"I don't know. He's been made director of the CIA. Jonson was killed in the attack."

"Fuck," Hunter said.

"Good for Hale though," Fawn said.

Hunter knew it was true. "He always wanted the job."

"Yes he did."

"Any idea what he's going to do now that he has it?"

"I'm not sure," she said. "I guess first order of business is to get El Sucio."

"You think he's back in Mexico?"

"That would be the first place to look."

"So what's the plan? Send me across the border and see what happens?"

"In a nutshell," Fawn said.

He could hear the apology in her voice. A poorly defined, open-ended mission like that was not what operatives wanted, despite what people thought. For Hunter, the more defined the mission, the better. When it came to killing people, he liked his orders to be as specific and defined as possible. The last thing he wanted was to be given a gun and told to go crazy.

But sometimes that couldn't be avoided.

He understood that.

"I suppose you're going to want to get me over the border as soon as possible after we land."

"That's correct," Fawn said.

"So is there anything we can go over before I get there?"

"Yes. I've got two psychiatrists, two psychologists, a lawyer, a doctor, a CIA handler, a DoD handler, and someone from the president's office for you to speak to."

"I'm going to be on the phone all night."

"I'm sorry about that," she said. "Just try to give them what they want and get through it as quickly as possible."

"I thought I'd at least get to watch some of these movies."

Fawn laughed. "They got anything good?"

"They've got my favorite. The Bourne Identity."

"If there's a Liam Neeson movie called The Grey you should watch that."

"I'll check for it," Hunter said.

The calls turned out not to be that bad. He was done with them in about two hours. The last person he spoke to was from the president's office. She told him that he had the president's confidence and if there was anything he needed, to get in touch with her.

Hunter said he wouldn't need anything.

TWENTY-THREE

Hunter watched half a movie before falling asleep. Denzel Washington going vigilante. When he woke they were two hours from El Paso and the hostess asked if he wanted breakfast.

"I'll take some coffee," he said.

She brought him a tray with a metal carafe of coffee, a glass bottle of orange juice, and some pastries and yoghurt. He stood up and walked around to stretch out. The chair had fully reclined and he was surprised how refreshed he felt. He hadn't slept that well in a long time. In a very long time in fact.

He sipped the coffee and the pilots opened the cockpit door and told him they'd be landing soon.

"We had some more bad news during the night," the senior pilot said.

Hunter wasn't sure he wanted to hear it.

"Two more bombings, one in San Francisco, one in Boston."

"Federal buildings?"

"No."

"What then?"

"High schools."

"What?"

The pilots nodded.

"I thought schools were closed."

"Many were, mostly elementary schools."

"I thought they were all closed."

"Apparently there are a hundred thousand public schools in the country. They're not run by the federal government. Closing them is a local decision."

"So we're under attack and the schools are open?"

"They're saying the country can't come to a standstill."

Hunter shook his head. "They're targets. They're easy targets."

"Yes they are," the hostess said.

"Do they know how the attacks were carried out?" Hunter said.

"They haven't said but it looks like they were similar to the attacks on federal buildings."

"Vehicles laden with explosives?"

"I think so," the pilot said. "They've been saying the bombs might have been meant for federal targets but were diverted when security was stepped up."

"Jesus," Hunter said. "This is all out fucking war."

"Someone's got to stop them," the hostess said.

She looked at Hunter. She and the pilots didn't know exactly who he was but they'd gathered enough to know he was needed for the response to the attacks. He was obviously important if a flight had been chartered for him.

"Whatever you're involved in," the second pilot said, "I wish you the best of luck, sir."

The captain touched his hat.

Hunter nodded at them.

"No one does this to our country and gets away with it," he said.

When they landed, Hunter saw for the first time just how different the country was from twenty-four hours earlier. They were at El Paso airport, not an air force base, and the entire terminal was closed. All traffic was grounded. There were tanks on the runway, humvees in front of the terminal, and soldiers everywhere.

The flags were at half-staff.

Hunter met Fawn in the arrivals area. She was the only person there.

"You didn't have to come in person," he said.

"The base is close by. I thought this would save time."

Hunter nodded.

He was still wearing the gray sweats from the plane. Fawn was wearing a tailored black suit, the pants cropped mid-calf, and the high-heels he'd rescued her from in Fairbanks. She looked like a million bucks. He was underdressed.

"Two more attacks," she said to him.

"Boston and San Francisco, right?"

"Yes."

"The pilots told me."

She nodded.

"I was afraid there'd been two more since then."

"No," she said. "None since those. The death toll is over eighteen thousand now, Hunter. And climbing."

"Including the ten thousand in New York."

She nodded.

She looked pale.

"Did you get any sleep?" he said.

"A little on the plane. How about you?"

"I slept."

"And you had your phone calls."

"I'm good to go. I've been reminded of my legal status, I've been counseled on my trauma, and I've been okayed by a shrink."

Fawn smiled. "That was a bit rushed, I know, but there really isn't time for the usual formalities."

"I prefer it this way," Hunter said. "I've had enough shrinks digging around my head to last a lifetime."

"I can imagine," Fawn said.

Outside the terminal a car was waiting for them. They got in and Fawn told the driver to take them to the air field north of the airport.

The drive took less than ten minutes.

"Let's go to the cafeteria," Fawn said. "I can tell you what we've got while we eat."

"Fine by me," Hunter said.

He followed her to the cafeteria, which was almost empty, and they each grabbed a tray. Hunter got eggs and sausage, beans and tortillas. Fawn got toast, muesli, and an apple.

They both got coffee.

They sat at a table overlooking the dusty runway, a sprawl of desert beyond it. Two fighter jets took off and Hunter watched them. Fawn put her briefcase on the table and clicked it open.

They had the area to themselves. There was no risk of anyone overhearing them.

"This is everything we've got," Fawn said. "The best intel available."

"DoD sent this?"

"Yes. Everything's been included. Special authorization by the president for some of it. It's very comprehensive."

The cafeteria ladies were getting set up for lunch. One

of them approached to clear up their trays but Fawn shook her head. She left them to it.

"What are these?" he said, picking up a computer printout.

"Delivery timetables across the border."

Hunter rose an eyebrow. There were hundreds of rows of data. The kind of details that weren't usually passed on to him. He didn't need it.

"And these are bank records?" he said, picking up some financial reports.

"Yes."

He flicked through the documents. "Forty pages, Fawn?"

"I know."

"What do they think I'm going to do with this? Audit him?"

"Isn't that how they got Al Capone?"

Hunter let out a laugh. "Very funny."

"I know there's a lot here. They didn't know what would be useful."

"These are dental records?"

"From the time of his first arrest."

"Twenty year old Guatemalan dental records?"

"Hunter, we told them we wanted everything."

"Have you ever overseen an operation like this, Aspen?"

"Fuck you, Hunter."

"I'm not trying to fight, Fawn. I mean it. I need to know where he's going to be. And when. And who's going to be with him. Who modified his vehicle. What kind of weapons they'll have. If his physiology provides an exploitable weakness, I'll take it, but fucking dental records?"

"If you don't want the dental records, don't read them."

"I don't want any of this stuff. I don't see a single actionable item in here. What's this map? It covers half of Mexico."

"The western half."

"The western half of the thirteenth largest country in the world."

"I didn't realize you were so into stats."

Hunter sighed. He leaned back in his seat and looked at her. This was not good. He didn't blame her for it, but she was the face of the agency right now, the only person he could voice concerns to, and this was concerning. He needed something actionable. He needed operational intel. This was a fucking mess.

"Hunter, I know this isn't ideal," she said.

"I'm one man. You do realize that?"

She looked out the window. She wasn't happy either. She'd probably had this exact argument already.

"I'm going in alone, right?"

"Yes."

"We need this man dead."

"Yes."

"We need him dead soon."

Fawn was getting angry.

"Fine," she said. "I get it. You don't want bank records."

She picked up the file and started going through it. She took out sections and put them back in her briefcase. She flicked through pages. There was a large black and white photograph of El Sucio, taken at the correctional facility in New York. She laid it on the table in front of him.

"This is your target. Male. Mexican. Sixty-six years old. Two hundred pounds. Five feet six inches."

"Do we have video?"

Fawn opened a video on a tablet and let it play. It was high resolution. It showed El Sucio walking into court. It showed him walking in his prison. It showed him giving testimony in court. It showed him sitting in his cell, doing nothing. She let it play and then opened another video. This was older footage, more grainy, but showed El Sucio in Mexico holding an AK-47. It showed him running from a helicopter to a truck. It showed him torturing a captured DEA agent.

Hunter watched the footage closely.

"Can I keep that?"

"Tonight you can."

He nodded. He wouldn't be bringing anything incriminating over the border.

"So you want me to go in tomorrow?"

"Tomorrow at dawn?"

"Why not today?"

Fawn held her ground. She opened the map that Hunter had scoffed at earlier.

"Tomorrow at dawn," she said. "You'll be taken by helicopter to the mountains west of Culiacán. You'll have some money. Identification. A handgun. Not much else."

"What's on the identification?"

"Texas. There's a legend that mirrors the contours of your life. Should be easy for you to remember."

She handed him a three page document outlining the legend. His name was Jack Morrow. Federal and Texas state records had been created to support the story that he was a big drug dealer in Dallas and Houston.

Hunter read it.

"Jack Morrow?"

"You don't like it?"

"Could be worse," he said.

Fawn slid him another piece of paper.

"There's a bank in Culiacán. Azteca. I've got some

weapons, money and documents in a safety deposit box for you."

Hunter looked out at the runway. Four more jets were taking off, loaded with ordnance.

"Air strikes started this morning," Fawn said.

"What are they hitting?"

The map was already open in front of them. It covered Baja, the Gulf, Sonora, Chihuahua, Sinaloa and Durango. She had a red marker and drew circles around the city of Culiacán and a number of neighboring towns.

"That's their stronghold."

"Right where you're sending me," Hunter said, grinning.

"You know how to take care of yourself."

"I guess I've been bombed by the government before."

"Experience is everything."

"So they say."

"The president is desperate to degrade their military capability before they have time to move it north and use it against us."

Hunter nodded. "I'd say that's a good idea."

Fawn drew an X on the map east of Culiacán. "This is where we're dropping you. In the mountains. The area is sparsely populated. It's their main growing region. Most of their military equipment is in this area too."

"And how are we getting air strike targets?"

"I think they're mostly coming from out of date Mexican sources."

Hunter looked closely at the map. The situation wasn't that different from what he was used to in Afghanistan. An arid, sparsely populated mountain region with little government presence, weapons stockpiles, outdated military equipment, and drug caches scattered throughout.

He knew how to fight in a place like that.

"If I ask for an equipment drop?"

"We'll get it to you."

"How will we communicate?"

"You'll have a cell. You can also use pay phones. They're everywhere down there."

"Is there an encryption protocol?"

She took another document from her briefcase and handed it to him. Any numbers given, such as an apparent phone number, time, or price, would be assumed to be coordinates for an air strike unless he said the word sunrise in the message.

"If I call in an air strike, how fast will it be acted on?"

"I can't guarantee. We'll pass it on to the military immediately but they'll have their own priorities."

"What if I find El Sucio?"

"If you find him, the best course would be to take him out personally."

"Personally?"

"Our first choice would be for you to have eyes on him when he dies. We want proof positive he's dead. If you can bring back the head, do."

"But if I need to call in a strike?"

"If you need a strike, call it in. You'll have to be able to find coordinates or describe the location. The codeword for El Sucio is Pimp."

Hunter smiled. "Who came up with that?"

"I don't know. Apparently that's what the DEA's been using for him for years."

"Is there anyone else looking for him down there?"

"We have no assets in the city. Neither do the FBI or DEA. The Mexican military will be going in eventually, but who knows how long that will take. Right now it'll just be you and the air strikes."

"Just me and the strikes."

"Correct."

"I'll try to stay out of their way."

"That would be smart."

"And do we have any idea where the pimp is hiding?"

"None," she said. "Since he escaped there hasn't been a peep. We're thinking he might still be in the US. He might have gone somewhere remote to hide."

"Or, he might have gone home," Hunter said.

"Exactly. Culiacán has always been his center of power. It's where he's always called home. He feels safe there. He defeated the Mexican government there. It's the most likely place you'll find him."

"Do we have a list of known addresses?"

"Memorize these," she said, handing him the list. "You can't take them with you."

"Are they being hit by air strikes?"

"Yes, I imagine they are."

Hunter looked at her. "He could be killed in a strike and we'll never know. That's happened with high priority targets before."

"I know."

"There's nothing worse than not knowing if he's still out there."

"That's why you're going to have eyes on him when he dies."

Hunter nodded. "That's right," he said.

TWENTY-FOUR

Hale was on his way to the White House. His security detail had been upgraded now that he was CIA head. Before, he had his driver, who was armed, and a Capitol Police detail that monitored his home on an hourly schedule. Now he had a full Secret Service security detail and was on the list of people to be evacuated from the capital in case of attack.

He wasn't sure how he felt about it. Everywhere he went there would be two armed bodyguards. If he was going to have a meeting, the person had to be vetted first. If he booked a hotel, the detail would put motion sensors in the corridor. At his house, an apartment was being installed in the basement for security service personnel.

It would cut into his privacy. His ability to conduct his affairs how he liked.

But there was also the prestige that came with it.

He was still using the same car and driver, but soon he'd be traveling in an escalade with tinted windows, two security officers in the car, and a follow up vehicle.

There was a bodyguard sitting up front with the driver.

"You always take this route?" the bodyguard said to the driver as they crossed the Rock Creek bridge.

"No," the driver said, annoyed. "I rotate routes."

"I'll need to see a plan."

The driver nodded. He looked in the rearview at Hale.

"Don't worry, Lou. I'll make sure they keep you."

"They're going to have their own guy," Lou said.

The truth was, Hale didn't know what the procedure was going to be. He didn't really care. If he had a choice, he would keep Lou on his detail, but he wasn't going to go out of his way to make sure it happened. They all worked for the same organization.

Hale enjoyed the process of pulling up outside the West Wing, despite the somber occasion, and being ushered inside by secret service agents. Outside, the media were going ballistic. The nation was in shock. It was also in mourning. No one knew what to think or what to feel.

All anyone knew was that they had entered a new era. Attacks were being reported constantly. Some were false alarms but too many were real. In the last seventy-two hours, there had been more bloodshed on US soil than at any point since the Civil War.

He noted the flag at half-staff.

He noted the roses and wreaths piled up at the gates.

He noted that reporters he didn't recognize were calling to him by name. He was a national figure now. He was about to hold a joint press conference with the president and the entire world would be watching.

This was a level of prestige he had never dreamed of.

Inside the White House, he was brought to a waiting area where a secretary offered him coffee. He declined. He sat on the couch and looked around. He'd been to the Oval Office before, but never for a one-on-one with the president.

He looked at his watch. It was two PM. The press conference was at four. Fawn would be calling soon. She'd been briefing Hunter on what they had.

Which wasn't much.

They were basically sending him in alone, with nothing to go on, and hoping he found his mark. Hale was pretty confident that if El Sucio was in Sinaloa, Hunter would manage to track him down and kill him. The problem was if he wasn't there. If he wasn't in Mexico. Then it was out of his hands. He prayed it wouldn't fall to the FBI to bring him in. They were the ones who'd lost him in the first place. And they'd just lost more than half of the staff at their head-quarters, scores of their most experienced personnel.

He hadn't heard yet who the president was going to call on to replace Moynihan.

The door to the Oval Office opened and the president came out.

"Jeff, glad to see you."

"Likewise, sir," Hale said.

He stood up and shook the president's hand before following him into the office. It really was going to be just the two of them. No National Security Advisor. No Chairman of the Joint Chiefs.

"I thought Antosh and Goldwater would be here," Hale said.

"We'll be spending a lot of time together, Jeff. You'll have to get used to me."

Hale smiled. The president had an easy air of familiarity. People enjoyed his company. He had a knack for making complete strangers feel at ease. That was what the British prime minister had said after their first meeting.

"First, let me give you my sincere condolences for the losses your agency has suffered," the president said. "A lot of federal employees lost their lives in the last few days, but Langley was hit very hard and I know it will be difficult for people to move forward."

"We're holding a ceremony tomorrow, sir. We've got personnel coming in from field offices around the world. We're going to take that moment to grieve, and then we will be one hundred percent ready to take out the monsters responsible for these attacks."

"I'm glad to hear that," the president said. "As you know, the DoD has already launched an attack. Operation Condor. We'll have launched more air strikes in the first twenty-four hours of this attack than we did in the first month against ISIS."

"How are we getting targets, sir?"

"We had a list. We had targets from the agency, from the DEA, we're getting more from the Mexicans."

"It won't take long until we've hit them all."

"No it won't," the president said. "That city, what was it called?"

"Culiacán."

"Culiacán," the president repeated, trying to commit it to memory. "Honestly, before this whole El Sucio thing, I'd never heard of the place."

"There's not much to know," Hale said. "About a million people in the municipality. An airport. They've got an Eiffel tower replica there that's about four stories high."

"I saw that."

"We've been patrolling the airspace ever since the Mexicans pulled out."

"That's given us more targets," the president said. "Between you and me, Jeff, I've told them not to be too picky."

"I'd be inclined to agree, sir."

"Just give me targets. I want that city on its knees."

"Have we given them an acceptable collateral casualty parameter?"

"One hundred thousand."

Hale wasn't known for his weak stomach when it came to civilian casualties, but that figure took the wind out of even his sails.

"You think that's high," the president said.

"Sir, we haven't accepted collateral like that since World War Two."

"I told them to destroy anything that could possibly be of use to the cartel, Jeff."

"You might as well tell them to carpet bomb the place. Save the missiles. They cost more."

The president looked grim.

"We're going in hard, Jeff."

"Very hard," Hale said.

"But it will all be for nothing if we don't get our man."

"Yes, sir. I completely agree."

"So tell me what you've got planned in that arena."

"Tooth Fairy is being flown into the region tonight. He'll be in position tomorrow morning. He'll be reporting to agent Aspen directly. If El Sucio's in Sinaloa, he'll find him."

"I want proof positive of the kill."

"Of course, sir."

"It won't do me a bit of good to kill this guy in an air strike and never know it happened."

"Agreed," Hale said.

"Now, what are we doing to cover the chance he didn't go back to Mexico."

"I've got our field offices all over the world on it, sir. Collation of the intel has been messed up because of the attack on Langley, but every CIA asset and informant in the world is listening for word of El Sucio."

"That attack really fucked us. If he's in the US we're in even worse shape. Honestly, I don't think the FBI will be operational for the next few months. They lost over a thousand people. Not just in DC. All over the country."

"Who are you naming the new head?" Hale said.

"I haven't decided yet. Any suggestions?"

"I'm sure you'll think of someone, sir."

The president nodded. We've got a few candidates. The problem is all the people we had vetted for a scenario like this were killed in the attack.

Hale looked out the window of the office and realized for the first time it was in the process of being replaced.

"Sir, I never asked. Was your wife hurt when the glass blew?"

"No, luckily she wasn't here. She's pretty shaken up though, I can tell you that much."

TWENTY-FIVE

Fawn spent the afternoon going over more briefing materials with Hunter. He wasn't a fan of all the background intel but when he saw that some of it was useful he quit giving her a hard time. She showed him files on all the cartel's top lieutenants, the people who were known to work closely with El Sucio and who would be an indication he was in the city. She also showed him pictures of every living relative El Sucio still had, including six sons, four daughters, and over forty grandchildren. There were four wives and ex-wives, and sixteen known lovers on the list.

After that, they watched Hale's press conference with the president.

It was strange to see the two men standing together at the podium. Hale was an inch taller than the president and Fawn could tell he was enjoying his moment.

The president went all out, calling Hale the man who was going to keep America safe. Some people in the press room actually began to chant Make America Safe Again and the president had to quieten them down.

"Our nation has weathered many storms," the president

said. "Right now, we are grieving. I have ordered all government flags be flown at half-staff until the monster, Segundo José Heredia, is dead in the ground."

Fawn thought the president was handling the situation well. He was saddened by the losses the country had suffered, but also brave and determined to bring El Sucio to justice.

The press was reacting well to the speech.

"In the past seventy-two hours, our nation has lost thousands of brave souls. Never have we suffered such a loss on our own soil at the hand of an external foe. Many of those lost were federal employees, judges, FBI agents, and law enforcement personnel. The attacks have struck at the heart of our government. The FBI and CIA headquarters, and over a dozen other federal buildings, were savagely attacked."

The president paused.

"But this enemy has also purposely maximized civilian casualties. Across New York, citizens of seventy-two countries lost their lives."

The room was silent.

"Two high schools were attacked."

You could have heard a pin drop. The president looked at Hale and then back at the cameras.

"But we are going to make sure those people did not die in vain."

The cameras were clicking furiously.

"We are going to make sure everyone we lost is remembered."

The president turned to Hale again and rose a hand toward him.

"The war we are about to embark on is not just a war of self-defense, it is not just a war to maintain global order," he stopped reading from his script and looked up at the crowd, "it is a war of vengeance."

There was a moment of hesitation, some people in the room looked at each other in surprise, and then, slowly, light applause broke out from some of the journalists.

"It is a war of anger, a war of rage, and mark my words, it will be a war of carnage unlike any the world has ever seen."

As the president continued, he grew darker and more menacing. His voice got louder. The people who had cheered stopped and went quiet.

"We are going to rain brimstone on these people," he said, his voice still rising.

"We are going to bring down the wrath of God on these people."

The atmosphere in the press room was getting icy. The president was letting his anger rise to a fever pitch.

"We are going to bring pain to these people. I swear to God. Every tear we shed, they will shed a thousand. Every grave we dig. They will dig a thousand. Every child we mourn," at this point, a presidential aide rushed onto the podium and said something into the president's ear.

The aide put his hand on the microphone.

The president seemed to have lost himself in the heat of the moment. There was a chatter among the journalists. He'd been one moment from threatening the death of thousands of Mexican children.

The president took a deep breath and composed himself.

He stretched a hand toward Hale.

"I am here today to introduce to you the man who is going to get this monster and bring him to the cold, icy hand of justice. I introduce to you the new director of the Central Intelligence Agency, Edward Hale."

The journalists applauded politely. They'd known in advance this was the purpose of the meeting. The jury was still out on what Hale's appointment meant for the country.

In the decades he'd been at the CIA, Edward Hale had avoided stepping into the spotlight. Not that he had any aversion to the attention. He would have relished the chance to put himself on the national stage, it was just that his role in black ops never afforded him the opportunity. He was completely unknown to the public, and virtually unknown in congress. He'd reported to cabinet on certain high profile-operations, but the rank and file on Capitol Hill had no clue what he stood for.

The president had already assured him his confirmation process would go quickly, that the senate hearings would be merely a formality, and, given the circumstances, Hale had every reason to believe that would be the case.

He was glad. Given his track record, he doubted he would have received confirmation during peacetime.

As the applause died down, Hale looked out at the assembled journalists and realized that for the first time in his life, he was addressing the entire nation. The entire world.

He was finally in a position of real power.

He found the camera and looked straight at it.

"Thank you Mr. President. I'm honored that you have chosen me for this grave mission during this time of unprecedented national crisis. There is only one thing I want to say to the American people today, and that is, I will fight for you. I stand by everything the President just said. Under my leadership, the CIA is going to take off the gloves and bring the fight to the enemy. We will not hold back. We will not be measured in our response. In a bitter fight like this, a fight to the death, the only way to win is to get blood on your hands. El Sucio's cartel has struck at the heart of our country while our guard was down. He struck while we trusted in laws, and judges, and lofty principles. That is not going to happen again. Next time the cartel throws a blow, we'll be ready. Under my leadership, the CIA is going to avenge every fallen agent we lost in the cowardly attacks of the past few days. We are going to bring this enemy to his knees, and we are going to make him beg us for mercy."

Spontaneously, the journalists broke into applause.

Fawn realized there'd never been a scene like it before in the history of the White House. Never, not even during the darkest hours against Hitler and Stalin, had US leadership embraced such aggressive rhetoric. The fact the press was applauding showed just how much the country had changed in the past seventy-two hours.

Hale strode across the stage and met the president between the podiums, shaking his hand firmly. The president grabbed him by the shoulder and pulled him toward him. They were like two linebackers after a successful blitz.

Fawn looked at Hunter.

"That was weird."

Hunter raised a single eyebrow in a high arch.

Fawn laughed. She rarely laughed in front of anyone, let alone someone like Hunter. He would think she liked him.

He would take it as an opening.

She shut her mind to the idea.

"I'm going to go for a run," she said. "I've been cooped up in too many airplanes lately."

"All right," Hunter said. "I'll stay here and keep going through these files."

"Someone from materials will come by and measure you," she said. "They'll get you some appropriate clothing."

Hunter nodded.

She hurried out of the cafeteria and made her way to the guest quarters where she and Hunter had been assigned rooms. The rooms were spartan but more comfortable than she'd expected. She'd seen a lot worse on military bases in the past.

She changed into her running clothes, a pair of black yoga pants and a tight, black racerback. Before she left the room she gave Hale a call to congratulate him on the press conference.

"I saw the briefing," she said.

"How was it?"

She could tell he was on a high after his performance. He thought he'd just hit a home run.

"Great. The media is eating it up. You're on every channel."

"I never felt anything like it, Fawn. It was like being ten feet tall."

"I'm glad you enjoyed it."

"The suit. Did you notice?"

Hale had charged a custom Tom Ford suit to his departmental expense card and somehow hadn't been called out for it. Not yet at least.

"I noticed it," she said.

"And?"

"It looked great. If anyone questions your dress sense, you're covered."

He noticed the tone in her voice.

"You have reservations about something."

"No, I called to congratulate you, that's all."

"Come on, Aspen. I can take it."

"It's just, I think it may have been a mistake to be so aggressive."

"They want someone who's going to take this guy out. You saw the applause."

"They liked it today, Hale, but if anything goes wrong, or if sentiment for the war changes, which it will, they're going to make you pay for those words."

"I'll be able to afford them by then."

"I hope you're not writing checks you can't cover."

Hale sighed. "Can't you just let me enjoy this?"

"Fine. You're one of the most powerful men in the world now. Relish it while it lasts."

"You're just afraid I'm going to forget all the little people who made it possible along the way."

"Are you?" Fawn said.

"I don't know," Hale said. "I'll have to see if they do anything especially memorable."

"Suck my dick," Fawn said.

Hale laughed.

"How's it going with our new recruit?"

"Good. He's going through the material now. If El Sucio's in Mexico, Hunter will find him."

"Let's hope so. I just promised the nation blood."

"That's what I was saying. You and your blank checks."

"Is he there? I want to talk to him."

"He's not here. I'm in my room."

"Can you get him? He doesn't carry a cell."

"I was about to go for a run," Fawn said, looking at herself in the mirror.

"Well run to him and hand him the phone, would you?"

Fawn sighed. She didn't relish the thought of showing Hunter what she looked like in spandex.

She hurried back to the cafeteria and found him, still sitting with the paperwork, a stack of notes in front of him.

He grinned at her when he saw what she was wearing.

"Don't," she said.

"Agent Aspen, my, my."

"Go fuck yourself, Tooth Fairy."

Hunter winked as she handed him the phone. He couldn't believe the body she had. She could have made a lot more money doing something else.

She turned away when he winked and he genuinely didn't know if she was playing hard to get or if she really did find him as repulsive as she let on.

He wondered if there would be time to find out.

"Hello?" Hale's voice said from the phone.

Hunter brought it to his ear.

"I guess you're pleased with yourself," he said.

"Why can't anyone just tell me I did well?"

"Because if we let you get a big head you'll be even worse to work with than you are now."

Hale laughed.

"How's the briefing going?"

Hunter was looking at Fawn. She had her back to him and was looking out the window at the runway, waiting to get her phone back. There was no way in hell a girl like that was going to leave her phone with a guy like him. In those yoga pants it was hard to look at anything else in the room so he leaned back and took in the curve of her ass at his leisure. It was a work of art.

His cock throbbed and he realized how long it had been since he'd had a woman. Over a month. Not since Chianne's death. The thought of it was hard, and every lustful desire he had was tinged with guilt.

He knew he should still be grieving.

He'd have to figure something out soon. He wouldn't be able to concentrate on his job if he didn't.

"Hunter? You there?"

"It's going well, chief. Aspen's run me through the basics. I'm going to need some concrete intel soon though. If we could even get confirmation he's in Mexico, I could take it from there."

"We're working on it, Hunter. SIGINT is a nightmare after the attack. They lost eighty members of their team in the Langley bombing. It will take a while to get them back up and running."

"I'm sorry about that," Hunter said.

Hale murmured some thanks.

Hale said goodbye and Hunter gave the phone back to Fawn. She left immediately.

TWENTY-SIX

Fawn went for a long run and it was time for dinner when she'd showered and got back to the cafeteria. Hunter was still there, poring over the files. He was committing everything to memory, even the tax records, the bank account numbers, the dental records. The man was a machine and when he said he'd do something, he meant it.

"You ready to call it a night?" he said when he saw her.

"You got everything you can out of those files?"

"I think so," Hunter said. "There's only so much use I can make out of twenty year old receipts for construction materials."

"They were thorough when they compiled those papers," Fawn said.

Hunter nodded.

Fawn looked at him. There was something in his eyes. He was up to something. He was going to ask her out, make a move, something. She could sense it.

"We've got to be up at two AM for the drop in," she said.

"We?"

"Well, you. I'll be on the runway to see you off though."

"That's nice of you."

"It's my job, Hunter."

"Heaven forbid you do it out of affection."

"Come on," she said. "Let's get some trays. Looks like they're serving meatloaf."

The cafeteria ladies had given Hunter room to do his work and none of the personnel from the base had come near him. Everyone knew he was with the CIA and was reading classified documents.

Fawn looked over at the food they were serving. Some soldiers were filling trays.

"Let's go into town," Hunter said. "I'll buy you a burger."

She knew it. The yoga pants did it every time.

"I don't know, Hunter. We've got to be up awfully early."

"It's my last night stateside," he said. "A burger's the least I can expect from my country."

"Did the materials guy come and measure you up?"

"Yes he did. I've got everything I need. Even a hat."

"Oh, God."

"They need me to look Texan for the legend. They took it pretty literally."

"Boots, buckle?"

"The works. I'm going to look like JR Ewing."

Fawn pictured it. She had to admit, going out in downtown El Paso with Hunter didn't sound like the worst way in the world to kill a few hours.

"Okay, but I'm driving," she said.

"Fine by me. I don't have a vehicle."

Fawn didn't either but she could get one. It was her way of maintaining a modicum of control over the situation. She wasn't giving him carte blanche. She definitely wasn't sleeping with him. She'd been propositioned by enough agents to know that business and pleasure never mixed well.

Celeste was the only exception.

Women were different.

There wasn't the same power dynamic at play. And she knew if there was anyone on earth she could trust to keep an affair private it was a lesbian at Langley.

No risk of locker room talk there.

On thinking of Celeste, she reflexively opened her messaging app.

She read over the last few messages she'd typed.

As soon as she'd heard news of the blast she'd sent Celeste a message.

"You okay?"

An hour later, "I'm sorry for what I said the other night."

During the night she wrote, "Celeste. Talk to me."

The messages said they'd been delivered, which to Fawn meant Celeste was all right. She couldn't bear the thought that something had happened to her. She forced it from her mind. The more time that passed, the more the lump in her throat grew.

"You okay?" Hunter said.

"I'm just worried about someone at work."

"They haven't checked in?"

Fawn shook her head. "Not since the blast."

"How often were you usually in touch."

"On and off."

Hunter nodded.

"We could check the official list," he said.

Fawn looked at him and smiled thinly. "I'm too afraid to," she said.

Hunter didn't say anything. She knew he was going to ask Celeste's name and then look her up on the list. She couldn't take it. She couldn't know for sure. As long as she didn't check the list, there was a chance Celeste was still alive.

"Come on," she said. "Let's get out of here."

They gathered up the documents and Fawn brought them to her room while Hunter went to his to change. When she was in her room she felt the emotion welling up inside her.

She pressed the call button, it was her third time trying since the attack. It rang out and went to voicemail like all the others. The fact the phone didn't go straight to voicemail, the fact the messages were being delivered, that had to mean the phone was operational. If the phone was okay, Celeste was okay. That's what Fawn kept telling herself.

She met Hunter back in the hallway and the way he looked at her brought her close to tears.

"I'm fine," she said. "It's fine."

"They've identified less than half the casualties," he said. "They're still pulling bodies from the rubble."

Fawn shook her head. "Could we talk about something else."

"I'm just saying, your friend, even if you checked the list, you wouldn't know for sure she was okay. The best thing to do is keep texting and hope for the best. If she's okay she'll be in touch."

Fawn wanted to change the subject. Hunter looked a lot different than he had a few minutes earlier. His new clothes were worn in so that he didn't look like he'd just been to the mall to buy a disguise. He looked like the real deal. He had on a Texan cowboy hat, boots, perfectly fitting jeans. A huge silver buckle of an eagle covered his crotch. His shirt was red and black plaid and the jacket was denim with fleece lining.

He looked good.

He looked like Jake Gyllenhaal in Brokeback Mountain.

They took a base vehicle and drove into the city.

She was surprised how much of a weight lifted from her shoulders as they left the base. The weather was a lot warmer than DC at that time of year and it gave her a feeling of optimism.

They stopped at an intersection and some kids from the University of Texas pulled up next to them. They were on Fawn's side and whistled at her.

"Pull down the window, honey," one of them shouted.

They couldn't see Hunter sitting on the passenger side so he opened his door and walked around the car and stepped in front of theirs.

"You boys lookin' to start something?" he said.

The kids laughed and tore off through the intersection, leaving a screech of rubber.

Fawn was impressed. The way he looked in the denim and boots, the way he walked, the swagger, he was like a new person.

"You play the role well," she said.

Hunter laughed. From somewhere he'd managed to find a tooth pick and was playing with it in his mouth.

"This ain't no role, sweetie. I grew up here."

She remembered it from his file.

"You like it here, don't you?"

"You know how home is. You can never get it out of your blood."

Fawn nodded. Her relationship to the place she'd grown up was a little more complicated than that, but she understood.

They got to a lively downtown neighborhood full of bars and restaurants and she parked the car. Live music was coming from every direction. The streets were busy with university kids, off-duty military personnel, rowdy local boys looking to get lucky.

Fawn liked it.

They walked down the street looking for somewhere they could eat and she was aware of what an odd couple they made. He was taller. He was older. He was about twice her weight. He had stubble and unkempt hair. She didn't have a hair out of place. Against his jeans and denim jacket, she was wearing an expensive black Lanvin turtleneck and cropped black pants.

She didn't look severe.

She wasn't dressed older than he was.

She looked hot.

It was just a different brand of hot to his.

They found a bar that had a good guitar player on the stage. The place had a half-decent menu by local standards. It was lively but not overly so. The town felt edgy, electric, like it was getting ready for something. War had just been declared. This was a military town. It was a border town. It was Texas.

Anything could happen.

That's how it felt to Fawn.

She checked her phone one last time before turning it off. Still no word from Celeste. The lump in her chest grew and when the waiter arrived she ordered beer and a shot of Jack Daniels. Hunter took the same.

When they were two rounds in, waiting for their steaks and french fries, Hunter asked if she wanted to dance.

"You're asking me to dance?" she said.

He shrugged.

The music was good. A few other people were on the floor. They were dancing slow, close, cheek to cheek.

"Only because this might be your last chance," she said.

She stood up and let him lead her to the dance floor. He put one hand around her waist and another on her shoulder and she let him pull her close. His body was pressed against hers. She could feel the bulge of his belt buckle. They danced to a rendition of Moon River and when the song was over, Hunter led her back to the table.

"I hope your friend is okay," he said.

Fawn was caught off guard.

He never seemed to do what she expected. He didn't act like any agent she'd ever worked with.

Their food arrived and they didn't talk much as they ate. When they were finished, Hunter went to the bar and paid the bill. They went back to the base and said goodnight outside their rooms.

When Fawn got in her room she felt restless.

The official death toll from Langley was still rising and the list of names of identified casualties was getting more complete. It was alphabetized. All she had to do was log in to her agency account to view it.

She didn't. She tried calling Celeste again and left her another message.

Then she went back out to the corridor. She stopped outside Hunter's room and looked at the door. She thought about knocking on it. She thought he'd let her inside. She shook her head and went to the cafeteria where Hunter had been working all day, half expecting to find him there. He wasn't there.

She went back out to the parking lot, to the vehicle, and without any specific destination in mind, drove back to the bar they'd had dinner at.

It felt like a different place now. The guitar player had been replaced by a DJ and the tables had been moved aside to make more room for dancing. The crowd was younger. There were more locals. Some soldiers from the base.

She saw a group of soldiers get in an argument with some tough-looking Mexican guys. The bar staff broke it up and the Mexicans left. The soldiers celebrated with a round of shots. Fawn walked up to the soldier who'd been most riled up, the most aggressive.

He was a big guy, about two-hundred-fifty, over six feet tall.

"You going to war, soldier?" Fawn said.

"What?" the man said over the noise of the DJ.

She put her mouth to his ear, letting her lips touch him.

"You going to war?"

"Got our orders today," he said.

She put her hand on his crotch and felt the bulge grow.

"Let me give you a little something to remind you why you're fighting."

She led him to the ladies restroom and he was all over her before they'd even shut the door. He turned her around and pressed her against the wall, her back to him.

He ripped down her pants and her panties.

The last thing she thought of was Celeste's face.

TWENTY-SEVEN

Hunter was on the concrete runway of Biggs airfield at two AM. Even for him, it was pushing the limits of what he considered morning to be.

He was dressed in some beat up Wrangler jeans, a pair of worn in Tony Lama boots, a buckle with a silver eagle on it, and the same red and black shirt and wool lined denim jacket he'd worn the night before. He was surprised at how good the clothes fit. They'd been broken in perfectly. He wondered where the agency got them on such short notice. He felt like he'd been wearing the boots for years.

On his back he had a civilian knapsack containing a water bottle, two packs of cigarettes, a lighter, a cellphone registered to the name of his legend, Jack Morrow, and a wallet. In the wallet was Jack Morrow's ID and credit cards and some Mexican and US cash.

He was standing close to a noisy, twin-engine Super Huey that had just flown in from Camp Pendleton.

A marine corporal ran from the helicopter to him.

"Ready when you are," the corporal said.

"I'm waiting for my handler."

"We're on your schedule," the corporal said.

"She won't be long."

The corporal stood with him, ducking unconsciously from the noise of the propeller, and when he saw Fawn approaching he ran back to the chopper.

Hunter could see three more marines in the back and two pilots up front. If they knew where El Sucio was located, that would probably be enough men to get the job done.

As it stood, they didn't even know if he was in Mexico.

"Bright eyed and bushy tailed," Fawn yelled at him over the noise.

Hunter looked at his watch and raised an eyebrow at her. It was ten after two. She looked like she hadn't had enough sleep.

"Good morning, agent Aspen."

"Don't agent Aspen me. You good to go?"

"More or less. I thought I was getting a handgun."

Fawn laughed. "I've got something nice for you."

She reached into her briefcase and pulled out a nickel-finished, two-inch barrel, .38 Chief's Special. It was the kind of gun issued to Texas Rangers in the 1950's as an off-duty gun. A five-shooter revolver that would fit in a pocket. It had a worn black rubber grip and plenty of wear and tear.

"I'm not going to be starting any wars with that," Hunter said.

"You're going to get picked up as soon as you cross into Sinaloa. If I give you anything too good it will look suspicious."

"It's still a .38," Hunter said. "It'll knock anyone over."

"Yes it will," Fawn said.

He looked at her. She looked strained.

"Any news from your friend?" he said.

She shook her head.

He grabbed her hand, gave her a handshake of sorts, then turned and made for the chopper.

"Good luck, Hunter. And stay in touch."

"I will."

"Use pay phones."

He nodded and got on board the helicopter with the marines. The corporal signaled to the pilots and they took off. Hunter looked out at the runway at Fawn's figure. She stood and watched until they were gone.

The plan was for the chopper to drop him in the mountains along the border between Sinaloa and Durango. There was a village, Tamazula de Victoria, that was on the Durango side of the border and still in government control. From there it wasn't more than a mile to cartel territory and less than thirty to Culiacán.

Hunter was to cross the border looking for a drug deal. The plan's finer details were hazy. He'd make his way to Culiacán and get in with the lowlifes and drug dealers that might know of El Sucio's whereabouts. He would drink hard, get in fights, and eventually, someone would notice him. There wasn't much more to the plan than that. He'd be in the right area, hanging out with the right people, and he'd keep his eyes and ears open.

It wasn't a bad plan as far as Hunter was concerned. His main worry was that El Sucio wouldn't be there, in which case he'd be wasting his time.

One of the marines looked at him.

"You going in alone?" the marine said.

Hunter was still holding the revolver. He showed it to the marine.

"I wouldn't say all alone. I'm bringing my old friends, Smith and Wesson."

The marine laughed. "Well good luck to you, mister. That's all I'll say."

"Thanks."

"The entire army's on the border and they're sending you in alone with a five-shooter," the corporal said.

"They've got other plans I'm sure," Hunter said, "but if you can win a war with a single shot, you might as well take it."

"Just don't miss," the corporal said.

"I'll hit him," Hunter said, "if he's down there."

The corporal nodded. "Lets hope you find the son of a bitch."

"And if I do, I never aim below the neck."

The marines seemed satisfied with the plan.

Hunter shut his eyes and tried to get some sleep. It was a five hour flight and they had to refuel at a Mexican air force facility outside Chihuahua. They continued through the night and the sun was just rising when the helicopter touched down on some high ground a mile from the village of Tamazula.

"So long," the corporal said as the helicopter took off.

Hunter got his bearings. It wasn't fully light yet and a mist was rising over the valley below. Over the crest of the hill he would find the village. Beyond that would be the border into the cartel's territory.

He turned on the phone and confirmed he was where he was supposed to be, then turned it off to save the battery and made his way down the slope.

The village was just beginning to stir. Until recently it was a quiet farming town in the middle of nowhere. Now, the government was stationing soldiers there and constructing a new barracks. He noticed some military heli-copters and lightly armed vehicles at the south end of the village. No one would have paid any notice to the sound of the helicopter that brought him in.

He walked down the main street of the town and when he found a woman cooking tortillas over an open grill he stopped and had some with ground beef. He asked if she had coffee but she only had soda. She told him he could get coffee at the hotel so after the tacos, he went straight there. The hotel was a little bigger than the surrounding buildings with a veranda and restaurant on the ground floor. It was full of police officers, state and federal. Hunter made a point of ordering loudly in English.

"Coffee," he said. "Black."

The woman working the bar didn't know what he meant. He tried asking louder. It didn't help.

"El quiere cafe," a policeman in a state uniform said to her.

"Con leche?" she said to the policeman.

"Sin leche," the cop said.

The woman went to get his coffee. She brought back a delicate china cup filled with the weakest coffee Hunter had ever tasted. It was lukewarm.

"Gracias," he said to the police officer in a heavy accent.

"De nada," the police officer said.

Hunter took a seat close to him and sipped his coffee. He took his wallet from his pocked and looked through it. He had some crisp hundred dollar bills, courtesy of the CIA, and he fingered through them as if counting.

"Maybe there's some business I can help you with," the police officer said.

"Who's in charge of the border?" Hunter said.

"Depends what you are doing."

"If I wanted to drive a truck out of Culiacán."

"A truck, that would be the army."

"Can you help me deal with them?"

"You don't want to deal with the army."

"How would I transport something out of Culiacán then?"

"What are you transporting?"

Hunter looked at the cop. He didn't have anything to lose, one way or another. Either he would get in trouble for trying to bribe a straight cop, in which case he could cross into Sinaloa to escape, or he would succeed in bribing a crooked cop, in which case his cover story would make a lot more sense if anyone looked into things in detail.

He counted out five hundred dollar bills and lay them on the table under his tea saucer.

"Packages," he said.

"How big are the packages?"

"Hunter made like he was holding something about the size of a football.

"A few kilos," he said.

"How many?"

"Not many," Hunter said. "Maybe a hundred."

"For something like that, you don't need to bring a truck across the border. You can unload on that side, carry the packages across, and load them on a truck on this side."

"And for that, who would I speak to?"

"You would speak to me."

Hunter smiled. He stood up and walked out of the hotel. The cop followed, taking a detour to Hunter's table to pick up the money first. Outside, the cop told Hunter to get in his car.

"Where are we going?" Hunter said, lighting a cigarette.

He offered one to the cop and the cop took it.

The cop took him to the border crossing, which was a mile further along the main street. The road was paved and well maintained. At the border, soldiers of the Mexican army had set up a checkpoint. They were armed with machine guns and heavy equipment and had built sandbag walls around their posts.

"This is the official crossing," the cop said. "It's very expensive to bring a truck across. You have to deal with the army. You have to deal with the federales. A lot of work. A lot of money."

"And if I don't want to deal with them?"

The cop pulled a u-turn and took him back to the village. From the village they took a road east into the mountains. It was unpaved. They drove about ten miles and joined another dirt road. That road led to an old creek. There had been a bridge crossing the creek but it had been destroyed. It would be very difficult to get a vehicle across the creek bed the way it was.

The cop pointed at the dusty road that continued on the other side of the blown bridge.

"That's Sinaloa," he said.

"The army doesn't patrol here?"

"We do," the cop said, pointing to the Durango state police insignia on his sleeve.

"And how would I arrange to make a crossing?"

"You would come to the hotel and speak to me. There is a bank in the village that accepts wire transfers. If you transfer the price, we will make sure you have no trouble with anyone."

"And what's your name?"

"Mendoza. If you call the hotel and ask for Capitán Mendoza you'll get me."

Hunter nodded.

He opened his door and got out of the car.

"Where do I get if I follow that road?" he said, pointing west.

"Little place," the cop said. "Las Milpas. A few miles."

"What's there?"

"A few farmers."

"Will they give me a hard time?"

The cop thought for a minute. "No," he said after a pause that was longer than it needed to be. "I don't think so."

"Will they take me to the cartel?"

"Can you speak Spanish?"

"Sí."

The cop smiled. "If they don't take you to the cartel, you'll be okay."

"Will it be difficult to get to Culiacán?"

"You'll need to find someone who can give you a ride."

Hunter nodded. He had more than enough money to manage that.

"I'll send someone to talk to you in a few days," he said to the cop.

"Be careful," the cop called after him. "Territorio enemigo."

Enemy territory, Hunter said to himself.

His mission had begun. From this point onwards, he would be a different person. He was no longer himself. He had no past. He had no family. He had never been in love. He had no God.

Hunter was from the school of thought that if you wanted your cover to hold up to scrutiny, it had to be true. If the legend said you were buying drugs, you had better make all the arrangements a drug buyer would make. If the legend said you used drugs, you better suck it up and put the shit in your arm. If the legend said you killed people, you had to kill people.

It was method acting. You became the legend.

You thought like the legend. You acted like the legend. You liked what the legend liked, and hated what he hated.

Not everyone in the modern CIA agreed with that stance. They didn't believe it was still necessary. But there was a time when every black ops asset had been trained to be the men they were pretending to be.

Hunter had read the files of agents who'd taken it to its limits. They'd killed, raped, and pillaged while playing the roles they'd been given. While the conventional military had been cleaning up its act, and soldiers were being tried for misconduct on the battlefield, no such change had been introduced to the CIA. Not a single agent had ever been censored for his actions while in the field. Not a single rule or guideline had been introduced.

Hunter had spent a lot of his life trying to forget the things he'd done to maintain his cover. He'd spent hours staring at the ceiling fan of his apartment, Chianne asleep next to him, trying to erase the deeds he'd done. Or trying to remember the deeds he'd forgotten, the missions erased or partially erased from his memory by experimental CIA neural transmittors he'd let them stick in his head.

They'd fucked him up.

And he was about to do it again.

All of it.

Whatever it took.

And if the memories haunted him to his grave, so be it.

He lit a cigarette and began walking toward the outpost of Las Milpas. The sun wasn't hot yet but it was getting warmer. He took off the jacket and threw it over his shoulder. A mile or two later he saw why the cop had tried to temper his expectations of Las Milpas.

It was little more than a single farm. There were a few small houses, a few large barns, and some groves of neatly planted trees. Hunter wasn't sure what they were growing.

There were dogs lying in the sun, some kids near the little houses, and a few women doing laundry.

There was a big house next to the main barn and he walked toward it.

When he was about halfway down the gravel driveway, someone came out the front door with a shotgun pointed in his direction.

Hunter knew how to act. It was like coming across a dog. You couldn't show weakness. You could never run.

He rose his arm in greeting and continued walking in the man's direction.

"I need a ride," he said. "To Culiacán. I can pay."

The man rose the gun in warning. Hunter was still too far away for it to do much damage.

"I can pay. Puedo pagar. Tengo dinero."

Another man came onto the porch to see what was going on. Hunter sized them up. They could have been farmers or they might have been tied up in the cartel. He doubted there were too many farmers in this province that weren't somehow tied to the cartel.

"Hombre loco," the older of the two said. He was the one holding the gun. He was about sixty.

The second man might have been his son.

He came down the steps of the porch and didn't look like he was armed. He had an honest face. Hunter felt he could trust him.

"Puedo pagar cincuenta," Hunter said. "For a ride to Culiacán."

"Dolares o pesos?"

"Qué prefieres?"

The man smiled. "Dolares, gringo."

Hunter took fifty dollars from his wallet and handed it to the man.

"Listo," the man said. He nodded toward an old pickup and hunter got in the passenger seat.

They got on the road and ten minutes later they were off the dirt road and on the paved road that the roadblock had been on. The man turned west and Hunter got his first look at life under the cartel. It didn't look that different from life under the Mexican government.

The land was dry scrub, mountainous, very little growing. There was the odd shepherd shack, a small hut, a gas station or restaurant along the side of the road that seemed to be in a permanent state of construction. Rebar poked out of the walls. Sacks of concrete and piles of brick lay against the sides of the buildings.

The man stopped at a gas station to fill his tank with the fifty dollar bill Hunter had given him. Hunter watched him go inside the store to pay. He took the key. He was gone thirty seconds, a minute, ninety seconds. Something was wrong. Hunter took the Chief's Special from his knapsack and put it in his waistband.

The driver came out of the store followed by four other men. They were in wife-beaters, muscled, with tattoos.

Time to get to work, Hunter thought.

He got out of the car and walked toward the men. They were surprised he was approaching them. It caught them off guard.

He looked at the driver.

"Teniamos un trato," he said. "We had a deal, you son of a bitch."

"Lo siento," the man said.

The man hadn't planned this. He was just stupid. Paying for gas with a crisp fifty dollar bill wasn't a smart move in these parts.

"So what do you assholes want?" Hunter said.

One of the men stepped in front of the driver.

"What's a gringo doing in Sinaloa?"

Hunter weighed him up. He was a big guy. From the tattoos, Hunter knew he'd done time in the US. The other three were similarly marked.

"I'm here on business," Hunter said.

"Negocios," the man repeated.

"Sí," Hunter said.

"Qué tipo de negocio?" one of the other men said.

Hunter looked at their waists. They were armed. The man who'd driven him moved off to the side, trying to put a little distance between himself and the gunfight that was about to happen.

The men were hesitant. They didn't know who Hunter was. They didn't know why he was there. The first rule in a place like Sinaloa is always know who a man is before you kill him. Kill the wrong man, kill someone who's protected by the cartel, and you could end up being boiled alive in a pot.

"Sólo hay uno," Hunter said.

The man in the lead laughed.

"Oh, there are many kinds of business here, gringo."

Hunter stared at the man. It was about to happen. The man to the left made to pull out his gun. Hunter ducked and drew his weapon. A shot fired above him. He rolled for cover behind a car as more shots followed him. He scrambled to the far side of the car and glanced around it. Bullets clanged of the steel chassis.

Bang. One of the men dropped to the ground, a .38 slug in his skull.

Hunter ducked back behind the car in time to dodge a hail of returned fire. The bullets continued to clang against the car's steel frame.

He put his chest to the ground and peered under the car.

Bang.

A bullet tore through the next man's ankle and he was on the ground, writhing in pain.

The third man had come around the car and was firing off shots, hitting the car and smashing glass. Hunter rose his gun and hit the man square in the middle of the chest.

He took a peek through the shattered windows of the car and saw the fourth man running back toward the store. The man who'd driven him was running into the scrubland.

Hunter dashed to the corner of the building.

The man who'd gone inside came back out with an M4. He sprayed bullets everywhere, eight-hundred rounds per minute, but didn't know where Hunter was. He shredded the car, flattening the tires, obliterated the glass. He hit the pickup Hunter had arrived in.

He hit the fuel pumps. Bullets hit each pump as the gunman cast around, searching for his target.

Hunter braced for an explosion. There was about five seconds when all he could hear was the mindless fire of the M4, and then, boom. The first pump exploded, sending a ball of flame and black smoke thirty yards into the sky. The explosion set off the next pump and a few seconds later the three remaining pumps exploded in the same way.

The black smoke billowed into the sky and would be seen from Culiacán.

"Mother fucker," Hunter said.

He'd been intending to draw the cartel's attention, but he'd have liked to get his bearings first. He wanted to get into town and get a lay of the land before they came looking for him.

He rounded the corner of the building, went to the door, and found the gunman reloading the M4.

"No," the man said, raising his hands in the air.

Pop, pop. Two bullets in the chest.

The man he'd shot in the ankle was still on the ground, screaming in pain. He'd been scalded by the explosion and his clothes were still on fire. Hunter picked up one of the men's handguns. It was a five-seven. Made in Belgium. The magazine held twenty .224 cartridges. It was a good gun. Three times, the US Congress had tried and failed to ban its importation. It was illegal in Mexico but easily obtained. Drug dealers called it the cop killer because it could penetrate a level IIA armored vest. When the NRA stood up for the gun and said it couldn't penetrate body armor, gun rights campaigners dared the NRA's executive vice president to take a hit while wearing a vest.

He declined.

Hunter weighed the gun in his hand. It was about half loaded. He went out to the lot and put the burned man out of his misery. Then he took a few extra cartridges from the bodies of the other men he'd killed.

He looked out over the chaparral. His driver could still be seen in the distance, running back in the direction of his farm.

Hunter didn't blame him.

He went to the pickup and got his knapsack. He checked that the fuel tank and engine hadn't been hit. Then he hot wired the vehicle and got back on the road toward the city.

TWENTY-EIGHT

Anyone interested in the history of tracking has heard of the Abbey of Saint-Hubert. It is a Benedictine abbey, originally called the Abbey of Andage, that was renamed in honor of Saint Hubert when his body was moved there in the ninth century.

For fourteen centuries its monks chanted and prayed, worshipped and fasted, sacrificed and did penance.

And they also had an unmatched talent for breeding dogs.

Over a period of a thousand years they bred the most highly prized hunting dogs in all of France. The long extinct Saintongeois and Norman hounds have been traced to their kennels. As have the Grand Bleu de Gascogne and the Artois Normande.

Over a thousand years ago they developed a pitch black hound that marked the pinnacle of their efforts. They were so proud of it that, starting in the twelfth century, they began sending six pups to the King of France each year.

They called the hound the Saint Hubert and it quickly became the most highly prized breed in the royal pack.

But over the centuries, something happened.

The blood became tainted.

The dog lost its distinctive black coloring.

The annual gift, once so prized, lost its value. The king turned to other breeds, the greffier, and the chiens blanc du roi. The annual gift was often destroyed without a single pup being kept.

People harked back to the true race, the lost blood, and the pitch black hounds it once yielded.

The monks spent generations trying to cure the breed, but the blood, once tainted, couldn't be purified. By the time of the Revolution they had stopped even sending the annual gift.

By then, the reputation of the breed was shot.

"Suitable for hunters with gout," Charles IX had said.

"Of no great strength," De Fouilloux wrote.

"Tainted blood," wrote D'Yauville.

And so the breed was lost.

Or almost lost.

And perhaps that would have been for the best.

Because the true talent of the breed, the tainted breed, was only just being discovered. And it wasn't for hunting deer.

In 1609, a year before he was assassinated by a fanatical Catholic, the Bourbon King of France made a gift to King James I of England.

King James was a hunter.

He hunted all the usual game, deer, boar, fox, but his favorite quarry of all was man.

He discovered that his new French hounds had an uncanny ability to track men on the run. The smell of blood, difficult for many breeds to discern, stuck out to them like a flair in the sky. He renamed them bloodhounds when a pack of them tracked an injured fugitive on a trail seven days cold, through the crowded streets of Edinburgh, to the upstairs room he was hiding in.

They could track men in any conditions, under any circumstances, days after the men had fled. And if the man was injured, the dogs would find them hidden in any city in the kingdom.

They only needed one thing.

A taste of the blood they were chasing.

And that's what Hunter needed.

As he entered the city of Culiacán, passing a group of men in pickup trucks heading toward the smoke of the blown up gas station, he knew he needed to find that taste, that trace of a scent. Once he had it, he'd find El Sucio if he was in this city.

He spent some time driving around the city, getting a taste for the neighborhoods, getting a feel for the different areas. The businessmen in Vallado Viejo, close to the main square, moving the money, protecting the money, handling the wire transfers and offshore accounts that gave the cartel its power. The younger guys in Primer Cuadro fixing cars in oil-stained shirts, upgrading their sound systems and suspension. The military thugs carrying AK-47's openly in Industrial Bravo.

He needed to get dirty. He needed to get the scent of the hunt on him.

He needed to raise a flair and see who showed their face.

He pulled over next to some guys at a fast food stand and whistled.

"Hey," he said, leaning out of the window. "Who speaks english?"

"I do," one of the men said.

"There a strip club in this town?" Hunter said.

The man put down his food and approached the truck.

"No me chingues, flaco," he said.

"Tranquilo," Hunter said.

He wasn't endearing himself to these guys. The rest of the group was standing now. No one was eating.

"Qué dijo?" one of the men said.

The man who spoke english told them he was looking for a strip club.

Some of the men took offense and looked ready for a fight. Hunter grinned at them. The more trouble he caused on his way to the club, the sooner he'd see results.

One of the men, a big fat guy with a CocaCola t-shirt stretched across his chest, pushed his way to the front of the gang. He was laughing, really going for it, a big, belly laugh, straight from the gut. It was contagious.

Hunter smirked. He raised his hands as if to admit his guilt.

"El quiere culo?" the fat guy said, unable to stop laughing.

"Sí," Hunter said. "Quiero culo."

That really set the fat guy off. He slapped the roof of the pickup.

"Quieres putas?" he said.

"Sí," Hunter said.

"Whores?" the fat guy said in English.

He stopped laughing. He grew serious. It only took an instant for his demeanor to change.

"You a real fucking cowboy, huh?"

Hunter sighed. No one in this place wanted to help out a stranger.

"No, for real, Homes. How you like it if I come to your home asking for whores?"

"I wouldn't care."

"Oh, you'd care if a fat Mexican came into your house looking to fuck your sister."

"I didn't know your sister was a whore," Hunter said.

The guy flew a fist through the open window and struck Hunter on the cheek.

Hunter threw the truck into reverse and flung it backwards a few yards. The men stepped back. He flung it back into drive and lurched forward, scattering them.

Someone flung a brick at the windshield. The windshield shattered.

"If you ain't going to show me to the strip club, I'd settle for your house," he shouted at the fat guy.

A gun fired. The bullet missed the truck.

There were seven men on the street and this could get out of hand. Hunter drew his gun and pointed it at the men.

"Fuck you, you fucking loco piece of shit," the fat guy said.

Hunter smiled at him and made a point of slamming the gun on the dashboard. He opened the door of the truck. Everyone could see his gun was in the truck.

"Órale," he said to the fat guy, pulling off his jacket and throwing it on the ground.

This was more to the men's liking. Pulling up and asking for a strip club was one thing, but being willing to take on the big guy was something they could live with.

"Oh, you want to get fucked up," the big guy said.

Hunter shrugged.

"If I win, you show me where to get laid."

The fat guy laughed again. "I don't know if I should like you or hate you," he said.

"You'll know when I'm done with you," Hunter said, stepping forward.

The big guy threw a beefy fist Hunter's way. It moved like a punch in slow motion. Hunter could have dodged it and broken the man's larynx in a single motion but he wasn't here to win fights.

He blocked the punch and then threw one of his own, leaving himself wide open. The big guy flung a wide left hook and Hunter took it on the chin. He hit the big guy in the gut but not too hard. The guy smacked him on the side of the head.

Hunter stepped back and spit blood. The crowd always loved it when a man spit blood.

He pulled his shirt up over his head and threw it on the ground.

What the hell.

Why not put on a good show?

He'd just insulted all these men's sisters, after all.

He lunged awkwardly toward the big guy and took an uppercut to the chin. He grabbed the man around the waist and let him land elbow after elbow on the back of his head. He hit him in the kidney a few times but took a hail of punches on the back of his head and neck while he did it.

He loosened his grip of the man's waist and gave him room to bring up a knee. It got him right in the face.

"Fuck," Hunter gasped.

His nose was bleeding.

He staggered backwards.

The fat guy took a moment to relish his victory, raising his arms in triumph to the crowd. Everyone cheered.

Hunter stumbled toward him and got swatted aside into the crowd.

The men in the crowd pushed him back into the fight and he stumbled toward the big guy again.

This time the big guy landed a clean blow on the side of

Hunter's face. Hunter let it spin him. It barely grazed him.
The big guy must have felt invincible.

That was one thing about men. All men. They never
felt a fight was too easy. No matter how easy you made it for
them, they always felt it was a victory well deserved.

Hunter let his eyes roll and stopped moving his feet.
His center of gravity rushed forward, ahead of him, and he
fell to the ground and shut his eyes.

The crowd went wild.

"All right," the big guy said, standing over Hunter, his
hands raised in victorious rapture. He'd woken up expecting
a completely ordinary day. Now he was Conor McGregor.

Hunter struggled to get to his feet. The big guy pushed
him over with his foot.

He struggled to get up again.

"Stay down, Homes," the big guy said.

"Fuck you," Hunter said, and swung a punch, hitting
him on the thigh.

The crowd laughed. The big guy feigned he was
in pain.

"I don't want to hurt you, Homes."

Hunter got to his feet and flung another wild punch.
Someone stepped in to end the fight and Hunter punched
him. The crowd laughed. The big guy came forward and
wound up a haymaker. Hunter ran into it, making sure the
contact would leave a mark on his eye.

Hunter went down and everyone cheered again. By
now, they would have shown him to any place in town
he asked.

There's no man easier to love than the man who just got
the shit kicked out of him at your hand.

The big guy stooped down to him.

"You okay, Homes?"

"A deal's a deal," Hunter said.

"What deal?"

"Tell me where to find some pussy."

The man laughed. "You had to win, Homes."

"I did win," Hunter said, leaning on the big guy, accepting his help to get to his feet.

"All right," the big guy said, still laughing. "You're right." He rose his voice to address the crowd.

"El ganador!" he announced to cheers.

Hunter gripped the big guy's hand and rose it in the air.

A few minutes later, the men were helping Hunter get his things from the pickup. They even made sure he didn't forget the five-seven from the dash.

TWENTY-NINE

Jeff Hale let the tailor finish measuring him before answering his phone.

"Director Hale speaking," he said.

He loved saying that. He loved the prestige of his new position. The trappings. The procedures for leaving his house, for entering a public building, for meeting a new person. There was nothing like being frisked before you could approach someone to show you who was boss.

"Sir, this is Jasper Marten."

"Ah, Jasper. How nice to hear from you."

There was a short pause. Then she said, "I got your new cell number from my editor. I hope you don't mind."

"Of course I don't mind. What is it? You can ask me anything. You know that."

"I was wondering, that is, my editor, we were wondering."

"What is it, Jasper?"

"There's a lot going on in Chicago."

Hale smiled. Chicago was where the FBI was concentrating its attention. There were a growing number of indicators that was where El Sucio had fled. Both Hale and the new FBI director had been shifting resources in that direction and it was only a matter of time before the media caught on to it.

"That's true," Hale said. "There's a lot going on everywhere, Jasper. We're not leaving a single stone uncovered."

"I know that, sir."

"There was a reported sighting this morning in Toronto and thirty minutes later, we were storming the Four Seasons with Canadian special forces."

"Yes, sir. There have been numerous false alarms."

"There was the raid in Miami."

"I know, sir."

"The army's preparing to enter Mexico. We're looking everywhere."

"I'm particularly interested, that is, we're particularly interested, in what's going on in Chicago, sir."

"You know I can't go into too many details on an open investigation."

"Of course, sir. Especially not on the phone."

Hale smiled. He signaled to one of his bodyguards to have the car brought round. There were a few things he needed to get done if he was going to be meeting Jasper later.

"Maybe we should discuss all this in person," he said. "It would certainly be a lot safer."

"The Ritz-Carlton lobby bar, like last time?" she said.

She knew exactly what she was offering.

"Oh, no, I don't think somewhere so open would be a good idea."

"Where then?"

"How about we take it straight to the room," he said. "They have truly exceptional room service at that hotel."

She hesitated only a second. "What time?"

"Two hours," Hale said.

First he had to go to the new FBI headquarters, which was being temporarily housed in the east wing of the National Art Gallery on Constitution Avenue.

As the town car pulled up outside, Hale was still wondering what he would give Jasper when he met with her. He knew he had to give her something useful. The *Post* editors wouldn't keep sending a girl like that if they weren't getting something good out of it. There was plenty he could give her that would further his interests. He just had to make sure none of it could be traced back to him.

The car pulled up outside the gallery entrance. The east wing of the building had been closed for maintenance earlier in the year. In the wake of the bombing it was offered as a temporary home for the FBI.

Hale walked up the steps and entered the modern building, its geometrical forms arching above him. It was a hell of a lot sleeker than the Hoover building. He'd have visited a lot more often if they'd always been here.

He paused in the lobby to look at a very famous painting, Gerard van Honthorst's 1623 masterpiece, the Concert. When the gallery purchased it in 2013 it created quite the stir. It had not been on display to the public in over two-hundred years. It was a big canvas, colorful, but Hale wasn't sure it was worth all the fuss, or the estimated twenty million that had been paid for it.

He walked past it to a makeshift security desk where a metal detector and x-ray machine were being set up.

"I'm Director Hale," he said to the security guard.

The guard had never heard of him and looked to Hale's bodyguards for help.

"He's the director of the CIA," the bodyguard said.

The man nodded. "We're not fully set up yet, sir," he said to Hale.

"I can see that," Hale said.

There were six guards, as well as the crew setting up the screening equipment. The museum had its own security but it wasn't up to the FBI's standards. So instead of using the system that was already there, the Bureau was making do with nothing while they installed their own. It was typical. They always insisted on getting things their own way or no way at all.

There'd been numerous times during Hale's career when the CIA had been in possession of critical intelligence that would have proved invaluable to the FBI. In the case of El Sucio, they'd begged to be allowed to provide greater assistance.

Chancey and Moynihan had refused point-blank.

Both men were now dead.

Hale stepped into an elevator with two of his own bodyguards and a member of the FBI's security. They got off on the next floor and walked through stunning galleries to a room that was being set up with computers and desks. Hale estimated that about two hundred agents would be able to work in that gallery alone. Most weren't there yet. They were still cleaning up the mess at the Hoover building, searching for anything that might be useful and seeing what could be salvaged.

Either that or they were dead.

The FBI had lost so many agents in the bombing that they would be understaffed for months. They were already making plans to draw more recruits from their training facilities as soon as possible.

The new director of the FBI, the third in less than a week, was Raquel Harris. She was a strikingly attractive

woman in her early fifties who'd been way down the line for
the job. Now that everyone above her was dead, she found
herself unexpectedly at the top of the pile.

"Mr Director," she said to Hale as she strode
toward him.

She was the epitome of professionalism, dressed in a
tailored blazer and knee-length gray skirt. Her shoes had a
solid four-inch heel that gave her a disciplinarian air. Any
man who'd had a crush on teacher would have found her
irresistible.

"Madam Director," Hale said, extending a hand.

She shook it firmly and led him to her private office
across the gallery. On the way, they passed paintings by
Vermeer, Botticelli, and the only Leonardo da Vinci in the
Americas. In her office hung a Rodin, a Degas and a Goya.

"Nice place," Hale said, taking a seat on the expensive
sofa by the wall.

"Thanks," Raquel said, taking a seat opposite him.

She still didn't have any of her FBI furniture or equipment so the room still had the style and panache of a
museum.

She pulled a pack of cigarettes from the inside pocket of
her blazer and lit one.

"Can you smoke in here?" Hale said.

Raquel smiled. "The detectors are off while they
renovate."

Hale raised an eyebrow.

"Who else can say they've had a cigarette while looking
at paintings like this," she said.

"Anyone who went to an art gallery before 1990,"
he said.

She nodded. "I should congratulate you on your
appointment."

"And I on yours," Hale said.

Neither of them mentioned the tragic circumstances that had led to their promotions. Between them, their two agencies had suffered over two-thousand casualties.

Hale would have been happy to make small talk all afternoon, at least until it was time for his meeting with Jasper, but Raquel got down to business.

"The president wanted us to meet," she said.

"Yes," Hale said. "I had a good working relationship with Chancey and Moynihan."

"Good isn't the word I heard," Raquel said.

"Well, we disagreed about everything. Especially security for the trial."

"If they were still alive you could tell them you told them so," Raquel said.

Hale was surprised by her bluntness.

"I think what I meant to say is I knew them well. I was used to working with them. We understood each other."

"Well, let's make sure you understand me," Raquel said. "I don't want there to be any hiccups while we get up and running."

"Okay," Hale said.

"The only thing that matters to me is catching this guy. I don't care if the FBI does it, or the CIA, or the fucking National Park Service as long as someone gets him."

"I'm glad to hear that."

"So any assistance you think you can offer us, any intel, anything, I'll take it."

"I'll have our people send you over what we have immediately," Hale said.

"And if I think we could use some of your operatives, some of your methods, I'll ask for them."

"What about the constitutional issues?" Hale said.

"Fuck the constitutional issues," she said, and took a long draw from her cigarette. "I saw your press conference. I heard what you and the president said. The gloves are coming off. If we need your help take out some military grade hardware the cartel is using, I'll ask for it."

Hale cleared his throat. "There seems to a lot of activity in Chicago."

Raquel smiled. "Nothing gets by you, does it?"

Hale shrugged.

Raquel stood up and went out to the main area. She came back a minute later with a file.

"This is what we've got. Cartel cell phone activity has increased dramatically in Chicago since the escape. Here's a map."

Hale looked a map of the country covered in red dots. There was a definite concentration in Chicago.

"Anything else?"

"Nothing yet. What we need is to let the cat out of the bag."

"I'm meeting with a *Washington Post* reporter this evening."

"What's her name?"

"How do you know it's a woman?"

Raquel rose an eyebrow. "You might be unknown to the senate confirmation committee, but I've read hundreds of pages about you."

"The FBI has a file on me?"

"We have a file on every senior CIA operative, Hale. I'm sure that doesn't surprise you."

Hale shrugged. His agency had files on all the FBI bigwigs too. He'd have to see what they had on Raquel when he got back to Langley. Unlike the FBI, the CIA would continue to operate out of its usual premises while the bomb damage was repaired. Langley was a large campus and the attack had not been quite as successful as the one at the Hoover building.

"All right," Hale said. "I'll tell the *Post* reporter that El Sucio's in Chicago. Then what?"

"All we can do is monitor traffic. See what changes. If he's really there, we'll notice something. If he moves, we'll notice something. We've got surveillance on every building known to be connected to his associates."

"If you want, I can get satellites on it."

Raquel blew out a plume of smoke.

"What about the constitutional issues?"

"Fuck the constitutional issues," Hale said.

Raquel smiled. "We see eye to eye then?"

Hale nodded, then looked at his watch.

"I'm keeping you," Raquel said.

"I've got to meet that reporter."

She smiled. "She's really taking one for the team, isn't she?"

THIRTY

Hale called Jasper from this car. He was running late.

"Would you mind getting the room?" he said. "I'll pay for it but I don't want to put it on my credit card."

"Why not?" Jasper said coyly.

Hale ignored her. "Will that be okay? Do you have an expense card from the newspaper or something?"

"I'm not important enough to have an expense card but I can put it on my own one."

"I'll pay you back with cash."

"You better," she said.

Hale smiled.

The Ritz-Carlton had a private entrance in the back for high-ranking dignitaries. Most of the top hotels in the city did. Hale had never been important enough to use them until now. His privacy had never been at issue. Now it was, and he was having a hard time coming to terms with the new rules, and the ways of getting around them.

He entered the hotel through the valet's office at the back and took an elevator to the fifth floor.

Jasper had already sent him a text message.

Room 524. Don't keep me waiting.

He grinned slyly when he read the message.

Jasper was dressed in black lace lingerie and Hale grabbed her the moment she opened the door. He pushed her back, kicking the door closed behind him, and fell on top of her on the bed. He wasn't one for foreplay.

He thrust and grunted until the surge of pleasure rushed through him. Then he collapsed.

"Jesus," he gasped.

"That was nice," she cooed, but he knew the entire process had taken less than a hundred seconds. Maybe that was why it was nice.

She lay next to him for a minute before getting up and going into the bathroom. He heard water running and she came back out in the white hotel robe.

"So?" she said without a hint of shyness.

She was getting used to their arrangement. He wondered if she'd let him see her at her home. It would take away the danger of being seen in public.

"Do you live alone?" he said.

She smiled. "You're not coming to my place."

"What if I give you something really big?"

"You just did."

Hale laughed. "You're too kind."

"I'm not kind. I'm ambitious."

"I see that."

"So whatever you have, it better be really huge, Mr. Director."

"You like big things?"

"The bigger the better."

"What about El Sucio's location?"

For an instant she looked surprised, then rolled her eyes. "If you knew that you'd have already made a move."

"What if I needed him to make a move first?"

"And our story would be that push?"

Hale nodded.

"We're supposed to report the news, not be a part of it."

"All right," Hale said. "There's a redhead at the *Times* who might be interested. I'm tired but I'm sure I could rally."

She leaned over and kissed him. He didn't often climax twice in the same night but he started to feel like it was a possibility. Jasper showed him he was right.

When they finished, Hale fell back on the bed and relished the sensation.

"You were so shy just a week ago," he said.

"I wasn't shy. I just didn't know what to expect."

"I thought you were so innocent."

"Men like you love to think women like me are innocent."

"I supposed I'm a bit old fashioned that way."

She nodded. She went back into the bathroom and he went to his briefcase and pulled out the copy of the report Raquel had given him.

When Jasper came back he handed it to her.

She looked through it and her eyes grew.

"Wow. So it is Chicago."

"Looks like it."

"Is this the only reason you think he's there?"

"No, but it's the only thing I can share with you."

"My editor will be thrilled with this."

"Will he give you a byline."

"I think so," she said. "I can be very convincing."

"You sure can."

"So are we done?" she said, letting her robe fall off her shoulders to the ground.

Hale feasted on the sight of her. The smooth skin, the round curves, the firm, ripe muscle.

"Not quite," he said, pushing her back on the bed.

He got down on his knees by the bed, his head between her legs.

"Oh," she said. "So you know how to give as well as take?"

THIRTY-ONE

Hunter walked up to the door of Culiacán's biggest strip club. It was also the best, according to the fat guy he'd let kick the crap out of him. He'd washed up a little, cleaned the blood off his face, but he still figured he'd have a hard time getting into a club with a gun.

"Armas?" the bouncer said, eyeing him up and down.

It was a tough place, you didn't have to look like you were attending the Oscars to get in, but Hunter was pushing it. His nose and eye were swollen, there was blood on his shirt, and he was carrying a knapsack that could have contained anything.

"Sí," he said. "Una pistola."

"Americano?" the bouncer said.

"Sí," Hunter said.

The bouncer looked at him closely, trying to decide if this was someone he was supposed to know, supposed to pay respect to, or if he could tell him to fuck off.

After a few seconds, he pointed to a sign behind him that had a gun on it with a line through it.

Hunter looked around. There was a motel next to the

strip club. He went to the motel office and found an old woman inside, knitting. There was a cat on the desk watching every movement of the needles as if it might pounce at any moment.

"Necesito un cuarto," he said.

She didn't look up.

"Pesos o dolares?" she said.

"Dolares."

"Por la noche o hora?"

"La noche," Hunter said. "The whole night."

She nodded. She looked up at him for the first time, assessing him, guessing what he'd pay.

"Cincuenta dolares," she said.

Hunter laughed. "Treinta."

"Cuarenta," she said.

He didn't have change so he handed her a fifty.

She took the money and handed him the key for room six.

"El cambio?" he said.

She sighed and opened her cashbox laboriously. She took out some pesos and handed him two fifties.

He was getting a shitty rate but he didn't care. It wasn't his money. He only bargained for appearances.

He left the office and walked down the gangway. Men were going in and out of the strip club. Someone in a black leather jacket was speaking to the bouncer. The bouncer pointed at Hunter and the man in the jacket turned and looked.

Hunter let them see him unlock the door to room six.

Inside, he washed his face with cold water. He took off his shirt and washed his body. He had no extra clothes and couldn't do much about the bloody shirt. He put it back on and put the jacket on over it. His hat had gotten beat up in the fight.

He reshaped it as well as he could and looked at it.

Then he put it on his head.

He left his bag and gun in the room and went back outside.

There was a group of tough guys standing with the bouncer now and he guessed they were with the cartel. He was in for a rough night but it was the only way he could think of to find out if El Sucio was in the city.

He lit a cigarette and strode toward the bouncer.

"Mejor?" he said.

"Better than what, gringo?" the leader of the cartel men said.

Hunter had been looking forward to at least getting inside the club before a fight broke out. He wouldn't have minded seeing the local talent.

Mexican music was coming from inside and he wondered how the girls managed to pole dance to it.

"I'm not looking for trouble," he said.

"Maybe I am," the man said.

"Maybe you can wait until after we've all had a few drinks before you find it," Hunter said.

The man laughed. The other men asked him what had been said and he told them. They nodded.

"Okay," the man said. "But maybe this night doesn't end the way you're thinking it will."

"You don't know how I'm thinking it will end," Hunter said.

The man let out a final laugh and told the bouncer to let him in. Hunter gave the bouncer one of the Mexican bills the motel lady had given him and went into the bar.

The bar was medium busy. There were a few younger

guys sitting up in front of the stage, watching the girls from as close an angle as they could get.

Some older guys were sitting at the bar, more interested in the soccer on the TV than the breasts and pussies that were on display.

Hunter went to the bar and ordered a beer in English. The girl behind the bar understood him. She was topless but for a pair of tasseled pasties.

"You got anything to eat?" he said to her when she came back.

"Quieres comer?" she said, arching an eyebrow.

"Sí."

She grinned. "Didn't anyone ever tell you never eat in a whorehouse?"

Hunter laughed. A few of the guys around the bar who'd understood laughed also.

"I know I shouldn't do it," Hunter said, "but that don't mean I don't."

The girl laughed and said she'd get him some tacos.

Hunter turned around in his stool and watched the stage. A fat woman with a black feather boa was walking around the pole while salsa music played. The guys sitting by the stage reached out and groped her.

One of the guys got up on the stage and a bouncer had to pull him back down.

Another girl, younger, with big brown eyes and expensive hair extensions asked him if he wanted to go in the back.

"How much?" he said to her.

"Pesos o dolares?" she said.

"Will you give me a good time for a hundred dollars?" he said.

He needed to know if she spoke English.

"Yes," she said.

She took him by the hand and he grabbed his beer before letting her lead him to the back of the club. They went into the next room, which didn't have a door, and he sat on a long sectional sofa that went the whole way around all four walls. There was another guy on the other side getting a dance. A big lady had her hands on his knees and her ass in his face. It looked to Hunter like the man, despite all the best advice, was eating in a whore house.

THIRTY-TWO

Hunter leaned back on the sofa and spread his legs. He took off his jacket and hat and left them by his side. The stripper threw a leg over him and sat on his lap.

"What's your name?" she said.

"Jack," he said. "How about you?"

"Adelita," she said, rubbing herself on him.

She reached behind her back and unclipped her bra. Hunter leaned back further and thrust upward like a buck.

She laughed.

"Adelita is a song, isn't it?"

"Sí," she said. "Una cancion muy hermosa."

"Sing it for me," Hunter said, reaching up and taking her breasts in his hands.

They were firm and pert. She arched her back and pressed them forward into his face. Hunter kissed them. She smelled like lilies.

"I don't sing," she said.

Hunter sang, "si Adelita ya fuera mi mujer, le compraría una vestido de seda."

It meant, if Adelita would be my woman, I'd buy her a silk dress.

"You speak Spanish," she said.

"No, I just like the song."

"And will you buy me a dress?" she said to him.

She moved in his lap, grinding against him.

"I don't know. Will you be my woman?"

She smiled and leaned forward, kissing his ear. "I'll be your woman," she whispered, "si te gusta."

She rose on her knees and reached for his crotch. He ran his hands down her back and let her unzip him. She reached into his pants and grabbed hold of him.

She moved her hand up and down his shaft and threw her head forward, letting her hair fall in his face.

Hunter leaned back and looked across to the other side of the room. The dancer was still holding herself up by her hands and was facing Hunter. Their eyes locked and she gave him a lascivious smile.

Hunter felt himself throb.

Adelita spat on her hand and wet herself, then lowered herself slowly onto him. He slid right into her.

It was a bad idea. He felt guilty.

But he couldn't hold back.

He had a role to play and this was part of it. Everything was part of it. The fights he fought, the drinks he drank, the women he fucked. He couldn't hold back on any of it.

He thrust up into her and pulled her close against his chest. He breathed in the scent of her. He shut his eyes. The image flashed across his mind of his dead wife. This was his first time since her death.

It was too soon.

If it was up to him he would have waited longer.

Adelita squirmed and swayed on his lap, kissing his neck and biting his ear. Behind her, the other woman was still looking at him.

"Yo siguiente," she mouthed.

Me next.

He felt the pulse of pleasure surge through him. He gripped at Adelita's back and pulled her closer, her breasts pressed against his face.

She moaned in pleasure, "Oh, mi amor."

Hunter squeezed her arms. The climax was long overdue and as soon as it was over he wanted more.

He pulled out of her.

"Thank you," he said quietly, doing up his pants.

"Wait here for me," Adelita said, and got up and left.

Hunter pulled the cigarettes out of his jacket and lit one. It tasted good. He finished his beer and sat there like an idiot, smoking and watching the fat Mexican with his whore.

He couldn't tell if the sight turned him on or disgusted him.

When Adelita came back she asked if he wanted to go back to the bar. He nodded and they went back out, taking a table close to the stage. A waitress came and Hunter ordered a bottle of champagne.

Adelita arched her eyebrows.

"You're spoiling me," she said.

"Wait until you see the silk dress."

She smiled. The champagne arrived in an ice bucket and the waitress poured them two glasses. Hunter handed one to Adelita and they clinked glasses.

"So you enjoyed yourself?" she said. "It was good?"

"Very good," he said.

She wanted him to pay her. She'd learned from experience if she waited, he would end up spending his money on other things. He thought about not paying her, getting in a fight and getting to the cartel that way, but he didn't want to put her through that. He took out his wallet and handed her two hundred dollar bills.

"Two hundred?" she said.

"One for now, one for later."

"Later?"

He smiled. "If you want," he said.

She nodded. Business was business. If he wanted another round and if he wanted to pay in advance, that was fine by her.

They watched some girls making out on stage. The girls began to finger each other and the bar, which was beginning to get busier, cheered and clapped.

"Do they sell cigars here?" Hunter said to Adelita.

Adelita called over the waitress and said, "el quiere cigarros."

"Cubanos?" the waitress said to Hunter.

Hunter nodded but then said, "no, Mexicanos."

"Mexicanos?"

"Son mejores."

The waitress looked skeptical. "Si lo dices," she said.

She came back with a cheap cigar and cut it in front of him.

"You want her to light it for you?" Adelita said, her hand on his leg, marking her territory.

"No," he said. "Do you want one?"

She shook her head and took a pack of cigarettes out of her jewel-encrusted purse. Hunter lit it for her.

They smoked and drank the champagne and Hunter kept an eye on the bar. There was a group of about ten men who he thought were from the cartel. Two of them were in suits but had their backs to him.

"Who's in charge around here?" Hunter said.

Adelita put her hand on his crotch and squeezed.

"I am," she said.

"No, I mean which man is in charge."

"Of the club?"

"Not of the club. Of the town. Of everything."

"Everyone knows who's in charge of this town," she said.

"But who's in charge right now? While he's not around?"

Adelita looked toward the bar then back at Hunter.

"Just enjoy yourself," she said. "If you ask questions you'll get in trouble."

Hunter nodded.

He looked at the bar, at the two men in suits. There was a good chance if he could see their faces he'd recognize them from the files Fawn had shown him of the cartel's lieutenants.

He stood up.

"Where are you going?" Adelita said.

She was jumpy. She didn't like him asking about the cartel.

"I'm going to get us some real drinks," he said.

He walked up to the bar. He was being watched by the group of cartel men. He leaned over the bar and blew out a thick cloud of smoke.

The bartender, a skinny guy in a white shirt, was serving the cartel men.

"Hey," Hunter said loudly.

The two men in suits who'd had their back to him turned. He saw their faces. He recognized them from

Fawn's files. They weren't particularly important but they were definitely associates of El Sucio.

"Two shots," he said to the bartender over the din of the crowd.

The bartender ignored him. There was no way he was making the cartel guys wait for their drinks.

"Hey," Hunter said again, louder.

Two of the cartel thugs started in his direction.

He knew he was on their radar. There'd been the shootout at the gas station. The smoke could still be smelled all across town. There'd been the fight across town. Now he was throwing money around their strip club.

It wasn't hard to stand out in Culiacán. An American in cartel territory was suspicious by definition. There was only a tiny handful of outsiders in the entire province, and the cartel would be suspicious of any of them. Why would anyone be in a pariah territory that was about to suffer the heaviest air strikes since the attack on Iraq?

They were definitely watching him.

The only question they would have was whether he was CIA, or some complete idiot with a death wish.

For Hunter's part, he knew they'd pick him up and bring him in. For him, the only question was whether he could get picked up by the right guys, the guys who could give him information, who could drop a clue, purposefully or by accident, on whether El Sucio was back in Sinaloa or not.

The two guys were standing next to him. Hunter nodded like he had no clue who they were and called out to the bartender again.

The bigger of the two guys slammed a hand on the bar. He was the muscle.

"Hey," Hunter said. "Tranquilo, buddy."

The guy looked at his friend. The friend was the brains. "He's not your buddy," the friend said.

"Okay," Hunter said. "I guess I can live with that."

"He's getting annoyed because you're being so loud."

"I didn't realize he had such tender sensibilities."

The big guy asked what they were saying.

The smaller guy translated for him.

Hunter turned away and the big guy pulled him back around by the shoulder. He wasn't used to being ignored.

Hunter looked at the man's hand on his shoulder. The man instinctively took it away.

It looked like there was going to be a fight but at that moment the bartender arrived. Hunter turned to him and ordered two shots of tequila. He paid with an American twenty and told the bartender to keep the change.

The smarter of the two cartel guys was looking across the bar at his bosses, the two guys in suits.

Hunter leaned in to him and said into his ear, "If your boss would like to talk business, my name is Jack Morrow. He might have heard of me."

They left and Hunter went back to Adelita. She'd been watching.

"What was that about?"

"Business."

She nodded. She knew all about that sort of business. She stood up and took Hunter's hand.

"Come on," she said.

He followed her back to the private room. It was busier now. There was a guy getting a lap dance on one side. On another was a guy getting a blow job. Next to him was a guy with two girls on his lap who were making out with each other.

"Not here," Hunter said.

"What?"

"I have a room at the motel across the way."

Adelita looked at him. She was scared of him now.

"I'm not a freak," he said.

She sighed and followed him back out to the bar.

THIRTY-THREE

Back in the bar, the music had switched over from salsa to hip hop. The place was really packed now and was becoming more like a nightclub than a strip bar. Guys were there with their girlfriends. The strippers were still dancing but they were more like background entertainment.

"Is there any man here who's going to get jealous if you go across the way with me?" Hunter said to Adelita.

He led her to the bar and got his bill from the waitress. He paid her with a hundred and looked back at Adelita. She hadn't answered.

He wasn't supposed to care about collateral damage. There was no amount of pain or destruction he could cause that wouldn't be justified given his objective. He also knew that whatever he did would pale in comparison to the damage the air strikes would cause.

But there was something about the girl. She was young. She acted tough, like she knew the ropes, but he could sense the vulnerability beneath the surface. It wouldn't have sat well with him if he caused her trouble.

"Of course not," she said. "I'd be in the wrong business if there was a guy like that."

Hunter nodded. "You tell me if there is, because I know things can get complicated."

"No one cares about me here," she said. "There's a hundred other girls just like me."

"You're not going to get in trouble for leaving the club?"

She hesitated. "Let me tell my boss where I'm going."

"He's going to ask how much you're getting paid."

"I'll tell him fifty."

"Is that what you usually charge?"

"I usually don't go across to the motel."

Hunter nodded. He looked over at the cartel guys. The men in suits were eyeing him. He nodded at them and they looked away.

They were sizing him up. They didn't know who he was. They didn't know what he wanted. They'd know soon enough when they looked up the files for Jack Morrow.

Adelita came back and he took her through the bar by the hand. At the door the bouncer asked Adelita where she was going and she told him she'd already cleared it with the boss.

Adelita was tall and thin, taller still in her six-inch heels. She walked across the parking lot like a gazelle, carefully placing each step.

Hunter admired her in the streetlight. She was like something from another world. A more innocent world. The big mistake she'd made was to be born in a place like this.

"I smell fire," she said.

Hunter nodded. On the horizon he could see the glow of fire. The air strikes had started.

"Hay una guerra," she said.

"Siempre hay guerra," Hunter said.

She nodded. The one constant in the world was war.

The moon above them was full and clear.

Hunter unlocked the motel room and they stepped inside. He switched on the light. Adelita sat down on the bed and looked up at him. She hadn't done this often. She wasn't sure how to proceed.

"How old are you?" Hunter said.

"Veintiuno."

"Verdad?"

She shrugged. "You don't really care what age I am, do you?"

Hunter pulled back a curtain and peered across the lot. The bouncer was still at the door. No one had followed them out.

Not yet.

They'd come.

He was sure of it.

He didn't answer Adelita's question. He went over to the bed and took her chin in his hand. She looked into his eyes. Here, in this new place, she looked different. In the club she'd been a stripper. Here, she was just a girl.

He felt the desire build up in him. He wanted her. He wanted to devour her.

He put his mouth on hers and they kissed. She didn't hold back. She moaned when their lips touched and he didn't know if it was real or if she was just doing her job.

She opened his pants and grabbed him. He pulled off her lingerie and stripped her. She stripped him.

He lay her on the bed and got over her. She looked up into his eyes.

"Hermosa," he said.

She smiled and shut her eyes, wrapping her legs around

him. The pleasure surged through him. With each thrust she moaned quietly in his ear. In a minute he was climaxing. He was sure she was too.

And then the door of the room burst open.

"Fuck," he cried out, as six cartel men poured into the room.

Adelita didn't make a sound.

The big guy he'd bumped into earlier pulled him off Adelita and threw him onto the floor. He was fully erect. Adelita pulled the blanket of the bed over her naked body.

"It stinks like a whore in here," one of the men in suits said.

Adelita hid herself under the blanket and edged away from the men.

Hunter stood up, fully naked, still erect.

He addressed the man who'd complained of the smell. He seemed to be in charge.

"You couldn't have waited two more minutes?"

The man looked at him, took in every inch of him, and grinned.

"Dos minutos mas?" he said laughing. "I think, gringo, you only needed one."

Some of the men laughed.

Hunter grinned.

"So what can I do for you gentlemen?"

The man was in his thirties, good-looking, with a shaped beard and an expensive suit. He stepped into the room. The rest of the men squeezed in behind him and shut the door.

The room was crowded now, eight people in a space designed for two.

"The question isn't what you can do for us," he said. "It's what the fuck are you doing here?"

Hunter picked up his shorts and three men pulled

pistols on him. Hunter rose the shorts to show them there was nothing to be afraid of.

"It's not a gun, muchachos," Hunter said, wiping his cock on the shorts. "Just a cock, but I can see why you're afraid."

The man in the suit scoffed.

"You talk a lot for a man who's about to die."

Hunter helped Adelita out of the bed. She took the blanket with her, wrapped around body.

"Gracias señorita," he said.

She made for the door and the men let her pass. She never looked back.

Hunter waited until she was back across the lot.

"I know what you're thinking," he said to the man in the suit.

"Oh, you do?"

"You're thinking, who the fuck is this fucking gringo piece of shit, showing up in my club, fucking my whores, killing my men?"

The man rose an eyebrow.

"So you're the one who shot up the gas station?"

"Who else in this piece of shit town would create a mess like that?"

"You'd be surprised," the man said.

"Well, I didn't mean anything by it. They tried to rob me."

"Is that any way to start a relationship?" the man said.

"I don't think it is," Hunter said. "That's why I killed them."

"And now you're here, telling my man your name, acting like anyone around here would give a shit about your business."

"Everyone gives a shit about my business."

"I looked you up, Mr. Morrow. You might be a big deal in Houston, but around here, I assure you, you're, how you say?" The man lifted his thumb and finger, showing about an inch between them. "Small cojones," he said.

Hunter threw his shorts back on the bed. His cock was rigid.

"I'm about to get a lot bigger," he said.

One of the cartel men laughed. Another asked what was funny and he translated. The boss looked at them and they stopped.

"Just tell us why you're here and I'll pass on the message."

"I want to buy," Hunter said. "I want to buy a lot."

"A lot?"

"I'll be your biggest customer."

"You don't now how big our customers are."

"I'll buy by the ton," Hunter said. "And I'll transport it myself."

"So you're a big business man?"

"Yes I am."

"Our best customer."

Hunter nodded.

"So tell me gringo, you buy by the ton, how are you going to get it into the US?"

"I'm not bringing it to the US."

The man looked at him.

"Our countries are about to go to war," Hunter said.

"I've heard."

"Who's going to supply all those thousands of US soldiers?"

The man rose an eyebrow. It was a market no one had given any thought to. It was a market that didn't even exist yet. He was interested.

"I'm already bidding for catering contracts. I'll be supplying and running every cafeteria on every forward operating base in Mexico."

The man shrugged. "Maybe you will," he said.

"And if I am, your bosses are going to want to speak to me."

The man in the suit looked at the other man who was in a suit. Hunter knew the one he'd been speaking to was the more senior. At least, according to the intel Fawn had given him. They'd both have to report this up the chain. It might be enough for Hunter to get a meeting, get a little closer to the heart of the operation.

The man sighed. "You'll be staying here?"

"I don't know where I'll be staying," Hunter said, "but I guarantee you'll be able to find me when you want me."

"If we want you," the man said.

Hunter smiled. "When you want me," he repeated.

The play seemed to be working. The men started making their way out the door and Hunter looked for his pants.

And then he heard it. The unmistakable, unforgettable, deafening thunder of a precision air strike. Everything outside the door of the motel lit up. The ground shook. Every window for five blocks shattered. And the strip club blew up like a firecracker.

THIRTY-FOUR

Fawn Aspen was the ranking CIA officer onboard the Ticonderoga class guided-missile cruiser, USS Lake Champlain, off the Sinaloan coast. The cruiser was part of Carrier Strike Group One, deployed in the Gulf of California to launch the air strikes that had been ordered by the president against the cartel.

It was one of four carrier strike groups currently in the gulf. Because of the speed of their deployment, and the nature of the cartel's organization, it was proving extremely difficult to identify targets suitable for the Tomahawk cruise missiles that the navy had allocated for the strikes.

The Pentagon was getting worried and was putting pressure on the CIA to provide targets since their usual methods were proving so ineffective.

The military used satellite imagery and military intel to target facilities like airfields, army bases, government buildings, bridges, railway tunnels, ports, and industrial facilities.

In 2018, when the Syrian government used chemical weapons against its own people, the Joint Staff was able to fire fifty-seven Tomahawks and nineteen JASSM missiles at the Barzah scientific research center in Damascus as soon as the order was given. Simultaneously, nine Tomahawks, eight Storm Shadows, three MdCNs and two SCALP missiles struck the Him Shanshar chemical storage facility west of Homs. The bunker at Him Shanshar was struck by seven SCALP missiles.

Syria's chemical weapons capability was neutralized in a matter of minutes.

That was the type of mission the Joint Staff liked.

They knew what to hit.

They knew how to hit it.

They knew who would be killed.

And they knew when it had been destroyed.

The cartel was not Syria. It wasn't a county. There was no army, none of the usual facilities, and the pentagon's satellites were useless in coming up with target lists.

The things that would really hurt the cartel, like drug stashes, safe houses, weapons stashes, and the homes of cartel leaders, was not what the satelites had been designed to find. It was not what the targetting teams had been trained for.

So they called in the CIA.

When Hale got the call from the Joint Chiefs, Harry Goldwater said, "You guys have your hands dirty down there. You've got eyes on the ground. I want a hundred targets per day or I'll just start picking them with a map and a dart board."

"We don't have hundreds of targets," Hale said. "We barely have a dozen."

"I've got marines flying one of your assets to the Sinaloan border as we speak," Goldwater said. "Get me targets Hale, or I'll have no choice but to fire blind."

"Blind?"

"The president wants one hundred hits per night, every night. I shot down every bridge, tunnel, port, and airport in the province last night. If you don't give me a list, I don't know what I'll hit tonight."

Hale understood. "I'll get you a list," he said.

Then he called Fawn.

Fawn was still watching Hunter's chopper fly off toward Mexico when she got the call.

"I've got all the intel here with me," she said.

"Everything?"

"I showed Hunter every last detail. The man's a computer."

"Okay," Hale said. "Just take it with you. I'm sending you straight down to join the strike group. You can help with the targeting from there. It'll be faster."

"How many targets do they want."

"How many do you think you have?" Hale said, curious what she'd say.

"I could probably come up with twenty good ones," Fawn said. "Fifty if we don't mind making a few mistakes."

"Oh, we don't care at all about mistakes. In fact, the more the better."

"What do you mean?"

"The president wants one hundred targets per night."

"A hundred?"

"Good luck," Hale said before hanging up.

Fawn could still see Hunter's chopper in the distance. She hoped he'd packed for heavy weather.

An hour later she was on a chopper of her own, making her way for the flagship of Strike Group One, the USS Carl Vinson.

On the way, she did her best to come up with a hundred targets, poring through her files and looking for patterns, locations, buildings, anything that could be used to justify a strike. It was an impossible task.

The first day of strikes had focused on traditional low-value targets like bridges and railroads.

Now, everyone was looking at her to provide the addresses and coordinates that would actually hurt the cartel if they were hit.

She had very little to give them.

There was the location of some meetings that had taken place a few months ago between El Sucio and his top men. The chance of any of the big players being present at the location now was next to zero.

She had three villas that El Sucio used before he'd been arrested. He'd lived in the houses with his family. His leadership had been at the houses. Again, the chance of anyone of value still being there was nil.

They navy was breathing down her neck.

They had to launch once darkness set and they had nothing to point the missiles at.

So Fawn improvised.

She had phone records of calls made by El Sucio and many of his top lieutenants before he'd been captured. From the records, she was able to come up with a short list of about two hundreds cell phones that likely belonged to important cartel operatives.

From the calls made by those phones, she'd been able to create another list, much longer, with about two thousand phones potentially linked to cartel activity.

The short list was good. Those phones had communicated directly with cartel leadership, usually multiple times.

The long list was not so good. A huge proportion of those phones belonged to perfectly innocent people. If a cartel member called his girlfriend regularly, or his grandmother, or his kid's kindergarten, that phone would have made it onto Fawn's long list. If he ordered pizza from the same place all the time, or if a number of cartel members ordered from the same place, the number would be on her list.

If they used her long list, innocent people would be hit.

They'd be basically carpet bombing Culiacán.

But the short list wasn't bad.

Would she have chosen it as the preferred method of targeting Tomahawk air strikes?

No.

But if the alternative was throwing darts at a map, this was an improvement.

It had the numbers dialed by El Sucio directly, and a handful of his most senior lieutenants. Unless El Sucio was ordering his own pizza, there would be a lot fewer collateral casualties by targeting phones on the short list.

That gave her two days worth of targets.

She sent the list of phones to Langley, knowing most of them could be tracked by CIA location tracking. The data would be provided by Google and Apple in a secret agreement signed by the president and representatives of the corporations that very day. If those phones were turned on, they were about to be hit by a Tomahawk.

After handing over the list, Fawn felt strange. She knew she'd just signed the death warrants of hundreds of people, many of whom had nothing to do with the cartel or the attacks on America.

If this was power, she didn't understand why so many people fought so hard to get it.

She'd been transferred from the flagship to the Lake Champlain so she could oversee the targeting in person.

Shortly before launch she went out to the cruiser's

observation deck for some air and threw up over the side of the ship.

She stood on the deck, looking across the water at the immensity of the supercarrier. The strike group consisted of six ships and they made an impressive sight on the gulf, the sun setting in the orange sky behind them. To the east she could just make out the lights of Sinaloa's coastline.

The strike group commander came out onto the deck.

"Aspen," he said, nodding at her.

She watched him from her side of the deck as he lit a cigar.

"We got a hundred-sixty-two live signals," he said to her.

That wasn't bad considering the numbers had been gathered a few months earlier.

"Are we targeting all of them?"

"Fourteen of them are in the US," the commander said.

Fawn pictured Tomahawk missiles honing in on those phones without any consideration of collateral damage. Her stomach turned.

"So those are out," he said. "The FBI is going to track them."

"The rest?"

"Twenty-two are in other Mexican provinces, or outside the country."

"So that leaves how many?"

"One-twenty-six."

"So that's it then," she said.

"Yes, ma'am. Most are in or around Culiacán. Some are in other towns. La Cruz. Eldorado. Navolat. Guamúchil."

The towns were just dots on a map to her.

The Block I Tomahawk missile was introduced into the US Navy's arsenal in the nineteen-seventies. The missiles on board the Lake Champlain were the more sophisticated Block IVs. They each weighed almost two tons when armed and fueled, and cost the US government one point eight-seven million dollars. There was a time when they were armed with a W80 two-stage thermonuclear warhead. Those days were over. Today, they were armed with a thousand pounds of conventional explosive. They would fly extremely low, at an altitude of about a hundred feet and a cruising speed of just five-hundred-fifty miles per hour. Their range was a little over eight-hundred miles.

They weren't fast.

They weren't overly sophisticated.

They were solid-fuel rockets that carried two tons of explosive to a GPS marked spot, where they would blow up.

"One rocket per target?" Fawn said.

The commander nodded.

The Block IV's targeting system allowed them to be launched with fifteen pre-programed GPS coordinates, allowing the targeting team to redirect the missile in mid-flight. Additionally, they had the ability to provide a completely new target, or to have the missile loiter over the battlefield until a more critical target was provided. They also had a bunker-busting capability, whereby the first detonation created a hole in a concrete hardened structure and allowed the second follow-through element to completely penetrate the concrete.

The missiles provided camera imagery of their targets in the moments before strike. It would be Fawn's job to analyze that imagery and determine what cartel or civilian damage was caused.

The first missile fired from a neighboring ship. Fawn saw it slide out of the launch tube in a cloud of smoke at what appeared to be an impossibly slow speed. Once in the air, the missile's six-foot wings extended and the missile took off, low over the water, toward its target.

The launch was quickly followed by another, and another. Three missile cruisers took part in the launch. One-hundred-twenty-six missiles, one-hundred-twenty-six targets, all over the province of Sinaloa.

When the boat she was on began launching, the sound was deafening and the commander had to grab her and bring back inside the ship.

"Wow," she said when he shut the steel door.

"They pack a punch," he said.

There was a windowed observation tower and he brought her up to it.

They arrived in time to see the flash of the explosions as the first missiles hit their targets near the coast.

The missiles kept coming. They took off every thirty seconds for over an hour. The air grew so thick with smoke that after the first dozen or so launches, they could only see the glow of the neighboring ships.

Firing a Tomahawk at a cellphone signal was like trying to kill one ant out of a group with a basketball. They were accurate to about ten feet, but created a blast crater of over twenty, killing everyone in a radius three to four times that.

"The first images will be coming back already," the commander said.

Fawn nodded. She would start her examinations imme-diately. She was scared to find out what they would reveal.

She went down the steel steps into the control room. The room was filled with computer screens, lights, switches, and the technical staff that targeted and launched the missiles.

There was a station set up for her with three huge, high-resolution screens showing the imagery coming in from the missile cameras.

Fawn sat down at her seat and opened the files from the first detonation. It appeared to have struck an apartment building in downtown Culiacán.

"What am I looking at?" she said to the naval officer who'd set her up at the station. "Why is there so much going on? What's this big circle."

"It's the cluster bomb radius ma'am."

"Cluster bomb?"

"Yes ma'am."

Fawn went cold. Cluster bomb packages contained one-hundred-sixty smaller explosives that scattered over a large area. They were less effective at destroying buildings but multiplied the human casualty potential of each strike.

Fawn's voice broke.

"I didn't know we were using cluster bombs."

"Directive from the pentagon, ma'am."

Fawn swallowed.

"I see," she said quietly.

"This operation is for revenge, right?"

"Right," she said.

"Fuck them, that's what I say."

THIRTY-FIVE

Hunter fell to the ground behind the wall. The cartel men scrambled back inside. Some of them were unhurt. Some were bloodied, concussed. All were panicking. One was screaming, still outside, the explosions going off all around him.

The cartel boss yelled for them to get the injured man. None went.

"I'll get him," Hunter said, and ran out into the chaos.

The man was writhing in pain about fifteen yards from the door. Hunter shielded his eyes and assessed the scene. Cluster bombs concentrated on the strip club. A strange target, he thought. And a strange choice of ordnance. Cluster bombs would spread damage around the building but would be less effective at destroying it or killing those inside.

They were shooting blind. Throwing spaghetti.

He ran to the injured man. There was a big piece of shrapnel lodged in his gut. Hunter couldn't tell if he was going to make it or not. He grabbed him under the arms and pulled him back toward the motel room.

The windows had blown out. Shrapnel and debris was everywhere.

"Necesita un médico," Hunter said.

The boss shut the door and they took cover behind it. The strike was already over but the chaos, but fear of follow up explosions kept them inside.

Hunter was the first to go back out.

"The stripper?" the cartel boss said.

Hunter shrugged. He was getting sentimental in his old age.

He ran across the parking lot. The area around the club had been packed with people. It was now a scene of carnage. There were body parts, pieces of flesh, a jawbone with part of someone's face still on it. Hunter could see the fillings in the teeth.

People were screaming.

He recognized the bouncer from earlier. The man's belly was open and his intestines mixed with the dust on the ground.

Inside there was panic but less blood. The club was solid, built of concrete, and above it was a second floor, also of concrete. Most of the injuries inside seemed to be from shattered glass, panic, stampeding.

People were coming out of the club. Hunter knew they didn't have much time. A follow up strike could already be in the air.

He scanned the faces of the women leaving the club, searching for Adelita. He told himself it helped his cover story if he showed an interest in her. No one should ever be as singleminded as an assassin has to be.

He found Adelita sitting on the ground behind the bar. She was unhurt.

"Tienes suerte," he said to her.

She looked up at him.

"Estás aquí?" she said, surprised to see him.

"Come on," he said. "There might be another attack. What's the best way out of here?"

"I have a car in the back."

He nodded. She led him back through the club to a fire escape. Hunter pushed open the door and instinctively looked toward the sky.

"Come on," he said to her.

They crossed the lot at the back of the club and went through a fence. She threw him the keys to her little Chevrolet which luckily had been parked out of range of the bombs. They got in and he floored it out of the parking lot. He wanted to put some distance between them and the air strike but he could tell from the plumes of smoke above them that they were hitting multiple targets across the city. Judging from the smoke, there had been dozens of strikes.

It was an all out assault on the scale used in Iraq or Syria or Yemen.

He quickly did some calculating. A city this size. The likely number of air strikes per night. How long it would take for the place to resemble a middle eastern war zone.

"Where do you live?" he said to Adelita.

"With my mother."

"What neighborhood?"

"La Conquista."

At least it was outside the city core. It was as safe a place as she was likely to find. He drove north across the river and left the highway in a relatively nice residential neighborhood. The further north he got, the less smoke there was in the sky. This part of the city had been less targeted.

"Left here," Adelita told him as they neared her home.

Hunter looked at her. She was still wearing her stripper clothes, her heels, her makeup. His semen was probably still inside her. There was some dirt on her forehead and he wiped it off.

"Does your mother know you wear clothes like this?"

She looked down at herself as if she hadn't realized how she looked.

"Oh," she said, and then, out of nowhere, she began to cry.

Hunter looked away, concentrated on the road. There was a large supermarket and he pulled into the parking lot.

"Wait here," he said to her.

She had stopped crying and gave him a thin smile. He went inside and bought her the supermarket's brand of jeans, a t-shirt, and a sweater with Minnie Mouse on the front. He also bought himself a fresh t-shirt.

Back in the car, she put on the clothes over her lingerie and smiled.

"How do I look?"

"Beautiful," he said.

She had some makeup in the glovebox and fixed her face in the visor mirror.

Hunter parked the car on a quiet street lined with trees. There were stores on the ground floor and apartments on the upper levels.

"This is it," Adelita said.

There was a nervousness in her voice.

"I can leave you here," Hunter said.

"How will you get back to the city?"

"I'll take a cab."

"You won't find a cab now."

"I don't mind," he said.

She shook her head. "No. I want you to come inside,"

she said. "My mother will be grateful you brought me home."

Hunter wasn't so sure about that but he followed her to the door. She opened three locks and they went up some stairs. There were two doors at the top. She unlocked the one on the left and they went into a small, tidy apartment with a tiled floor and lace curtains on the windows. There was a TV on one wall, book cases on the other and a balcony directly across. To the left was the kitchen and to the right a hallway leading to the bedrooms and bathroom.

Hunter had pictured an old woman but Adelita's mother was barely in her fifties. She was attractive, with a good figure and smooth skin. She had the same eyes as her daughter. She was watching the news on the TV and jumped when she saw Hunter standing over her.

When she saw Adelita she got up and ran to her.

Adelita began crying. She asked her mother why she was still awake. Her mother looked at the TV screen which was showing the carnage across the city. Dozens and dozens of air strikes were wereaking their havoc. Adelita said Hunter had helped her get away.

"Muchas gracias," the mother said.

Hunter said he should leave but the mother insisted he let her make him some tea. He sat on the sofa and the two women went into the small kitchen. He could see them and hear them talking. Outside, the street was quiet and through the window he could see the plumes of smoke rising from the attack sites.

He turned down the sound on the TV and looked around the room. There was a graduation photo of Adelita with the year written under it. She'd told him she was twenty-one. This photo put her at twenty-seven or twenty-eight. There was also a photo of her with a baby. There was another of Adelita with a little girl.

The women came back with the tea and Adelita told him they wanted him to spend the night on the couch.

He shook his head and then the mother spoke in English.

"They won't shoot an American," she said, referring to the air strikes.

Hunter knew that wasn't true but he didn't say that. He only nodded.

The truth was he liked it there.

THIRTY-SIX

Hunter woke at dawn. The apartment was quiet. He'd slept surprisingly well. He got up and left the apartment as quietly as he could. From the street he noticed either Adelita or her mother watching him from a window. He didn't look up.

He walked two blocks and found a payphone. He called Fawn and waited. An automated voice asked for a numeric password and performed a voice analysis. Then he was connected to Fawn's cell and heard the dial tone.

"Hunter?"

"Worried about me?" he said.

She ignored the question. "You're in Culiacán."

"Yes. I made contact with the cartel last night. I'm going to need some money in that account."

"You're a buyer?"

"Yes. And if you could give Jack Morrow a contract to supply FOBS in Mexico that would be great."

"The United States doesn't have FOBS in Mexico."

"Just get my name on a list of some sort?"

"Catering contracts?"

"Yes."

"I'll see what I can do."

"And I told them I'm going to be a player, so I'll need to be able to wire the kind of money that will get me a seat at the table."

"How much did you have in mind?"

"Twenty?"

"Twenty million dollars?" Fawn said, letting out a quick laugh.

"You'll be able to trace it."

"No we won't."

"Well, who cares?"

"Some pencil-pusher somewhere."

"Get me as much as you can."

"If we were going to buy our way in, we didn't need to send you," Fawn said.

"Yes you did, and twenty million's a drop in the ocean. You spent a hundred million on air strikes last night. Destroying fucking strip clubs."

"So that's where you were."

"That's where the cartel was."

"That's why we hit it."

"With a cluster bomb?"

"That wasn't my call."

"Anyway, is there a hotel or something you can put on a safe list?"

"Okay," Fawn said, "wait a second."

She did some typing.

"The Hidalgo downtown. It's on the square."

"Thank you."

"You'll like that one."

"I'm not sure I'll be enjoying the amenities."

"Well, it won't be hit by us so you can sleep easy," Fawn said. "Anyway, that's a hundred seconds."

"I'll check in again soon. Try to get me some money. I'll send you an account number from the cell. Otherwise I've got no in with these guys."

"I'll get you something."

"Thanks, Fawn."

"One more thing," she said.

"What is it?"

"They're zeroing in on Chicago. Cell traffic and other indicators. See if you can hear anything."

"Okay," he said.

He hung up and went into a convenience store. He bought a cup of coffee and some Marlboro cigarettes. He scanned the front pages of the newspapers, *Primera Hora, El Sol, Norte.* Journalists from all of them had been gunned down in the past by the cartel. Every word they published was now censored. Hunter grabbed a copy of each. There were no newspapers from outside the state.

He paid and asked the clerk where he could find a cab. The clerk directed him around the corner. In the taxi, Hunter flipped through the newspapers. The main news was the air strikes. There had been over a hundred across the state. The strikes were concentrated on known cartel properties like villas, drug stores, and nightclubs, but there had been a lot of collateral damage. For all their precision, bombs had hit fields in the middle of nowhere, residential buildings, two churches, a school, a cemetery, lonely stretches of highway. Hunter guessed they were targeting cell phone signatures. He'd seen the CIA's data. They didn't have much else they could have used.

There were also reports of a US troop buildup along the border. The agreement with Mexico had been that the US would provide military support, but wouldn't send ground troops over the border. Everyone believed it was only a matter of time before they crossed in strength.

Refugees were fleeing Sinaloa. The newspaper criticized them for abandoning their home and said they would be destitute once they crossed the border. They added a dose of deterrence by pointing out that many refugees were being killed by the cartel for cowardice.

One of the newspapers also reported a buildup of US law enforcement personnel, as well as military units, around Chicago. Hunter wasn't sure what to make of that. El Sucio was smart. If Chicago was in the newspaper he'd be anywhere but there.

He got out of the cab at the square and checked in to the Hidalgo hotel. He got a room on the top floor with a view south over the city. After checking in, he went to the lobby and had breakfast. At eight-thirty he went out onto the street, crossed the square, and entered the Azteca bank.

The bank was in a grand colonial building similar to his hotel, and he asked to see his safety deposit box. He showed ID for Jack Morrow. The bank staff treated him deferentially and he had no doubt the cartel would hear of his visit. They might also know what was in his deposit box although in theory it couldn't be opened without his key. He prayed the agency hadn't fucked up when they paid for it. The paper trail would have to be perfect around here. The cartel had even tighter control over their territory than a government would have.

Hunter watched everything. He noted the clerk opening a steel drawer behind the security desk. From the drawer she took a set of keys which she used to unlock a door leading to the deposit boxes. The boxes themselves required that the same key be used as well as a key held by the customer. That key was small and Hunter had it in his wallet.

The deposit box contained ten thousand dollars in US currency and about the same in Mexican. Hunter filled his wallet with as much of each as he could reasonably carry. He planned to throw some money around to win over the lower level cartel guys. It was amazing what a few grand at a night club could do for your reputation. There was a good quality Nikon camera and some lenses in the box. Hunter didn't touch them.

There were two handguns. Both Glock twenty-two's. Hunter preferred the FN Herstal Five-Seven he'd taken from the cartel men at the gas station so he left the Glocks in the box. There was also a Remington Mk 21 Precision Sniper Rifle. He lifted it out of the metal case and looked it over. Everything was in order. There was also ammo. He left the guns and ammo. They were safer here than anywhere else.

After checking the box, he went back to the lobby and asked to speak to a manager. A few minutes later he was taken to an office to wait. He was served coffee and a few minutes later an overweight man in an expensive suit joined him.

"Mr. Morrow," the man said. "My name is Calderón."

"Mucho gusto," Hunter said, shaking his hand.

"What can we do for you?"

"I'm expecting a wire," Hunter said. "Can you receive it for me?"

"Of course."

"I don't want an account. I just want you to receive the wire and pay the money on to whoever I say."

"I see."

"I take it that won't be too complicated."

"It depends who you are sending the money to."

"To local sources," Hunter said.

Calderón nodded. He understood what that meant. "We're not subject to Mexican financial regulations any longer," Calderón said, "but that could change in the future."

"If things change in the future, we can change the way we do business."

Calderón nodded. He wrote some routing information on a piece of paper and handed it to Hunter.

"You can wire money here."

"Thank you," Hunter said.

"Can you give me an indication of how much we should expect?"

Hunter thought about it. He'd asked the CIA for twenty. The case was high priority but the agency never gave anyone what they asked for.

"Maybe two, maybe five," he said. "Depends how business goes."

"Million?"

Hunter nodded.

"Dollars?"

"Dollars."

THIRTY-SEVEN

Hale strode across the gravel driveway while a crowd of reporters shouted questions. His security detail and the White House secret service guys flanked him on both sides. When he reached the steps he stopped to savor the moment. He turned to the reporters. Cameras clicked and flashed like it was a red carpet event.

"What can you say about the sightings of troops in Illinois?"

"Are troops being deployed to Mexico?"

"What is your comment on the bombings along the border?"

Hale heard of the latest attacks just minutes earlier. He'd been in his car on his way to Langley and was immediately called to the White House. He had no idea how the press knew so quickly.

He looked to see who'd asked the question. It was Antonio Perez from the *LA Times*. The question caused an uproar among the reporters. Apparently they hadn't heard either.

"What's your information?" he called to Perez over the noise.

"I just got a message from the office," he said. "Literally this second."

Hale wasn't sure what to say. It would be a huge breach of etiquette for him to address the nation from the steps of the White House, especially on something as big as these latest attacks.

But on the other hand, it was also a huge opportunity.

He weighed the options and decided on the safer strategy. He turned away from the reporters and entered the building. The National Security Advisor, Andrew Antosh, and Raquel Harris were already inside.

The three guests were escorted to the Oval Office where the president was sitting behind his desk massaging his temples.

"It's a zoo out there," the president said.

None of the visitors said anything.

"I'm going to speak to them. I have to. I just want to make sure I have something concrete to say first."

"What are the details of the attacks, sir?" Hale said.

"It's still coming in. Looks like suicide vests at border crossings."

"Suicide vests? That's fucking new," Antosh said.

The suicide vest was a weapon generally limited to religious extremists, for obvious reasons. Drug dealers were motivated by material gain, not heavenly reward. Cases of soldiers using suicide attacks were not unheard of. The Japanese Kamikaze and Kaiten units during the Second World War. Chinese soldiers during the Sino-Japanese wars.

Hale was at a loss to come up with a single case of a criminal organization using them.

"Dozens of border personnel and civilians were killed," the president said. "I'm going to order troops to enter Mexico and secure the area south of the border. If there are going to be attacks, I want our military on the front line."

"Understood, sir," Antosh said.

"What do the Mexicans say?" Hale said.

"I don't give a fuck what the Mexicans say," the President said.

Hale nodded. "For what it's worth, sir, I don't think they'll put up much of a protest."

"I've got a meeting at the pentagon in fifteen minutes," the president said, "so let's keep this brief. Raquel, what's going on in Chicago?"

"It's all hands on deck, sir. We planted a story in the *Post* and as soon as it hit the stands the cartel's cell traffic went through the roof."

"So our man's in Chicago?"

"We think so, sir."

"You think so?"

"We've got all available agents and local law enforcement working round the clock. The CIA is providing support. National guard units are on stand by."

"What about black ops?"

Raquel looked at Hale. The question made her uncomfortable. Everyone knew the president was willing to cross the line on this. He didn't care what the law said and he knew the country would back him up if he broke a few eggs to catch El Sucio and end the madness.

Raquel's problem was that she wasn't so sure they would back her up. The same went for Hale and Antosh. No one wanted to be the fall guy on this.

"Sir," Hale said, clearing his throat.

"I don't want to hear excuses."

"It's not that, sir," Hale continued.

"I've had congress repeal *Posse Comitatus*. I've federalized the national guard. I've done my part."

"Sir, the repeal doesn't take effect until the first."

"I know when the repeal takes effect. Fucking senators." He turned to Raquel. "Just lock down that city. If he slips out, it'll be your head."

"Yes, sir."

"I'm on my way to the Pentagon. The army is going to set up road blocks along Interstate forty-three to Beloit, from there along thirty-nine to Bloomington, then through Champaign, Lafayette and up to Elkhart. Every road. Every highway. Every farmer's dirt track through the fields. If he's in that box, he's not getting out."

"Thank you, sir."

"And the lake, too. Not so much as a skiff gets out of the city."

"If he's in Chicago, we'll find him, sir."

The president nodded. The measures he'd undertaken were unprecedented. Never had a US city, especially not one the size of Chicago, been sealed off before. As well as the physical barrier which enclosed an area roughly the size of Wisconsin and cut through four states, all air and rail travel within the zone had been halted and special FISA orders had been made allowing for the monitoring of all communications of any kind.

The president was assembling forces larger than those used to subdue Baghdad during the height of the Iraqi war.

He turned to Hale. "And now, plan B. Our man in Sinaloa."

"Yes, sir. He's made contact with the cartel. He's killed some of their members. He's also had eyes on some of the air strike sites."

"Any word on El Sucio?"

"Not yet, sir, but he's set up a meeting to buy drugs from the cartel. We've wired him two million dollars to pose as a dealer."

"Are they going to fall for that DEA style crap?"

"We're setting up some fake military supply contracts now to cover his story."

"Correct me if I'm wrong, Hale, but El Sucio doesn't show up in person every time someone tries to buy two million dollars worth of drugs, does he?"

Hale glanced quickly at Raquel and Antosh, trying to gauge if either of them was going to pounce. His position was weak. They had nothing. He needed to buy Hunter more time.

He knew his agent and if El Sucio was in Culiacán, Hunter would find him.

"Sir, he's going to get into their inner circle. Then he'll be in a position to determine if El Sucio's back in Sinaloa."

Raquel butted in. "He's not in Mexico. He's in Chicago."

"Cell phone chatter," Hale said. "We all know what that's worth."

"And one off-the-rails agent in Mexico with a gun and an expense account. We all know how that goes, too."

The president rose his hands. "I've got to go. Both of you, I want more. Just give me more. Whatever you have, throw it at this. Hale, I want another asset in Sinaloa. We can't have all our eggs riding on this one guy."

"He's not just one guy."

"Give me another asset. Raquel, get on board and start coordinating with the army. They're going to be all over Illinois in the next few days. It's martial law time. Quit sitting on the fence."

Raquel nodded. "Yes, sir."

The president and Antosh left and Hale and Raquel were escorted out of the building.

Hale gave Raquel a withering look. She rose an eyebrow at him, daring him to challenge her.

THIRTY-EIGHT

Hunter spent most of the day in his hotel, drinking coffee and smoking cigarettes at the fancy restaurant patio overlooking the square. It was the most visible place he could put himself. He knew the cartel was watching. He would play the role of a man waiting to do a deal and at night, he would play the role of a man who would make mistakes, let his guard down, get in trouble. It was the fastest way to get in with the people who would know where El Sucio was hiding.

At about noon, Calderón called from the bank and a waiter brought Hunter the phone.

Two million dollars had been received by wire from a bank in Panama. Hunter told him that was correct and then cursed the CIA for sending him one tenth of what he asked for. Two million might be enough to get him a meeting with someone important but twenty would have been better. He'd have to play it off as a taster of what was to follow.

In the afternoon he swam in the rooftop pool and ordered Aperol cocktails. There were some pretty women sitting around the pool catching sun. Hunter didn't know if they were working or if they were the girlfriends of cartel guys. Probably both. He flirted with them and asked where would be a good place to party that night.

They told him the name of a club near the hotel called El Diablo.

He asked if there would be women like them there and they laughed.

He forced himself to sleep a few hours in the afternoon and when he woke up he had dinner at the restaurant over-looking the square.

After his steak he ordered a cognac and smoked a cigar.

It hadn't been a bad day, all things considered. He could have played that role for a week without tiring of it. It was a shame he had to blow it all up so soon.

He asked his waiter if he could buy some coke. The waiter left and came back with a gram in a plastic bag. Hunter asked how much he owed him and the waiter told him it was on the house.

Hunter left him a fifty dollar tip.

He did a small line at his table and made sure people saw him do it. It felt good but he didn't like it.

At dusk, air strikes started up but the city remained remarkably calm. It was as if they were already used to them. None landed on the square and the evening drifted on like nothing unusual was happening.

Hunter sat at his table nursing a beer and waited for it to get late. He watched the people coming and going to and from the hotel. It was a popular place for the cartel, the best hotel in town, and it made sense he'd be staying there if he was who he said he was.

On the square he saw the rank and file cartel guys in their Gucci clothes and tattoos, their scantily dressed women on their arms. There were bars around the square that all seemed to be full of players. Some came to the hotel bar and Hunter watched them. They watched him too. He sent them a bottle of Ace champagne. The hotel had a bottle list to rival any club in New York or Los Angeles.

One of the cartel guys came over to him. Hunter was ready. He had cocaine, a cigar, and a beer on the table.

"Join us, gringo," the man said.

Hunter recognized him from Fawn's intel. He had a goatee and a mop of curly hair. In the file he was called Juan but he introduced himself as Jesús.

He was sitting with two other guys and three women.

Hunter accepted the offer. They were all smiles. Jesús asked what he was doing in Culiacán. Hunter said he was there on business. He knew Jesús knew who he was.

One of the girls toyed with his feet under the table but he ignored her.

After about fifteen minutes of making small talk, Jesús and his friends left.

Hunter sat alone at their table and a few minutes later he asked for the bill. The waiter told him Jesús had already paid it. Hunter gave the waiter another fifty and walked out of the hotel and across the square to the club.

El Diablo was a lot higher end than the strip club from the night before. It had the look and feel to rival any club in any city in the world. There was a long line outside the door and girls in tiny bikinis were serving shots from glasses held in their mouths. One of them approached Hunter and he took a shot of some blue, sugary liquid from the glass in her mouth.

He walked straight to the front of the line and the bouncer took one look at his Texan hat and boots and knew who he was. He patted him down. Hunter hadn't brought a gun or a phone.

"Entrar, vaquero," the bouncer said.

Hunter gave him some money and walked in. The door led to a large anteroom made of marble, the high ceiling held up by Roman columns. It would all be a death trap if an air strike hit. There were girls taking people's jackets but Hunter kept his. He walked through the room to the ballroom which had a huge bar at the center. Around the bar, people were standing around, talking over the music. Beyond was a dance floor and beyond that a balcony with a DJ on it. Above it all were a series of massive chandeliers.

Hunter was the only outsider. Everyone noticed him. He was dressed to stand out.

He walked up to the bar and got a scotch and soda. Then he walked through the crowd to the VIP area overlooking the dance floor. A bottle girl looked to her boss and when he nodded she led him to a table surrounded by leather sofas. She left and a minute later another girl came over to him. She spoke English.

"What can I get you?" she said.

She was barely wearing anything. The top of her bikini was a few neon pink straps with small patches of fabric over the nipples, barely big enough to cover them. A similar sized patch of fabric covered her pussy and a thin strip of lace ran up the crack of her ass. She had brown hair and blue eyes.

"What have you got?" Hunter said.

"At the bar I'd give you a shot. Up here I'd recommend you order a bottle of something expensive."

"I'll take ten bottles of the most expensive thing you have."

The girl's eyes grew. She knew a tip when she saw one.

"You're waiting for friends?" she said.

"I don't have any friends."

"I can bring you some company if you like."

"That would be fine," Hunter said, "as long as you're one of them."

The girl left and when she came back it was like a birthday party at a kid's restaurant. A group of six girls dressed just like her followed. They were all carrying sparklers and ice buckets and even a cake covered in cream. They made a big show, giving him his money's worth.

Hunter wouldn't have ordered like that if any of the cartel bigwigs were already there, you didn't want to outdo those guys, but it was still early and no one important was there yet.

The girl with the blue eyes sat next to him and put a leg on his lap. He took her chin in his hand and kissed her on the lips. He sat back and tried to relax. The cocaine and alcohol was affecting him but not as much as it should have.

The CIA had fucked with his body in every way they could come up with, and one of the effects was to desensitize him to recreational drugs. To this day, Hunter was grateful they hadn't fucked with his sex drive.

The girl was still on his lap and the other six were all looking at him. To his side, another girl had her hand under his shirt and was playing with his chest. Hunter kissed both of them and then sat back to watch them kiss each other. Across the table, across the ten ice buckets and the ten bottles of champagne, the other girls teased him, flashing him, kissing each other, touching each other.

Hunter played with all of them while watching every person who entered the club.

The girls asked him if he wanted coke and he said he would take everything they had to offer him. A minute later, a pile of cocaine sat on the glass surface of the table like a mound of flour in a bakery.

Hunter took some from the breasts of the girls and they all helped themselves, snorting it off each other's bodies.

He made sure not to get carried away and ordered cigars to give himself an excuse not to drink and snort as much as they expected.

The club was taking notice of him but it wasn't until some of the cartel big shots came in and took the VIP booth next to his that he knew it would lead to anything.

The cartel men were middle-ranking leadership. He recognized four of them. They ordered like he'd ordered and they got the same birthday show. Girls were all over them in no time and Hunter noticed the gold-plated handguns in their waistbands, the designer clothing, the piles of cocaine.

Hunter continued his show, making out with his girls and making a fool of himself. He pretended to be drunker than he was. More fucked up.

When Jesús arrived, Hunter saluted him and then pulled the blue-eyed girl onto his lap. He did more coke off her breasts and kissed her. She straddled him, making out with him, and before he even realized it, they were fucking.

He stole a glance at Jesús and saw that he was laughing. Laughing at the gringo who'd had too much coke and couldn't control himself.

Hunter stood up and fell over the table onto the other girls. Bottles smashed, coke flew everywhere, and the girls laughed and screamed. He grabbed one of them and started making out with her.

Security was beginning to take notice.

Everything was going perfectly to plan and then there was shouting. A woman's voice. He strained to focus through the haze and smoke and saw Adelita's face. She was dressed like she was out for a good time but she was not happy.

"You fucking pig," she yelled at him.

"Baby," he said, but he was covered in champagne, surrounded by broken glass and naked women, and she was jealous as hell.

He was surprised. She was a stripper. They'd only spent one night together. What did she expect?

But her Latina fire was burning and it suited his purposes perfectly. The bigger the scene he created, the bigger the meeting he'd get with the cartel.

He got to his feet and feigned dizziness, falling back on the ground and smashing more drinks and glass.

"You fucking pig," she screamed. "I knew you were no different."

She continued swearing at him in her own flowery language and then turned to leave.

The girls were laughing. Hunter saw that Jesús and the cartel guys were watching intently. Every word of this exchange would make it back to the cartel.

Hunter did up his fly and took out his wallet. He threw a thousand dollars on the smashed table and told the girl he'd fucked it was for her and her friends. The club could send the bill to the Hidalgo hotel.

He ran after Adelita and caught up to her right as she was passing Jesús and the cartel guys.

"Baby," he said. "Don't be mad."

"You love to make us look like fools," she spat.

"No I don't."

"No, it's my fault for even thinking someone could be different."

"I never told you I was different."

"No you didn't," she said and turned away.

He grabbed her arm and she struggled to free herself. The cartel guys rose and grabbed him.

"Tranquilo, gringo," a low-level cartel guy said.

Hunter swung a wild punch and it grazed the man's face. It wouldn't have hurt but the man took it personally and hit Hunter on the chin. Then he grabbed him and rammed a knee into his face.

Hunter's nose was bleeding. He staggered back and knocked over the velvet rope that separated the VIP area from the dance floor.

Everyone laughed.

Hunter got back on his feet and looked at Adelita.

She was shaking her head.

She reached out and took hold of the arm of the man who'd hit Hunter.

He shoved her off, pushing her. She tripped on her heels and fell to the ground.

Hunter was on the guy in a second, punching him repeatedly in the face. He didn't lose his temper. He didn't hit the guy hard. He didn't want to do any real damage. But it was enough that Jesús and some other guys had to pull him off.

"It's time for you to get out of here," Jesús said.

Hunter looked at him and then at the scene he'd created. Tables were knocked over, champagne bottles were smashed, there was blood all over the floor.

"Lo siento," he said.

Jesús made a gesture with a flick of his wrist.

"Don't worry about it," he said.

Hunter nodded. He helped Adelita to her feet. She was a lot calmer than she'd been now that Hunter had defended her.

"Come on," he said.

She didn't say anything but she let him lead her away. On the way out, Hunter grabbed the manager by the sleeve.

"Pagaré el daño," he said.

"Don't worry about it, señor."

"No. Insisto. And I'll pay for them too," he said, pointing at Jesús. "Send the bill to the Hidalgo. Everything will be paid."

The man nodded and Hunter turned to Adelita.

"You coming with me?" he said.

THIRTY-NINE

At the hotel Hunter told the concierge to pay whatever bill the club sent over.

He led Adelita to the elevator and they rode it to the top floor. She was impressed with his room, the most opulent in the hotel.

She sat on the bed and watched him.

"Sorry about all that," he said.

"Don't speak to me," she said.

"You know that was just business."

She looked away.

"Mentiroso," she said.

"No," he said. "It's true. That's how you do business with these people."

"Why do you want to do business with men like that?"

"Why do you?"

She didn't answer. She wasn't dressed like she'd been the night before. She was wearing a pretty yellow dress that showed her neck and cleavage. Her hair spilled over her shoulders and some strands were loosely braided.

"They'll kill you. Those men. Sooner or later."

"Lets hope it's later," he said.

"Everything's a joke to you. Fucking girls. Spending money. Doing drugs."

"It's not a joke, Adelita."

"You play with fire."

Hunter said nothing.

"Juegas con muchas cosas."

"I never played with you."

"You're the only man I ever brought home."

"The only one?"

"The only one since ...", her words trailed off.

"Since what?"

She didn't answer.

He sat next to her on the bed and kissed her. She let him.

He was glad she'd seen him with the other women. There was a part of him that wanted to protect her, or at least not fool her. He didn't want her falling for him. He'd be gone in a few days and there was a good chance that everyone he came into contact with would be dead. The idea of her being among them bothered him.

It shouldn't have.

Collateral damage meant nothing.

But he was still human, despite the agency's best efforts.

"You don't know what kind of man I am," he said to her.

"Que tipo de hombre," she said to herself. "I thought I did."

"Adelita. I met you last night at a strip club."

She looked into his eyes. "Would you say I've looked into the eyes of more men than you have?" she said.

He thought about that. He thought about all the men he'd killed. That last moment when they realize where they're going and their eyes give away everything. In

Hunter's experience there were two types of men. Those who were surprised at the end, and those who weren't. Everything boiled down to that.

Then he thought of Adelita's life. The lap dancing. The fucking. There was probably a look in the eyes of men she'd seen a thousand times that Hunter never had. Adelita would have come up with her own way of reducing the world into two types of men. Her two types would be different than his.

"Yes," he said.

"Tell me this, Jack Morrow. Do you think it takes a long time to know a man?"

Hunter wasn't sure what she meant.

"Because it doesn't. Ask any whore. Everything you need to know about a man, you can tell in a single second."

"So you think you know me?"

"I know I know you," she said.

"You don't, Adelita."

"Sí, Jack. Lo sé. I know you better than you know yourself."

"What do you think you know?"

"I know you do bad things."

Hunter let out a laugh. That wasn't saying much.

"I know you do them for a good reason."

He looked at her.

"I know you feel every bit of pain you inflict."

There was a mirror over a desk at the end of the bed and Hunter caught himself looking at it.

"I know you feel more pain than you show."

"Everyone feels pain."

"I know you lost everything you ever loved."

He wanted her to stop talking.

"I know you think you've lost your faith."

"I was never religious."

"Yes you were. And you think you've lost your faith in God because you think he's lost faith in you."

"Enough, Adelita."

"You live like you're on borrowed time. Like your death is overdue."

"Maybe that's because it is."

"You don't fear death but you know you have to get right with God before it comes."

"Adelita," he said, taking her face in his hand.

She looked into his eyes. "You know you could love me. You could love any woman like me. You could give your life for a woman like me."

"A woman like you?"

"A woman who...".

Her words trailed off as he tried to kiss her.

She pushed him away.

"A woman who needs you. A woman who will ask you to love her."

"Is that what you're asking?"

"I would, but I already know the answer."

"What's the answer?"

"You would say no."

Hunter didn't know what to say. He looked at her. She was beautiful.

"You would say no and you would tell yourself it's because you're protecting me."

"I would be."

"You're lying. If you wanted to protect me you would say yes. Saying no doesn't protect me. It just means you're not responsible for what happens."

Air strikes had been hitting the city all night and the glow of them over the city was like the distant lightning of a storm. As Adelita spoke the last sentence, a strike hit closer to them, just a few blocks away, and the ground shook.

"Nothing's going to happen to you."

She smiled.

"You know that's not true," she said, and pushed him onto his back.

She opened his pants and climbed on top of him. She locked her eyes on his and didn't release them until they finished.

FORTY

Hunter woke with a start. Adelita was still asleep next to him, her naked body entwined with his. Someone was outside the room.

He reached beneath the bed for his gun and went to the door.

There was a knock.

Hunter looked under the door. There were at least four men out there.

He was jumpier than he should be. Maybe it was the cocaine in his system. Maybe it was the fact Adelita was there.

"Quién es?" he said.

"Abre la puerta."

"Who is it?"

"Jesús."

"What do you want, Jesús?"

"We want to talk."

Adelita was awake and Hunter told her to hide in the bathtub.

"Draw the curtain," he told her.

He went back to the door and opened it. Jesús and four men came into the room. Hunter looked at his watch. It was three. They'd come from the club.

"That was quite a scene you made earlier," Jesús said, smiling.

Hunter went to the mini bar and all four of the cartel men drew their guns when he opened the fridge.

Hunter ignored them and grabbed the little bottle of bourbon.

"Can I get you something?" he said to Jesús.

Jesús shook his head.

Hunter knocked back the bourbon.

"There have been some discussions," Jesús said.

"Discussions?"

"In my organization. They have been discussing your proposal."

"Tenemos un trato, Jesús?"

Jesús smiled.

"Sí."

"Troops are already crossing the border."

"And according to our sources, you will have the contracts for the bases."

Hunter smiled. Fawn had been hard at work.

"I'm going to need one kilo per week per thousand troops."

"That's not enough."

"It's a start."

Jesús nodded. Once combat started, or the boredom of waiting for it, he'd go through five times that much.

"That's twenty kilos this week. Fifty next week. Probably one hundred per week after that."

"At a minimum."

"At a minimum," Jesús said.

"Shall we say ten thousand a kilo?" Hunter said.

Jesús laughed. "You're paying twenty-five in Texas."

"We're not in Texas."

"You'll pay fifteen thousand a kilo."

Hunter nodded. "Once I exceed a hundred kilos a week, I want a better price."

Jesús sucked air through his teeth. "From what I hear, you spoke earlier of buying by the ton."

"By the time the bases are set up I'll need two tons a week."

Hunter did some quick arithmetic. At fifteen a kilo, that would make Hunter a thirty million dollar a week customer. That was enough to get the kind of access he needed.

God bless the troops.

"When you're buying a ton a week, we'll talk again about the price."

Hunter nodded.

"We'll need three-hundred thousand tomorrow. Seven-fifty in a week."

"I'm ready when you guys are."

"Oh, we're always ready."

"Good," Hunter said.

While they talked, Hunter watched the four men Jesús had brought with him. They were moving around the room. One was at the mini bar helping himself to a beer. Another was by the balcony. Another glanced into the bathroom. The fourth was looking at the bed.

"Donde esta la puta?" he said.

Adelita's underwear was on the floor by the bed.

Hunter gave the answer to Jesús.

"En el baño."

"Why is she hiding?" the man said.

"She's shy."

The man went into the bathroom and a moment later Adelita screamed. There was the sound of some struggling, a mirror smashing, the shower curtain coming down. Then the man reemerged pulling Adelita by the hair. Her lip was bloodied and she'd been hit in the eye.

"Why did he go and do that?" Hunter said to Jesús.

"Es mi puta," the man said.

"She's his whore," Jesús said.

Hunter strode over to the man and punched him in the face. The man fell back and the other men drew their guns. Hunter ignored them. He got down on top of the man and began pummeling him in the face. The man rose his hands in self-defense but Hunter kept the fists raining down. He didn't stop when the man lost consciousness. The other men looked at Jesús but he didn't say anything.

He was watching to see what kind of man he was doing business with.

Hunter landed a few more punches into the unconscious man's face and Jesús finally spoke to stop him.

"Please, Mr. Morrow. That's enough, I think."

"He comes into my room and acts like that?" Hunter said.

"He doesn't have any manners."

"I'm going to kill him," Hunter said.

It was the type of thing Jack Morrow would do, but more than that, Hunter knew the man would take this out on Adelita if he let him live.

"Is that necessary?"

"Yes," Hunter said. He turned to Adelita. "Go back in the bathroom and close the door."

She looked into his eyes and Hunter couldn't tell if she was thinking she'd been right about him or wrong about him.

She did what he said and Hunter glanced at Jesús to see if he would stop him.

Jesús said nothing.

Hunter lifted the unconscious man from the ground. He held him like a man talking his bride across the threshold for the first time. He carried him past the other cartel men out onto the balcony, extended him over the side, and let him go.

The man regained consciousness in time to let out a scream before landing on the roof of a car five stories below. The car's alarm went off but apart from that, the event garnered no response from the people in the square.

"Come to the nightclub tomorrow night," Jesús said, and left.

FORTY-ONE

Fawn was on her way to Hale's office when the cell rang. It was Hunter. She went into a conference room and shut the door.

"Good morning, sunshine," she said.

"Two million?" he said to her. "I asked for twenty."

"Is that all they wired?"

"Yes."

"Cheap bastards, I'll get more."

"Get a lot more."

"What have you go to report?"

"No word on El Sucio."

"Anything about Chicago?"

"Not yet, but I'm inching my way up the totem pole. I've got another meeting tonight."

"How's the Hidalgo treating you?"

"It's fine."

"I saw a satellite feed of someone plunging off your balcony last night."

"What can I say?" Hunter said. "He disrespected my woman."

"I saw her on some feeds too."

"Jack Morrow doesn't sleep alone."

"How thorough of you to flesh out the story."

"Anyway, I better go. The timeline is twenty kilos this week for three hundred. Fifty next week. A hundred the week after."

"You'll be long gone before then."

"Yeah," Hunter said.

Fawn took a breath. "There's one more thing."

"You know I hate surprises."

"We're sending in another asset."

"Fuck," Hunter said.

"He'll steer well clear of you."

"You know how this will end if the place is suddenly crawling with CIA agents."

"President's orders."

"Fucking president."

"They record these calls, you know."

"Fucking president and his fucking big gun."

"What big gun?"

"Barrett M82."

"What are you talking about?"

"Doesn't matter. Whoever you send in isn't Praying Mantis, is he?"

"Your the last Mantis."

"They'll skin him alive."

"The president doesn't think so."

"I've got to go," Hunter said.

"Happy hunting."

The line went dead. Fawn looked at her phone. Hunter had called from the cell rather than a payphone.

Fawn put the phone away and went back out to the temporary area set up for black ops in the wake of the bombing. Hale's office was a former locker room. She knocked on the door.

"Come in," Hale said.

She went inside. Hale was pouring himself a cup of coffee from the little station in the corner. It was like the coffee making area in a business hotel room.

"Settling in?" she said.

He nodded at a newly framed picture of himself and the president during their joint press conference. It was on the wall above his desk, just below the agency mandated portrait of the president himself.

"Very nice," she said.

He brought her some coffee and offered her the seat across from his. They sat and Fawn began filling him in on the latest report from Hunter.

"He's got another meeting tonight."

"Another meeting? We need results."

"He needs more money in that account."

"I'm working on that."

"No one's going to meet with a guy for two million."

"No one asked him to become their business partner."

"What else was he going to do, Hale?"

"He's been trained to do a lot of things."

"And most of them would scare the target into hiding."

Hale conceded the point and took a sip of his coffee.

"What else?"

"He wasn't happy that another asset is going in."

Hale didn't put a very high priority on Hunter's happiness.

"What else?"

"Nothing. No word on Chicago. No word on El Sucio. The FBI's operation is still our best bet."

Hale sighed. He would have preferred if it was his agency to bring El Sucio in.

"Is that it?"

Fawn nodded. She rose to leave.

"What did he say about that guy he threw from the balcony?"

"It was something to do with a woman," Fawn said.

Hale laughed.

"You ever wish it was you down there?" Fawn said.

"Not for a second."

"Come on, admit it. Shooting and fucking your way through an entire city."

"Do you?" Hale said.

Fawn wasn't sure. She'd often wondered what it was like for someone like Hunter. The man had the sort of power ordinary people didn't even bother to fantasize about. In Washington, power meant the ability to sit behind an important desk and sign important documents. Hunter didn't need a desk. He didn't need documents. If he didn't like something he could break it. Or kill it.

"Sometimes," she admitted.

Hale nodded. "Are you going to Arlington now?"

"Yes."

There'd been funerals every day for the agency members who were killed in the attacks. As director, Hale had gone to a ceremony every day at Arlington. Usually he was required to say a few words.

Today was Fawn's first time attending. They'd never found Celeste's body, they were still digging in the rubble for a lot of missing people, but she was now numbered among the fallen. Today's ceremony would be in her honor.

"We'll ride together," Hale said.

It rained through the ceremony. Hale held his umbrella

over Fawn the whole time. He knew she had something with Celeste though he didn't mention it.

Afterwards he told his driver to take her home in his car. He would get a ride with his security detail.

Fawn was glad of the ride, the rain had soaked through her coat and she was beginning to feel like a drowned rat in her wet cashmere. She'd been emotionless during the ceremony but as soon as she was in the car she broke down.

She rarely cried, even when she'd lost her parents and baby brother in a car accident when she was a kid, but this day she did. Her relationship with Celeste had been short, but it was intense. She realized how much of her decision to break up with Mitch had been based on Celeste. Mitch had pulled the trigger but she was the one who'd let it die.

She knew what she was doing, even if she hadn't been ready to admit it to herself. She'd been passively deciding to leave a great guy, a guy everyone expected her to end up with, in order to be with a woman.

She pulled out her cell and without thinking dialed Mitch's number.

"Fawn?" he said, surprised to be getting a call from her, or maybe surprised that it had taken her this long to make it.

"Mitch," she said, tears flowing down her face.

"Why are you calling me?"

"I'm sorry, Mitch. I'm so sorry. Please give me another chance."

It didn't take much more than that, and thirty minutes later she was at his parents' house in Silver Spring.

The moment he opened the door she threw her arms around him.

He tried to speak but she covered his mouth with hers. She pushed him back into the hallway and began pulling open his shirt.

"Fawn," he gasped.

He wanted her. She could feel his lust. She kicked the door closed and was on her knees before he knew what was happening.

"Good thing no one's home," he said.

She opened his pants and took him in her mouth, something she never did when they were together.

It was only afterwards, as he struggled to catch his breath and process what had just happened, that he realized she was soaking wet.

"Where were you?" he said, taking her coat and hanging it for her.

"Arlington," she said.

"Arlington cemetery?"

She nodded.

"For a funeral?"

"A memorial service."

"For who?" His tone changed and it was only then she realized how mad he was going to be.

She made to take her coat from the rack but he grabbed her arm.

"Mitch," she said.

"For who, Fawn?"

"What does it matter?"

"You fucking cunt," he said quietly.

"Don't," she said, trying again to grab her coat.

He stopped her again.

"You fucking used me."

"I didn't use you. I needed you."

"Celeste died, didn't she?"

"What does that have to do with anything?"

Mitch tore the coat from the hook and something

ripped. He didn't care. He threw it at Fawn with such force the belt buckle hit her face.

"Get the fuck out of here," he said.

"Mitch," she said, but she knew he was right.

She was embarrassed.

"I'm sorry," she said.

"Don't," he said, turning to leave.

Fawn turned and struggled to open the front door. There was something tricky with the latch and it took her a few seconds. It was raining heavier than before and Hale's car was gone.

She was in the middle of nowhere. A suburban street in a sprawling neighborhood with no transit and no cabs.

She walked a mile before reaching Georgia Avenue where she could hail a cab.

By the time she got home she was shivering. She'd cried the entire cab ride back and didn't know if it was for Celeste or for what had happened with Mitch.

She could still taste him when she got in the shower.

FORTY-TWO

Sarin is a colorless, odorless gas that is lethal at low concentrations. It is an organophosphorus compound not found in nature. Direct inhalation leads to death in one to ten minutes unless an antidote is administered. Non-lethal doses lead to permanent neurological damage.

Its production and storage has been a war crime since 1997.

It is a nerve agent, acting on neurotransmitters at neuromuscular junctions. It affects the brain's ability to control muscles. Death occurs by asphyxia when the brain can no longer control the muscles necessary for breathing.

The minutes following inhalation are not pretty. The pupils constrict and the chest tightens. The nose runs uncontrollably. The subject begins to drool. They vomit, urinate, and shit themselves. They begin to twitch and jerk, collapsing in a convulsion of spasms before breathing stops.

The gas is highly volatile and if not inhaled it can still be lethal by absorption through the skin. Contact with a contaminated person or their clothing can be lethal for up to thirty minutes after the initial exposure.

Pure sarin is twenty-six times more lethal than cyanide, forty-three times more than phosgene, twenty-eight times more than mustard gas, and five-hundred-forty-three times more lethal than chlorine.

There are numerous ways to produce sarin. Its chemical composition is readily available on the internet or in textbooks. Detailed descriptions of various production methods, used by different militaries around the world, are well documented.

But it is not easy to produce. Sophisticated lab processes are required, measuring and mixture methods are delicate, small mistakes can lead to the batch being rendered useless, and any leakage during the process can be lethal. Rabbits or lab rats must be kept on hand at all times to warn of contamination.

Once produced, the gas is highly acidic, creating difficulties for storage and transportation. Experiments were performed in the fifties and sixties by the US and British militaries to increase the shelf life of sarin but no completely effective methods were found. Army scientists at the Rocky Mountain Chemical Weapons Arsenal at Commerce City, Denver developed a method of adding tributylamine to sarin that increased its shelf life by up to six months. This was the most effective method developed by any military but it was difficult and complicated to perform. In other countries, triethylamine was tested with less success.

To this day, the gas remains highly volatile and cannot be reliably stored for long periods or transmitted over great distances without significant deterioration. Militaries that still possess it must renew or re-distill stocks regularly.

After the invasion of Iraq it was found that Saddam Hussein's stock's lasted for as little as two weeks.

The properties of the gas were first discovered by IG Farben at the Wuppertal-Elberfeld complex in 1938. At that time, IG Farben was Europe's largest corporation with over three-hundred-thousand employees. At its height, a full half of all the company's workers were slaves, leased from the SS and put to work at custom-built facilities near Nazi concentration camps. The company's products, such as Zyklon B, used in the Auschwitz gas chambers, made the Holocaust possible. The US Justice Department concluded in 1978 that were it not for the expertise, technology, and concentration of economic power at IG Farben, Hitler would not have been able to start World War II when he did.

The Bayer group at IG Farben conducted numerous medical experiments on concentration camp inmates at Auschwitz and Mauthausen. At Birkenau's Block Twenty, the women's hospital, they deliberately infected patients with typhoid, tuberculosis, and diptheria, and tested a number of experimental antidotes with horrific results.

To test a new anesthetic, Bayer ordered one-hundred-fifty women from Auschwitz. When the SS charged two hundred Reichsmarks per woman, Bayer objected and negotiated the price down to one-fifty. When all one-hundred-fifty women died, the company ordered a second batch of the same number and quality at the same price.

The Nazis quickly recognized the potential of sarin when its formula was sent by IG Farben to the German chemical warfare section. The Nazis immediately made plans for mass production and started construction of a number of facilities. The largest of these were still under construction when the war ended. It is estimated that the Nazis successfully produced up to ten tons of weaponized sarin and had begun incorporating it into artillery shells. None had been used by the time the war ended.

Soon after the war, both NATO and the USSR adopted sarin as a standard chemical weapon and began industrial production for military use.

In 1953, Britain tested the gas on living subjects resulting in the death of Royal Air Force Engineer Ronald Maddison at the Porton Down chemical warfare testing facility in Wiltshire.

The United States halted sarin production in 1957 but re-distilled its existing stocks until 1970.

In 1976, the Chilean Dirección de Inteligencia Nacional developed portable sarin spray cans which were used in a number of assassinations by the regime of Augusto Pinochet.

In 1988, Saddam Hussein used sarin and mustard gas against the Kurds in Halabja, northern Iraq. Five thousand civilians died in the attack and tens of thousands were injured. The cancer rate in the affected area remains elevated. The following month, the Iraqis used sarin four more times against Iranian soldiers on the al-Faw peninsula, helping them retake the area.

When one-hundred-sixty-two nations signed a UN chemical weapons treaty in 1993 banning sarin, there was an estimated fifteen thousand tons of the gas in military stockpiles globally. It is estimated that a tenth of that amount still exists today, despite being in breach of international law.

The Japanese doomsday cult, Aum Shinrikyo, used sarin to kill eight people in 1994 when a converted refrigeration truck released the gas into a residential area close to the home of three judges overseeing a real-estate lawsuit expected to go against the cult. Three gallons of sarin was heated in the back of the truck and a fan was used to spread it around the vehicle. The resulting cloud resulted in two-hundred-seventy-four people being rushed to hospital. The day after the attack, dead fish were found floating in a nearby pond. The bodies of dogs, birds, and a large number of caterpillars were also found, and the leaves of plants and trees in the vicinity turned brown.

Nine months later, the same cult released a gallon of sarin in the Tokyo subway system, killing twelve and causing over a thousand people to be hospitalized.

The Russians used sarin in assassinations in Chechnya in 2002.

Iraqi insurgents used it against a US convoy in 2004.

The Syrian government used sarin in the Khan al-Assal attack in Aleppo in 2013, killing twenty-six. Five months later, they launched rockets containing sarin at opposition controlled suburbs around Damascus, killing up to seventeen-hundred. Four thousand patients displayed symptoms of neurotoxic poisoning at Médicins sans Frontièrs hospitals in the city.

A Syrian government air strike against the town of Khan Shaykhun in April 2017 used sarin to kill over a hundred people. Another air strike in Douma in 2018 also used sarin.

The US congress has sarin listed as a potential terrorist attack agent and has ordered research into potential emergency response procedures in case of an attack.

It was not known that the Sinaloa cartel had hired Syrian and Russian chemists with expertise in sarin production, or that they had constructed specialized labs in the mountainous area of Surutato, about fifty miles north of Culiacán.

Two precursor compounds that were more stable and

easier to transport were produced in high volume and loaded into specially modified tanker trucks. The trucks had a capacity of eleven thousand gallons and each truck contained one of the two compounds. Twelve trucks set out from Surutato and crossed the state border into Chihuahua at Soyatita. From there they drove east to the Mexican Gulf, and crossed the US border at Reynosa, just south of McAllen, Texas.

From there, the trucks split into six pairs, each pair consisting of one truck carrying each part of the binary compound. All that was necessary to form sarin gas was for the two trucks' cargoes to be mixed.

One pair followed US highway eighty-three from McAllen to Laredo. Another went north to Corpus Christi. The third went to San Antonio, the fourth the Austin, the fifth to Houston, and the sixth to Dallas.

The drivers chose the mixing locations at random. In Houston, they dumped their cargoes into a downtown, concrete-lined city park pond that had been emptied for cleaning. In Houston, they did it in the lowest level of an underground parking facility beneath a mall. In San Antonio they used an empty suburban swimming pool. In Dallas, it was the foundation site for a major construction project.

In every case, the materials mixed slowly and vaporized into a fog that wafted from the mixing site. Within minutes, people close to the site were coughing and their eyes were watering. After thirty minutes, everyone within a radius of half a mile was affected. After an hour, people up to five miles away, if they were outdoors or close to open windows were being rushed to emergency rooms.

Close to the attack site, depending on ventilation and weather conditions, fatality rates were as high as seventy percent, or as low as thirty. Wind in Corpus Christi brought the cloud out over the gulf and reduced casualties. In Houston, the parking lot's ventilation system was tied to the systems for a number of buildings overhead including an office complex, a shopping mall, and hundreds of residential condo units.

The effects were catastrophic. All six attacks caused mayhem in panic in the affected cities. The least deadly attack, in Corpus Christi, created four thousand hospital emergency room visits and led to over four hundred deaths. The deadliest, in the Houston building complex, killed over five thousand.

FORTY-THREE

Hunter watched the news of the sarin attacks on a Sinaloan news channel. He was in the lobby of the hotel. He was angry and he didn't bother trying to hide it. He was playing the role of a Texan and that was his home. The news footage seemed to revel in showing scenes of disorder in the affected cities. People were screaming, holding their necks, clawing at their faces. Bodies littered the streets and para-medics were afraid to collect them for fear of contamination.

The president addressed the nation from the oval office, announcing the deployment of four hundred thousand additional troops and preparations for a ground invasion of Mexico.

It was horrific, but more than that, there was something about it that gnawed at Hunter.

It didn't make sense.

The cartel was a business. Its purpose was to make money. Its customers were in the United States. The continued attacks, the continued provocations, they were leading to a ground invasion of Mexico. How could that be in the interest of the cartel?

How could it play out in their favor?

What the hell was El Sucio's end game?

Hunter finished his beer and went to the bank. Then he went up to his room. Adelita was still there. He was afraid to let her leave after what had happened the night before. He'd killed her pimp. A lot of people had seen her with him. They'd seen her leave the club with him.

He wasn't sure she was safe.

"You've got to stay out of sight for a while," Hunter said.

"Where will I go?"

"Get out of the city. Get out of the state. Go anywhere. Somewhere in Mexico. Somewhere in the states."

"How will I go to the states?"

"Go to Mexico City then."

"I don't know anyone there."

"You can see what's happening here," Hunter said. "There's going to be a war. A full war. The kind of war you see on television."

"I've lived with war all my life."

"This is different. They're going to turn this entire city to rubble. They're going to wipe it off the map."

"They've been saying that for years. The cartel always survives. The worse things get, the stronger the cartel gets. War forces everyone into the hands of the cartel."

"Not this time."

"Sí, Jack, this time too. Nothing will change. The army will come in, the army will leave, and the cartel will be stronger than ever, with or without El Sucio."

Hunter was carrying a leather shoulder bag and he threw it on the bed.

"Open it," he said.

Adelita looked inside and immediately shut it.

"No," she said.

"Yes. It's the only way."

She looked at him and he noticed that tears were filling her eyes.

"You're trying to buy me off. Get rid of me. You think money is a substitute for love."

The bag contained a quarter million dollars cash. It was enough for her to take her mother and disappear forever. She was a stripper. No one would look for her. She could go to the capital, or leave the country, and start a new life.

"When this is all over," Hunter said, "I'll come find you."

"How would you find me?"

"I would find you, Adelita. And you would be safe."

"You're a coward, Jack. Cobarde. You're a fucking coward."

"Take it and go," he said.

He lifted the bag and threw it at her. The force of it surprised her.

"Go," he said. "Get out of here. Get out of Sinaloa. And take your mother. As soon as you're out, you'll see that there's a new life for you."

Adelita was crying. She knew what was happening. She knew what it meant. The money was nothing. The money could disappear in an instant. What she needed wasn't a bag of money, it was a man.

And she wasn't going to get him.

She took the bag and slammed the door behind her. Hunter took a deep breath. At least he didn't have to worry about her blood being on his conscience after this was all over.

He took a shower and got dressed. He didn't wear the hat this time.

Texas was in mourning.

He killed some time in the hotel lobby before heading back to El Diablo. The air strikes started up as he was crossing the square and they seemed to be heavier than the night before. That didn't surprise him. He wondered how long it would be before American soldiers were in that square.

The center of Sinaloa

If they wanted, they could be there in a week.

But to what end?

Occupying forces never accomplished their objectives as easily as people imagined. Like Adelita said, every time there was trouble, it just drove the people closer into the grip of the cartel. When the government closed off the province, everyone was suddenly a cartel member. Whether they dealt in drugs or not, they were with the cartel because the rest of the country was against them. With American troops entering, Hunter could see a very real chance that all of Mexico would begin to identify with the cartel.

Was that the plan?

To turn Mexico into a real narco state?

An entire nation of millions that saw only two sides, American guns and cartel money. And how many would side with the guns that were pointed at them?

The scene at El Diablo was a repeat of the night before, with scantily dressed women sidling up to low-level cartel runners dressed like rappers. He went inside and found Jesús and some other guys waiting for him.

Jesús nodded at him.

Hunter had told Calderón to transfer three-hundred thousand dollars to the cartel earlier and he was expecting to arrange a delivery for the first batch. Twenty kilos. Crossing at Tamazula de Victoria. From there it didn't really matter to Hunter what happened to it. He'd tell Fawn where to pick it up and she'd arrange something that would support Hunter's cover story. Twenty kilos didn't require much. Just a guy in a car.

The arrangements were simple.

It was winning the cartel's trust that was difficult. This twenty kilos was the beginning of a relationship that could be worth over a hundred million dollars a month.

He was sure it was time for them to introduce him to someone higher up the food chain.

"We're not staying here, Gringo," Jesús said. "We've got a ride to take."

"Where to?"

"Not far. There's a car outside."

Hunter followed Jesús and six other men through the club and out the back entrance. Two black G-class Mercedes SUVs waited. One of the men frisked Hunter and checked for weapons before letting him into the backseat. Jesús got in next to him. Two men got in the front. The remaining two got in the second vehicle. They left the square heading northwest. After a few blocks Jesús took out a black hood and handed it to Hunter.

"Really?" Hunter said.

"For your security," Jesús said.

Hunter acted insulted but put the hood on. He concentrated on the movements of the vehicle and was pretty sure they left the city on the road north through Culiacancito. They drove for half an hour and when they stopped they were at a beach resort on the coast. The beach was sheltered by a long sandbar. He'd studied the aerial photography and recognized it as Isla Altamura.

Jesús opened the door and got out. Hunter followed him. They were in the driveway of a luxurious villa. There was a Greek marble statue in the middle of a fountain and in front of the steps a Lamborghini, a Ferrari, and three more Mercedes like the one he'd arrived in.

"Who are we meeting?" he said.

Jesús didn't answer.

He led the way into the villa. The door led to a large, marble hall with a staircase sweeping up to the second floor. Beyond the staircase he could see a huge room with floor to ceiling glass walls overlooking the ocean. There was a modern fireplace in the center of the area and Jesús nodded toward it.

"Wait up there."

Hunter walked up to the fire and sat on a white leather sofa. There was a humidor on a table by his side and he opened it and took out a Cohiba. He cut it with the puncher on the bottom of the tabletop lighter and began smoking.

He sat about ten minutes. Along the coast he could see the glow of air strike explosions, and toward the horizon he thought he could see US navy ships flashing in the distance.

The villa was opulent. The styling was modern. It felt like he was in Miami or LA. It wasn't lived in. There was nothing personal there. It was more like the showroom that a developer would use to sell the rest of the units.

"Jack Morrow," a voice said from behind him.

Hunter turned.

He couldn't believe it.

Before him stood Ernesto Pérez Masón, El Sucio's brother in law.

Hunter stood up. "Señor," he said.

"Do you know who I am?" Masón said.

Someone in Jack Morrow's position, if he'd done his

research, might know that Masón was El Sucio's brother in law, and one of six men who led the cartel in El Sucio's absence.

"You are Ernesto Pérez Masón," Hunter said.

"You are well informed," Masón said.

"In this business, you're either well informed or you're dead."

Masón nodded.

"So you're the man who will be supplying the US troops while they are guests in our country."

Hunter nodded.

"There is always money to be made in war," Masón said.

Hunter nodded again. "I think it was Machiavelli who said the time to buy is when blood is in the streets."

Masón laughed. "It was Baron Rothschild, actually."

Hunter smiled. "I hope you don't mind, I helped myself," he said, holding up his half-smoked Cohiba.

"You can smoke my cigars," Masón said. "Unlike in your country, we have no difficulty importing things from Cuba."

Hunter looked around the villa admiringly. "If you don't mind me saying," he said, "you're not safe here."

"You don't think so?"

"They love to hit places like this," Hunter said, nodding toward the ocean. "They've been hitting targets along the coast."

"Yes they have, but they've been hitting targets in the city as well. I might as well be somewhere I like."

Hunter shrugged. "You're used to dealing with this better than me," he said.

"But you have experience with air strikes?"

"I served in the Middle East."

"I see," Masón said. "My people tell me you are a Texan."

"Yes I am."

"Born in El Paso."

"Yes, sir."

Fawn set up the legend perfectly. If there was one thing you could rely on the CIA for, it was to create ghosts.

"You'll have heard we attacked your state today."

"I did hear."

"It's nothing personal."

"Of course," Hunter said.

"It's all strategy."

"You don't need to explain."

Masón nodded. He looked at his watch, a jewel encrusted monstrosity that covered his wrist like a handcuff, and called out to one of his men.

"Traer el Americano," he said.

Hunter's heart sank. He'd been through scenes like this before. It was the reason he'd been so upset when Fawn told him more assets were being sent in.

"We caught this American entering the province through the mountains today."

Jesús and another man came up the stairs, dragging their captive.

Hunter had no doubt he was the CIA asset Fawn had told him about. He was young, about twenty-five, a shag of blonde hair coming down over his eyes. He looked like a surfer. Hunter could have been him if he hadn't been selected for Mantis.

"A test of loyalty," Masón said, holding out a handgun.

"I've killed better men than this," Hunter said.

He took the gun and walked over to the captive. The man's face was bloodied. His lips and eyes were swollen from where he'd been punched. There were cuts on his arms and his finger nails had been ripped out.

He'd been interrogated.

"DEA?" Hunter said.

"CIA," Masón said.

Hunter looked the man in the eye. He was a kid. He was scared. He didn't know who Hunter was but he was nurturing the hope he wasn't alone. The agency wouldn't have told him about Hunter, but he'd have guessed he wasn't the only asset in the state.

Hunter could have saved him.

He had a gun in his hand, which was more than he needed.

He shoved the barrel of the gun into the man's mouth. The man began struggling. He tried to scream but the gun muffled his cries.

Hunter shoved the gun far into the man's throat, far enough that he began to gag. Then he pulled the trigger.

FORTY-FOUR

When Hunter got back to the hotel he went straight to the bathroom. Adelita was in the bed but he didn't speak to her.

He washed his hands.

The CIA guy's blood was on them and he kept washing them with soap and water until the water began to scald him.

"What's the matter?" Adelita said.

He took a deep breath and buried the memory of the man's face.

"Why are you still here?" he said. "I told you to run. It's not safe here."

"I couldn't run. They would have come after us."

"Why would they come after you?"

"Because of you. Because I sided with a gringo. An outsider. Even if they do business with you, they wouldn't allow someone like me to make a decision like that."

"And if you stay? What then?"

"I don't know, Jack. But I couldn't run. They had someone outside my house. If I ran, they'd know. They'd have stopped the car. They'd have brought us back. Or hurt us."

Hunter sighed. He'd fucked her. He'd drawn too much attention to her. Her only hope now was if he made it look like she meant nothing to him. Any more special treatment and it would only cement their suspicions.

He looked at her. She looked back into his eyes.

He'd have to break her heart.

He'd have to make her hate him so much that when she went back to work, they'd believe her when she cursed his name.

It was the only way to save her.

The right thing to do.

He wouldn't go easy on her. He wouldn't show weakness. Hurting women had never come naturally to him but he'd been trained to do anything to anyone.

He pictured his hands around her throat.

He pictured her screaming and trying to get him off her.

He wondered if the violence would be enough to get rid of her. She'd seen a lot of that. She'd seen him throw a man off the balcony and hadn't flinched.

It might take more than that to get her to leave.

He shook his head.

She had her arms around him and was looking into his eyes.

"Jack, what's wrong?"

"Nothing."

"Something's wrong. You look like there's a monster inside you."

"There is a monster inside me," he said.

"Well let me tame it," she said, opening his jeans.

"No, Adelita. I have to get rid of you. The more time

you spend with me, the less your people will trust you. When I leave, you'll have no one."

She nodded. "I know," she said.

"So what are we going to do?" he said.

"I'll leave you, Jack. After tonight I'll leave you. I promise."

"That won't be enough."

"I'll cry. I'll go back to the club and I'll say nothing. They'll ask me what's wrong and I'll tell them you raped me."

"Will they believe that?"

"Why would I lie?"

Hunter thought about it. She was right. "I'll act violently when they're watching me again. I'll make them believe it."

"They'll tell me I deserve whatever happened and then they'll let me get back to work."

Hunter noticed that she hadn't brought back the money he'd given her.

"When things settle down, when they forget about me, I'll get out of here."

"Okay," he said.

"But let me have one more night with you," she said.

He should have told her no. He should have sent her away there and then, but he wanted her. His mind was full of her. His fingers were in her hair and her scent filled his nostrils. He threw her on the bed and began to strip her. His mouth was on hers. Then it was on her breasts. Then he was inside her, and a pleasure that erased everything else.

She screamed his name when he climaxed.

Afterwards he called down to the lobby and ordered a bottle of champagne and two glasses. She lay with her head on his chest and he played with her hair.

They didn't get up when the waiter brought in an ice bucket, the bottle, and two flutes.

"I can't wait to get away from this place," she said when the waiter left.

"And where would you go?"

"I don't know."

"If you could go anywhere in the world, if you were completely free to have whatever you wanted, where would you go?" Hunter said.

"More important than where I was going is who I was going with," she said.

"What would you like?"

"What every girl would like."

"And what's that?"

"I'd like a nice man, a handsome man, with a good heart, who loved me. I'd like him to take care of me, to protect me. And for him to love the people I love."

"I think you could find a man like that."

"You show me where he is and I'll go there," Adelita said, smiling, but there was a sadness in her eyes.

"With your looks, you could have whatever man you wanted."

"You think in Texas the men would go for a girl like me?"

"I know they would."

"I don't know," she said. "They like bigger breasts in America."

"Who told you that?"

"All the girls know it. That's why we have so many cosmetic surgeons here. We have the best cosmetic surgeons in the world here. Better than Los Angeles. Better than New York. Better than Miami."

"Really?"

"Of course. Where do you think all these whore's come from? The cartel pays for everything. You want bigger tits, they pay. You want bigger ass, they pay. Nose, cheeks, everything."

"Have you had any work?"

She laughed. "Not yet, but I have a wish list."

"I wouldn't change a thing," Adelita.

"No, really," she said, standing up. She was naked and she showed him her body. "These breasts, they should be bigger. I think they should be really big."

"How big?"

"The implants, they measure them in cc's. They go all the way up to eight hundred cc's."

"You wouldn't need that much."

"No, I think three hundreds would look nice on me. High profile."

"High profile?"

"They stick out more. Pointier."

"Like two torpedoes."

She laughed. "Exactly."

"So that's what you'd get?"

"I wouldn't stop there. I told you. We have the best in the world. The cartel pays for everything if you're one of their girls."

Hunter nodded. He wondered if she was still one of their girls. She had been when he found her. He might have permanently fucked that up for her.

"What else would you get?"

She turned and arched her back, sticking out her ass. "Ass. Definitely ass. I'd never find a good American man without more ass."

Hunter grabbed her ass in his hand.

"Not this ass. This ass is perfect."

"It's perfect," she said, "but it could be more perfect if there was more of it. After I did that, and maybe some facial contouring, then I could go to America."

"You don't need all that to find love in America."

"But it would help. It would give me an advantage."

"I guess so," Hunter said.

"Unless you want to bring me home with you," she said.

She reached over and pulled the blanket off him, admiring what she saw. He grabbed her and turned her onto her hands and knees. She teased him with her ass, swaying slowly from side to side.

"It's perfect, Adelita."

She reached back and grabbed it. "Imagine it was bigger," she said. "Rounder. Like a cherry." She gave herself a smack to emphasize the point.

"It's like a cherry now," he said.

"Imagine it was all yours, Jack. Whenever you wanted it."

He knew what she was doing. She hadn't given up on him yet. She was still holding out hope.

She'd never leave.

She'd stay in Culiacán and spend the money he'd given her on a boob job.

He thrust into her and the pleasure, the desire, flowed through him like a drug.

FORTY-FIVE

Hunter woke early and left Adelita sleeping in the bed. He went to the lobby and asked if he could use their phone to make an international call. He made no effort to hide the number, which would trace back to an invented Texan drug trafficker, or to prevent anyone from overhearing what he said.

The phone reached Fawn but did not go through the verification measures he usually used. She would know he was calling as Jack Morrow.

"This is Morrow," he said into the receiver.

The cartel would be listening to every word he said.

"Mr. Morrow. How are you enjoying your trip?"

"It's nice," he said. "Fruitful."

"I'm glad to hear that," Fawn said.

"I'm going to have a small package delivered."

"How small?"

"Thirty keys."

"Where to?"

"Tamazula de Victoria in Durango."

"I know it."

"Go to the hotel there and ask for Capitán Mendoza. He'll handle the arrangements at the border."

"Understood."

"There will be a bigger delivery in a week. Tell Mendoza."

Hunter hung up. That should put everyone's mind at ease.

He went to the bar and watched the waitress setting up. It was still early. She was wiping the bar top, polishing cutlery, folding napkins.

He asked her for coffee and she brought him some, black, the way he'd had it last time she served him.

"You're up early," she said.

She spoke English well but with more of an accent than Adelita. She was younger too. She was very attractive. Hunter wondered what she'd done to avoid ending up under the cartel's thumb. Then again, maybe she was under the cartel's thumb here.

He was upset with himself for what was going on with Adelita. All he had to do was smack her in the face and tell her he didn't love her and she'd be gone. That's all it would take to potentially put her out of harm's way and get her back to her old life.

But instead, he kept letting it drag on.

Each time she touched him he told himself it was the last time. But each time, he let it happen again. Even as he sat there, she was upstairs in his room, in his bed, tying her fate ever more tightly to his.

He ordered more coffee and sat at the bar, waiting.

Something would happen.

Fawn was taking steps. She knew what he needed.

The cartel knew he was getting ready to ramp up busi-

ness. They'd be eager to get that first shipment across the
border.

On the TV screen above the bar he saw footage of US
troops crossing the southern border in force for the first time
in over a century.

"More coffee?" the waitress said.

He nodded.

An hour passed. Hunter was thinking he should go back
upstairs to shower and get rid of Adelita, she would be
awake by now, but the concierge came over with the phone.

"Who is it?" Hunter said to the concierge.

"Señor Calderón, señor. From the bank."

Hunter looked at his watch. It was still too early for the
bank to be open.

"Mr. Morrow."

"Yes."

"This is Calderón from Azteca."

"Yes?"

"We have received another wire."

"How much?"

"Eighteen million."

"Dollars?"

"Yes, sir."

"Thank you, Calderón," Hunter said and hung up.

That would cement it. He had no doubt the cartel knew
about the money. Twenty million would get him a seat at
whatever table he wanted.

He was about to go upstairs when he saw Adelita
coming his way. She was wearing a light blue dress that he
hadn't seen her in before. She looked like a breath of
fresh air.

His mind leapt back to the image of her wiggling her ass
in his face and he wanted her again.

That was the problem. He wanted her too much. She'd sensed it and she wasn't letting him go.

She sat on the stool next to him and asked the waitress for coffee. The waitress looked her up and down and then looked at Hunter. He nodded.

"The more people see you with me, the more they'll want to kill you if I do anything to upset them," he said to her.

"But you wouldn't do anything to upset them."

"I threw that man off the balcony."

"For me," she said, smiling.

She thought he was immune, above the law.

"You've got to leave."

"I want breakfast."

Hunter sighed. He asked the waitress to bring them something to eat. She brought eggs and salsa and tortillas. They ate together at the bar and then Adelita got up from her seat.

She leaned in to kiss him and whispered in his ear, "Don't treat me like a whore. If you treat me well, they will."

Then she strolled through the lobby and Hunter felt the pang in his heart. He'd killed her, as surely as if he pulled the trigger himself.

The waitress looked at him as she cleared away the breakfast things.

"I know that girl," she said.

Hunter nodded.

"Her daughter goes to school with my sister's daughter."

Hunter didn't speak.

He went upstairs and had a shower and dressed. Adelita had arranged for the hotel to do his laundry and it felt good to put on clean clothes. When he went back to the lobby, Jesús was waiting for him at the bar.

"Mr. Morrow," he said.

"You're alone," Hunter said.

"We're business partners now. No need for all the extra men."

"Where I come from, we call that progress."

Jesús nodded. He was sipping a cocktail and asked Hunter if he wanted one.

Hunter nodded and the waitress brought him one. It was bourbon with sugar.

"To your health," Hunter said and they touched glasses.

They each drank and the waitress watched them. She was looking at Jesús like she had designs on him. She wasn't so different from Adelita after all.

"Your delivery is ready," Jesús said.

"Can you send it to Tamazula de Victoria?"

"Of course."

"Someone needs to call the hotel there and ask for Capitán Mendoza. He's a Durango policeman."

"Okay."

"He'll take the delivery and pass it on to my man."

"You're going to need to speak to the army men soon."

"How much will they let Mendoza handle?"

"A few kilos. Not more than a hundred."

"Okay, and how will I get in contact with the right person."

"You'll come to a party tonight."

"Another party?"

"Yes. It will be at the villa. I'll pick you up at eight."

FORTY-SIX

Jeff Hale was back in the east wing of the National Art Gallery, waiting in the lobby for Raquel. The place as beginning to take shape. It had come a long way in the few days since his last visit. The security screening was in place, the FBI had hired hundreds of new people from other government agencies, and was laying the ground for the largest raid in the history of US law enforcement.

They'd been zeroing in on El Sucio's location for days and had thousands of Army and National Guard troops on the ready.

They would act on Raquel's orders.

In the space of a week, Raquel had been catapulted from the depths of the FBI's middle-management, to arguably the second most powerful person in the country. With army and national guard units no under her direct control, only the president had more forces at his disposal. And the president's actions were strictly monitored.

Raquel was freer to act.

When she stepped out of the elevator, Hale noticed the change in her.

The fact he was even waiting for her, and not the other way around, showed the subtle shift in the dynamic.

Raquel had become dangerous.

She was flanked by six aides, all men, all carrying iPads, all talking at once.

"Jeff," she said, crossing the lobby. "So sorry to keep you waiting. The security here's still a shambles."

He was Jeff now. They were on a first name basis.

Hale eyed the armed guards who were stationed at every conceivable entrance to the building. They wore full body armor and carried automatic weapons. Their faces were concealed behind balaclavas.

This wasn't the America they'd been accustomed to.

It was a country at war now.

Raquel hadn't wasted a second exercising the new powers congress had given her. She was making far greater use of them than the CIA was, that much was clear.

"Come on upstairs," she said.

They all went back into the elevator, Raquel, Hale and the six aides.

"You sure you got enough guys?" he said.

Raquel smiled, unamused. "We're about to execute the largest law enforcement operation in history," she said.

"It's more than a law enforcement operation," Hale said. "You've got troops involved."

"And the Air Force," she said confidently.

They passed the paintings, the Vermeers, the Botticellis. In her office still hung the Rodin, the Degas and the Goya, but behind her desk she'd hung the Da Vinci that was previously in the main gallery.

"I see you've done a little redecorating," Hale said.

Raquel lit a cigarette and took a deep drag.

"Let's get down to brass taxes," she said.

Brass taxes, Hale thought. He wanted to laugh. Who did this woman think she was?

"We're zeroing in on a location."

"I heard the city is emptying out," Hale said.

It was all over the news. With rumors flying that El Sucio was in Chicago, people had started fleeing.

"How do we know El Sucio's not among them?" he said.

"We've cordoned off a square mile around the DuSable Bridge. No one gets out with passing a checkpoint."

Hale had a hard time believing that. It was chaos down there. The DuSable Bridge was the very heart of the city, where Michigan Avenue crossed the river. The most important buildings in the city were clustered around it.

"This man has escaped every prison he's ever been in."

"What do you want me to do, Hale?"

"I want to know what the plan is."

"I've got more troops massed around the city than have ever been deployed on US territory. I've got the Air Force, the CIA, the Army, every single federal agent watching that patch of ground. I've got military satellites and even ballistic missiles pointed at it."

"And what good are they?"

"What do you mean?"

"What good are they? All those men. All those weapons. What are you going to do? Open fire on our own city?"

"Of course not."

"Exactly."

"Exactly what?"

"What's the point in having a big gun if you can't use it?" Hale said.

She could see where this was going. It was the same place these arguments always led with Hale.

"You want to send in one of your special agents, your *enhanced operatives?*"

"Of course I do."

"But your man is all the way down in Mexico, fucking whores and spending taxpayer money, from what I hear."

"I can get him back."

"I'm not handing this over to you, Hale. You've got your shot down in Mexico."

"And El Sucio's not down there."

"You keep looking."

Hale let out a sigh. "You're just like Chancey and Moynihan. You don't care what happens as long as you're the first one in."

"Just because I don't have a dick doesn't mean I'm not going to get into a dick measuring contest," she said.

Hale laughed. "There's a sentence you don't hear every day."

"You know what I mean."

"Yes, I do. You're putting your own career before the interests of the country."

"Aren't we all?" she said.

Hale looked away. His eyes rested on the Da Vinci. It was a portrait of a Florentine aristocrat, Ginevra de' Benci, done in 1478. It had been commissioned to celebrate her marriage.

"She looks miserable," he said.

Raquel turned to look at the portrait.

"I've been doing a little reading on it," she said.

"And?"

"Arranged marriage at sixteen. You'd look miserable too."

Hale looked at his watch. "I should be on my way," he said, getting up from his seat.

"So soon?" Raquel said.

Hale looked at her. What was she cooking? He sat back down.

"Is there more you'd like to say?"

"I have something, delicate, I'd like to discuss," she said.

"I'm all ears."

She got up and locked the office door. Then she went to her desk and opened the drawer. She took out a small electronic device that looked like an old iPod and pressed play. It was a signal jammer. If anyone was listening in on their conversation, now would stop them.

"There's talk of impeachment," she said.

Hale scoffed. "You can't be serious."

She looked him in the eye.

She was serious.

Hale looked back to the portrait. He didn't know who looked more fierce, Raquel or Ginevra. Of course he'd heard the impeachment talk.

Ever since Nixon's time, the definition of high crimes and misdemeanors had pretty much been whatever a majority of the house of representatives wanted it to be. In a situation like this, with thousands dead, the question was bound to arise.

Failure to protect the nation from the most heinous attacks in its history could certainly fall within the definition.

The president had enemies.

Impeachment was always on the table.

But Hale hadn't seen this coming.

"Do you really think now is the time to be turning on our own?"

"We've got more civilian casualties than at any time since the civil war."

"And the president's doing everything he can to stop them."

"He's weak, Jeff."

"He just named you head of the FBI. Show a little gratitude."

"Gratitude?"

"And loyalty."

"He's not my lover, Jeff. If there's an opening, we should pounce."

"What are you talking about? What opening is this?"

"I know there's a majority in the house."

"Bullshit."

"I can get there."

"But why would you even want to?"

"Maybe it's time for a change of leadership."

"We've just lost hundreds of our best people. We're the embodiment of a change of leadership, Raquel."

"I want more, Jeff."

"You want to impeach the president. On what grounds?"

"Failure to protect the nation."

"And you think there's support in the house?"

"I know there is."

"I don't get it, Raquel," Jeff said. "I don't see the play. The end game."

"The point is, this is an opening. The president isn't going to get out of this intact, Jeff. You must know that."

"But at least let him bring in El Sucio first. This is the opening round. Let the dust settle."

"When do you think the head of the FBI is going to have a better chance to take a stab then now, when she's controlling the army and has troops in the streets."

"Jesus Christ, Raquel. If anyone heard you speak like this."

"I'm not talking to anyone."

"No, you're not."

"I'm talking to you, Jeff."

"And what the hell would be in this for me?"

"A shakeup."

"I'm already head of the CIA. That's the top of the ladder for me."

"You're thinking too small, Jeff."

Hale shook his head.

"I don't like this talk, Raquel. I don't like it one bit. And I don't see how pushing for impeachment right now would be anything other than naked opportunism."

"This is going ahead, with or without you."

"The senate will never remove him from office."

"You let me worry about that."

"You need a supermajority."

"We're at war Jeff. The world is a different place than it was a week ago. There are people dying of asphyxiation in the streets. The people want someone to pay."

"El Sucio will pay."

"They want more blood than that."

"We'll blow Mexico to shit."

"It won't be enough."

"You think they want to remove the president from office?"

"I know they do. And you know who they're going to want to replace him?"

"Let me guess. You?"

"Us, Jeff. Us."

"Us?"

"You as president. Me as vice president. Can't you see it?"

"You've lost your mind."

"The heads of the CIA and FBI, leading the country in this new era when every danger is possible, every threat is real. Keeping the country safe. Taking the fight to those who would hurt us. The people are scared Jeff. The people want the power back. They want to be back on top."

"We are on top."

"It doesn't feel like that, Jeff. They see bodies in the street. They think if a drug dealer can do this, what the hell can the Chinese do? Or the Russians? Or the Arabs?"

"You've lost your mind."

"Just think about it, Jeff."

"I will not. Raquel, frankly, I don't even trust you. You'd set me up for this and then watch it blow up in my face."

"How could I show you I can be trusted?" Raquel said, leaning forward, letting him see down the front of her blouse.

"Forget about it. I can get tail a lot easier ways than this. This is edging on treason."

"No it's not. We're talking about a lawful vote in congress. There's nothing treasonous about it."

"Well it tastes like treason. Like betrayal."

"What if I let your guys go in and take out El Sucio?"

"My guys?"

"You've got assets on hand, don't you? Other programs. You've got eight guys in Graylock."

"Seven."

"What happened?"

"One of them was killed in Culiacán last night."

"How many of them are available right now?"

"Five. The other two are in Sinaloa."

"Well, what if I let your Graylocks go in and take out El Sucio. You come out with the head of the devil. Congress announces impeachment proceedings against the president. Even if the senate doesn't vote our way, you'd be the top candidate to run in the next cycle."

Hale shook his head. What the fuck was this bitch up to? It didn't make sense.

"You're crazy," he said.

"All I'm asking is you lean in favor of impeachment when you're asked about it. Don't oppose it."

"And you'll let my Graylocks take out El Sucio?"

"You just send them to Chicago. I'll let them get the glory."

Hale was flabbergasted. It really was a new world. Just days ago, letting Graylock agents operate on US territory would have put Hale in prison. Now, Raquel was talking about using them to launch a presidential bid.

"I've really got to go," Hale said.

"Just think about it."

He paused. Weighed things. She wasn't asking for much. Not yet.

"I'll send the Graylocks to Chicago."

"That's all I ask," Raquel said.

She got up from her seat and walked around her desk. She stopped in front of him and leaned forward.

He could see all the way down her blouse. She was flaunting it. Her bra was an expensive, black, lace number.

"Just keep an open mind and maybe you'll be the next president of the country."

Hale rose to his feet and backed away from her. He unlocked the door and hurried out of the office without another word. He was spooked. Something very strange had just happened. That was not how the heads of the CIA and FBI were supposed to talk.

It was tantamount to plotting a military coup.

Outside, he got in his car and told the driver to take him to the hospital. The car pulled up outside the visitor entrance and he insisted on going in alone.

"Protocol, sir," his guard said.

"My wife's in a fucking coma," Hale said. "There's no protocol for that."

The security detail agreed to wait outside and Hale hurried in. He stopped at the gift store and grabbed a bunch of flowers.

"How much?" he said, pulling out his wallet.

"Twenty dollars, sir."

He stuffed a twenty in the clerk's hand and rushed up to the visitor desk.

"Jeff Hale," he said. "I'm here to see Martha Hale."

The nurse looked up the visitor list and found his name.

"There have been a few changes since your last visit, Mr. Hale. You'll be going to the third flood."

Hale stormed away from her. Last visit. She didn't have to sound so judgmental. His wife had been in a coma for nine years, to the day, and he hadn't always let so many months pass between visits.

He got in the elevator and pushed the button for the third floor. When it stopped he stepped out into the corridor and searched for the nurse's station. He asked for his wife's room. Room fourteen.

As he neared the door his hand began to shake.

Three months. How had he not been here in three months? He suddenly felt overcome with guilt.

He pushed open the door and the staleness of the air hit him. There was a vase on the dresser and it was empty. He put the flowers in it but didn't bother unwrapping them. He didn't give them any water.

He walked to the bed and sat down next to his wife. He looked at her for the first time in three months. She looked the same. She always looked the same.

"Sorry it took me so long," he whispered. "I didn't want to miss your anniversary."

Nine years to the day. He could remember every detail, every second of what had happened. His wife had been in this hospital ever since.

He sat there for a while, mulling over the things Raquel had said. It was a trap. He was sure of it. But it was tempting.

As Raquel had said, even without impeachment, there were a lot of reasons why the head of the CIA might be a top contender in the next election. Especially if he was the one to bring in El Sucio.

He stood up and went back to the corridor. He pulled his cell from his pocket and dialed Fawn's number.

"Has he checked in?"

"He's getting closer, boss."

"Tell him to find out about Chicago. I need to know what's happening there."

"He's working on that."

"At any cost, Fawn. I want anything he can get about Chicago."

"At any cost?"

"You know what that means?"

"Yes, sir."

He hung up.

He looked up and down the corridor. It was empty.

He went back in to Martha's room.

FORTY-SEVEN

The next time Hunter called Fawn it was Hale's voice that answered.

"What's your status, soldier?"

Hunter was surprised. "Where's Fawn?"

"You don't have to sound so disappointed."

Hunter let out a laugh. "This isn't what I signed up for."

"Relax," Fawn's voice said. "I'm here too. We've got you on speaker."

"Anyone else there?"

"Just the two of us."

Hale's voice came on again.

"We just got word the first transfer was successful."

"Someone picked it up."

"Thirty kilos. One of our guys took delivery."

"Worked with that cop down there? Capitán Mendoza?" Hunter said.

"All worked fine. Everything's set for the next delivery."

Hunter cleared his throat. "Hale, did you send a Graylock guy into Culiacán?"

"Yes. President's orders."

"I had to kill him."

"I know, Hunter."

"It's not exactly my favorite thing."

"I know. I'm sorry. The president forced my hand."

"How many more of them are down here?"

"Two."

"Call them out."

"I can't. President wants them both in Culiacán tracking down different angles."

"There are no different angles."

"Don't break my balls, Hunter."

"Fuck," Hunter said, more to himself than to Hale. "You know they're going to make me kill everyone they catch. Prove my loyalty."

"They won't be caught, Hunter."

"They better keep their heads down."

Fawn broke in. "What's next, Hunter? I got you twenty million. That's got to get you to the people that matter."

"Yes. I'm going back to the villa tonight. It belongs to the guy I finalized the deal with."

"Who was that?"

"You'll never guess."

"No I won't," Fawn said.

"Masón."

"Ernesto Pérez Masón?" Hale said.

"The one and only," Hunter said.

"He's the second in command after El Sucio, isn't he?"

"More or less," Fawn said.

"I'll be with him and his top guys tonight."

Hale spoke up. "Hunter. We need you to zero in on Chicago. Anything at all you can find out."

"You still think that's where he is?"

"The FBI is certain of it. The city's surrounded by

troops. There's a square mile downtown and they think he's in."

"Okay," Hunter said.

"Find out anything at all," Hale repeated. "No matter the cost."

The phrase, 'no matter the cost,' was a code in the Black Ops division. It meant that Hunter was should find out about Chicago even if it meant his own death, assuming he could get the information back to Hale. There was no amount of collateral damage that was too high.

"No matter the cost?" Hunter said.

Repeating the phrase was protocol.

"That's right, Hunter."

Hunter was quiet for a second. "Okay," he said. "I'll bring the cell."

If he had the cell he could take greater risks because he didn't have to think about getting back to the city. He only needed time to make a call.

"You know Chicago, Hunter?" Hale said.

"Yes, sir."

"You know the bridge on the Miracle Mile? Right where Trump Tower is, and all those old newspaper buildings?"

"Yes, sir."

"They think he's within a mile of there."

"I understand, sir."

Hale really had a hard on for this Chicago theory. Hunter wondered what had changed.

"Don't you want to send me in there?" Hunter said.

"You stay where you are. We're putting five Graylocks in and besides, there's always the chance the Chicago theory's a bust and he's in Sinaloa."

FORTY-EIGHT

Jesús arrived at eight on the dot. Hunter was in the bar waiting for him. He had the cell in the inside pocket of the fleece-lined denim jacket, the location tracker on. Any data on it was accessible to Fawn. He didn't bring a gun.

"Listo, gringo?" Jesús said.

"Listo," Hunter said.

He left some money on the bar and followed Jesús to the car.

Jesús had two girls in the back of a stretch limo with opaque windows. There was a driver who patted down Hunter and ignored the phone. The driver's compartment was separated by a glass partition that was also opaque. Once inside the limo, you couldn't see out.

"This beats a blindfold," Hunter said.

Jesús shrugged.

"Ladies, this is Jack. Jack, this is Estrella and Catalina."

The girls gave him their hands and he kissed them.

Jesús sat next to Catalina and she wrapped her arms around him. Hunter figured that left Estrella to him.

He put his hand on her thigh and she turned to him.

"Welcome to Sinaloa," she said, and took out a vial.

She poured some cocaine from the vial onto her cleavage and leaned in to him.

Hunter snorted it from her chest and then kissed her. It felt good. The coke flooded his veins and made him feel confident. He hoped it wouldn't make him careless.

"So, Estrella," Hunter said. "You speak english?"

She nodded.

"Tell me then, what can I expect from a party like this."

Estrella opened her top and showed him her breasts. She took one in her hand and pulled it toward her mouth, sucking the nipple.

"I see," Hunter said.

Jesús laughed. "Don't worry, gringo. It's going to be fun. You haven't lived until you've partied with the Sinaloa cartel."

Catalina spread her legs and pulled up her skirt. She was wearing pink lace panties and she pulled them aside and sprinkled cocaine on her skin.

Estrella leaned forward. She licked the coke from Catalina's skin.

Jesús looked at Hunter.

Hunter nodded.

"Something to drink?" Jesús said.

He opened a fridge in the center console and pulled out a bottle of champagne and some glasses. He poured the drinks and the girls immediately began pouring it over their bodies and licking it off each other.

Hunter watched.

The ride seemed longer than the first time but when they arrived he saw they were at the same place. He left the car with Estrella on his arm and they walked up the steps of the villa on a red velvet carpet.

There were cars everywhere.

Armed security guards watched the guests.

"Welcome back," Jesús said, and let Hunter and Estrella enter first.

The villa looked a lot different from when he'd been there the night before. There were hundreds of people at the party. They were everywhere. Up in the the balcony overlooking the entrance, in the area by the big fire where he'd shot the Graylock, on the porch beyond it leading to the pool.

There was a DJ playing techno music by the window.

"Come on," Hunter said to Estrella and lead her toward the fire.

Dozens of chandeliers had been hoisted to the ceiling since the night before.

A naked woman with a tuxedo collar around her neck came up to him with a silver tray. Hunter took two glasses of champagne and handed one to Estrella.

"Thank you," she said, eyeing the server like she was a threat.

They walked up past the fire and Hunter took everything in. Cartel guys were partying, drinking, doing coke and other drugs. The women all seemed to be prostitutes. Anyone could fuck anyone.

They went out to the back and torches lit up the entire pool area. The pool was a glowing turquoise jewel and it was full of naked women and senior cartel guys, fat with hairy backs, or the more junior guys, tanned and ripped with long hair and shaped beards.

Beyond the pool, down on the beach, spits were grilling meat.

Hunter estimated about four hundred people were there.

He hadn't seen Masón yet, or any other of the cartel's top generals, but he was sure they were there, most likely on the upper floor overlooking the pool.

"Wait here for me," Hunter said to Estrella and went to the washroom.

The washroom was like something you'd find at a club, built for the public, not for a family. The men's and women's stalls were separated by a long sink that anyone could use.

Hunter went into a stall and checked his location on the cell phone. He was on the coast, close to where he'd estimated the night before.

He sent the location to Fawn.

An air strike was the last thing he needed.

When he got back to the pool, Estrella was gone. He was glad. He got another drink and a cigar and sat by the pool watching girls making out with each other.

Some cartel guys were watching too, encouraging them. They all knew who Hunter was but had been told to let him be.

Hunter lit the cigar and was just sitting back to smoke it when Masón, Jesús and some other men came out onto the balcony overlooking the pool.

Masón had a microphone. He welcomed everyone and made a toast.

Then the party continued and Hunter sucked on the cigar.

About five minutes later, a junior cartel guy came to him and told him his presence was requested upstairs.

Hunter followed the man through the villa and up the stairs. The entire second floor was one large area opening onto the balcony that stretched the length of the building.

Masón was on the balcony with the other senior cartel members.

"Ah, Mr. Morrow," he said, "so good of you to come."

"My pleasure," Hunter said.

There were thirteen men on the balcony including Jesús and Masón. Masón introduced the three most important of them. Hunter recognized all of them from Fawn's intel.

There was Dr. Enrique Belmar, El Sucio's fixer who handled many of the finer details of the cartel's operations in the US.

There was Sebastian Mendiluce, an Argentine banker who handled financing.

There was Mauricio Cáceres, a former general in the Mexican army who handled many of the arrangements that the cartel required to get their cargoes up to the US border.

"I understand that you are going to need help at the Durango border," Cáceres said.

"That's correct general", Hunter said. "I'm sure Masón told you of the current arrangement."

"Yes. The current arrangement with the police will not work. My men are already tracking down your friend, Capitán Mendoza."

"Capitán Mendoza gave me good prices," Hunter said.

Hunter thought back to the meeting at the hotel. Poor Mendoza. The army would skin him alive.

"The army will give you reliable performance at," the general paused, "fair prices," he said.

"And if I pay Masón, he can pay you and you can take care of the army for me?"

"Yes, that will work very well."

"What's the cut?"

"Thirty percent."

Hunter looked toward Masón. Maybe Cáceres really was that greedy, or maybe they were just seeing how he'd react. He was going to react how any sane man would react.

"I'm afraid that's not going to be possible," he said.

Cáceres laughed. "What's possible can change very quickly when your life is on the line," he said.

"Is my life on the line?" Hunter said, looking Cáceres in the eye.

"Every man's life is on the line, every minute he is alive."

"I see," Hunter said. He looked at Masón. "Thank you very much for your hospitality," he said. "Please, don't let me keep you from your other guests."

Hunter turned his back on them and made for the door. If Cáceres wanted to put a bullet in his back and fuck up a hundred million a week for Masón, that was on him.

"Mr. Morrow," Masón said, "don't leave."

"I don't have time to stand around, pretending to nego-tiate with a delivery boy," Hunter said.

Cáceres stepped forward.

"Who are you calling delivery boy?"

"You, you fat fuck," Hunter said.

Cáceres drew a gun. It was some gold-plated, jewel-encrusted statement piece that was triple the weight it needed to be. He pointed it at Hunter's chest.

Hunter didn't move.

Cáceres rose the gun a little higher, so it pointed at Hunter's forehead.

The men were about ten feet apart.

Cáceres pulled the trigger. At the last moment he flicked his wrist slightly, so that the bullet grazed the top of Hunter's hair as it flew over him. It was a nice trick. For a split second, Hunter thought he'd called the wrong man's bluff.

All the men laughed. Cáceres put his gun back in its holster beneath his jacket.

Hunter took two steps forward.

"Do that again," he said to Cáceres.

Cáceres hesitated.

"Pull your gun again," Hunter said.

Cáceres thought about it. He was about to do it. Hunter was about to grab it from him and kill him. But Masón stopped them.

"Gentlemen," he said. "I think we should give our new friend a chance to say what he wants."

Hunter looked at them.

"I want the same deal anyone else would get."

"No one else is trying to move this much product."

"Bullshit," Hunter said.

Cáceres looked at Masón.

Masón gave him a nod.

Cáceres sighed. "Diez por ciento."

Hunter looked at Masón. "Ten percent and he guarantees everything from the border of Sinaloa to the gates of the US bases.

"He can't guarantee."

"For ten percent he can fucking guarantee," Hunter said.

Masón looked at Cáceres. Cáceres nodded.

It was done.

"Okay," Hunter said. "Is that it? Are we good now? I'll get the money ready for next week. My guy will pick it up again from Tamazula."

"No need," Cáceres said. "Your guy can drive through Tamazula on the highway, all the way to Culiacán."

"Really?"

"Of course. I *guarantee* it."

Hunter didn't like the way Cáceres said that but it didn't matter. This deal would never take place. Hunter would be gone.

"Okay, okay," Masón said. "Enough business. We're here to party, no?"

Jesús handed Hunter a glass of scotch, neat, in a heavy crystal tumbler.

"You're going to need this, gringo," Jesús said.

Hunter wondered what he meant when some men entered the room and told Masón everything was ready.

Masón was excited. He led everyone down the stairs and through the party out to the pool area. Hunter followed, Jesús by his side.

"What's he got planned?" Hunter said.

"You probably won't like it," Jesús said.

Hunter nodded.

They walked past the pool, gathering more of the crowd as they went to the beach. Torches lit their way and the moon over the ocean looked beautiful. Even the distant glow of air strikes looked pretty.

On the beach, men were grilling meat on spits over huge fires and as they got closer, the smell of the meat hit Hunter.

"Tienes hambre," Masón said to him when they reached the fires.

Hunter nodded.

"I could eat."

"I'm glad to hear it," Masón said.

There was a cheer back in the direction of the villa and Hunter looked up. Beyond the crowd, Hunter saw group of four men dragging two prisoners onto the beach.

"Fuck," Hunter said under his breath.

Jesús heard him but was not surprised. "No one really likes this," Jesús said. "But we must pretend."

"Why?"

"It's tradition," Jesús said.

The men pushed the prisoners and Hunter could tell they were Americans. They were naked, bruised, their hands tied in front of them. If they slowed, the men pushed them. When they saw the fires and spits they began to beg and cry.

"No, please, no," they begged, but the men just laughed and kept pushing them forward.

They were Hale's Graylocks.

"We caught these men entering our territory," Jesús said.

Hunter nodded.

"Well if they're fucking feds, I'm not going to lose any sleep watching them die."

"You're a harsh mother fucker, Morrow."

Hunter shrugged. "Guerra es guerra."

"Cierto," Jesús said.

They watched as Masón made a big display of pulling the men toward the fire. The men struggled, begging for mercy. They weren't faking it. They were really scared. They knew what was coming.

As men began tying them to steel rods, their wrists and ankles attached to the rod with steel wire behind their backs, Masón gave a speech. He talked about how the cartel was growing from strength to strength. He said he was not taking over. He said no one could ever take over from El Sucio, who he referred to by his full name, Segundo José Heredia.

He told them not to think for one second that every-thing that was happening wasn't part of a plan. The US invasion. The trial of Heredia. Even the air strikes. All of it was playing into their hands, was going to make them more powerful than they'd ever been, and was going to ensure that their power reached right to the very heart of the American government.

Everyone applauded, and then four men lifted the first captive from the ground and placed the rod on specially erected stands over the fire. The man screamed a bloodcurdling scream as the flames licked his body.

The skin singed and tightened instantly.

The screaming even made the cartel men cringe.

They cheered and cringed at the same time as the man was slowly rotated over the fire.

The spit was lowered slowly and as the man cooked, the screaming grew and grew, until it stopped.

Hunter watched it all. He watched the man's body hair, and the hair on his head and face burn away. He watched the skin tighten and crackle. He watched the fat begin to render and drip from the body.

He looked at the second prisoner and wondered what that poor bastard was thinking.

Did he know that if the president had kept out of it, he'd be in Chicago right now, preparing to become famous as one of the men who brought in El Sucio?

The man's eyes were like big orbs of terror.

"Poor bastard," Jesús said, also looking at him.

Hunter nodded.

"At least for the first one it's over."

Hunter nodded at that too.

Then Masón stepped forward. They took the cooked body down from the spit and Masón, brandishing a butcher's knife, cut a slice of meat from the man's thigh.

In front of the crowd, he put it in his mouth and began chewing.

Everyone cheered.

Then he called Hunter to join him.

Hunter stepped forward and everyone cheered again. The loved it. Hunter took a piece of meat and put it in his mouth. He chewed it, cursing the president and Hale with each bite.

Then he swallowed.

As the second man was put over the fire, Hunter and Jesús went back up to the pool.

"How do you feel?" Jesús asked him.

"I don't know," Hunter said.

He went to some bushes and threw up. Then they got some scotch from a naked waitress. When they got to the pool, they sat on sofas and Jesús started talking business.

"You're going to make me a very rich man, gringo."

"How's that?" Hunter said.

"As your handler I've moved up a few rungs in the organization."

"Congratulations," Hunter said.

They touched glasses and then Hunter saw someone he recognized.

"What the fuck?" he said.

FORTY-NINE

"Adelita?" Hunter said. "What the fuck are you doing here?"

"Happy to see me, babe?"

"Don't call me that."

"I'm your woman now."

"Fuck me," Hunter said.

He turned to look at Jesús, who seemed amused by the situation.

"This isn't funny, Jesús."

Jesús kept laughing.

"If people think you're my woman, they're going to use you to get to me."

Hunter turned to Jesús, seeking backup.

"Es verdad," Jesús said to her. "Es peligroso."

Adelita looked at the two of them. She was uncomfortable, vulnerable.

Hunter made room for her and she sat next to him. She was wearing a silver, sequined dress. Most of the people were still on the beach watching the Americans die. Adelita looked in that direction.

"What's going on?" she said.

"They're cooking American cops," Hunter said.

She nodded. She'd seen that sort of thing before.

"Tu novio comió," Jesús said.

"I had to," Hunter said.

He looked at Adelita.

This was where she'd always wanted to be. On the sofas by the pool with the big shots. It was where all the women in Culiacán wanted to be. It was their only ticket.

"What do you think of my ass," she said to Jesús.

She turned to show him and he grabbed a cheek in his hand.

"Poco pequeño," he said.

"I told you," she said to Hunter.

Hunter smacked it. "Looks fine to me."

"I went to the cosmetic surgeons today."

"Why?" Hunter said.

"To make an appointment."

Jesús was nodding in approval. Hunter sighed.

"They're going to make it rounder?"

"Yes," she said.

People were coming back from the beach. The Americans were dead. Hunter could smell the meat.

Masón's staff were setting up a screen in front of the pool. It was the kind of screen people used with projectors. There was going to be some kind of show.

"What's that for?" he said to Jesús.

"I'm not sure. The boss has some surprise planned."

"Another one?"

Jesús nodded.

They waited, sipping scotch and smoking, and Adelita looked back defiantly at every woman who glanced their way.

When Masón arrived, Jesús got up and went to him.

"Are you happy I'm here?" Adelita said when Jesús left.

Hunter looked at her. She was beautiful. In a way, he was happy she was there. But the smell of the cooking American agents hit his nostrils and he remembered what was at stake.

"I told you not to come," he said.

"You're ashamed of me."

"I'm not ashamed of you."

"You want to fuck these other whores."

Hunter shrugged.

"I won't stop you. If you fuck them I won't say anything. Just don't do it in front of me."

"It's not that, Adelita."

"What is it?"

"If anything goes wrong with my business. If I disagree with the cartel on the price, or some drugs get seized, anything."

"They'll come for me."

"Yes."

"I don't care."

"You'll care when it happens."

"Every woman I know wants a boss. Every one of them. Can't I want one too?"

"I'm not a boss."

She put her hand on his crotch. "You, Jack, are a very big man."

"You're playing with fire."

She pouted. "I have friends who've had cartel boyfriends."

"And how did it turn out for them?"

"Good. They got money. They got surgeries. They got

clothes and jewelry and purses. They went to Miami and Las Vegas."

"Christmas all year long," Hunter said.

"Yes. And if their boyfriend got killed, no one hurt them. Even if the cartel killed the man, no one came after the women."

"It will be different with me. I'm not in the cartel. I'm American. They'll use you against me, Adelita. You know that."

She looked into his eyes. "Then let me enjoy the time we have. Maybe we'll have five years together. Maybe ten."

"Maybe much less," Hunter said.

He knew they'd be lucky to have five more days together, but he couldn't tell her that.

"Don't come after me," he said, getting up. "Find another man. Your ass is plenty round for these guys."

He walked away. He was already detaching himself from her in his mind. If she kept playing this game she was going to get herself killed and she was smart enough to know it. As soon as he left the city, as soon as they put things together, they'd kill her. There was no point hoping otherwise.

"Jack," she called but he didn't stop.

He wanted to see what was going on with the screen.

An audience had gathered in front of it and they made room for him. Masón was clearly excited. He was speaking to his men, pouring them tequila, getting ready for another big show.

When everyone was gathered, he got in front of the crowd and addressed them.

He said they were in for a special surprise. A projector had been brought out and he turned it on. The screen lit up with footage of an American city. Hunter recognized the skyline.

It was Chicago.

The footage was being taken from a helicopter.

"Es en vivo," Masón said.

The footage was live.

Hunter suddenly got a sinking feeling in his stomach. He had to contact Fawn. The phone in his jacket pocket had been modified so that any data on it was immediately accessible to Langley. He took a risk and reached into his breast pocket, took it out, and switched on the camera. He held it down by his pants pocket and pointed it at the screen.

"Chicago," he said aloud, for the phone's benefit. "Live. I can't believe it."

Masón continued his speech.

"Todo sucede por una razón," he said.

Everything happens for a reason.

He said everything that was happening was part of the cartel's plan and that it would make them all richer and more powerful than ever.

The crowd applauded.

Hunter noticed that Adelita was by his side and he put the phone in his pocket. The sound would still be recording.

Langley would have seen enough anyway.

A helicopter over Lake Michigan. It would be intercepted in a matter of minutes.

The camera in the helicopter panned across the skyline.

The crowd watched patiently.

"Pronto," Masón said.

Soon.

And then the camera panned left. They were looking at the Willis Tower.

Formerly the Sears Tower.

It had been the tallest building in the world at one time. One-hundred-ten stories high, seventeen hundred feet. The height was limited not by the architects or engineers, but by the Federal Aviation Commission. When Sears commissioned the building in 1969, they were the largest retailer in the world. They were long gone and now, United Airlines was its current main tenant, their global headquarters occupying twenty floors of the building.

After 9/11, several high profile tenants left the building for fear of a terrorist attack. That fear was well founded. The tower was the only building in America taller than the World Trade Center, with the sole exception of the new World Trade Center.

The camera zoomed in on the building.

"Fuck me," Hunter said.

He pulled the phone back out of his pocket and pointed it at the screen.

"The Sears Tower," he said. "They're going to hit it."

In 2006, the FBI arrested Narseal Batiste and six other men for plotting to destroy the tower. The men were all members of a bizarre religious cult known as the Universal Divine Saviors. The FBI said the group lacked the means to carry out the attack but it raised the profile of the building as a potential target.

El Sucio was about to prove that. He was about to succeed where the Universal Divine Saviors had failed.

Hunter knew it.

Beyond the tower, he noticed two lights in the sky. They were growing rapidly and he realized they were fighter jets intercepting the helicopter.

So they were paying attention to the cell data.

Missiles flew from the jets and hit the helicopter but it was already too late.

As the missiles hit the chopper, the base of the tower, still visible in the feed, lit up in a series of bright lights, like strobes.

The helicopter was in trouble. The cameraman was screaming at the pilot. It began to spin out of control. The camera remained on the entire time. As the pilot struggled with the controls, the cameraman kept recording.

The chopper was rapidly losing altitude.

As it spun, the camera panned across the city and the collapse of the tower was visible each time the camera panned past. In the time it took for the chopper to rotate seven times, the tower collapsed in a mountain of dust and smoke.

Three more spins and it hit the water.

The feed died.

Hunter put the phone back in his pocket and scanned the crowd. Even Masón was speechless.

They'd just witnessed the perfect attack. The perfect statement.

The cartel's 'fuck you' to the world.

There was a moment of stunned silence and then a slow applause began from Jesús and the other men standing with Masón. The crowd picked up the cue and soon everyone was cheering.

Adelita squeezed Hunter's hand.

She wasn't cheering.

Neither was Hunter.

Masón looked at him but Hunter didn't applaud. The legend said he was a drug dealer, not a traitor. He left the crowd and went inside the villa.

Adelita tried to go with him but he told her to let him be.

His plan was to get rid of the phone. The chopper getting shot down so soon was a potential giveaway.

He walked past the big fireplace. The area was empty now apart from servants. He was heading toward the washrooms when he heard Masón's voice.

"Mr. Morrow," he said.

Hunter turned to face him.

"You didn't enjoy our little show?"

Hunter shrugged. "It's still my country," he said.

Masón nodded. "We're your country now."

"El tiempo lo dirá," Hunter said.

Time will tell.

He wanted to get away, somewhere private where he could ditch the phone, but he thought of Hale's words.

At all costs.

He had to get them information. They would be watching the read from his phone like hawks. As far as he knew, he was their only chance at getting a read on El Sucio's location before another attack took place.

"Can I ask you a question?" he said to Masón.

"It depends," Masón said.

"I don't suppose you'll have an answer," Hunter said. He walked back toward Masón and sat on the sofa by the fire.

Masón took a seat across from him. He took two cigars from the humidor and cut them. He handed one to Hunter.

"Why is your boss waging this war?" Hunter said.

Masón lit his cigar and handed the lighter to Hunter.

"He has his reasons."

"It seems dangerous."

"Life is dangerous," Masón said.

"He's provoking them. Poking the bear, we call it."

"Poking the bear," Masón said, testing the words in his mouth. He liked the sound of it. "Yes, he's poking the bear."

"Why would he do that?"

"Why would anyone?"

"Because he had a death wish."

"Or because he wants to fight with the bear."

"You can't fight a bear."

"But you can kill them," Masón said. "You can't fight them, but you can kill them."

Hunter shook his head. He puffed on the cigar. Out by the pool he could see the crowd getting back to the party. He could see Adelita sitting alone by the pool. She was looking at him through the open doors. Jesús was with his men, talking business.

It was time to take a risk.

"When they find him, they'll kill him," he said.

"So they kill him," Masón said.

Hunter nodded. He drew on the cigar and exhaled a cloud of smoke.

"But it could have all been avoided. If he didn't make all these attacks. If he just disappeared after the escape."

"Some men like to go out swinging," Masón said.

Hunter looked at him skeptically.

"And now the army is coming. Ground forces. They'll beat this land to a pulp"

"We've been fighting back armies our entire lives," Masón said.

"Not this army," Hunter said. "You've never seen an army like this."

Masón rose an eyebrow.

"Tell me this," he said. "You're planning to buy thirty million dollars a week to supply American soldiers in

Mexico. That makes you a billion dollar a year customer.
You'll triple your money. That makes you two billion dollars
if the war lasts one year."

"Yes," Hunter said.

"Two billion dollars," Masón said again.

"Right. The war is good for me. I'm not questioning
that. I'm questioning how good it is for you."

"Just you," Masón said. "A common dealer from Texas.
Just one man. Two billion dollars."

"So what?"

"So don't you think if you're making that much money,
that other people are making money too."

"I don't doubt they are."

"So for you at least, this war makes sense."

"For me, yes."

"And for others, it's good for them too."

"For some people."

"So maybe for my boss, for my organization, maybe for
us it makes sense too," Masón said.

Hunter smoked. He had no doubt the cartel had an
angle, but he couldn't see what it was.

"How is it good business to get invaded?"

"How was it good when the US invaded Iraq? It was
good for ISIS. It was good for the people they left in charge.
It was good for a lot of Iraqis. A lot of money changed
hands."

"But it wasn't good for Saddam."

"My boss is not Saddam Hussein."

"Then who is?" Hunter said.

Masón laughed.

"You know, for us it's always war," he said.

"That's true," Hunter said.

"Siempre guerra," Masón said again.

"Siempre guerra."

"And the winner is not the man with the biggest gun."

"No?"

"No."

"Who is the winner then?"

"The winner," Masón said, "is the man who can see what is right in front of his face."

"Can't everyone see that?" Hunter said.

"Very few can."

Hunter had to keep digging. He needed more, something to tell Fawn, something about Chicago. He got the sense Masón was enjoying the conversation but they were interrupted when Jesús came into the room. He'd brought the two girls from the limo, Estrella and Catalina.

"I've got a present for you, gringo," Jesús said.

Hunter glanced toward the pool but Adelita wasn't there. When he turned back, he saw for the briefest second Jesús give Masón a look.

Something was up.

"Ladies," Jesús said to the girls, "please take Mr. Morrow upstairs and show him why our hospitality is so famous."

Hunter looked again for Adelita but she wasn't there.

He let the two girls take a hand each and lead him toward the stairs.

"Remember, Mr. Morrow," Masón said, letting out a loud laugh. "It's not the man with the biggest gun."

Hunter smiled.

Then he followed the two women up the stairs. They led him to a grand bedroom with a four-posted bed in front of doors leading to a balcony. The balcony overlooked the ocean.

The women pushed him onto the bed and he lay on his

back watching them. They put on a show for him, making out with each other and undressing. They were in front of the balcony, the lace curtains flowing around their naked bodies in the breeze.

He began to take off his clothes.

He let the girls get on the floor between his legs and make out with each other. Then Estrella straddled him and lowered herself onto him.

While they fucked, Catalina poured a prodigious amount of cocaine on Estrella's breasts.

She snorted more coke than Hunter had ever seen anyone take in a single go and threw her head back in satisfaction.

He followed her lead, leaning down to the breast, but instead of inhaling, he exhaled, and when he came up, the coke was gone. It looked like he'd snorted it.

Catalina poured more coke, this time on her own breasts, and Hunter did the same trick, blowing away the coke without taking any.

After the look Jesús had given Masón, he couldn't afford to get fucked up.

Something was definitely going on.

Estrella gripped his shoulders so hard she drew blood. She screamed in pleasure.

"Holy fuck," Hunter gasped.

She looked into his eyes like she had even naughtier things she wanted to do to him, but she got up and made room for her Catalina.

Catalina got on his lap and began grinding against him, coaxing him back to life.

She made out with him while Estrella played with his nipples, licking them and pinching them.

He got hard again and Catalina put him inside her.

He wasn't quite ready for action and while she swayed back and forth, he said to her, "What's going on?"

She stopped moving and looked at Estrella.

Then she looked back at him with eyes that seemed to ask why he wanted to spoil a perfectly good fuck with a question like that.

He reached up and put his hands on her neck. He didn't squeeze, but he left her in no doubt that he could.

Estrella was on her knees next to him and she stood up.

"Sit down," he said to her.

She looked toward the door.

"Sit down or I strangle your friend."

"My sister," Estrella said.

Hunter looked from her to Catalina and back. It was true. He'd missed the resemblance.

He had to scare them. He had to scare them and he had to get them to talk.

He willed himself to stay hard and began rocking back and forth, sliding in and out of Catalina as he swayed. He squeezed her neck, just slightly, and felt her body tense.

She got the message.

"You know," he said, "some guys where I come from, they like it when the girl is in pain."

"Don't hurt her," Estrella said.

"They like it best of all if the girl is dying," he said, and he squeezed her neck ever so slightly harder.

"Please," Catalina croaked.

"Don't," Estrella said.

He swayed back and forth while Estrella pled with him not to hurt her.

"So," he said. "Why am I in this room with the two of you?"

"Jesús told us to get you high."

"Why?"

"I don't know why," Estrella said.

Getting him high wasn't a big deal. The order hadn't come from Masón. It could be Jesús acting on his own initiative, getting him to let his guard down.

Hunter was going to let Catalina go but the pleasure was building in him. He thrust up into her and climaxed, relaxing his grip with each surge of pleasure.

Estrella was pulling at him.

"Let her go," she cried.

He fell back on the bed.

"Fuck," he said.

"Estas bien?" Estrella said to Catalina.

"I'm okay," she said. "He didn't hurt me."

Estrella calmed down when she saw her sister was unhurt.

Hunter lay on the bed staring at the ceiling. The women seemed in no hurry to leave the room.

"Why does he want me high?" he said.

"He just wants to get to know you," Estrella said, getting on the bed next to him.

"I want to get to know him too," Hunter said.

"He's a good guy," Catalina said.

"And we know everyone's secrets," Estrella said.

"You mean you know what everyone likes in bed."

"Not only that," she said. "You can tell a lot about a man after you fuck him."

"What can you tell about me?"

"You've got your guard up," she said.

"Will you tell Jesús that?"

She looked at Catalina.

"I'll tell him you like to act tough but your grip is softer than it looks."

He looked at her. He could have killed her, she knew that, but he'd been gentle. He'd scared her, but that was all. In fact, if he wasn't mistaken, and if she hadn't been faking, she'd climaxed when he had.

"So how do two sisters end up in a place like this?" he said.

They were both sitting on the bed and Catalina put a hand on his chest, playing with his nipple. He wondered how long this moment of peace would last.

"The same way every other girl does," Catalina said.

"Who's older?"

"Me," she said. "Four years older."

He'd see them kiss. He'd seen them play with each other's pussies. He knew it was wrong but he couldn't help being aroused by it.

He wondered how it was from their perspective.

"You can't tell," he said.

She smiled.

"Do you know Adelita?" he said.

They shrugged. "We've seen her around."

"We've known her our whole lives," Estrella said. "But we've never been close."

"I need your help," he said.

They looked at him.

"I want to get rid of her."

"Why? What did she do?"

"She thinks she's my woman but she's not."

"So tell her," Estrella said.

"I want you two to tell her."

"Tell her what?"

"Tell her I'm taking you to the United States."

"Are you?"

"No, but she'll get the picture if she thinks I am."

"Why don't you just hit her," Estrella said.

"He won't," Catalina said.

"Then tell her to leave you alone."

"She won't listen."

"So we have to tell her you're with us now?" Estrella said.

"Tell her I'm taking you to the States. That's all."

"Where are you taking us?" Estrella said.

"Miami?" Catalina said.

Hunter shook his head. "Chicago."

"Why Chicago?" Estrella said. "It's freezing there."

"Have you been?" Hunter said.

"Been all over," she said.

Catalina looked at her like she was saying too much but it was too late.

Hunter reached up and grabbed them both by the neck, one hand on each.

He forced himself to forget who he was. He forced himself to turn off the feeling. He looked them both in the eye and they saw it. They saw the change.

He spoke very quietly and very slowly.

"What did you do in Chicago? I'll only ask once. Then I'll squeeze one of you like a chicken and get the other to talk."

Estrella's eyes were wide.

Catalina spoke up.

"There was a woman there. An important woman. We were at a party at her house."

"I need a name."

He clenched his grip.

"Harris," Catalina said.

"Harris?" he said.

"Raquel Harris."

Hunter let them go. They fell to the bed, coughing. Tears were in their eyes.

"I'm sorry I had to do that," he said.

"If anyone finds out we told you that, we're dead," Catalina said.

"They won't find out from me," he said. "We're the best of friends, right? The three of us, best of friends."

They looked at each other and nodded.

"Come on. Put your clothes on. We're the best of friends." As they got dressed he added, "actually, tell Adelita we're going to Texas."

FIFTY

Fawn couldn't believe her eyes. She was already in Chicago for the search and when the tower collapsed, she was just twelve blocks away at the FBI's base of operations. Hale had wanted her to oversee the operation, coordinate with the FBI, and make sure Harris kept her word on allowing the Graylocks to make the kill.

The analysts said they were eighty percent confident El Sucio was in the Willis Tower.

Now, the whole thing was a pile of rubble on the ground.

Raquel came up to her and put a hand on her shoulder.

"It's shocking, I know."

"I'm so sorry, Raquel."

"We both lost good people."

"You had hundreds of agents in there. We only had five assets."

Raquel sat down on the chair next to Fawn. Fawn was staring at her computer monitor. The footage of the explosion was playing over and over, from a million different camera angles. It would take months to go through all the feeds.

"Do you think El Sucio was in there?" Raquel said.

Fawn looked at her. She felt sympathy for her. She'd only just been made head of the FBI and now she'd lost hundreds of agents in the one of the worst disasters in the history of the agency. She looked pale, like she might faint at any moment.

"I think it was a trap, Raquel. A big fat trap."

Raquel nodded.

"Why don't you go home and get some rest?" Fawn said.

Raquel was from Chicago. She had a place there.

"Maybe I should," she said.

Fawn looked back at her screen and was surprised when Raquel hugged her. It was awkward, sitting in the chair, a hug from the side.

"Go on," Fawn said to her. "I'm going down to the site."

"Don't you want to wait until morning?" Raquel said.

The building had collapsed two hours ago. The National Guard was closing off the area and didn't want people coming and going.

They'd had to issue a direct order to the FBI not to crowd the site.

The field office was just blocks away and there were hundreds of agents overseeing the operation. They'd just sent hundreds more into the tower. They were in shock. Their natural impulse was to rush to the site and help in the search for survivors.

It would have just added to the chaos.

"No," Fawn said. "I have to go now. I have to see it. You go home and get some rest."

Raquel nodded and got up to leave.

The first men into the building were Hale's Graylocks.

They'd been equipped with multiple body cameras and Fawn had been monitoring every move they made. They swept each floor, one at a time. It was a huge job, over a hundred floors, but the intel all pointed to one place, the office of a private investment firm on the twentieth floor, and they were sure that was where they'd find their man.

As the Graylocks swept the floors, they were followed by a tactical team from the FBI.

Letting Hale's guys take the lead was a favor, a gift, to Hale.

Fawn wasn't sure how he'd managed it. She knew how ambitious Raquel Harris was and giving up the capture of El Sucio seemed like the last thing she'd do voluntarily. Hale must have found a way to twist her arm. If he had, he hadn't told Fawn about it.

She rubbed her eyes.

She was tired.

Everyone was tired. Since El Sucio's escape, the entire nation was at battle stations. The men and women in that office were on the front line.

She looked across the office. Raquel was still there, by the door, talking to some agents.

Fawn got up and walked over to them.

"Raquel," she said.

Raquel turned to her. "Yes?"

"Can you send us the intel again? Everything you've got."

"You already have everything," Raquel said.

"I want the internal work too," Fawn said. "All our analysis. All your people's work. Every document, every file, every note. I want to know how we were so sure this was our spot. How could we be so wrong?"

"I'll get someone on it," Raquel said. She turned to the

men she'd been talking to. "Mathew, you'll see to it. Give them whatever they want."

Mathew nodded.

Fawn thanked them and grabbed her coat. Chicago was colder than DC and she'd learned her lesson in Alaska. As soon as she got home she went to Nordstrom and bought the warmest winter coat she still felt stylish in. It was from a Canadian company, black with a fur trim. Not the most politically correct choice but she didn't care.

In knee-high, black leather boots and the warm coat she felt equipped for the twelve-block walk to the Willis Tower, but when she got to the street, she was shocked by what she saw. A thick dust, like a fog, blocked her view. She could barely see a hundred yards in front of her. The traffic lights at the next intersection were a dim glow.

She coughed and pulled her scarf in front of her face.

Above her, she could hear the sound of helicopters.

The army was everywhere.

The city was on lockdown.

Martial law was in effect.

Tanks were forming road blocks and troops were setting up positions at intersections and on bridges.

How quickly the world could change. How vulnerable it all was. There was nothing simpler than making a bomb. Some instructions on google, a trip to the hardware store, some high school chemistry.

Dozens could be killed.

Hundreds.

In the really big attacks, thousands.

And how was a nation to react?

How much should things change?

How hard should the response be, how deep, how merciless?

She was part of that reaction, that response. She already knew she would spend the rest of her career reacting to these events, even after El Sucio and all his henchmen were dead and in the ground.

After 9/11, the United States had gone to war in Iraq and Afghanistan. Within a decade, ISIS had declared the Caliphate and was beheading women who didn't wear the veil.

Action. Reaction. Action. Reaction.

What would this action lead to?

She'd walked four blocks but already it was getting hard to go on. The air was so thick with dust that she had to go into the entryway of an office building just to catch her breath.

There were so many soldiers on the street, so many emergency vehicles, it wasn't safe.

When she heard gunfire up ahead she decided to turn back.

What had she been thinking? She didn't walk twelve blocks at the best of times. She wasn't about to start in a war zone.

Her phone began vibrating and from the tone, she could tell it was Hunter and that he was verified. She pulled it out of her pocket and cleared her throat before speaking.

"What have you got?" she said.

"What's it like down there?" Hunter said.

"We didn't have time to do anything," she said. "We got your footage."

"I saw you took out that helicopter."

"Yeah, divers are getting the bodies now. But the Willis Tower is down, Hunter."

"I saw it happen."

"All the Graylocks were inside."

"Apart from the two who were killed here tonight." .

"Oh, Jesus."

"They cooked them over an open fire, Fawn. Like pigs on a spit."

"Fuck."

"They were feeding them to the party guests."

"Did you eat any?"

There was a second's pause. Would he lie to her?

"I had to. Masón was testing me."

"You're going to make me sick."

"It was like pork."

"I don't want to know, Hunter."

"Sorry."

"Where are you now?" she said.

"Back at the hotel."

"I saw the phone went dead."

"I got rid of it," Hunter said.

Fawn began coughing.

"What's the matter?" Hunter said.

She made her way back toward the field office. Some soldiers were approaching her.

"It's the dust."

"You're at the site?"

"No, I'm ten blocks away but there's so much dust. It's like a war zone here. Hold on. Some soldiers are coming."

She flashed them her credentials and they let her go on.

"That's cuckoo," Hunter said.

Fawn stopped walking. Cuckoo was a code word. The next name Hunter said would be the signal.

He said nothing for a few seconds.

"Cuckoo," she said, confirming the message.

Then he spoke.

"How's Raquel Harris handling all this?"

"Raquel Harris?"

"Yes."

Fawn's head spun. She coughed again and had to stop and take shelter in an entryway to catch her breath.

"Raquel's holding up okay," she said. "I should go."

"God speed," Hunter said.

FIFTY-ONE

Hale was impressed. The driveway was lined with statues. It was paved with red stone. At the end it formed a circle, at the center of which was a sixteen-foot-high fountain.

"Pretty snazzy," the driver said.

Hale let out a little laugh.

"Her father invented some sort of flange used on aircraft," Hale said. "He sold the company to Boeing in 1998 for a billion dollars."

The driver nodded. "Flanges," he said. "I'm in the wrong line."

"You and me both," Hale said, stepping out of the car.

He walked up to door and a soldier guarding it knocked on it for him.

Some sort of butler opened the door.

"Jeff Hale?" he said.

"That's right."

"You're expected, sir," the butler said. He stepped aside to let Hale pass.

Inside, he led the way up some stairs and into an office overlooking the grounds behind the house.

They were north of the city, less than twenty miles from the site of the Willis Tower, but Hale felt as if he was a million miles away, in England or northern France. Everything was perfect. The pool, the rose garden, the little maze made out of hedges.

In the distance he could see the nighttime skyline of the city. He wasn't sure if the tower should have been visible, but it definitely wasn't there now.

"Like the view?" Raquel said as she entered the room.

"It's not bad," Hale said.

"Can I get you a drink?"

He took a seat and gave her a nod. She called out to a servant who came to take his order.

"Whiskey," he said.

"For us both," Raquel added. "And bring some snacks. I haven't eaten in hours."

"Have you spoken to Fawn?" Raquel said.

"Yes. From the car."

Raquel took a seat across from him. The room wasn't that different from the Oval Office. There was a comfortable seating area, a big desk with its more formal chairs, and on the walls, bookshelves, maps, portraits of people in outdated hairstyles. Many were on horses.

"Everything's in motion," Raquel said.

Hale looked at her. She seemed pleased with herself.

"You seem remarkably calm for someone who just lost hundreds of personnel."

"I didn't know any of them," she said.

Hale was surprised. She wasn't even pretending to hide her true motives.

"They were your men."

"They were never my men."

"You're their commander," he said.

"I've got a thick skin, Hale, as I'm sure you have. I know what it takes to make an omelette."

She gave him a pointed look. She was sizing him up. She was going to reveal something.

"This is more than some cracked eggs."

"It doesn't matter."

"Jesus, Raquel. This is your fucking city for Christ's sake."

"None of it matters, Hale. None of it."

"You've been underestimated, haven't you?" he said.

She smiled. "You didn't think a woman had the balls to talk like this?"

"I didn't think you did."

"Well, now you know."

"You've come out of nowhere."

"Or did I?" she said.

He looked at her. As FBI director she was a national figure, but she hadn't even been one of the top five names for the job until the attacks wiped out everyone above her.

How deep did this go?

Had she taken advantage of events to get where she was, or had she been in on masterminding the whole thing?

"You're plotting to overthrow the president," he said.

"Plotting is the wrong word, Hale. Congress is going to vote to impeach. That's not my doing. That's the mood of the country. He's failed to protect us. Now he's getting fired."

"When's the vote."

"It will be raised in the House tomorrow. And it will pass."

"How can you be sure?"

"I've made it my business to know."

"And then the vice president will take his place."

"For now."

"For now?"

She said nothing. Hale needed to know more. He needed to be certain he was doing the right thing. All Fawn said was that Hunter had flagged her. That wasn't enough.

"You said before that we could take power."

"Yes I did."

"Me as president and you as vice president."

"If that's how you want to play it."

"How else might we play it?"

"I could be president."

"Is that what you would prefer?"

She shrugged.

"Forgive me for being so blunt," Hale said, "but what the fuck are you talking about?"

"All I'm saying Hale, is that you and I could have more power than any two people in the history of the nation. They've handed us everything. Internal powers. Martial law. Special investigatory provisions. They're in the process of passing us even more powers, and they're about to impeach the sitting president."

"So you just think all this has fallen into our laps, and it's too good an opportunity to pass up?"

"Don't you?"

"What I'm uncertain of, Raquel, is whether all this really did just fall into our laps."

"What's that supposed to mean?"

A servant in a black suit came in with a crystal whiskey decanter and two glasses. He set the tray on the table between them. A second servant, a young woman, carried ice and a platter of hors d'oeuvres.

"Shut the door," Raquel said to them.

She poured them each some whiskey and then said,

"Hale, what I'm proposing is very simple. There's an opportunity here. There's chaos. We can snatch the opportunity while it lasts. You and I."

Hale took his glass from her.

"Help yourself to ice," she said.

He took a sip. It was smooth as honey.

His mind raced over what he knew. She wanted to seize power. She'd been implicated by Hunter.

It was time to cut to the chase.

He was armed with his agency issued Glock.

"When was El Sucio here?" he said.

Raquel didn't miss a beat. She kept his gaze. She took a sip of her whiskey.

Hale suddenly knew he was vulnerable. There was no one in the room but the two of them but he knew he'd made a mistake. She'd known he was coming. She didn't care what he knew.

She was rotten to the core, more than he'd realized, and he was in more danger than he'd guessed.

"He's been here many times."

"I see," Hale said, looking around the room for signs of a gunman.

"He and my father knew each other for years."

"Your career was his idea?"

"Sort of," she said. "He knows an opportunity when he sees one."

"So all this," Hale moved his hand in front of him, searching for the word.

"Chaos," Raquel said.

"Yes, all this chaos."

"It's a decoy. A distraction."

"The real plot is to put you in power?"

"Us," she said.

"It will never happen," Hale said.

"It will," she said. "You don't have to be part of it, but it will happen. Here and in Mexico."

"And the drugs will flow like a torrent."

"How's that any different from what happens now?" she said. "Apart from the fact that if everyone's on board, there'll be less violence."

"Less violence?"

"You think the casualties of the past week are something major. Do you have any idea how many people have died in the past ten years while the cartel fights for every package to cross the border?"

"This isn't about saving lives," Hale said.

Raquel nodded. "No, it's not."

"It's plain old money and power."

"It's about being sensible, Hale. The people want drugs. The government must get out of their way. Give them what they want."

Hale was looking at her but his attention was on everything else in the room. The windows. The door. The light coming in from the hall. She must have known he'd be armed.

"If you don't mind me asking," she said, "how did you know El Sucio had been here?"

"Part hunch," Hale said.

"And part your operative in Culiacán?"

Hale nodded.

"So I guess it comes down to this, Jeff Hale. Do you want to be part of the solution, or do you want to die tonight?"

Hale took another sip of whiskey.

"Well, I definitely don't want to die," he said.

"You're calculating right now, aren't you?" she said.

He nodded.

"You're wondering if you could draw your Glock, put a round in my forehead, and make it out that window before my guy kills you."

"Would I make it?"

She smiled and shook her head.

She nodded toward the wood-paneled wall and said, "Come on out, Luis."

The paneling slid open and a short man with a mustache and dark eyes stepped forward. He had a gun pointed at Hale.

Hale looked from him back to Raquel.

"So what's the plan? You're going to kill me?"

"I'd prefer if you'd join me. I'm not really sure why you'd turn this down."

Hale leaned back and stretched out his legs.

"Why me?"

"I've looked at your career, Hale. I've looked at every detail. If there's one word to describe you, it's pragmatic."

Hale nodded. "I don't disagree."

"Time and again, you've shown yourself to be ruled by what's practical."

"I've never betrayed my country."

"That's debatable," she said. "You've allowed foreign forces to kill our forces on multiple occasions."

"It was in our best interest."

"It was pragmatic," she said. "As was killing your own enhanced operatives when their existence became inconvenient."

"I make sacrifices, but for a greater good."

"Sometimes it's hard to see the greater good when so many sacrifices are being made," she said.

Hale looked from her to Luis and back to her. "So that's

it? You think I'm the one. The amoral, rudderless pragmatist with no loyalty other than to what will get me ahead?"

She nodded.

"Yes I do. And that's why I think you'd make such a good president."

Hale sat back in the sofa and finished his scotch. He let her pour him another glass.

She was right, of course.

He had no moral compass.

He did what needed to be done to further whatever ends he was pursuing at any given moment. Often, he sent men to their death. Often, he ordered their death. Good men. Patriots. Men who were risking their life for their country.

If Jeff Hale had any loyalty, it was to Jeff Hale.

And now, Raquel was offering him the presidency of the United States.

FIFTY-TWO

Hunter slept alone in the hotel room. He half expected someone from the cartel to come in and try to kill him. He wasn't sure how good Estrella and Catalina were at keeping secrets. If they let it slip that they'd mentioned Raquel Harris to him, they'd both be killed, but that was no guarantee they'd keep their mouths shut.

He took very basic precautions but he was drunk and tired and the coke was beginning to wear off.

He put a chair in front of the door, pillows in the bed in the shape of a sleeping body, and slept in the bathtub with the curtain mostly drawn, a gun by his side.

It wasn't CIA operating procedure but neither was anything else he ever did.

No one came.

Fawn would be taking steps to find out how compromised Raquel was. Everything else would follow. They'd tap her phone and get El Sucio that way, or they'd interrogate her in a cell until she spoke. Either way, he figured there wouldn't be much more for him to do down in Sinaloa.

He could start wrapping up loose ends.

He had to decide what his next move would be.

Could he go back to the US? To his place in Fairbanks?

Would Hale let him go back to his life?

Would Hale offer him a job?

He had a sore neck when he woke and lay flat on the floor to stretch out. He called downstairs and ordered coffee, Tylenol and some eggs.

He did some pushups and waited for the breakfast to arrive.

He watched TV in his room while he ate.

The news was all about the Willis Tower. It had been one major terrorist attack after another and the newscasters were beginning to run out of ways to express the magnitude of what was happening.

CNN showed the president in Chicago telling people to remain calm and to cooperate with the military who were taking over from the police as the source of government power on the streets.

Reporters shouted every question imaginable and soldiers had to raise their hands to quieten them.

"Will there be another attack?"

"Was El Sucio in the tower?"

"How long will martial law last?"

"What are the troops in Mexico doing?"

Hunter had never seen the nation swing so wildly. He'd been in on some of the darkest and most underhanded actions of the government, but no one had ever thought of taking the steps that were now on the table.

The borders were closed.

The airports were closed.

The army had unprecedented power to maintain public order.

Buildings were collapsing. Bodies were piling up.

And Raquel Harris had hosted Estrella and Catalina at her home at some point in the last few years.

Hunter wanted to know more. He wanted to know where she'd come from. How had she arrived at the top of the pile of potential FBI heads? What was her plan?

He wished he was in Chicago. He wanted to be the one to bring El Sucio in.

The entirety of the events of the past few weeks stacked up in his mind.

What the fuck was going on?

Cui bono was how Roman judges got to the bottom of things.

Who benefits?

Hunter couldn't see it.

El Sucio wanted to escape. Sure. But the follow up attacks? What were they? They only guaranteed the entire country would track him to the ends of the earth.

Did he care?

Was this a smokescreen for something else?

Why set off sarin gas in Texas?

Why blow up the tower in Chicago?

Why bomb the federal buildings?

There was another phrase that the people at Langley taught him.

Cherchez la femme.

Look for the woman.

It wasn't rocket science. It came from an Alexandre Dumas novel. "In every clusterfuck, look for the woman. Every man is obsessed with a woman and will do anything for her."

Hunter couldn't see it. Whatever was going on, whatever El Sucio was up to, it wasn't for a woman.

Maybe Raquel would have something to say.

He would have to decide soon if he was going to go back to the States. Hale would call him back, he knew that much, but could he trust Hale?

He thought of Adelita.

What had he gotten her into?

Would Catalina and Estrella pass along the message?

He decided to find out, and after a hot shower and a shave he went down to the lobby and had the bellhop hail him a cab.

He went to Adelita's apartment. At the door he rang the buzzer. There was no answer.

He buzzed again.

Still nothing.

He took a few steps back from the door and looked up at the windows. Someone was coming out onto the balcony and he saw that it was Adelita's mother.

"Esta aqui?" he said.

"She doesn't want to speak to you."

From the tone of her voice, he could tell Adelita had received the message. Now all he had to do was seal the deal. A little harshness. A little meanness. She'd forget about him in a matter of days.

He'd given her some money. He didn't need it back but it gave him the excuse he needed. He'd take it and he'd make her want to forget she'd ever met him.

"I need to speak to her."

"Go away. She hates you."

"Let me in."

Adelita appeared. She'd been crying.

"Me mentiste," she said. "You fucking liar."

"Necesito el dinero," he said.

She'd been holding out hope that he was there to make

up with her. Now she saw he was only after his money. It was the only thing he'd ever given her and he wanted it back.

She lost it and began to wail loudly.

Her mother put her arms around her.

"Let me up or I'll kick in this door," Hunter said.

"Fuck off, you fucking gringo fuck," the mother said.

Hunter was calm. This was the remedy, the medicine. If it saved them it would be worth it.

He rose his foot and stamped down on the lower part of the door. It broke and the latch separated from the frame.

He pushed his way in and went up the stairs.

He banged loudly on the door and the women yelled out at him to go away.

A neighbor, a man in his fifties, came out of his apartment and asked what the noise was about.

"Vuelve adentro," Hunter yelled at him.

The man came forward and Hunter punched him in the gut. Then he pushed him back into his apartment.

He went back to Adelita's door and kicked it. It flung open, swinging wildly on its hinges. He pushed through the women and began searching for the money. He smashed as many things as possible as he searched.

"Where is it?" he yelled at them.

They weren't going to tell him.

That was fine by him. It gave him more of a reason to create a mess. He pulled books from the shelves. He broke plates in the kitchen. He knocked over chairs.

When he made for the hallway Adelita got in front of him.

"No," she said.

He leaned around her to look down the hall. There were three doors. A bathroom and two bedrooms. There was something back there she wanted to protect. Her kid, he thought.

"Bring me the case and you never have to see my face again," he said.

He said it coldly. It hurt him to see the look on her face. It hurt him to do this to her.

She slapped him across the face and a ring she was wearing was turned inwards. The gemstone tore into his face and cut a gash in his cheek two inches long.

Hunter reached up to his face and felt the blood.

Adelita looked at him, looked into his eyes, and saw nothing.

No trace of emotion, no hint of the man who'd been there before.

"I'll get your fucking money," she spat.

She turned and went into one of the rooms.

When she returned she was holding a gun. A nine millimeter. Nothing too heavy.

He thought about letting her shoot him. Maybe that would be better. It would give her back her status as a loyal Sinaloan. It would also mean she could keep the money.

He felt he owed her that much. Her and her mother and daughter.

In all this mess, in all this violence, something good had to happen to someone innocent at least once.

"What age is your daughter?" he said to her.

Her eyes grew, she was suddenly terrified, but she also recognized him again. He was himself. She was torn.

"Seven," she whispered.

"Shoot me in the arm," he said.

"What?"

"You have to, Adelita. I'll be gone soon and the cartel is

going to come after you. For your daughter's safety, shoot me in the arm."

He put his hand on his shoulder and showed her where to shoot.

"Here," he said.

She shook her head.

He went toward her and took the gun from her hands. She offered no resistance. Her mother was watching, speechless. Hunter pressed the gun against his shoulder at an angle that would give it a clear path through.

"Don't stand behind me," he said to Adelita's mother.

"What are you doing?" she said.

He took a deep breath. Then he fired.

The sound was deafening. The pain leapt through him.

Blood soaking into his shirt and jacket.

Adelita was crying. Her mother was looking at him like he was crazy, but when she nodded he knew she understood.

Hunter was trained to go into situations and create as big a mess as possible. This was his way of minimizing at least one part of that mess.

The mother grabbed him some towels and he pressed them against the wound.

"If anyone comes, you tell them I came here for my money and you shot me," he said.

Then he left.

FIFTY-THREE

Fawn's eyes were glued to the satellite feed.

Eight CIA operatives surrounded the home of the FBI director. It would have been unthinkable before.

"They're in position, Mr. President," she said.

"Well, better send them in," the president said.

"That's a go, alpha," she said.

"Copy," the lead said.

She watched the dots begin to close in on the building. The blue pulse of Hale's location was coming from a second floor office overlooking the back of the building.

The heat signatures of Raquel's people were scattered throughout the building, about twenty in all, but Fawn was most concerned with the one in the room with Hale and Raquel.

That was Raquel's safety net.

Fawn had no doubt he had a gun pointed at Hale at that very moment.

"We're in position, Ma'am," the lead said.

"Have you got eyes on Hale?"

"Yes we do."

"We don't want Harris killed," she said.

"Copy that."

She watched the units on the screen. The pulse of weapon discharge showed up. Eight shots, simultaneously fired, and eight of Raquel's men were down, including the assassin in the office.

Hale's dot leapt forward onto Raquel. He was either restraining her or protecting her from gunfire. They had to get her alive. She might have El Sucio's location.

The agents continued through the building, clearing it of Raquel's people with tactical precision. It helped that they knew exactly where everyone was. They took out everyone and secured the building without a single shot being fired against them.

Fawn saw them converge on the second floor office and waited for Hale.

When his voice came through the feed she gasped in relief.

"Fawn?"

"Boss? You okay?"

"Fine."

"Is Harris alive?"

"Yes she is, and she has something she wants to say to us."

"Go fuck yourself, Hale," Raquel said to him.

Fawn switched to the bodycam of one of the men in the room. Raquel was on the ground and Hale had his foot on her neck.

"You know we don't have time to dance around this," he said to her.

"Fuck you, Hale."

"Where is he?" Hale said.

He put weight on Raquel's neck and she began to

squirm under the pressure. She clawed at his leg and struggled wildly but there was nothing she could do. A little more pressure and she'd be in trouble.

"Agent," Hale said. "Put a bullet in her foot, would you?"

Fawn knew the president and the Chiefs of Staff would be scrambling to get on the feed. This was it. This was the moment they were going to find out where El Sucio was hiding. No one would want to miss this.

"You know I'll never tell you that."

Hale laughed. He nodded at the lead agent, who put his gun against Raquel's foot and pulled the trigger. The foot is a painful place to take a bullet. It's full of bones. They shatter on impact. There are so many nerve endings in there that it can feel like the pain is everywhere in the body at once.

Raquel screamed.

"Hit her in the other foot too," Hale said. "And the hands."

"Fuck you," Raquel screamed.

The agent didn't hesitate. He put a bullet in Raquel's other foot, and then moved to her left hand.

A second agent was already bandaging her feet, making sure there was no risk of her losing too much blood.

Raquel was in agony. She'd lose consciousness soon but Hale was good at this sort of thing. He knew how much she could take.

The agent's gun went off again and Raquel's left hand was a mess of blood, flesh, and shattered bone.

The agent went to her right hand and Raquel told him to stop.

"He's on a ship," she said. "A container ship."

"Where?"

"North."

"North?"

"Northern end of the lake. Up by Cheboygan. Lake Huron. Near the Canadian border."

"You get that?" Hale said.

"We got it," Fawn said.

FIFTY-FOUR

Hunter was in a bar off the square.

He'd gone to the hospital to get his arm seen to, which wasn't necessary, but he wanted to make sure the cartel knew Adelita had shot him.

Now, he was waiting for orders. He'd reported all the bigwigs in the cartel he'd come in contact with. He just needed to know what the government wanted him to do.

He could take out a hundred men in a single bloody night and be out of the city before dawn. That would do some serious damage to the cartel's post-Heredia leadership, but they still hadn't given him an order.

The live news coverage was on every channel. The bar he was in had CNN and his eyes were glued to the screen.

The container ship was in the northern sound of Lake Huron, between Rogers City, Michigan and Cockburn Island, Ontario. There'd been some debate but the ship was still in US waters.

After a lot of back and forth between agencies, it was the Coast Guard that would be mounting the assault.

The decision to have the press televise the event came

straight from the White House. There was a chance the operation would be unsuccessful, but after the carnage of El Sucio's attacks, it was felt the risk was outweighed by the nation's need for closure. The president wanted the country to see El Sucio die. He wanted the cameras present when the final bullet was fired.

The country needed it.

The people needed it.

The president knew his political future was on the line.

Hunter ordered another beer. Everyone in the bar was watching the screen.

Four coast guard helicopters were flying above a ship and a dozen speed boats were circling around it in the water.

The cartel had men on deck who were armed with assault rifles but sharpshooters in the helicopters were taking them out, one by one.

It was shocking to see it being televised, to hear the commentators talk about each death like they were calling a sports game, but after the destruction of the past few weeks, Hunter agreed the people had a right to see the battle play out.

The CNN commentator noted that at that moment, more people were watching than had watched the moon landing.

The choppers circled until there were no more cartel shooters on deck, then the boats moved in.

As soon as the agents boarded, things got bloody fast. Cartel men poured up from the hold. The initial team of coast guard agents were massacred. They were followed by more teams who battled along the length of the deck, taking cover behind shipping containers and pushing forward until they reached the entrance to the ship's control room.

Once inside, the helicopter cameras switched to live feeds from the agents' body cameras. The footage was being delivered live and unedited by the coast guard to every major news agency in the world.

Hunter had to admit, it made for riveting television.

The agents battled, room to room, through the narrow corridors of the ship's quarters. The steel walls made for treacherous ricochets, especially with the cartel using submachine guns.

More and more boats unloaded more and more coast guard teams onto the ship and over the next half hour they fought their way to the deepest part of the cargo hold. A steel door was the final obstacle between the US government and the man who'd caused more death to American citizens than anyone in decades.

Hunter's eyes were glued to the screen.

This was it.

This was the end of the mission.

When the moment finally came, it was eerily devoid of drama.

An agent opened the reinforced steel door and no one fired at him. The camera showed the inside of the hold. It was dark but for the beam of the agent's gun-mounted flashlight.

The light settled on a man sitting on a chair. Steel barrels flanked him on both sides. His hands were on his head in a position of surrender.

Hunter looked at the waitress. She shook her head.

"That's him?" Hunter said.

She nodded.

The look on El Sucio's face was one of confusion, like he wasn't quite sure how he'd arrived in this situation.

This was how it always ended.

All the chaos. All the death. And at the end of it, the mastermind was just another Joe Schmo who wiped his ass the same way as everyone else.

The agents swarmed around him and put him in hand-cuffs. El Sucio offered no resistance.

They got him to his feet and led him back along the corridors they had just battled through.

And then, with a manic grin on his face, El Sucio reached for the collar of his jacket with his mouth, found a wire, and with a jerk of his neck, pulled it.

All the feeds went black.

The footage switched to the helicopter cameras, which showed a massive explosion taking place inside the ship. The booms were followed by smoke and shattered material flying from every opening in the hold of the vessel.

The whole ship had been boobytrapped.

El Sucio was going out on his own terms.

Death was preferable to facing the repercussions of the worst attacks ever made on US soil.

The newscasters reported in horror as flames and black smoke billowed from the ship. There was no footage now from the inside.

The only view was of the ship, which began to list and go under.

The choppers continued to circle. Gradually, some of the body cams came back online.

The feeds showed the desperate struggle of their last moments as the coast guard agents tried to make it back to the deck through fire and falling steel. Some made it but many were still inside when the ship went under.

Hunter knew the explosives had been positioned in a way to make the ship sink as quickly as possible. It also looked like secondary explosives had been placed to block exit routes.

Even in death, El Sucio wanted to take down as many people as possible.

The cameras showed gut-wrenching views of the faces of the men as they realized they were going to drown.

The compartments were filling with water.

It rose to their knees.

Then their waists.

Then their necks.

One of the feeds showed El Sucio himself. He was being submerged, the water rising above his face. He was still in handcuffs.

He didn't make a sound.

FIFTY-FIVE

Fawn and Hale were staying at the Drake hotel. The government had requisitioned two floors for senior officials who were in Chicago for the operation. Many of them were now in the Coq d'Or, the hotel's bar. In the thirties, it had served the city's first cocktails following the repeal of prohibition. The rich wood panelling and tobacco-infused leather gave the bar a warm glow.

It invited you to drink to something strong.

And that's exactly what Hale and Fawn were doing. Hale was into his third old fashioned, while Fawn was drinking something called a Scofflaw, which contained a six-year-old Templeton rye, dry vermouth, lemon, and pomegranate.

Fawn had left the main group of agency personnel and was at the far end of the bar. Hale came to join her. They'd clinked glasses a dozen times already but did so again. He sat next to her and they watched their colleagues celebrate.

"Doesn't feel like much of a victory, does it?" Hale said.

"I'm sorry," Fawn said, trying a thin smile.

"Don't apologize, I feel the same way."

"It's just, so much death, you know?"

"It was a war," Hale said.

"It was. And they brought it to us this time. Not some far flung corner of the world."

"It's scary," Hale said.

"It's terrifying."

"It's the new normal."

"I know."

Hale shook his head. "It was bound to happen. Why set off a car bomb in Kabul or Baghdad or Mexico City, when you can do it in Washington or New York or Chicago and actually get the attention of the people you're trying to target?"

Fawn took another sip of her Scofflaw. She liked it. It was her second but she'd already decided she was having another. It might not feel like much of a victory but their job was done, their target was at the bottom of a lake, and the biggest terrorist threat in the history of the nation had been neutralized.

At least, that was the official story.

"How long until they find the body?" she said.

"A day or two at most," Hale said. "They had to stop searching when it got dark."

She nodded. She wanted that body. If they didn't recover the body, no one would be satisfied. They would say it was all some grand hoax. And Fawn would agree with them. El Sucio had been one step ahead of them at every turn. This tidy little ending would only add up when they had the body.

After everything he'd done, recruiting the head of the FBI, masterminding an impeachment of the president that might still happen, pulling off all those attacks, this seemed a little bit too simple for Fawn's liking.

"They better find that fucking body," she said.

"I know, Fawn."

"Without a body, none of it counts. No one will believe he's dead. The cartel can pull off some two-bit attack and everyone will think El Sucio's still calling the shots."

"I know, Fawn."

"Even with the footage."

"Jesus, I know. Can't we just savor this moment?"

"And what about Raquel? How are you going to play that?"

"We're going to call it what it was."

"A plan to overthrow the president? A plan for the FBI and CIA to take over the government?"

"Right," Hale said skeptically. "That's just what the county needs."

"What then?"

"We're going to say she was cooperating with the enemy. That he'd bought her off. That he was going to help her attempt some sort of coup."

"Without going into so many details."

"Right."

"When's the story being released?"

"At a press conference tomorrow. There's only one story anyone's interested in today."

Fawn nodded.

There was a TV above the bar and it was showing the president's press conference.

"There are a lot of young journalists in town," Fawn said, looking at Hale.

He shook his head. "What's that supposed to mean?"

She sipped her drink. She shouldn't have teased him but she didn't care. They were blowing off steam. If she didn't take advantage of moments like this, she'd never get to know him, the real him.

"I mean, I wouldn't be surprised if the story leaked," she said.

"It won't leak."

"Isn't that little *Post* reporter staying in this very hotel?"

"You know," Hale said, "if the women in my life didn't shoot me down so badly, I wouldn't have to go looking for it from little *Post* reporters."

"The women in your life?"

"You for instance."

Fawn laughed.

"What's so funny about that?"

"Well, let me think. You're thirty years older than me. You're my boss. You're married."

Hale nodded. "See what I mean."

"Maybe if you went for women your own age," Fawn said.

"Like Raquel Harris?"

She shook her head. "She's not the only woman in the world your age."

Hale sighed. "I've got nothing against women my age," he said, "except they all see right through me."

"They see you for what you are."

"Exactly."

"And what's that?" she said.

He thought for a moment. He finished his drink and ordered another for them both.

"I'm a womanizer," he said. "A good old-fashioned womanizer."

Fawn looked him in the eye. "And is that so wrong?"

"It's out of fashion."

"For the time being."

"You think it's going to come back?"

She thought about it, then said, "wouldn't you rather a world where men acted like men?"

He looked at her. His leg pressed against hers.

He moved his hand to his knee.

She knew it was only a matter of time before it jumped the gap and was on her knee.

Why was she flirting with him?

Maybe it was the Scofflaws, the six-year-old rye, the fact they'd killed El Sucio.

She decided to change the subject, but as she did, she opened her legs, ever so slightly, just an inch.

"What should I do with Hunter?" she said.

Hale looked up from her legs.

"Get him to make a mess. We got their boss but I want to take out their entire leadership. Every guy who could possibly succeed to the throne."

Fawn nodded.

"And then?"

"And then call him in."

"Are you sure about that?"

"Why wouldn't I be?"

"He didn't come in last time."

"This time is different," Hale said.

"Is it?"

"Of course it is."

"I read his files."

"I know you did. I was the one who signed off on that."

"Hale, he thinks his final mission was that Butcher of Kabul job. The one at the market with the air strike."

"He thought that once, but I doubt he still believes it."

"I think he does."

"What makes you say that?"

"Something he said about that gun. The one the president ordered him to take."

"The M82."

"The Barrett. Right."

"What did he say?"

"Nothing really. He just didn't like that we were sending in more agents. He didn't like the president butting in on something operational."

"That doesn't mean anything."

"It's not just that," Fawn said. "It's everything. The way he talks about the president. The way he talks about you."

Hale nodded. He knew it was true. Maybe he hadn't admitted it to himself, maybe he'd been holding out hope for some sort of redemption, some sort of closure.

"You see it don't you?"

"Of course I see it, Fawn."

"If he remembered his actual last mission, if he knew what you really put him through...".

"I'd already be dead."

Fawn nodded.

His leg was no longer touching hers. His mind was on his neck now, not his cock.

For once.

It was an improvement, she thought.

"Let's not think about that now," he said after a long pause.

"It's not going to go away."

"If he hasn't remembered by now, he probably never will. That was the whole point of the memory wipe."

Fawn shuddered. Just the mention of the procedure made her skin crawl.

"The point of the memory wipe was that he wouldn't

remember anything at all. He remembers almost everything."

"But not that last mission."

"And you're happy with that? That's a risk you're willing to take?"

"What choice do I have?"

Fawn shrugged. He was director of the CIA. They both knew what choices he had.

She looked at him. She could see it in his eyes. He was drunk. He wanted to fuck her. He wanted her to spread her legs and take him just like every other woman.

Hale was lucky he lived in Washington. It was the world capital of daddy issues. Every woman in the city would give it up for a man with power.

She looked at him and she knew what he was going to do. His mind was already made up.

He would have Hunter killed the moment he got back.

FIFTY-SIX

Fawn was toying with him. Those eyes. That voice. The way her hair hung in front of her face like she was always half hiding.

Fuck, he was drunk.

She was too.

Hale reached across and put his hand on her lap.

That skirt, barely half way to her knee.

Those stockings.

His hand was on her thigh and the warmth of it, the electricity. It flowed from her.

She was looking at him. Reading him. And then, in an instant, the blink of an eye, everything changed.

What was it?

What did she see?

It was Hunter. She saw he was going to make the order. She knew.

Those two were close. Maybe they'd fucked. He shouldn't have sent her to Texas alone to brief him.

She slapped him across the face. He knew it wasn't for the hand on her thigh.

It was for Hunter.

He put his hand to his cheek.

It didn't matter. She'd handle it. She was a professional. The best he'd ever worked with. There was no way she'd put personal feeling above professional duty.

She was sentimental, but what woman wasn't?

He took one last glance at her legs. He'd been so close.

"I'll see you tomorrow," she said, her cheeks flushed with anger.

Hale nodded. He didn't mind that she'd hit him. If that was all the blowback she gave him over ordering a hit on Hunter, he'd consider himself lucky.

He watched her march out of the bar, a little wobbly but stable enough to make it to the elevator.

As soon as she was gone, his mind moved to Jasper.

Fawn was correct. She was staying in the same hotel. She might even be in her room as they spoke. He thought about the pale skin on her breasts, the light pink of her areola.

He wanted her.

He pulled out his phone and typed a text.

Front page if you're interested.

He ordered another drink and watched the news footage. There were celebrations across the country. Real celebrations. Spontaneous ones. Block parties in New York. Fireworks in Texas and California.

The raising of flags on navy ships.

His colleagues across the bar had thinned out. It was well past happy hour now.

His phone vibrated.

He read Aspen's response.

Where are you?

The hotel bar.

She was there in five minutes, wearing a long gray coat that came almost down to her ankles. She also had on black pumps and her ankles were bear.

"Want a drink?" he said, holding the side of the bar to steady himself.

She pulled open the belt of the coat and let it open. Beneath, she was wearing nothing but black lingerie, complete with garter and stockings.

He smiled.

She pulled her coat closed before anyone saw, and Hale took her by the hand and led her to the elevator.

Inside the elevator, he opened her coat again and groped every inch of her pristine flesh.

She got on her knees and unzipped his pants.

The elevator dinged and they stumbled out. A moment later she was on her hands and knees with her back to him. He had his hands on her hips and was thrusting forward with a frenzy that was extreme even for him.

Despite the alcohol he was hard as a bat.

He dug his fingers into her hips and she arched her back and tilted her ass.

He grabbed her hair and wrapped it around his fist. He pulled it hard and she cried out as he thrust deeper and deeper into her. She was completely under his control. She was completely at his mercy. He could have done anything he wanted to her.

She was his.

He yanked her hair mercilessly and she moaned and cried out.

As the pleasure surged through he cried out her name. Or at least, what he thought in that moment was her name.

"Fawn," he cried. "Fawn, Fawn, Fawn," over and over with each forceful thrust.

Afterwards he collapsed on her and the weight of him pushed her down.

"So good," she moaned.

He had no idea if she'd climaxed.

He closed his eyes and began to fall asleep, the alcohol finally getting the better of him.

But to his surprise, Aspen didn't let him fall asleep.

"Not so fast, old man. We have some business to attend to.

He was still in his suit, his cock sticking out through his fly like a limp attachment.

He reached his hand into his pocket and pulled out his wallet. She watched as he opened it, and when he came out with a couple of hundred dollar bills she lost it.

"What the fuck, Hale?"

He was slow. Drunk.

"That's two hundred," he said.

"I'm not one of your fucking whores, you son of a bitch."

He struggled to come out of the daze of drunkenness.

"You promised me a front page story."

"Oh," he mumbled.

She grabbed his cock and squeezed it.

"What is it, you old, fat fuck?"

"Story?"

She squeezed his balls and that got his attention.

"Aspen, you kinky slut."

She squeezed harder and the pain brought clarity.

"Fuck," he said. "The story. Raquel Harris was involved."

"Involved in what?"

"Everything. She was helping El Sucio. He was helping her. He'd been to her house."

"What are you talking about?"

She let go of his balls and he took a deep breath.

"She's dead, Aspen. Raquel Harris is dead."

"Harris is dead?"

"I killed her."

FIFTY-SEVEN

Hunter was at the same bar he'd been at for two days, sipping beers and watching the news while he waited for orders from Fawn. His arm had healed and he hadn't seen head nor tail of Adelita. The gunshot did the trick. She'd gotten the message.

He was watching CNN and another major news story was breaking across the screen. It felt like a day couldn't pass anymore without something major happening.

Yesterday, El Sucio had been killed.

Today, a bombing.

A major bombing.

The president of Mexico had been in the middle of a live televised address to parliament. The entirety of Mexico's government had been present. The president, his cabinet, parliament, even judges and senior civil servants.

And then boom.

The cameras blacked out.

Then came the stunned reactions from newscasters as they reported the scraps of information that were coming in from the parliament.

And then the footage began to stream in.

It was unbelievable. The entire Mexican parliament building, the National Palace, was rubble.

Hunter looked at the plume of smoke rising hundreds of feet into the sky and shook his head.

The National Palace had been built from the ruins of Moctezuma's Imperial Aztec capital. It was built by Hernán Cortés in 1521. It was a fortress with embrasures for cannon and musketeers.

For half a millennium it stood in the center of Mexico City, housing the government.

Now it was gone.

Even the disloyal Sinaloans were stunned.

Mexico was without a government, and with the palace in ruins, it almost felt as if it was without a history as well.

Hunter looked around the bar and wasn't sure which way the mood would go. Maybe the cartel had finally gone too far.

They'd gone to war with the government and the people had gone along with it. They'd pushed the government out of Sinaloa and made the state a de facto rogue nation, and the people stayed quiet.

Now, they'd attacked the very history of the nation, the palace built from the rubble of the Aztec sacrificial pyramids.

The people were stunned.

The people would have watched the cartel destroy almost anything.

Almost anything.

Hunter felt uneasy. He'd felt that way since the killing of El Sucio.

This added to it.

Nothing was right. The attack on the ship had been too

easy. The protection for El Sucio had been laughable. The live footage of his final moment didn't alleviate the suspicion Hunter felt in his gut.

Where was the body?

Without the body, how could anyone accept that this was over?

And with Mexico now on its knees, a perfect decapitation, how could anyone claim this war was over?

It was not over.

Hunter felt it in his bones.

Nothing was right.

He went back to the hotel and sat at the bar. He ordered a beer but didn't drink it. He was waiting. Waiting for Jesús. He'd come soon enough. They had business to discuss. There would be another delivery. Transportation needed to be arranged. Payment had to be finalized.

El Sucio's death wouldn't halt the business of the cartel. Not even for a minute.

He watched the news on the television. They were discussing who would take over the Mexican presidency with so many of those in the chain of succession killed in a single attack.

It seemed the front runner was a little-known politician from Guadalajara called Luiz Fontaine Da Souza. The man had lost his leg thirty years ago in an accident while serving in the Mexican navy, and he walked on his prosthetic with a strange limp. He was a member of the former president's cabinet, something to do with fisheries, and the news commentators were already calling him el Pirata. No one thought it had been anyone's plan that this man would one day ascend to the presidency.

It was about dusk when Jesús showed up.

Hunter had just eaten. He'd been playing his role all

day, sitting at the bar watching the TV, not overly interested in the news. At one point he asked the waitress to switch it to sports. He ordered beers and let them go warm. He smoked.

He knew he was being watched and he played everything right.

When Jesús showed up it was with another guy.

"Jack," he said. "I hope you don't have plans for the evening."

"Someone want to see me?"

"I have a driver outside. We must go back to Masón's villa."

This was exactly what Hunter wanted to hear, but he pretended it was an inconvenience.

"Is that necessary? We've agreed to all the details."

"It's necessary," Jesús said.

Hunter looked at the man he was with. The man had a tattoo of a scorpion on his neck, just under the ear.

Something was up.

That was fine by him. He wanted to start shaking things up. He had a feeling everything was just a little too calm, too business as usual, for a cartel that had just lost its boss.

According to the news, the coast guard still hadn't pulled Heredia's body out of the lake.

If an organization as cutthroat as the Sinaloa cartel had really just lost its boss, there would be a war.

"Fine," he said.

He followed them out to the car and this time they didn't even bother with the blindfold.

These guys weren't that lazy. They were going to kill him.

"No blindfold?" he said.

"We're business partners now," Jesús said.

Hunter smiled.

He wasn't wearing his gun. He focused on his breathing as the car wound its way to the coast. He visualized the possible scenarios.

He thought what he would do if the car stopped.

What he would do if Jesús pulled a gun.

What he would do if the man with the neck tattoo pulled his.

It was relaxing. Hunter had been playing dead for days. He'd let that general fire a bullet over his head. He'd let Masón feed him the flesh of a CIA agent. He'd even killed one of the agents.

He'd followed orders. He'd let himself be pushed around. He'd been exactly where they wanted him to be, every time they came looking for him.

He carried a cellphone but rarely used it.

He had a few guns but rarely carried them.

He drank too much.

He got fucked up too much.

He let things get way too complicated with the first whore to put his dick in her mouth.

They thought they knew him.

They thought he was soft.

They thought he was lazy.

They thought he was like every other American drug dealer who came south of the border thinking he knew what he was doing.

Everything was set.

And he was ready to start getting to work.

When they got to the villa he counted nine cars. There were other vehicles parked at a separate lot beyond the lawn but those seemed to be for staff.

There were four guards outside, two sitting on the edge

of the fountain, smoking, and two standing by the door. They carried AK-47s. Some of the cars had drivers sitting in them.

He scanned the building and it didn't look like there was much happening inside.

From what he'd seen of the interior, no one lived in the house. Masón didn't keep his family there. It was a place for meetings, for parties, for business.

Jesús led the way into the house. The guy with the tattoo stayed outside with the guards.

Inside, Hunter saw Masón and seven other men sitting by the fireplace.

He could also see two sets of ankles dangling from the ceiling. He couldn't see who they belonged too but they were female.

Hunter was surprised when they kicked and jerked. They weren't dead.

The men had their backs to them, they were finished with them, and were smoking and drinking and talking.

As he got closer, he saw further up the two bodies.

They had loose nooses around their necks and were struggling to breathe, holding the nooses, clawing at the ropes, trying to keep the weight on their arms.

It was a slow torture that could only end one way.

The women were naked. Their bodies had been beaten. Their faces were almost unrecognizable. But he could tell who they were.

Estrella and Catalina.

"Masón," Hunter said, raising his voice. "Was that necessary?"

Masón stood and turned to face him. He had a lazy grin on his face.

The men with him were the most important men in the

cartel. Hunter had already met some of them. Belmar the fixer, Mendiluce the Argentine financier, and Cáceres, the general who was going to handle transportation for Hunter's shipments for a ten percent cut.

Masón nodded at Jesús and Jesús calmly took a pistol from his waistband.

"Get those girls down," Hunter said.

They were still struggling but they were losing the fight.

"I hear you had a nice time with them at the party," Masón said.

"So what?" Hunter said.

"I heard you were asking a lot of questions."

"I don't think I was asking questions."

"Questions about Chicago."

"Maybe it came up."

"Questions about Raquel Harris."

Hunter ducked. Jesús was the first one he went for. He pounced at him, grabbing him around the shins like he was making a low tackle. A shot fired. Jesús hit the ground hard and Hunter jammed a fist in his crotch. He doubled over in pain and Hunter was on his feet. In a single motion he grabbed Jesús by the hair, pulled his head up, and slammed it back against the marble floor once, and grabbed his pistol.

He kept rolling and stayed a hair in front of the hail of gunfire that followed him across the room.

He kept moving, crawling along the back of the sofa as bullets pelted through it. He emerged from the far end and fired three shots as he dove for the wall.

Three men hit the ground.

The first was Cáceres.

The two guards who'd been at the door came into the hallway and Hunter shot them both in the forehead. He ran toward them and dived through the door, grabbing an AK.

From the steps of the villa he rained gunfire on the remaining two guards by the fountain.

The man with the neck tattoo took two bullets in the face.

Hunter ran along the front of the villa and got back inside through a side door.

The men were still inside.

They were confused.

Masón, the banker, the fixer. Two other guys. The guards were down.

There might be a few more guards around but they wouldn't know who they were looking for or what was going on.

The only one inside Hunter needed to be wary of was Belmar, the fixer. He was a wiry, muscular guy with dirty black stubble and the dead eyes of a killer.

Hunter knew he'd killed hundreds of men.

He slung the AK over his shoulder and checked the cartridge of the pistol.

He had eleven shots.

He went back to the main area. Four men stood there like idiots.

Hunter methodically put a bullet in each head and scanned the room for anyone else.

The sisters were no longer struggling. They'd been hit by the hail of bullets that chased Hunter out of the room.

Hunter went to Jesús and checked his pulse. He was still alive, but barely.

Another firm yank of the head by the hair, another slam back down onto the marble floor, and another, and he felt the crunch of the skull.

As he'd expected, Belmar was the man who was missing.

Hunter kept moving. Back out to the hallway where he'd killed the guards. Back around through the kitchens where he'd entered.

Back to the main area with the fireplace.

He did a circuit of the other half of the ground floor. He found an open window from an office and climbed through it. He crossed the lawn to the landscaped area beyond it. Belmar had left this way.

He'd gone through the flowerbeds toward the beach.

Five hundred yards away he saw Belmar.

Hunter wondered why he was running. He wasn't the type to leave a gunfight.

If he had a rifle he'd have capped him.

He watched him run along the beach and enter into the grounds of the next villa.

Hunter wondered what was there.

He went back to the villa and checked the bodies.

All were dead. He took a photo of each for Fawn and then shot the ropes suspending Estrella and Catalina. They fell to the floor and he lifted them onto the sofa and lay them next to each other. He spread the blanket from the back of the sofa over them.

Then he went to the front door.

The drivers were still alive. Four more guards had shown up also.

"Don't fire?" he shouted out at them.

The guards answered with gunfire.

Hunter still had the AK and swung it to his hip.

With his left hand, he sprayed bullets over their heads and into the vehicles. He stepped out into the doorway. In his right hand was the pistol and he pointed it at the only guard he could see, crouching behind the fountain. He hit him between the eyes and kept sweeping bullets over the whole area with the AK.

Another guard stood up and fired. Hunter crouched and fired back with the pistol. The man's head flew backward and smashed the window of the car behind him.

The third guard was crouched behind a red Lamborghini and rose up to fire. Hunter hit him in the chest before he even got a shot off.

The last guard threw his gun over the hood of one of the SUVs.

"Está bien?" Hunter said, coming toward him. "The car?"

The guard looked it over.

"Sí, sí," he said.

"Las ruedas?"

The man quickly checked the four tires.

"Sí señor."

"Las llaves?"

The man looked in the driver side window and saw the keys.

"Sí," he said.

Hunter walked right up to him and opened the door.

The man came closer and Hunter knew what he wanted.

He jammed the butt of the AK into the man's face, breaking his nose. The man fell back, hitting the hood of the car behind him.

"Gracias," he said.

"De nada," Hunter said and gunned the Mercedes back toward the city.

FIFTY-EIGHT

It wasn't until he got halfway back to the city that Hunter thought of Adelita.

The image of Estrella and Catalina dying on the ropes kept running across his mind and he knew he had to check on her.

He drove to her neighborhood and parked a block away.

When he saw the door, he didn't know if anything was wrong.

He'd kicked it in and broken the frame. The fact it hadn't been fixed yet didn't mean anything.

He went inside and up the stairs. The door of the neighbor's apartment was okay and Adelita's mother's door was shut, but when he touched it it opened.

It was then that he knew he'd fucked up.

He'd tried to save her but it wasn't enough.

Adelita's mother was laying on the sofa, the same sofa he'd slept on. She was dead and her blood was pooled around her head, staining the upholstery. There was a second blood stain between her legs. She'd been raped, maybe with a weapon.

Around her, the apartment had been smashed up. Not completely. There hadn't been a search. Just a fight.

He pulled the mother's head back. She'd been shot between the eyes at point blank range. Whoever shot her, she'd looked him in the eyes.

Hunter followed the trail of destruction to the hallway. He'd never been to the bedrooms that way. At the end of the corridor was the bathroom and he could see Adelita's arm hanging over the side of the tub.

As he got closer, he saw she had no fingers.

The fingers were in the bathtub with her. They'd been removed with a bolt cutter at the second knuckle. Before they were removed, the nails had been pulled out.

It was the same on the other hand.

Between her legs, blood had soaked into her nightgown. There'd been more rape. There'd been torture. They'd interrogated her.

The image of Chianne flashed across his mind, lying on a Gurney at a police morgue, her face so mutilated he only recognized her from her necklace.

Adelita had suffered the same way. Her teeth hadn't been knocked out of her head. Her body hadn't been ritualistically sacrificed. But she was dead just the same, a bloody, messy death with fucking and raping and agony.

He'd cursed her.

The moment he told her his name, he'd signed her death warrant.

Everyone he got close to suffered for it.

And he'd known all along this was how it would end. It was the only way it could end. The moment he took her to the motel. Or when he went back inside the club to get her after the air strike. Or when he slept in her home.

He'd known.

He'd fucking known down to the last detail.

All that bullshit about trying to give her an out, warning her to stay away, all of it was just for show. It was for him. So he could tell himself afterward he'd tried. Something that would make it just a tiny but easier to live with himself when it was all over.

Adelita had been fucked with a knife while her fingers were cut off, her mother was raped and killed in the next room, but he'd done his best. He'd warned her. He'd tried to protect her.

Hunter wiped his face with his hands.

He rubbed his eyes.

He felt tired.

He went to the sink and poured cold water over his face.

He'd done this. Down to the finest detail, this was his fault. The men who'd carried out the order, didn't know her. They didn't know how connected she was to him. They didn't give a fuck who she was.

But Hunter, he knew everything. And he knew this was how it would end.

He looked at his reflection in the mirror, then smashed it with his fist.

And then he heard something. One of the bedroom doors opened. Then footsteps, light, tentative, coming his way.

The bathroom door opened slowly. Hunter stared at it. He had the pistol in his belt but he didn't draw it.

When the door opened he saw a girl looking up at him. Adelita's daughter. She looked like her mother. The same knowing eyes. The same smooth hair, like she spent a lot of time brushing it.

Her skin was pale and her eyes were wide.

She was terrified.

She was about seven.

She stood there and looked at Hunter. She didn't care what he was going to do. He could save her or he could kill her. She was already gone. Her mind had already brought her away from this place.

Next to them, Adelita's body was still bleeding in the bathtub, but the girl's eyes were fixed on Hunter.

"What's your name?" he said in English.

She looked at him and said nothing.

He stepped toward her and she didn't flinch. She didn't run. He lifted her into his arms and took her down the corridor. He covered her face with his hand as they passed her grandmother. He brought her out of the apartment and down to the street.

On the street he put her on the pavement. She stood next to him. He wasn't sure what she would do. He began to walk toward his car. She followed him. He walked slowly and she came up next to him. He didn't look at her.

She rose her hand to his and he took hold of it.

He led her down the street and when they got to the big Mercedes, he lifted her into the passenger seat and put her seatbelt on.

There were tears on her cheeks but she made no sound.

FIFTY-NINE

Hunter drove out of the city in the direction of the beach. He had no destination in mind. It was dark and the child was in a state of shock.

After about thirty minutes he pulled over at a roadside restaurant.

"Are you hungry?" he said to the girl.

She looked at him but said nothing.

"Tienes hambre?" he said.

She looked at him. She moved her mouth. She wanted to speak but she was unsure of herself, as if she was no longer certain she could make the sounds.

They sat in the car and looked out at the restaurant.

Ten minutes passed.

Hunter tried to keep his mind blank.

Every now and then a car drove past and they watched the lights approach and then recede.

When the girl spoke, the sound brought Hunter back to the present.

"I can speak English," she said.

He smiled at her.

"That's very good."

She nodded.

"Who taught you to speak English?"

"My mother and my grandmother," she said.

Hunter nodded.

"They live in Culiacán," she said.

He looked at her.

"I used to live there too," she said.

Hunter thought about what she was saying. He got out of the car and went to her door. He opened it for her and took her from the vehicle in his arms.

The restaurant was closed but Hunter knocked on the door.

A woman in her fifties opened the door.

"Estamos cerrados, señor."

Hunter smiled at her. He took his wallet from his pocket and unfolded four hundred dollar bills.

"No telefono," Hunter said.

The woman nodded.

"Gente morirá si lo haces," he said.

She understood. "No telefono," she said.

She stood aside and let them enter. The restaurant was a plain, cinderblock building with windows overlooking the parking lot. Hunter had the gun at his waist.

He'd parked the vehicle in plain sight and had taken no steps to hide his tracks when leaving the city. He wouldn't have minded if the cartel showed up, it was a decent place to stand and fight, but he doubted anyone was coming.

Unless the woman made a call.

He'd told her not to, which made it about a fifty fifty chance.

The girl might have tipped the odds.

They ordered food, there wasn't much to choose from,

and when they finished, Hunter asked the woman if she had ice cream. She didn't but she had a plain cake and they had some of that. She made hot milk for the child and black coffee for Hunter.

They didn't speak while they ate but the food seemed to do the child some good.

When they finished, they went back to the car and drove north along the coast. They passed Masón's villa and Hunter saw the cartel men mulling about. They passed the next villa, the one Belmar had run to, and he saw that there was even more activity there. He couldn't see exactly what was going on but there were lights from dozens of vehicles in front of the villa. The building was larger than Masón's villa.

There was no one on the road and they drove on.

Twenty miles further along the coast, he pulled off at a dirt road that led down to a beach. He drove onto the sand and parked in a spot that was sheltered from the road.

"It's time to sleep," he said to the child.

She nodded and he took off his jacket and put it over her. He put her seat back. She curled up and closed her eyes.

He could tell she was asleep when her breathing slowed. He closed his eyes also. He slept a few hours and when he woke he got out of the car and lit a cigarette. It was a crystal clear night. He walked down to the sea and looked south along the coast. Every now and then he saw the distant glow of an air strike.

He smoked the cigarette and when he was done he took off his clothes and washed in the salt water. He swam out a hundred yards and wondered what it would be like to keep going, swimming farther and farther from land until the only things he could see were the moon, the stars, and the light reflected on the surface of the water. It would be a good way to go.

He went back to the beach and dressed. He checked on the child. She was sleeping soundly. He turned on the engine and got back on the highway. He drove as far as the villas and pulled off the road into a forested area about a mile from them.

It was three AM.

The car was well hidden.

If the child woke up she would be afraid but she would wait.

He took off through the forest in the direction of the villas.

Something was going on.

He got to Masón's villa first and approached carefully under cover of dense vegetation. There were dogs and electronic devices to detect intruders but the perimeter was not well maintained. The sensors were turned off.

In front of the villa a guard had a dog on a leash but it was too far away to notice him.

Hunter watched the villa.

There were a few men around. Most of the signs of the killing Hunter had done there earlier were already cleared up. The damaged cars were gone. The bodies were gone.

He knew something going on at the larger villa and he made his way through the brush toward it.

Hunter had just killed a number of the cartel's top lieutenants, and supposedly El Sucio himself had also been killed.

The cartel should have been in mourning.

They should have been preparing for war.

And there should have already been the signs of a power struggle.

But from what Hunter could see, someone was planning a celebration. There were catering vans unloading crystal chandeliers and cases of champagne. Stone statues in the style of a Roman piazza had been set up along the beach. Flowers were being arranged on tables under canopies. There must have been a hundred workers making arrangements. And all of it happening in the dead of night.

El Sucio had escaped.

Hunter would have bet his life on it.

He knew when he checked in with Fawn she'd tell him they still hadn't found the body.

He would have to go back to the city to call her. He would go back and check in and then be back here in time to witness the celebrations.

He was about to leave when the sound of a military helicopter rumbled in from the west.

He waited for it. It came in over the water and landed on the lawn between Hunter's position and the villa. He was close to it. Scarcely a hundred yards away.

He was certain he was going to see El Sucio come out of it, running from the helicopter, his head ducked, a coat around his shoulders.

Four men exited the chopper and Hunter got a clear look at all of them. None were El Sucio.

But the fifth man was someone unexpected.

It was El Pirata himself, Luiz Fontaine Da Souza, the peg-legged new president of Mexico.

SIXTY

The child was still asleep when Hunter got back to the vehicle. He got back on the road in the direction of the city. On the outskirts he stopped for gas and bought some pastries and milk.

He woke the girl and they ate together in the car.

Hunter wasn't sure what to do with her. She seemed calm with him, comfortable. She was obviously in shock but while she was with him she seemed able to block the memory of what had happened in the apartment.

He wasn't sure what would happen if he left her with someone else.

"Good pastries," he said.

She nodded.

He opened the milk carton and she drank directly from it.

"Do you go to school?" he said.

She nodded.

"Do you want to go to school today?"

She thought for a minute and then shook her head. "My grandmother takes me to school."

Hunter nodded.

He thought about cutting her loose. He could drop her at a police station or a hospital.

"You got a name?" he said to her.

She looked at him but didn't answer.

"My name's Jack," he said.

She nodded.

"Do you have any place you want me to take you?"

She didn't answer.

"Some family?" he said. "Some relatives?"

Nothing.

They drove toward the center of the city and when he passed a children's school he stopped the car.

"Come on," he said to her, getting out.

She didn't move.

He went around to her door and opened it. He opened her seatbelt. He took her hand.

"Please," she said.

He looked at her.

"Please what?"

"Please don't throw me away."

"I'm not throwing you away. I need to put you somewhere safe. This is a school."

"This is not my school."

She was calm. There was no panic in her. She wasn't crying. She wasn't raising her voice.

But he knew there was an abyss of emotion beneath the surface. It would be better for her if they didn't get down into it.

"Don't worry," he said, reaching for her hand.

She pulled it away.

"Don't throw me away," she said again.

"I'll come back for you?" he said.

"You won't."

He sighed. He didn't know what to do. He could have pulled her out of the car but he knew he wouldn't. He couldn't.

He got back in and drove to the square. He pulled up across the street from his hotel.

"Wait here," he said.

She nodded.

He got out of the car and left the key. He went quickly into the hotel, through the lobby to the elevator. He went up to his old room and stopped outside the door. He listened. He looked under the door. There was no one there. He opened the door and went inside. The room had been searched. He checked where he'd hidden the five-seven and it was still there, loaded. He put it in the back of his jeans and went back to the elevator.

When he got to the ground floor he let the elevator door open but he didn't step out. He watched the lobby.

Everything was normal.

No one had come.

He didn't have much time though. Someone would be watching, waiting in case he came back.

He went to the bar and the usual waitress was there.

"Give me a beer," he said.

There was a notepad and pen on the bar and while she got his drink he wrote on it.

"Adelita's daughter is in a black Mercedes across the street. Adelita and her mother are dead."

He left the note and five hundred dollars cash on the bar and left.

He went to the staff door and exited at the back through a separate entrance for laundry and deliveries. He got back to the street about two hundred yards from the main entrance. He stood there and watched.

Four SUVs pulled up out front and cartel men with AKs swarmed out of them. Hunter waited. The waitress come out of the hotel and crossed the street. She got in the Mercedes. He waited until she turned it on and drove off. No one noticed.

Hunter walked away from the hotel, turned a few times, checked to see if he was being followed. He was clean. Four blocks from the hotel he entered a cafe.

There were no customers in the cafe and the owner was an old man sitting by the door with a pipe in his mouth.

"Hay un teléfono público?" he said.

The owner pointed to an old phone in the corner.

"Hay otro telefono?"

The man showed him the other phone which was on the wall behind the counter. Hunter would be able to see it from the payphone.

He stood still for a moment and listened. They were alone in the store.

He went to the telephone and began dialing the verification codes to speak to Fawn.

When she picked up she said, "Great news."

"Great news?" Hunter said.

"We found the body."

"El Sucio?"

"Yes."

"Where was he?"

"In the ship. The divers found him."

"Hmm," Hunter said.

"What's wrong?"

"You know who I saw flying in this morning?"

"Who?"

"El Pirata."

"Da Souza?"

"Yes."

"So we killed El Sucio but the cartel captured the country?"

"They almost captured both countries," Hunter said.

"They were trying," Fawn said.

"This is messed up."

"Something's not right," she agreed.

Hunter said, "If you were masterminding something huge, something that would start a war, that would get the president impeached, that would give you control over the Mexican government, would you hang out on a boat on Lake Michigan while it played out?"

"No," Fawn said.

"Would a drug dealer sacrifice himself for some grand plan?"

"I don't see why."

"This ain't right, Fawn."

"No it isn't."

"Who's benefitting from all this?"

"The cartel. El Sucio. If he was still alive."

"There's no way he planned all this and then got caught with his pants down."

"They've run DNA tests, Hunter. It's a match. It's him. We got him."

"Really?"

"Yes."

"What's the certainty on that DNA?"

"It's certain, Hunter. They had good samples. They got all the DNA they wanted from the corpse. It can't be faked."

"It's definitely him?"

"One hundred percent."

Hunter thought. What the hell was the point of all this? Was El Sucio someone's puppet? Was someone else running the whole show?

The Mexican government was gone.

Masón and his lieutenants were gone.

Who the fuck was throwing this party at the villa?

He looked at the old man, still sitting by the door, his pipe billowing smoke.

The door opened, the bell clinked. Hunter reached for his gun but it was just a customer.

A woman.

Hunter looked her up and down.

She was something else, a cool drink of water, with a short skirt and high heels.

She had an ass like a ripe peach, breasts like melons, and lips that seemed custom-made to be wrapped around a cock. The old man got up to serve her and barely seemed to notice her looks. There were a lot of women in Culiacán that looked like supermodels.

"Remember those dental records?" Hunter said.

"El Sucio's?"

"Yeah, the one's from his first arrest."

"The twenty year old Guatemalan records that you couldn't be bothered reading?"

"See, I was paying attention."

"Yes you were," Fawn said.

"Get them checked."

SIXTY-ONE

Hale was sitting in the oval office across from the president. Everyone was there, Antosh, Goldwater, the Secretary of State, the Attorney General.

"He's not the same man," Hale said.

"How the fuck is that possible?" the president said. "We have a fucking DNA match."

"It's not the DNA," Hale said.

"What do you mean it's not the DNA? It's always the DNA. Don't try to tell me he's got some way of faking the DNA."

Hale sighed. He'd already been over this with Antosh and Goldwater.

"Sir, we took the DNA from the prisoner," he was calling him the prisoner now, not El Sucio, "when he entered US custody."

"On the aircraft carrier."

"Correct, sir."

"And?"

"And, we were taking DNA from a double."

"A double?"

"A double, sir. Like what Saddam Hussein had."

"A decoy."

"Yes."

"So we never fucking had him in the first place?"

"We never had him."

"Fuck," the president shouted.

He slammed his fist on the small table in front of him and Hale's coffee spilled all over the documents he'd spread out.

"Fuck, fuck, fuck," the president said.

"Sir," Andrew Antosh said, "we've got contingency plans already in motion."

"Don't fucking talk to me about contingency plans you dumb fuck," the president shouted. "This guy fucking plotted my downfall."

"Yes, sir," Antosh said.

Hale was relieved Antosh had spoken up. It took some of the pressure from him, however briefly.

"He was going to have me impeached. He was going to get that cunt, Harris, to take my place."

Hale mopped up his coffee with a napkin, avoiding making eye contact with the president.

"And you're telling me, with all our intel, with all our fucking bullshit agents all over the world, we had the wrong fucking guy right from the get go?"

"Yes, sir," Hale said, rescuing Antosh.

"Why?"

"It was a plan to raise hell, sir."

"Raise hell?"

"Yes, sir."

"Raise fucking hell?" the president said, his voice rising once again. "What's that supposed to mean?"

"Sir, we believe the cartel's goal was to get you

impeached, put Harris in your place, and put Da Souza in power in Mexico."

"They planned all that?"

"Yes, sir."

"And El Sucio's escape?"

"They were rescuing the double, sir."

"After they'd served him up to us on a silver platter?"

"Yes, sir."

"Why?"

"So that we'd hunt him down and kill him, sir."

"I'm sorry, Hale, but that doesn't make an ounce of fucking sense."

"Sir, he kept attacking us, kept provoking us, so that we'd keep hunting the double. He left the double in Lake Michigan to make him an easy target. Maybe they were even hoping the body would be lost in the explosion."

"They wanted us to think we'd killed him?"

"Yes, sir. The world would think El Sucio was dead, and meanwhile, Harris would take over your position following an impeachment, and Da Souza would take power in Mexico."

"That's one hell of a fucking plan."

"Exactly, sir."

"So how do we know we had a double?"

"We have old dental records, sir."

"Are we sure the old dental records are the real thing?"

"Yes, sir. They were made twenty years ago, the first time El Sucio was arrested. Before he had all this sophistication. Before he had body doubles."

"And how did he manage that?"

"They have amazing plastic surgeons in Sinaloa, sir. The best in the world."

"But they couldn't fake the dental records?"

"They never thought they needed to."

The president was shaking his head. He couldn't believe it. The escape had been a national disaster. And now he was learning they didn't even have the guy they thought they had.

"You still got your man down there in Culiacán?" the president said.

"Yes, sir," Hale said.

SIXTY-TWO

That night, Hale met Aspen in the hotel room.

She'd come straight from work, he hadn't given her much notice, and she was wearing a blazer and pants.

When she entered the room she threw the blazer over the back of a chair.

She was getting more comfortable with him.

Hale wasn't sure he liked that.

The whole thrill was that the girl wasn't supposed to know him. She was supposed to be shy. She was supposed to be scared even. Once they got like this, the thrill of the chase was over.

Taking something innocent.

That was the thrill.

He knew this would be the last time he called her. There'd be other reporters, whether at the *Post* or at the *New York Times* or the *LA Times*. Maybe someone from a television network.

There was always someone new to pursue.

Hopefully someone who put up a little more resistance than Aspen had.

Someone who appreciated the thrill of the hunt.

"What have you got for me tonight?" she said.

She went to the minibar and helped herself to a beer.

It had all happened so quickly. Just a few encounters, a couple of weeks, and they were like an old married couple. She'd gone from virginal innocence to being an old hand. She hadn't even spritzed her perfume.

Last time, he told himself.

Make it count.

Give yourself something to remember.

"I've got photos of the body," Hale said.

"Is that all?"

"That's the biggest story of the century, sweetheart. We got our man. He's dead. The biggest terrorist in history. Here's his face, bloody and bloated from lake water."

She nodded. "Okay, sorry. I just thought maybe it would be some new information."

"There is no new information, sweetheart."

She was in for a rude awakening if she thought photos of a dead man's face weren't a scoop. These past few weeks would be the highlight of her career. She'd never break anything this big again.

"Okay," she said, stepping toward him.

He was sitting on the bed and she straddled him, sitting on his crotch. He began to stiffen.

She brushed her bloused breasts against his face.

He put his hands beneath the blouse and ran them up her back, unhooking her bra.

"Make it a big success," he said. "We got our man. We're safe again. That's the story."

She smiled, leaning into him and running her tongue over the contours of his lips.

He grabbed her hair and pulled back her head.

"The country needs it," he said. "We need this win. Play it up."

She opened her mouth and he put his tongue into it. She moaned but he could tell she was pretending.

He opened the buttons on her blouse, one by one, and grabbed her breasts. He caught her nipples between his thumb and forefinger and squeezed. She moaned. He sucked them, first one and then the other. He sucked them hard and she arched her back and pushed them forward, moaning in his ear.

He ran his nails lightly down her back and kissed her neck. He wanted to leave a hickey. He wanted to mark her. This was the last time he would have her. If he could have made it so that she'd never be with another man again, he would have.

The thought of that, of ownership, of possession, made him stiffen completely.

SIXTY-THREE

Hunter checked in with Fawn that evening. She had three words to say.

"Go get him."

And that was all he wanted to hear.

He was close to the center of the city and felt conspicuous in his boots and shirt.

From a street vendor he bought a black windbreaker and put it on.

He didn't have the heart to part with the boots. Sneakers would have been less noticeable but he was far from the only man in town in boots.

He walked a few blocks to the square and crossed on the side opposite the hotel. He spotted some cartel guys watching the hotel but they weren't looking in his direction.

The Azteca bank was closed.

He walked past the entrance.

The windows on street level had metal bars in front of them. The bars were decorative and he tried them but they were solid. The glass doors had them too.

The windows on the second and third floors only had

wooden shutters, no bars. They were closed but could be overcome easily enough.

He crossed the street and lit a cigarette, watching the bank as he smoked.

Things were quiet inside. The employees had gone home but he could make out the silhouettes of two security guards at a desk in the lobby.

The street was also quiet. It was too early for the evening revelers to be out at the bars around the square.

Hunter threw the cigarette on the ground and crushed it with his boot, then crossed the street, glancing to his left and right.

All clear.

He checked the five-seven at his waist.

He rounded the corner and walked along the side of the bank. When he reached the first window, and without slowing down, he hopped onto the sill. He climbed the bars and used a street lamp to help reach the sill of the second floor window.

He pulled himself onto the sill and stood with his back to the window.

He only had six inches of sill to stand on.

With his heel, he hit the wooden shutter hard and heard it crack. He reached down and pulled some of the slats loose.

He let them fall to the street below without making any effort to keep quiet.

Then he kicked the window, smashing it.

The whole block erupted in alarms. A yellow light built into the eave of the building every twelve feet began flashing.

He climbed into the bank through the broken window and pulled the five-seven from his waist.

He was in a large gallery with a parquet floor and paintings on the walls. He crossed the room in the direction of the staircase and crouched behind the door. He could hear the guards scrambling up the stairs.

He let the first enter the room, and swung his leg into the doorway to trip up the second. He leapt on the fallen man and yanked his neck ninety degrees with a single jerk. Then he lifted him and used him as a shield against two shots fired by the first guard.

Hunter drew the five-seven from his waist and fired a shot. It hit the guard between the neck and collar bone and he fell backwards onto the floor. He was still breathing and Hunter kicked away his gun and left him there. Maybe he'd make it, maybe he wouldn't.

Hunter guessed he had about five minutes before the security firm responded to the alarm. They would be poorly trained local boys with bad aim and no plan.

He hoped he could get to the deposit box before they arrived so that he wouldn't have to kill them.

He hurried down the stairs and into the lobby. Behind the guards' desk was a steel drawer. It was locked but a single shot from his gun opened it. Inside was a set of keys and Hunter recognized the one used to access the deposit boxes. He took it and went across the lobby to a steel door. The key opened it and he went inside and found his box.

He was aware of the irony of robbing a bank just to get to his own deposit box, but the cartel would have been all over him if he'd come earlier. He also knew that if they saw that he was picking up a sniper rifle they'd take steps to protect El Sucio.

This was simpler.

Using his own key and the key from the steel drawer he opened the box and removed the steel container. He glanced at the contents and took the documents, which contained his photo and could have been used against him at some point in the future, and the sniper rifle.

The weight of the rifle felt good in his hands after all those days with a handgun.

The rifle was a Remington Mk 21 bolt action. It weighed about seventeen pounds. It had a Leupold and Stevens mark four sight which he put in his pocket, and a suppressor. The cartridges in the box were .338 Lapua Magnums.

The effective range with that ammo was just shy of a mile, and according to the military it would pierce level four body armor at five hundred yards.

It was a good gun.

They'd given him a five and ten round magazine and he took them both, as well as the suppressor and all the ammo. He also took two Glocks and put them in his waistband with the five-seven.

The box was full of cash but he left it. He placed the box back in position among the others and locked it shut. He put the key back in the steel drawer he'd shot open.

He unlocked the front door of the bank, walked out, turned right, and was around the corner before the security guards arrived from the other direction.

It wouldn't take long for word to get to the cartel that he'd broken into the bank but they'd assume he was there for money. It would take time for them to realize he'd opened his deposit box.

If they'd known what was in his box they'd have taken it.

With the rifle under his arm he was a lot more conspicuous and he took the first car he could hot wire easily. It was an old Ford pickup.

He got the engine going and drove it to a strip mall he'd passed earlier.

He parked outside a dentist's office and kicked open the door. There was no alarm. He went inside and searched through the supplies until he found what he was looking for.

Then he went across the lot to a camping store and took two big hunting knives.

There was a white sedan in the lot and he moved his things from the pickup to the sedan and hot wired that.

· He drove back out to the coast toward the villas. He watched every car that came the other way. Nothing looked out of place.

He wondered if El Sucio had been in his villa the entire time.

Probably.

He definitely hadn't been on a fucking boat in the Great Lakes.

He peered at the two villas as he passed them. The celebration at the second villa was in full swing.

He parked the car in the forest and walked back to the bigger villa, taking a different route than before and approaching from a different angle. From his position he had a good view of the pool and beach, as well as the rooms overlooking the pool where he knew the bigwigs liked to do business.

On the beach, servants were grilling meat over open fires. It didn't look like it was human meat this time.

Da Souza's helicopter was still on the lawn on the far side of the villa.

Hunter had to hand it to El Sucio. From this place, while under constant air attack, he'd successfully taken out all the top players in the Mexican government and had their replacement in his pocket. He'd almost succeeded in achieving the same north of the border.

All that from a guy who'd grown up on the streets of Culiacán cleaning windshields.

Hunter watched the party for a few minutes and got an idea of where the security was. There were guards all over the villa, most armed with AKs but some with handguns. He counted thirty but there was probably close to double that.

As for guests, there was a similar number to the party he'd attended at Masón's villa. Hunter looked at the girls in bikinis by the pool and thought of Adelita, Estrella and Catalina. The only thing he could do now was hope he hadn't caused the death of the little girl too, or the bartender from the hotel.

He doubted anyone would care what happened to Adelita's kid but nothing was ever for certain in this place.

He scanned the villa.

One the ground floor, party guests were putting on costumes of some sort. On the beach, they were setting up effigies. Hunter smiled when he realized what they were planning.

El día de los Muertos.

El Sucio was celebrating the report of his own death, which was on the front page of the *Washington Post*. Hunter had read the story. It was a classic Hale plant. He'd even given them photos of the bloated face of the corpse.

Adelita had been right about Sinaloan plastic surgeons.

They were the best in the world.

He assembled the Remington, attaching the scope and suppressor and propping it up on its bipod.

He began examining the guests through the scope. Some he recognized. Many of the top lieutenants he'd already killed, but there were others waiting in the wings. Trying to take them all out would be pointless. He couldn't kill an entire city.

He had one objective.

Find and kill El Sucio.

The knew this was the place.

It added up.

Chicago had not.

He watched the party, scanned the windows, and tried to recognize the faces of the men around the pool. They went inside frequently and there was a lot of activity on the second floor.

From his knowledge of the other villa, he suspected that the important business was being conducted in the second floor room overlooking the pool.

If Heredia and Da Souza were inside, that's where they'd be.

There was one window in particular that he favored.

It had a lace curtain over it that obscured the faces of the figures inside, but he could make out their outlines.

There were people in there.

He watched it for about an hour and noticed that when someone important left the party, he showed up in the room soon after.

He stayed put and let another hour pass.

The party was heating up and people were getting more and more fucked up.

Four women were having sex in a hot tub. A crowd of men watched them.

Other couples were fucking by the pool.

The alcohol and cocaine were flowing freely.

In the room behind the lace curtain, things seemed to be heating up also. There was more activity. More movement.

Hunter had been in position for three hours and had assessed his options. With that curtain obscuring everything but the silhouettes of the people in the room, none were ideal.

He could try shooting everyone in the room through the curtain. It was unlikely he'd be fast enough to get off six shots before people started diving for cover. He also never had a line of sight of all the people in the room at the same time.

The likely outcome would be that he'd take out three or four people at most.

There were usually about seven or eight in the room.

That gave him a fifty percent chance of killing his target.

He'd give away his position and would have to content with hundreds of men. If El Sucio wasn't one of the first men he killed, he'd be long gone. He'd know there was an assassin after him.

He'd go into hiding and might not come up again for months. Years even.

The other alternative was to abandon the rifle and enter the room. He knew he could get to the balcony without being seen. H would enter through a window.

He'd be in the room before anyone knew what was happening and he could kill El Sucio with certainty.

He'd also be able to get confirmation of the kill once he'd cleared the room.

He'd have to fight his way back out of the villa but that didn't matter. Only the target mattered.

El Sucio would be dead by then.

He traced the path he'd take to the balcony through the rifle scope. He would run across the unlit lawn to the side of the building. He would get to the balcony using the porch pillars. There were guards on the balcony but they weren't paying attention. He would get to the balcony behind the first and break his neck without the others noticing.

If one of them saw, he'd shoot.

He'd be in the target room in seconds, well before El Sucio could escape.

He'd shoot him.

That was it.

The chance of success was almost one hundred percent.

The chance of getting back out alive was close to that.

He knew the layout of the building. In three directions it was surrounded by dense forest that would aid his escape. Everyone inside was drunk and high.

He checked his handguns and was about to abandon the rifle and make his move when the curtain moved.

He aimed the rifle at the window.

A hand was on the curtain and pulled it aside.

Suddenly, Hunter could see clearly into the room.

The man at the window was Da Souza. He had a glass of champagne in his hand and was looking out the window while the head of a blonde woman bobbed back and forth in front of his groin.

Behind him, across the room with his back to the window, a man with white hair was fucking a woman who was bent over, her legs splayed open and her hands on the wall. The man had a cigar in one hand. His other hand was on the back of the woman.

Hunter kept the scope trained on him.

He wouldn't shoot until he saw the face.

The man climaxex and was about to turn around.

Hunter put the crosshairs on his head. He put his finger on the trigger.

This was it. The single headshot that would end a war.

One head.

One bullet.

The .338 Lapua Magnum was a rimless, bottlenecked, centerfire cartridge. Developed for military snipers, it was perfect for this shot. It was the preferred sniper cartridge in both Iraq and Afghanistan. Hunter was intimately familiar with its ballistics. Half an inch in diameter, three and a half inches in length, lethal against armored combatants at over a thousand yards. Maximum effective range was closer to two thousand. It was the perfect bullet.

The man's head turned.

It was El Sucio.

Hunter pressed the trigger and instantly, El Sucio's head exploded. Blood spattered on the wall and on the woman who was still holding herself up against the wall.

Hunter took a second shot and Da Souza, also at that moment orgasming, lost the top half of his head.

Hunter put down the gun and abandoned his position, moving the entire way around the building so he could approach from the far side.

The remaining men in the second floor room were on the floor taking cover.

The guards on the balcony were running toward the shattered window.

The majority of the revelers by the pool and on the beach hadn't even noticed the suppressed sound of the gunshots.

Some were looking up at the balcony, and then in the direction of Hunter's shooting position, but Hunter was already gone.

He moved stealthily through the brush around the building, crossing the driveway about a hundred yards from the house. When he got to the other side, he ran across the lawn, leapt onto a pillar, and climbed onto the balcony.

He drew the five-seven.

He entered the building through an unlocked door and was in a large arcade similar to the one at Masón's villa.

There were three men at the far end of the arcade, just outside the door to the room El Sucio had been in.

Hunter popped off three shots and the three men's heads jerked, blood spattered, and they fell to the floor.

He ran across the arcade and kicked open the door. Two men were in the room, crouched over El Sucio's body. They looked his way abut he shot them before they could get a shot off.

There was a guard at the window, climbing in from the balcony and Hunter shot him too.

The two women who'd been fucking El Sucio and Da Souza were also in the room. One was screaming and the other was in shock.

Hunter left them.

He pulled the dental mould from his pocket and opened El Sucio's mouth. He put the mould between his teeth and pressed the jaw shut. The teeth left a pattern in the mold and he put it in his pocket.

Another guard approached. Hunter watched the shadow approach the window.

He jerked to the side to dodge the bullet just as it came for him. Then he rose his arm and fired off a shot, killing the guard.

He kept low and made his way back to the door. He peered around it and then rounded the frame of the door. The arcade was clear.

He ran across the room to the door he'd come in through and was back on the balcony while the people at the pool were still trying to figure out what was going on. Men were coming into the villa now, rushing up the stairs and entering the arcade through the large wooden doors that separated it from the landing at the top of the stairs.

They didn't see Hunter at the far end of the arcade.

He watched them, then crossed the balcony and leapt down to the lawn.

As he reached the brush he heard gunshots from the building behind him. They weren't being fired in his direction.

As he crossed the lawn he shot a guard who spotted him. The guard's dog ran toward him and he killed it too.

Then he was back in the forest, moving quickly and quietly, the noise of the villa getting fainter in the distance.

SIXTY-FOUR

Hunter drove to the hotel.

The air strikes were bad as he entered the city, possibly the worst since the night they'd started, and columns of black smoke rose into the sky.

He had no idea what they could still be targeting but it didn't matter. They would be raining down for as long as was politically expedient.

At the hotel he didn't conceal his arrival. It was more important that he was fast. He pulled up in front of the main entrance and went inside. The bar was closed but the night manager was at the desk.

"The girl who works at the bar," Hunter said, "where does she live?"

The manager took one look at Hunter and then typed something into his computer. He printed it out and handed it to him.

"If anyone knows I asked for this, they'll kill her," Hunter said.

The man nodded.

Hunter looked at him, trying to assess if he could be relied on.

"If anyone asks why I came back, tell them it was for my documents."

Hunter turned and went back outside. He scanned the square. Three men were running toward him and he dropped to one knee, supported his right arm with his left, and shot the three men with headshots at three hundred yards. He had to arc the shots, firing over their heads.

He got in his vehicle and drove to the address the night manager gave him. It was an apartment building four blocks from Adelita's. He rang the buzzer and waited for an answer.

He was buzzed up and when he got to the door the bartender from the hotel let him in.

"Thank you," he said to her.

"The girl is sleeping."

She led him to the living room where her sister was sitting on the sofa. It was the middle of the night but there had been air strikes in the neighborhood and it was difficult to sleep.

The sister went into the kitchen and put on a kettle to make tea.

"How was the girl?" he said to the bartender.

"Upset you left her."

"Was she happy with her friend?"

"She was okay."

"Will your sister be able to keep her?"

She laughed.

"No. She's terrified. If anyone finds out we helped her we'll all be killed."

Hunter nodded.

He wondered what her name was but he didn't ask.

The sister came back with a tray of tea and cookies. She put it on the table and poured Hunter a cup. Then she made the bartender go back into the kitchen with her.

The two of them argued in hushed tones and when they came back, the sister said in English, "I'm sorry, but the child must leave. I have to think of my daughter. If Adelita did something to upset the cartel, I can't be involved."

Hunter sipped the tea. He thought for a few seconds. He'd seen this coming but he wasn't sure what to do. He shouldn't have come here, but he couldn't abandon the child.

There was a flash of light outside the window, followed by a huge boom. The ground rumbled and a photo on the wall fell to the floor. The glass smashed.

The two women let out cries. Hunter stood up and rose his hands to calm them. He went to the balcony and found the source of the explosion. It was an air strike about three blocks away.

"What's over there?" he said to the bartender.

"I don't know," she said. "Nothing important. Homes. Stores."

"Why would they target it?" Hunter said.

She shrugged.

The noise had woken the children, and the two of them emerged from the hallway and ran to the women. When Adelita's daughter saw Hunter she burst into tears.

"You said you wouldn't leave me," she cried.

The bartender held her in her arms but she was looking at Hunter.

"You said you wouldn't leave me," she cried, over and over.

Hunter went to them and took her in his arms. She

stopped crying. He thanked the women and then carried her down the stairs and back out to the street.

He put her in the passenger seat and got in the driver's seat. They drove out of the city as more and more air strikes landed. The strikes were more intense than anything he'd seen in Iraq or Afghanistan.

They drove on the main highway east in the direction of Durango. In less than half an hour they were approaching the border crossing where Hunter had entered Sinaloa.

Hunter slowed down as they approached the checkpoint. Two men came out of the hut and approached the car. Hunter told the child to get on the floor. He put his jacket over her.

Then he shot the two men, as well as two others still in the hut holding AK47s.

He gunned the car and drove past the Mexican army checkpoint a few hundred yards farther east. They didn't open fire and he didn't stop to explain himself.

He drove northeast through the night and the girl slept in the seat next to him. He stopped for gas once and as the sun rose in front of them, they stopped for breakfast in the town of Delicias, Chihuahua.

They stopped at a roadside diner and sat at a booth by a window. They ordered eggs and Hunter made a phone call from the payphone. He watched the child from the phone.

"It's done," he said when Fawn picked up.

"Are you sure?"

"As sure as I can be. I got a dental mold so you can make sure."

"Good work, Hunter," she said.

He noticed something in her voice.

"What's wrong?" he said.

"I don't know what to tell you."

"I can't come back, can I?"

"Hale might have you killed," she said.

"Why's he so afraid of me?"

"I don't know," she said.

He thought he detected evasion in her voice but it didn't matter. She was warning him. That was what counted.

"What do you want me to do with the dental mold?" he said.

"If I was you," she said, "I'd put it in the mail."

Hunter let out a little laugh.

"I'm sorry, Hunter," she said.

"It's not your fault."

"I wish there was something I could do."

"You warned me," he said. "I appreciate that."

He hung up and went back to the booth. The child had finished her eggs. He still didn't know her name.

"You ready?" he said to her.

She nodded.

"Where do you want to go?" he said.

She shrugged.

He looked at her and then out at the rising sun.

"You ever been to the beach?" he said.

Stay in touch with Rawlin to get free books and offers.

SIGN UP NOW